D0981309

MARY'S HOME

BOOKS BY
JERRY S. EICHER

THE ADAMS COUNTY TRILOGY

Rebecca's Promise
Rebecca's Return
Rebecca's Choice

THE BEILER SISTERS

Holding a Tender Heart
Seeing Your Face Again
Finding Love at Home

EMMA RABER'S DAUGHTER

Katie Opens Her Heart
Katie's Journey to Love
Katie's Forever Promise

FIELDS OF HOME

Missing Your Smile
Following Your Heart
Where Love Grows

HANNAH'S HEART

A Dream for Hannah
A Hope for Hannah
A Baby for Hannah

LAND OF PROMISE

Miriam's Secret
A Blessing for Miriam
Miriam and the Stranger

LITTLE VALLEY

A Wedding Quilt for Ella
Ella's Wish
Ella Finds Love Again

**THE ST. LAWRENCE
COUNTY AMISH**

A Heart Once Broken
Until I Love Again
Always Close to Home

PEACE IN THE VALLEY

Silvia's Rose
Phoebe's Gift
Mary's Home

STANDALONES

My Amish Childhood
The Amish Family Cookbook
(with Tina Eicher)

MARY'S HOME

JERRY S. EICHER

HARVEST HOUSE PUBLISHERS
EUGENE, OREGON

Scripture quotations are from the King James Version of the Bible.

Cover design by Garborg Design Works

Cover image © Yanika, volgariver, Dean Fikar / Bigstock

The author is represented by MacGregor Literary, Inc.

This is a work of fiction. Names, characters, places, and incidents are products of the author's imagination or are used fictitiously. Any resemblance to actual persons, living or dead, is entirely coincidental.

MARY'S HOME
Copyright © 2017 by Jerry S. Eicher
Published by Harvest House Publishers
Eugene, Oregon 97402
www.harvesthousepublishers.com

ISBN 978-0-7369-6934-5 (pbk.)
ISBN 978-0-7369-6935-2 (eBook)

Library of Congress Cataloging-in-Publication Data

Names: Eicher, Jerry S., author.
Title: Mary's home / Jerry S. Eicher.
Description: Eugene, Oregon : Harvest House Publishers, [2017] | Series:
 Peace in the valley ; 3
Identifiers: LCCN 2017006751 (print) | LCCN 2017010983 (ebook) | ISBN
 9780736969345 (paperback) | ISBN 9780736969352 (eBook)
Subjects: LCSH: Amish--Fiction. | BISAC: FICTION / Christian / Romance. |
 GSAFD: Christian fiction. | Love stories.
Classification: LCC PS3605.I34 M37 2017 (print) | LCC PS3605.I34 (ebook) |
 DDC 813/.6--dc23
LC record available at https://lccn.loc.gov/2017006751

Printed in the United States of America

17 18 19 20 21 22 23 24 25 / LB-GL / 10 9 8 7 6 5 4 3 2 1

ONE

Mary Yoder drove Danny Boy toward Deacon Stoltzfus's place with Betsy on the buggy seat beside her. Spring had arrived in the valley, and the trees were draped in a fresh hue of green. The colorful Adirondack flowers would soon blossom and dot the roadsides in their brief display of glory. Tonight, the breezes from the foothills to the north bore the last memory of winter snows that had blasted the community with drifts along the road, four feet high in some places.

Betsy pulled her shawl tighter under her chin and muttered, "Why didn't I go to the *rumspringa* gathering with Enos tonight?"

Mary gave her younger sister a bright smile. "Because there's a load of young people coming in from Lancaster, and Enos changed his plans when he found out. Everyone will be at the volleyball game instead. Just think!"

Betsy's face darkened. "I don't want to meet any young people from Lancaster."

Mary didn't answer as Danny Boy's hooves beat a steady trot on the pavement. Betsy's attitude toward the community and the Amish way of life was a grave family concern. Lately, Betsy expressed her views with greater frequency—even in public, much to *Mamm* and *Daett*'s chagrin. They would have to pray that the Lord would see fit to draw Betsy's heart toward the right ways.

"You don't have to be so critical of me." Betsy gave her sister a sharp sideways glance, as if she had read Mary's thoughts. "I have my reasons."

"I didn't say anything," Mary protested. "And I do understand."

"How can someone with your plans understand me?" Betsy huffed. "I know why you are so excited. You plan to snag an Amish man, perhaps even tonight. I know that's why you left your *rumspringa* time early."

"I saw Jonas Troyer making eyes at you at the last hymn singing," Mary encouraged her sister. "I'm sure he'll talk to you soon. Jonas might even ask you home on a date—once you've both decided to settle down in the community."

"Jonas!" Betsy snapped. "The man has straw in his hair, and he goes barefoot in the winter—well, most of the winter. Stomps right through the mud! How would that look in a woman's home? He'd leave tracks all over the house, and not just in the kitchen. If I have to settle for that sort of man, I'm not settling."

Mary laughed in spite of herself. "I'm sure Jonas can be cleaned up a bit. If not, there will be others. You're a nice girl."

Betsy grunted and fell silent.

They had been over this ground before. Betsy bore the scars on her face from a childhood accident, but her saucy attitude did more harm than the burn marks on her skin.

Mary tried another tack. "I found a poem this afternoon in the old cedar chest upstairs that I wrote when we were in school. You like *Englisha* things. This one is about the Mona Lisa in Paris."

"See, you are more *Englisha* than you admit," Betsy said. "You know about such things, and you write poetry. We should jump the fence together."

Mary ignored the suggestion to quote by heart,

The world is drawn to your face,
To your quiet beauty and your grace.
They hang your portrait in their lofty halls;
They captured you upon their walls.

Some man conceived with paint and brush
To touch your heart and show the hush,
Which sorrow wrote upon your life,
The peace that came amidst the strife.

For beauty does not rise in mortal eyes,
Unless the lines are written from the skies.
With pain you showed us heaven's touch,
And so your smile is loved so much.

"Not bad," Betsy allowed. "But my point stands."

Mary didn't answer as they bounced into Deacon Stoltzfus's lane. Further conversation on the subject would get neither of them anywhere. She would have to think of something else to say. Ahead of them lantern light glowed in the windows of the barn, where the volleyball game would be held. Several boys stood chatting near the door. When they noticed the buggy, they came toward Mary and Betsy to help them unhitch.

"Those are Lancaster boys," Mary whispered out of the corner of her mouth. "One of them might be your future husband."

Betsy pretended not to hear as she hopped down from the buggy. She chirped, "*Goot* evening, boys."

There was a chorus of *goot* evenings in response. Betsy could project a cheerful and happy attitude if she wished, but the subject of an Amish husband and her future in the community brought out her dark side.

Cousin Enos came toward them with a wide smile and made the

introductions. "These are two of our Yoder girls, Mary and Betsy. Both of them are charming, sweet, and available."

Laugher rippled around the buggy, as two men from Lancaster nodded to Mary.

"Josiah Beiler and Ronald Troyer." Enos waved his hand to include both of the girls. "They are staying for the weekend, and maybe for another week if things work out."

Laugher filled the air again, and heat rushed into Mary's face. Everyone knew what Enos referred to. If one of the Lancaster men found a love interest in the valley and took a girl home from the hymn singing, he would wish to stay another weekend to cement the relationship before being reduced to letter writing for communication.

Mary snuck a long look at the two men. The truth was, her decision to end *rumspringa* early was a risk. There were no unmarried men in the valley who had given her more than a passing glance, but faith was firmly fixed in her heart. Her dream of home and family in the community would be fulfilled. She believed the Lord would lead her to a man who would love her and hold her close to his heart, so she had stepped forward with confidence.

One of them, Josiah, caught her look. He was handsome enough. In fact, Mary thought him quite handsome. His eyes twinkled as he said, "So you are Mary Yoder."

"*Yah.*" Her eyes met his, and shivers tickled her spine.

"You live far from here?"

"A little ways." She sent a nod toward the Adirondack foothills. "Down Duesler Road, just outside of town."

A smile filled his face. "Don't know where that is. I've never been here before."

"Are you staying over the weekend?" As she spoke, Josiah didn't appear to notice the heat that rushed up Mary's neck.

"Everyone's staying over for Sunday," he said, chuckling. "Longer than that? Depends, I guess. You're not dating, are you? A girl like you?"

Now her whole face flamed red.

"Sitting on the edge of your *rumspringa*?" Concern had crept into his voice.

"No! Not at all. I..." The words stuck in her mouth. Was the Lord answering her faith this soon?

"Are you coming, Josiah?" Enos had his hand on Danny Boy's bridle.

Josiah grinned. "In a little bit. But don't worry. I'll bring Mary with me."

"Oh..." Enos cooed. "Has Cupid shot his arrow and hit the mark?"

Laugher rose again, but Mary kept her eyes on the ground. Thankfully, the others moved toward the barn as Betsy cast her a baleful glance. At least Betsy had engaged the other Lancaster man, Ronald, in conversation.

"Sorry about the teasing," Josiah said once the others were out of earshot. "Are you okay?"

"*Yah*, I'm fine." Mary caught her breath. She clearly wasn't, and Josiah noticed.

"What is life like here in the valley?" he asked, as if they were sharing a normal conversation on the couch in *Mamm* and *Daett*'s living room. Dizziness swept over Mary at the image of Josiah seated in that familiar place with her beside him.

"Not much different than Lancaster," she managed. "The country is beautiful, but so is Lancaster."

"Do you visit often?"

Mary shook her head. "Most of our immediate relatives are here in the valley."

He regarded her for a moment as a buggy trotted past them and parked at the end of the line. "How old are you and Betsy?"

Mary rushed out the words. "I'm almost twenty, just coming off my *rumspringa*, and I took my first baptismal class two weeks ago. Betsy is a bit younger."

He appeared impressed. "That's exceptional. I joined last year. A little early, but I was ready to settle down." Josiah gave Mary a warm smile. "What does everyone do for *rumspringa* around here?"

Mary tried to breathe evenly. "There's not much going on. The biggest town nearby is Utica, which is still a good distance away. Most of the Amish boys don't get automobiles, so we'd have to drive with *Englisha* friends to get there."

"Pretty tame then?" His pleased expression didn't fade. "I broke down and got an automobile. I kept it hidden in *Daett's* barn, but cars aren't what they are cracked up to be. I guess that's what *rumspringa* is about, though. Finding out that the world doesn't offer what's advertised." He gave her a glance. "I was never one to dream of jumping the fence. Not many of our people do, I suppose, but there are some."

Mary looked away. What would Josiah say if he knew of Betsy's determinedness to find herself an *Englisha* husband?

"What happened to your sister's face?" His chin motioned toward the glowing loft windows. "Or was I seeing things?"

Mary shook her head. "Betsy's scarf caught fire when she was small. She was tending the stove, and *Mamm* didn't get there in time. There was scarring, as you can see..." Mary let the words hang.

Mary often wanted to tell Betsy that her scars were not that bad, but how could she say so when men like Josiah noticed them? Other men obviously did the same, which went to the heart of Betsy's complaint about Amish life.

"Such things happen." He shrugged. "There will be a man for your sister. Scars shouldn't scare them away."

"Betsy has her struggles," Mary managed.

Josiah would hear the truth from someone, perhaps even from Betsy's lips if he stayed in the community long enough. Better to give the impression that she was not hiding the matter. Even if Josiah was an open door from the Lord straight into Mary's dreams, honesty was still the best policy.

"Should we go inside?" Josiah suggested.

Several young people from the other buggy had paused to stare at them. Who was this handsome young man Mary Yoder was speaking to? Mary could practically hear the question rippling through their minds, and heat tingled at the base of her neck again.

Josiah's clear blue eyes twinkled as if he had read their thoughts too. He turned toward the others, and she fell in beside him. The introductions were up to her if she could find her voice.

"Josiah Beiler from Lancaster," Mary heard herself saying as everyone shook hands.

Josiah stayed near her as they made their way to the barn loft. The other girls clearly noticed. They whispered to each other, and she could guess at their remarks.

"Did Mary know this would happen?"

"And he's so goot *looking."*

"How did she do it?"

"Snagged the handsome fellow with a twirl of her finger!"

She would not be proud, and this was not a sure thing. Josiah might leave after the Sunday services and not ask her home for an evening date. If he didn't, she would not allow disappointment to grip her heart or sow discouragement—but the wound would sting deeply. Very deeply!

As the group entered the barn, the light of the lanterns burst around them. Two buggies had been set up a short distance from each other with their wheels blocked up on hay bales, and a volleyball net was stretched between them. This was not the usual *rumspringa* gathering, but a calmer, approved community event. Here, both the young people who had joined the baptismal class and those still on *rumspringa* could attend.

Mary glanced at Josiah. She had no regrets about leaving her running-around time behind. Risky experiences, such as local *Englisha* rock band concerts, did not compare to her dream of home and family with a man like Josiah Beiler. Thankfully, she had made the decision to join the baptismal class before Josiah appeared, so she would be assured for the rest of her life that the choice had been made for the right reasons.

"We want Josiah on our side!" Ronald Troyer hollered from his place beside one of the buggies. As a visitor from Lancaster, Ronald had been given one of the honored positions of team captain for the evening.

"Maybe he can't play volleyball!" Enos retorted from his post beside the other buggy.

Everyone laughed. They could tell that Josiah Beiler knew how to play volleyball. Mary stole a glance at his limber frame and guessed he would be an excellent player.

"Well, I guess visitors have privileges," Enos declared with a grin. "Let's stop arguing and get to playing."

"You're playing by my side," Josiah told Mary out of the corner of his mouth.

Mary's knees weakened, but she managed to follow Josiah to their assigned places. Ronald gave Josiah a slap on his back as they passed, and whispered to Mary, "Looks like you are in the game."

Which meant more than playing volleyball tonight.

Josiah must have overheard because he laughed good-naturedly, which turned her face the color of red beets. She kept her head down, wondering if she was nothing more than Josiah's latest conquest. But what a horrible thought! She decided to banish it from her mind forever.

The game began with the ball flying back and forth across the net. The other men from Lancaster were also great volleyball players. They spiked and set up with abandon, and Josiah outdid the others with ease. He even gave Mary some chances to play. She managed to hit the ball back over the net each time and avoid total embarrassment.

"You're *goot* at this," Josiah said as they caught their breath.

Mary stilled her protest and kept her gaze straight ahead.

"Can I take you home on Sunday evening after the hymn singing?" Josiah asked in a low tone.

Mary nodded as the ball arched in the air high above them.

TWO

On Sunday evening Mary drove into Deacon Stoltzfus's driveway with the buggy seat empty beside her. She stopped by the barn with a flourish and then hopped out as several Amish men loitering nearby hurried forward to help unhitch the buggy. Josiah was not among them, so she assumed he hadn't arrived at the hymn singing yet. At the church service this morning, he had sent warm smiles her way for the whole three hours. Her face had remained one solid flame of red, but no one had objected to the new couple's behavior. Rather, several of the older women had whispered kind words into Mary's ear while she served tables afterward.

Rachel, Deacon Stoltzfus's *frau*, had said, "The Lord has blessed you with a handsome young man."

"We wish you nothing but the best," another woman had added.

"You are such an encouragement to our young girls," said Annie, Bishop Miller's *frau*. "The Lord is smiling on you indeed."

Mary smiled now when Enos walked up to her buggy with Ronald Troyer, his new friend from Lancaster, by his side. "I see I started quite the thing," Enos teased. "Happy to see you settling down so early, Mary. But then, we expected that of you."

Ronald chuckled. "I didn't know Josiah was looking for a girlfriend, so you must have taken him right off his feet."

14

Mary bowed her head and scurried toward the house. She had heard enough compliments for the moment. The thought of her first date with Josiah had sent her heart pounding since the volleyball game on Friday evening. The only dark cloud over the occasion had been Betsy's reaction.

"You shouldn't have said yes to that man," Betsy had scolded on the way home. "Ronald Troyer would have been a much better choice."

"Please don't be so negative," Mary had begged. "If you were so impressed with Ronald, maybe he will remember you in the future."

Betsy had glared at Mary and fallen silent. They both knew that the pain in Betsy's heart was real, even if few in the community could understand.

Mary paused at the front door of Deacon Stoltzfus's house to catch her breath. The buzz of conversation inside grew louder when she opened the door. Mary made a beeline for the kitchen, which was filled with women. "Is there anything I can do to help with supper?" she asked Rachel.

"Give the mashed potatoes another whirl, and check them for seasoning," Rachel suggested. "We'll be ready to serve in a moment. With the Lancaster load here tonight, I'm running a little behind."

Mary nodded and grabbed the bowl of potatoes to stir them vigorously with a wooden spoon. That she was given this task was a great honor. Mashed potatoes were a staple in Amish meals and must be prepared to perfection, especially with the Lancaster visitors present.

"Here's the sample spoon," Rachel said in her ear.

Mary dropped a small glob of potatoes from the wooden spoon into a smaller utensil and tasted a bite. More salt was needed. She added a small amount plus two pinches of pepper from the cupboard.

Mary whipped the potatoes again, and Rachel appeared at her side. Mary handed her the spoon for another test.

"Perfect," Rachel pronounced.

Two women behind Rachel descended on the bowl of potatoes to fill smaller dishes. Then they disappeared in the direction of the dining room.

"We're ready to serve," Rachel told Mary. "Thanks for the help. You are the best."

Mary's face burned again, and she tried to hide behind the warm stove. Why did everyone draw attention to her this evening? Thankfully, Deacon Stoltzfus called for the prayer of thanks from the kitchen doorway, occupying everyone for a moment.

"And now, gracious heavenly Father," Deacon Stoltzfus prayed. "Let this evening be pleasing in Your sight. We give thanks for the bounty You have blessed us with and from which we are about to eat..."

Mary listened as Deacon Stoltzfus gave thanks for the visitors from Lancaster and prayed for their safe travels home. Would Josiah be staying for another week? Did she dare hope? Their first date hadn't even begun. She had prepared coconut ruffles for their evening snack, and a party mix made with pretzels, Cheerios, and Cheetos. If Josiah stayed another week, she could bake a cherry pie for him, plus a few extra pies to pacify the family. Gerald would eat a whole pie by himself if *Mamm* didn't keep an eye on the boy.

"Amen," Deacon Stoltzfus pronounced, and Mary lifted her head as the buzz of conversation resumed.

With the visitors present, supper was served cafeteria-style at the dining room table, with a line on each side—one for the men and one for the women.

"Go!" Rachel ordered, and Mary fell in with the other unmarried girls who streamed into the dining room. Betsy should have come tonight, but she had refused. Enos was here, so there was no *rumspringa* gathering to attend. Instead, Betsy was probably brooding in her room, which wasn't *goot* for anyone. They would have to pray even harder for Betsy's full healing now that Mary was dating Josiah—or, at least, was going on one date with him.

Mary glanced up and caught Josiah's clear blue eyes fixed on her from across the food-laden table. The plate in her hand almost slipped out of her fingers. She had never been in love, but if this was what love felt like, they should be married in a few years. Mary took a deep breath and dared to glance across the table again. Josiah's smile was still there, and it dazzled her. The food dishes became blurry, and she had no idea what she put on her plate.

Josiah leaned toward her to whisper, "Can I sit beside you?"

Mary nodded, and they found chairs toward the back along the living room wall.

"Perfect!" Josiah declared.

He clearly referred to their secluded position in the room, but from his smile he could have been speaking of her too.

Mary's heart pounded in her ears.

Several of the girls with their boyfriends in tow gave them pleased glances as they walked past to find seats together. It seemed that everyone approved of Josiah Beiler and Mary Yoder. The only person with a scowl on his face was Stephen Overholt, a bachelor who rarely came to the hymn singings. Where had Stephen come from? Why would he choose tonight to attend the young folks' gathering? Likely he knew someone who had come in from Lancaster, but that didn't supply a full explanation. Was there a girl who had sparked his interest? If Stephen had spoken with her earlier in the evening, a rejection would explain his fallen face.

"Is that Stephen Overholt over there?" Josiah asked, his spoon moving just slightly in Stephen's direction.

Mary kept her voice low. "*Yah*. How do you know him?"

"My cousin Linda..." Josiah motioned with his spoon again.

Mary nodded. She'd met Linda Friday night after the volleyball game, but Josiah's face was all she recalled clearly from that evening.

"Linda came to me, but not for advice." Josiah grinned. "She already had her answer, and now I can see why. She said this Stephen Overholt talked with her outside the mudroom door after the church services and asked her for a date this evening. When Linda said no, he wouldn't back down. He prattled on and on about the Lord's will, and how Linda should think long and hard before risking going against what the Lord wanted. I guess the man still hasn't given up."

"I'm sorry about that," Mary whispered. "I guess Stephen must be desperate."

Josiah grunted as if he totally agreed. "I'm thinking the man should ask some widow for a date. Don't you have any of those? Someone who would fit the man better than my cousin Linda?"

"I'm sure we do," Mary managed. "There's Sadie, for one, and Lavina has two small children."

"There you go." Josiah appeared satisfied with himself.

"I didn't know Stephen acted like that," Mary told him. "I knew he was a little strange."

"I thought you might know from experience," Josiah teased with a wicked grin.

Heat flamed into Mary's face, and she quickly took a bite of food.

"Am I right or not?" Josiah persisted. He was obviously drawing the wrong conclusions.

"Stephen has hardly ever spoken to me, let alone asked me for a date," she told him.

He tilted his head sideways. "Okay. Just sympathizing with you, that's all."

"Thank you," she told him.

What he said didn't make sense to her, but little did at the moment. Josiah couldn't be jealous, could he? Or did he think her the kind of girl whom Stephen would ask for a date?

"I've been waiting all day to spend time with you," he said with a twinkle in his eye.

Was Josiah still teasing?

"I was," he insisted, as if he read her thoughts. "I wasn't expecting to find someone like you in the valley."

"Josiah, please," she managed. "I'm embarrassed enough. I am quite thrilled to say the least. I've...it's..." Words failed her.

"Did you think no *goot* could come out of Lancaster?"

She met his teasing look. "It sounds like you expected no *goot* to come out of the valley."

"That would be right," he agreed. "But look what I've found: a diamond at the foothills of the Adirondacks."

"Josiah...I...stop it, please," Mary sputtered.

His smile only grew. He obviously enjoyed her discomfort.

"Are you ready for dessert?" he asked.

She cleared the last of her plate and nodded. Thankfully Josiah knew when to break up an embarrassing conversation.

They stood, and he whispered, "You first."

Mary made her way through the crowd with Josiah at her shoulder. The smiles and nods sent their way were plentiful and sincere, and Mary noticed that Stephen Overholt appeared to have vanished.

"You have a nice community here," Josiah told her as he filled his plate with chocolate cake, rice pudding, and shoofly pie. "You even have Lancaster's best food." He bent his head low to draw a deep breath over the pie on his plate. "Ah, the smells of home!"

"Most of the people moved here from Lancaster," she reminded him. "We know how to make shoofly pie."

He grinned. "I know. Just making sure they still know how to bake."

Mary took a piece of pie for herself. Shoofly pie would be a staple in their home if Josiah and she were to wed. Lancaster might be miles to the south, but they were connected in so many ways by community, by the generations who had gone before, and by their desire to live a life that was pleasing to the Lord.

Josiah took a bite of his pie as they walked back to their seats. "I should have taken a second piece!" he declared. "This is amazing. Exactly like home."

"You can have mine," she offered.

"Thanks, but I have to watch the pounds." He patted his flat stomach.

They laughed together, the sound muffled by the voices that rose and fell around them. Already she felt right with this man, so comfortable, so at home.

"Can I see you again next Sunday?" he asked in between bites of pie.

"You haven't even taken me home yet," she retorted. "How do you know you'll want to see me again?"

"I know," he said. "Can I stay over the week?"

Mary nodded, not trusting her voice. Josiah wanted to continue their relationship. She couldn't believe he wanted another date before he had eaten the food she had prepared for him.

"I hope I'm not being too forward," he said. "I know we only met each other Friday night, but rarely have I been so certain of anything, Mary. I would like to see a lot more of you this week. Maybe we could sneak in an extra evening at your place, considering the circumstances. I'm not very good at letter writing."

Mary's voice trembled. "I'm sure *Mamm* and *Daett* would not object. *Mamm* wasn't totally sure this morning which one of you Lancaster men was Josiah, but she said you all seemed decent."

"Then we will have to work on your *mamm*'s poor impression of me," Josiah said with a broad smile.

"I didn't mean it that way," Mary protested. "*Mamm* just...well, she couldn't—"

"I understand," Josiah interrupted. "I will do my best to get your *mamm* on my side."

And he would. Josiah would succeed. He should be able to charm any woman he wished to impress. Mary was so grateful that Josiah had chosen her, and she wondered if maybe this was the answer to their prayers for Betsy. Her relationship with Josiah might bring healing to her sister's heart, if only Betsy would withhold her quick judgments.

Josiah finished the last piece of his shoofly pie and sighed deeply. "*Wunderbah!*" he said. "Absolutely, *wunderbah!*"

Mary leaped to her feet to hide another rush of heat up her neck. "Time to help with the dishes," she tossed over her shoulder.

As she approached the dining room table, the girls in the kitchen began singing, "Praise God from whom all blessings flow!" Mary gathered up a handful of dishes and joined in the song. How could she praise the Lord enough for the blessing He had brought into her life since Friday evening? There seemed no way to fully express her joy, but the words of the song helped. Mary sang with her heart full. She deposited the dirty plates on the kitchen counter and returned to the dining room, where Josiah gave her a wink from across the table.

THREE

A year passed, and spring arrived in the valley once again. Mary sat on the front porch swing with a letter from Josiah on her lap. So much had happened in the past twelve months—the beginnings of Josiah's attentions, the letters that flew to and from Lancaster, her baptism, and now her new job at the food co-op in downtown Fort Plain. With her *rumspringa* in the past, her *mamm* had raised no objections to this increased exposure to the *Englisha* world. Mary's future in the community was secure. Even her friendship with Mrs. Gabert, the widow whose house was on her route to the co-op, raised no eyebrows. Mrs. Gabert was a sweet and spry grandmother who lived alone, and Mary stopped by often to check on her. Most of the time, Mrs. Gabert's conversations centered on her grandson Willard, who had recently begun work overseas at a mission in Kenya.

"Willard is such a brave, sweet boy," Mrs. Gabert had declared. "He always was. He left for Kenya as he'd planned, even after Carlene broke his heart. They were engaged, the two of them. A perfect couple bound for the Lord's work."

Mary nodded and listened. Kenya was a world away from the community and a place she knew little about. Her attention was fixed on places closer to home.

"I'm so sorry to hear that," she had commiserated with Mrs. Gabert. "I hope things work out for your grandson."

"Oh, they will," Mrs. Gabert had assured her. "I have prayed long and hard, and the Lord will answer in His own sweet time."

"*Yah*," Mary had agreed. "The Lord does all things right."

Like sending me Josiah's love. But she had not said as much to Mrs. Gabert, other than to say that she did have a boyfriend. There were some things not meant for *Englisha* ears. Mary smiled at the thought, and her gaze dropped to the letter again.

"My dearest, sweet Mary," Josiah had written. "How I long to see you again. Your smile lights up my whole life in the brief moments when I am with you. Your memory keeps my heart warm in the months when we are apart. I go upstairs after the evening chores and supper are over, and I think of you. I can hardly wait until the next time I am able to make the trip up to the valley and spend a few blissful hours in your presence."

A wistful smile lingered on Mary's face. How blessed she was with such a love. Her faith had been rewarded to the fullest. As the letters passed each other between the valley and Lancaster, the only cloud that hung over the Yoder family was Betsy's continued determination to jump the fence into the *Englisha* world. From time to time, Betsy mentioned being impressed with Ronald Troyer, but there was no hope in her heart that such a man would give her attention. She went out with Cousin Enos almost every Friday night, and Gerald wasn't old enough to join in the *rumspringa* activities, which was just as well. Betsy's attitude didn't seem to affect Enos, who had firm plans to settle down in a year or so—but Gerald was young and easily influenced.

Mary pulled her gaze back to the written pages. Josiah might propose soon, perhaps in time to plan a wedding this fall? Betsy could serve as the witness for the Yoder side of the family, and Mary would ask Josiah if they could approach Ronald to sit with Betsy. If Ronald could give Betsy a *goot* time on such a *wunderbah* day of joy and happiness, surely she would see the error of her ways and soften her heart.

Mary turned over the last page of the letter. There she had written some words that had bubbled up from her heart. Poetry had always come easily to her, but the fountain had opened since Josiah starting showering her with love and affection. Someday she would show him his letters with the poems on the back, but she didn't dare now. They were not yet husband and wife, and some things could only be shared once the sacred vows had been exchanged. She was a serious woman by nature, but love made everyone silly. At least that's how she had been feeling for the last year.

Mary whispered the words of the poem.

> My dearest, my dearest, Josiah, my dear.
> Your blue eyes sparkle like sun-washed skies,
> The bluest, the bluest, of blues they be,
> Your face so near, so dear you are.
>
> Your heart like a river, your eyes so blue.
> We gaze, we look, we tremble with joy.
> I hold your hand, so strong in mine.
> The Lord has so blessed me; how is He so kind?
>
> My faith was turned upward,
> Oft whispered in prayers.
> Thinking and wondering, not knowing what man
> The Lord would choose—yet the best was His plan.
>
> Now you have arrived, Josiah, my dear.
> My dreams but shadows before the sun shines through.
> My hope is alive, now that you're here.
> I bless the Lord, and I love you, I love you, so much.

Heat flushed Mary's cheeks, and she turned the page over again. What if someone discovered the stash of letters in her dresser drawer with her poems scribbled on the back? *Mamm* would smile and know not to read them without her permission, but Gerald...he would think she had taken leave of her senses. Betsy would sympathize but raise her nose in the air. No man compared to Betsy's opinion of the out-of-reach Ronald Troyer.

Apparently this was what love did to a person. Mary almost floated along, feeling as though the hardest tasks in life would be easy with Josiah by her side.

Surely he would propose soon, and Mary guessed he would want to live in Lancaster after the wedding. He hadn't mentioned anything about his plans, but he wouldn't until after proposing. His *daett* was well established in Lancaster, so Josiah and Mary could move into a small farm there and make it their own. Mary loved life here in the valley, but with Josiah, anywhere would be heaven on earth.

The front door swung open behind her, and Betsy's face appeared. She frowned as Mary buried the letter in her apron. "What are you doing out here?"

Betsy knew the answer, but Mary still spoke with a smile. "Thinking about Josiah and reading his letter."

Betsy's frown deepened. "You mean rereading it ten times. I saw you with that letter before you went to bed and now first thing this morning."

"It is a beautiful one," Mary replied. Engaging Betsy's negativity would do no one any *goot*.

Betsy sighed and settled onto the swing beside Mary. "I saw a really handsome *Englisha* fellow while I was out with Enos last weekend. He smiled at me and might remember me, unlike Ronald."

Mary didn't respond. Instead, she studied the range of the Adirondacks beyond the rooftops of Fort Plain.

Betsy carried on. "I am going to find my dream, Mary. I'm just telling you. Somewhere there is a man who will love me, one without straw in his hair and the smell of manure on his clothing first thing in the morning."

"Betsy!" Mary scolded. There were limits to her sister's complaining. "This is not how things are at all. Look at Josiah—"

"Josiah!" Betsy sniffed. "I don't trust the man, and Josiah's not a farmer."

Mary drew a long breath. "Farming is a blessing from the Lord, Betsy. *Daett* and Gerald are farmers. You should open your heart to whatever blessing from the community the Lord sends your way."

"I want an *Englisha* husband," Betsy continued undeterred. "Maybe a factory worker or a banker's son. Wouldn't that just be the dream?"

Mary tried again. "The Lord's will is what is best."

Betsy seemed not to hear. "I danced with two Amish boys last weekend at the local rock concert. Both of them stepped on my toes and didn't know the last thing about how to move with the music. Now that *Englisha* fellow..." Betsy's face drifted into a faraway look. "He could twirl across the room like the wind over the cornfields."

Enos shouldn't be taking you to such places, Mary almost said, but enough words had been spoken on the subject. "Are you ready to wash the dishes?" she asked instead.

Betsy sighed. "I would already have them done if *Mamm* and *Daett* had enough sense to install an electric dishwasher. I'll have one of those someday, and a husband who doesn't believe in slave labor."

"Come, let's go." Mary tried to speak cheerfully, but Betsy was like a thundercloud this morning.

Betsy glared at her sister. "You know my opinion of Josiah hasn't changed. He's playing with you. Who knows what the man is doing in Lancaster while he keeps you entertained with sweet letters."

"Betsy!" Mary gasped. "How can you say such things?"

"Because they are true!"

"Why? Because..." Mary searched for words. "I know that the accident with the fire has deeply affected your life, Betsy. I'm sorry you haven't gotten attention from the man you admire, but the Lord can heal the deepest wounds."

"Heal this?" Betsy lifted her chin to reveal the familiar scars, which ran almost from ear to ear. "They don't appear very healed to me."

"Beauty is in the soul of a woman," Mary replied, but the words sounded hollow.

The wounds from Betsy's childhood foiled her dreams in a world that placed great value on a woman's looks. That Amish men usually overlooked such injuries did not remove the scars from her. Mary wondered what she would do if the situation were reversed. Would she believe Josiah's affections were genuine? Would he have offered them to her in the first place?

"See, I do have a point," Betsy said, as if reading Mary's thoughts.

"*Yah*, I guess you do," Mary allowed. "But we must pray. The Lord can work in your heart to draw you back to His ways."

Betsy didn't answer.

"Do you want to read the letter from Josiah? You can see for yourself what a decent Amish man is like."

Betsy wrinkled her face. "I already know what he says, or I can imagine. So no thanks!"

Mary took a deep breath. She was glad that Betsy had declined, but any attempt to bridge the gap between them was worth the effort.

Mary turned the page over. "Do you want to see what I have written?"

"Your letter to him?"

"No, a poem to myself. I wouldn't show Josiah this—at least, not until we are wed."

Betsy shrugged and took the letter. She read it quickly, and a smile crept across her face. "If this were about my *Englisha* boyfriend, I would agree perfectly."

Mary took the page back and led the way into the house. Betsy's defenses were impenetrable. Only the Lord could breach them.

Mamm looked up with a smile when they walked into the kitchen. "Are both of you coming with me to the monthly sewing circle today?"

Betsy simply turned on the hot water at the sink without responding.

Mary waited a moment before saying, "I suppose I could come."

"I'll be ready in half an hour," *Mamm* told her before leaving the kitchen.

"You should come," Mary said to her sister.

Betsy busied herself with the dishes and remained silent. Even with Betsy's constant complaints about Amish life, she could handle herself well with household duties at the Yoders' home. She washed dishes and knew the intricacies of cooking and bread making. On the counter sat pecan pies she had made yesterday, two of which would go along with *Mamm* to the monthly sewing and would impress the best of the community cooks. If only Betsy's heart could be turned.

"Help us, dear Lord," Mary prayed as she wiped the dishes dry.

Betsy concentrated on her work.

Mary tried one more time. "Sure you don't want to come?"

Betsy shook her head. Mary grabbed her shawl and the pecan pies before leaving the house. She found *Mamm* beside the hitching post with her hand on Danny Boy's bridle. Mary hurried up to slide the pies under the back buggy seat before she lifted the shafts, and *Mamm* twirled Danny Boy expertly into place. They fastened the harness before climbing in and driving out of the lane.

"How are things going with Josiah?" *Mamm* asked as Danny Boy's hooves beat steadily on the pavement.

"Really *goot*. He's coming to visit soon. He didn't say when, but..." She paused. Sharing Josiah's sweet words out of desperation with Betsy was one thing, but saying them out loud to *Mamm* was another.

The smile on *Mamm's* face grew. "I'm glad to see you two doing so well. Our prayers are being answered for you, for which we are thankful. Now if only..." A cloud passed over her smile.

There was no need to speak the words. They both felt the pain that lay heavily on their hearts.

"The Lord will help us," *Mamm* finally said. "There must be an answer somewhere."

Mary nodded. "We must keep our faith."

Deacon Stoltzfus's home appeared in front of them, and Danny Boy turned into the familiar driveway with only the smallest pull on the reins. A row of buggies sat alongside the barn, and after she and *Mamm* parked, Mary hopped down to unhitch Danny Boy. *Mamm* left with the pecan pies while Mary took Danny Boy into the barn.

Deacon Stoltzfus met her at the door with a broad grin. "I can take him from here," he offered.

Mary returned the smile and offered a soft, "Thank you."

She turned to go, but Deacon Stoltzfus wasn't finished. "I hear Josiah's keeping the mailman busy," he teased.

Mary colored and looked away. The community's approval of their relationship gave her such a *wunderbah* feeling—a blessing Betsy would miss if she didn't change her ways.

"Your example in coming back early from your *rumspringa* even when you didn't have things sewn up with a man was exactly the example our young girls need," the deacon continued. "I want to compliment your faith, Mary."

Now her whole face was red under the deacon's praise. "Thank you," Mary managed to say.

"The Lord's blessings on the both of you," Deacon Stoltzfus continued. He disappeared into the barn with Danny Boy in tow behind him.

Mary turned her face toward the sun on the walk up to the house.

Maybe the day's warmth would serve as an excuse, but there was no shame in her blushing face. She should feel happiness and a great thankfulness for what the Lord had granted.

"*Goot* morning," Rachel greeted her at the door. "I'm glad you came with your *mamm* today."

Rachel didn't ask why Betsy hadn't come. Her intentions were well known in the community.

Mary nodded and returned the greeting, turning next to the other women gathered around the quilt frames set up in Rachel's living room. They would finish several today if things went well. She might even finish one to hang at the food co-op in Fort Plain where she worked. The regular customers wouldn't buy it, but the occasional tourist who passed through might pick up a quilt. The funds would go toward needs in the community. This month's sewing was intended to pay a portion of Emery and Laura's hospital bills incurred from their baby's premature arrival. Little John was home now, and Mary had seen him at the church services on Sunday. He would be a handsome man someday and charm a girl's heart the way Josiah did hers.

Mary settled herself in front of a frame, looked down, and began stitching across the intricate web of flowers. The quilt would be beautiful when finished, and as she worked, she thought about Josiah coming to the valley soon. What had she done to deserve such blessings from the Lord?

FOUR

On Sunday evening, Mary and Josiah departed the hymn singing together. As the buggy wheels spun beneath them, Mary leaned against his shoulder.

"Sorry about this horse," Josiah said with a laugh. "Your cousin Enos told me he was new but perfectly safe."

"I'm okay," Mary whispered as they hurtled along. A kicking, bucking horse was fine with her. That was how much she trusted him.

Josiah chuckled. "I think Enos wants to embarrass me when I spill the buggy in the ditch." He managed to pull up for a brief pause at the stop sign at Highway 163. "Is there some secret admirer of yours in the community you haven't told me about?"

Mary laughed. "There's no one. Trust me. Cousin Enos just wants to see if you can handle his wild horse. I know you can."

"Sure about that?" Josiah said, clutching the reins.

"Which point do you refer to?" She peered up at his face.

"You know which one I mean."

Mary nestled against his shoulder again. "If there is an admirer, I haven't noticed. I was too busy gazing toward Lancaster, waiting for your next visit."

Josiah roared with laughter. "Now that's the kind of answer that warms the heart. Letter writing gets a little wearisome."

"But you write so well." Mary sat up straight. "So cultured and..."

Words failed her when it came to Josiah. Only poetry fully expressed her deepest feelings, and the time to speak or show them to Josiah had not arrived. Someday his face would glow with happiness when she showed him all of his letters with her scribbles on the back pages.

"I should have brought you a bouquet of flowers like the *Englisha* do," he said.

"That isn't necessary," she protested. "You know the customs of the community. Your being here is enough for me."

"I feel the same about you." He smiled. "But there's a little something I brought for you under the buggy seat."

"Josiah! You didn't have to."

"I wanted to."

His eyes twinkled. She wanted to reach up, touch his face, and pull him close, but they had not yet kissed. That would be Josiah's move when the time was right. Maybe if he lived in the valley, they would already have arrived at this point.

"Penny for your thoughts," he teased.

She didn't answer as they turned into the Yoders' driveway. Josiah expertly pulled to a stop right by the hitching post, with the head of Cousin Enos's wild horse inches from the tie rail.

"Aren't you going to see what I brought you?" he asked, thankfully moving on from his other concerns.

Cousin Enos's horse blew his nose as if impressed with his frisky performance. Mary ignored the horse to reach under the buggy seat. At first her fingers found nothing. She leaned forward further and touched paper. Slowly she lifted the package into her lap. "What is it?"

"You'll have to see." Like Cousin Enos's horse, Josiah sounded pleased with himself.

Mary opened the paper bag to reach inside and lift out one of the items—chocolate candy with fancy wrapping. There was a card and a small journal, leather bound and expensive. Finally, she pulled out some perfume in a small bottle. The scent of roses wafted into the air as Mary touched the glass with her finger.

"Josiah!" she chided. "This is too much."

He kissed her lightly on the top of her *kapp*. "Nothing is too much for you, dear. After all this time, I couldn't arrive with empty hands."

"But...but..." Mary gave up and clung to his arm, the items strewn on her lap. "Thank you so much, Josiah. So very much."

"Considering that response, I should have brought more!" He laughed and held her hand for a moment. "Shall we go inside before this horse decides to dash on home?"

Mary nodded and gathered up her gifts. Josiah jumped down to secure Cousin Enos's horse, and then he offered Mary his hand from the bottom of the buggy step. Her face felt flushed from all his attention, but she hoped he didn't mind. He kept her hand in his on the walk up to the house.

Mary paused to glance back when Gerald pulled in the driveway with Betsy beside him. She was grateful Betsy had decided to attend the hymn singing tonight, but she didn't want Josiah ensconced on the living room couch when Betsy came in. Her sister's dislike for Josiah had yet to diminish. By now Josiah must have heard about Betsy's search for an *Englisha* boyfriend, but he didn't know about her deep distrust of him.

"Are we going in?" He tugged on her hand.

"Can we stay a moment? Watch the stars?" She peered upward at the heavens. Josiah's face was the only star she wanted to see, but that was something one shouldn't say aloud just yet.

"I suppose so," he allowed. "Do you like stargazing?"

"I do."

"Come then." He tugged her hand in the opposite direction.

As they stepped out from under the tree, Betsy jumped out of the buggy and dashed up the walk without a word to them.

"*Goot* night," Josiah hollered after her.

Betsy took the porch steps two at a time and never slowed.

"I'm sorry about Betsy," Mary whispered. "She doesn't mean to be rude..."

"I've heard. Don't worry. We all have our injuries in life. That's just the way things are. I'm sure Betsy will eventually become more comfortable around me."

"It's not you," Mary protested.

Josiah didn't seem to hear as he led her farther out beneath the open skies. "There they are." His hand swept from horizon to horizon. "Beautiful. I don't often think to stop and look. You are *goot* for me, Mary."

"I hope so." She clung to his hand.

"You are!" He smiled down at her. "Shall I take that?"

Mary nodded and handed him the paper package. "I wish I had something to give you."

"You have food inside, don't you?"

"*Yah*! Brownies and shoofly pie. But that's not much compared to this."

"I disagree," he said. "You are like coming home. Much better than the store-bought things I brought you. Even my card is from Walmart."

They laughed together, the sound muffled under the open heavens. "I'll have to read your card once we're inside."

He pretended embarrassment and covered his face with his free hand.

"*Goot* evening!" Gerald hollered from a few feet away, making Mary jump.

"You're scaring your sister," Josiah scolded.

Gerald grinned. "I think she'll get over it." He held out his hand. "Welcome to the Yoders' house again."

"Thanks." Josiah shook Gerald's hand. "Did you leave any shoofly pie for me?"

Gerald's grin grew. "No danger there. I'm a pecan pie man. Betsy makes the best in the community."

"Ah...you don't know what you're missing," Josiah told him. "But that leaves more for me, I guess."

"*Daett* likes shoofly pie." Gerald held open the front door. "I guess he remembers Lancaster better than I do."

Josiah laughed. "Can't live without shoofly pie. Or marry a *frau* who doesn't know how to make shoofly pies."

Gerald joined in Josiah's laugher. "I'll be sure to check out her pecan pie-making abilities when I find the perfect girl."

"Oh, she'll know how to make pecan pie if she's perfect," Josiah assured him. "Otherwise she wouldn't be perfect for you."

"Now that's a thought." Gerald closed the door behind him. "What's in your bag, Mary? Any dating lessons for me in there?"

Josiah chuckled but didn't answer while Mary made a beeline for the kitchen. Josiah must be teasing about matching a woman with a man's pie tastes. Surely he wouldn't have rejected her if her shoofly making abilities had been horrible. Mary pushed the thought away as Gerald's footsteps faded up the stairs. She should have invited Gerald to sit at the table and eat a piece of pie with them, but she wanted every moment possible alone with Josiah. He would leave the house tonight and travel back tomorrow by the Greyhound bus to Lancaster. Many weeks would pass before his return.

A soft touch on Mary's shoulder turned her around, and she melted into Josiah's arms. She had not dared before, but neither had he offered her the opportunity. He held her close while she tried to breathe evenly. Had their relationship progressed to a proposal yet? Perhaps tonight?

She pulled away to slide pieces of shoofly pie onto plates. He bent low to take a deep breath over them. "Perfect as always," he said. "And so are you."

Mary ducked her head. She should change the subject. "Where is the package?" she asked. "I should take a better look at your gifts now that we are inside in the light."

He pulled her close again. "You can look later. I want to be with you right now."

"And eat shoofly?" she teased.

He grinned. "*Yah*. A man must eat." He let go to admire the pieces of shoofly pie. "How many can I have?"

"The whole pie if you wish."

"I might just take you up on the offer."

Mary filled glasses of milk, and Josiah picked up their plates to lead the way back to the living room. He seated himself on the couch and motioned for her to sit beside him. She handed him a glass of milk, and his fingers lingered on hers. A smile spread across his whole face. "You have no idea how many times I think about this moment when I am away from you. Always it seems so far in the future, and yet now here we are, you and I, alone and enjoying each other's company. Do you know how much these visits mean to me, Mary?"

She seated herself and didn't answer.

He continued undeterred. "I have never spent much time planning my life. Did you know that?"

He glanced at her, and she forced a smile. "I never thought about the question."

"I don't," he stated. "I just live life as it's given to me. Never did I imagine I would find you here in the valley when I visited almost a year ago, or think I would spend my time writing letters to a girl. Letter writing certainly wasn't in my plans...not that I had any, but just saying. Now I'm enjoying myself immensely. Well, certain moments at least. I doubt if any man is happy writing letters for very long." He gave a little laugh.

Mary clasped and unclasped her hands. "You could write less,

Josiah. I'm not trying to be a burden, although I would miss your letters. You bless and inspire me. I doubt if you know how much."

His smile didn't dim. "I'm just rambling, sweetheart. I like what life has given me, and I thank the Lord often for the gift I found in the valley. You are a precious girl, Mary. Any man in the community would count himself blessed to call you his beloved."

Mary tried to breathe. Tears swam in her eyes, and she guessed her face must be burning brighter than the noonday sun.

"I have wanted to ask you for some time, Mary." He set down his pie to take her hand. "I even thought to write you the question, but that would have spoiled so much—this moment, this preciousness, this sweetness in your presence. Letters just don't carry all of that, so I waited until I could make the trip again."

"*Yah?*" Mary managed.

He touched her cheek with his hand. "I said that in a rambling way, because that's how I found you, Mary. I don't regret one second or one turn in the road. You are very dear to me. Would you marry me, sweetheart?"

The room spun in circles, and then Josiah's blue eyes finally filled Mary's vision.

"Would you?" He moved closer.

"*Yah,*" she whispered. "Oh, Josiah, you don't know how I have longed for this time to come."

"Really?" A pleased look filled his face. "I do love you, Mary."

"And I adore you, Josiah. I love you with my whole heart, with everything in me. Perhaps too much even, but how can I ever love you enough? I comfort myself with that thought. Oh, Josiah! To be your *frau*! That would be such an honor, such a privilege, such—"

His face came closer, and he gathered her in his arms. "Hush, sweetheart. Soon you will be my *frau*," he whispered into her ear. Then his lips found hers, and she clung to him.

"Ah...what a girl. Your kisses are much better than I imagined."

She reached for him again, and he didn't resist as she snuggled against his chest. "I will miss you, Josiah, so much more now that we are promised to each other."

He grinned. "Maybe we should begin to plan our wedding next year."

"Next year!" Mary gulped. "I was hoping that..." She hadn't known Josiah would propose tonight, but he had to know how much she had longed for this hour to arrive.

"I have to save up for a farm," he said. He reached for his piece of shoofly pie. "That's what *Daett* told me. I don't plan things, but *Daett*'s the businessman, and if I want his help I'd best listen. Surely we can wait until next year's wedding season? Maybe the first Thursday in November?"

Mary gathered herself together. "*Yah*, of course we can wait. You are worth the wait, Josiah. So...whatever you say. I know you're right."

He swallowed his bite of shoofly pie before he answered. "I love you, Mary. So very, very much. You are so sweet."

FIVE

With a blast of black smoke from its rusted muffler, the blue-and-white striped bus maneuvered around a pile of garbage in the street. Willard Gabert paused at the corner near a tumbledown shanty and squinted his eyes in the late afternoon sun. In front of him a boy, scrawny and thin, stumbled into the refuse with a sharp twist and a somersault. The boy must have been ejected from the bus, and not from the passenger door.

Willard moved closer. *Another homeless child has landed in Nairobi,* he thought to himself. Nairobi was considered the land of Eden in the disenfranchised countryside. It was a mistaken view, but one held by many. "Death trap" was a more apt description for the city.

Willard knelt beside the child and took his hand. There was a pulse. Willard was not a medical doctor, but he knew to do that much. He had come to Kenya a year ago as a minister of souls, even while his own bled. The pain subsided at moments like this, when he saw the reason he had come, when he touched the pain of others whose injuries were deeper than his own agony.

He had come from America, a society Kenya sought to emulate. Many people came to Nairobi with dreams that usually went unfulfilled. At worst, lives were destroyed.

39

"Hello," Willard called to the fallen child. "Can you speak English?"

There was no answer. He should carry the child to the mission center some ten blocks away. In America you would dial 911 and wait until help arrived, but here, Willard was the help—a disturbing thought when prayer and a heart to serve were usually the best things he had to offer. Tambala, the nurse and midwife he had hired, would do what she could for the boy, but funds were limited at present.

Carlene's father, Alfred, was the senior pastor at Lighthouse Baptist Church back in New York. The man had connections everywhere, but his planned funding of the mission had dried up with the cancellation of his daughter's marriage. Willard was on his own except for his grandmother's prayers. The Lord seemed distant at times, but Grandma had a warmth and faith that reached all the way across the Atlantic.

"Be strong and of good courage, Willard," her email had declared last week, echoing the familiar words of his youth. Grandma had learned to use email in her old age, mostly to communicate with him. She had other grandchildren, but her mastery of the web's secrets had coincided with his departure for Kenya. She had begun her effort soon after Carlene had rejected Willard. Grandma had known that he would answer the call of missions, even with a broken heart.

"The Lord will give you healing, son," she had told him. "Just follow Him when the storm blows its hardest. The waves cannot overflow His love for you."

He had gulped down the pain, smiled, and continued with his plans, but the void had remained. He and Carlene had dreamed together and looked into the future. Carlene's father had a heart for missions, a passion perhaps greater than Willard's own. Together they would have gone far. Alone, Willard placed one foot in front of the other and hoped he would have the strength to finish each day.

Before him in the dirt of the street, the child had begun to stir. "Hello?" Willard said. "How badly does it hurt?"

A soft groan was the only answer. Willard moved the boy's arm slightly higher. No protest came. He did the same with the other arm, and both legs. The boy let out another groan, but apparently he felt no sharp pains. Likely just bruises that made his whole body ache.

Willard understood. Perhaps soon his own pain would lessen and eventually disappear. But how could he forget Carlene? He guessed she was engaged again. No one had told him as much, but the silence spoke clearly enough—and he knew her well. She would not be single for long. Not such a woman. A treasure had slipped from his hand to another's and left him destitute.

Carlene should be here with her arms around him, her face upturned and smiling brightly. The woman was lovely beyond belief. She likely now smiled into the face of another, a man more worthy than Willard. Perhaps a business executive, someone on the upward climb of the corporate ladder.

Willard placed his arm under the child and gently lifted him. The boy's dust-encrusted head rested softly against his shoulder. Willard closed his eyes and pressed onward. He stumbled over the garbage in the street and caught himself with only a slight jolt to the injured child. Carlene had been spared the slums, the despair that rose from the streets, the hopelessness that haunted many faces. He would have brought her here, where she would have suffered with him. Maybe the Lord had been right to spare Carlene from their work. Willard was destined to walk alone, and somehow his heart would adjust.

He navigated the turn of the street and avoided a head-on collision with an old man, whose burlap bag dangled over his shoulder.

"Excuse me," Willard muttered, but the courtesy was not expected.

The man barely paused in his shuffle down the street. A block later Willard heard a muffled cry behind him, and he turned, the boy still cradled in his arms. Three young boys had assaulted the old man and thrown him to the street. The gang was in the process of shaking the bag's contents into the surrounding garbage, and two of the boys were on their knees, rifling through the debris. They came up with something and held the object aloft. With cries of delight, they vanished into a side street.

Willard retraced his steps and laid down the injured boy. The old man was already on his knees.

Willard held out his hand. "Are you okay?"

A grunt was the only answer. The old man surveyed the strewn contents for a second before bending over to pick up the bag. He resumed his shuffle down the street, hopelessness written large on his face. What had been in the bag? Perhaps a half-eaten piece of beef scavenged from a restaurant downtown, or nothing more than a head of rotten lettuce that would stave off hunger for a few hours. Healthy boys had attacked him—the ones who kept the gang going before succumbing to the terror of the streets. Eventually, those boys might find themselves addicted to sniffing poisonous glue bottles, or worse. The cruelty of the slums in particular drove most to seek relief from a life they could not change.

Willard gathered the abandoned boy in his arms again. What was the use? He struggled against impossible odds. He sought to reach human varmints, the hated of the hated, but no one encouraged Willard's effort. Who was to blame for the city's problems? Everyone and no one at the same time. America's opulence, Africa's poverty, the missionaries' intentions... Maybe this whole mess should be left alone? That would leave Kenya to its own devices, and America to its abundance. Yet he had come, and he would stay. Not because he had failed back home, but because his heart called him. He would do what could be done or die trying.

The mission was located in a calmer district, in an area of town that would provide safety and quiet to the children and the missionaries. It took a bit of time for Willard to make the trek as he gently carried the injured boy. He turned the last corner and approached the double doors of the mission that opened directly into the street. These buildings had been here when he arrived, a month before the last missionaries departed. Rose and Donald Petersheim, a young American couple, had finished their two years of service. Rose and Donald had not asked for a detailed explanation when Willard had shown up alone, without Carlene. Their smiles were compassionate.

Can you stay another year? he had almost asked, but the sadness in their eyes restrained him. They appeared weary and broken, casualties of the city's corruption.

Willard crossed the front lawn and entered the double doors of the mission, calling out, "Tambala. Can you come?" He deposited the boy on the low table in the living room and was propping up the boy's head with a blanket when the elderly woman entered.

"Willard!" she scolded. "You are ruining my best blanket."

"Can you see to the boy? See what is wrong with him?"

Tambala continued her scolding even as she obeyed. "You cannot save the whole city, Willard. This one is almost dead. Why didn't you leave him where you found him? They are best dead anyway! Don't you know that by now?"

Willard ignored her words. "How badly is he hurt?"

"Nothing broken," Tambala confirmed. "He may have internal injuries. How was he injured? Beaten up by the others?"

"He let go from the bus chassis, I guess," Willard responded. "I didn't see the whole incident, but he came out from under the vehicle."

Tambala clucked her tongue. "Then he was half dead already. They ride those buses in from hundreds of miles out. You know that. And you can't make him stay here."

"We can try." Willard forced a smile. "Kindness and godly teaching can change anyone if they will open their hearts and believe."

Tambala snorted in disgust. "Our whole country rattles on and on about faith. Believe in American values, believe in prosperity, believe the Lord, and He will bless you. What a lie this is. We die and we live for reasons we cannot understand. That's the truth, Willard."

He closed his eyes and rested his hands on the table. He missed Carlene the most in moments like these. He missed her support, her words of faith in the darkest hours, when evil appeared triumphant.

"I will clean him the best I can," Willard said. "We will see where we go from there."

"I know you barely have the funds to keep this place open," Tambala continued. "You need to think about yourself."

Willard reached for the boy again, but she shooed him away. "I will clean him." Her face softened. "You do enough."

He gave in, his body weary. Was his faith failing him? With faith a man could outlast any storm. How Tambala knew about the mission's financial condition, he wasn't sure. Maybe such things were obvious from his efforts to live on a tight budget. Then again, didn't all missionaries live on lean budgets? He would have to return stateside eventually to build up his base of support. He should have done more fund-raising before making the trip over, but there hadn't been the time. Plus, his heart had failed him. That was his problem—his heart. With a broken heart, a man died, even if he had the faith to move mountains.

Willard filled a bowl of water and followed Tambala into the bedroom, where she laid the boy on the floor. The simplest accommodation in this house was luxurious compared to life on the street.

She glanced at the bowl of water and stood to retrieve two washcloths. "You can help," she told him, handing him a cloth.

Willard knelt and began to wash the child's callused feet. Broken skin ran along his soles, and crusted blood filled the wounds. Willard wet his cloth and dripped the water over the foot before touching the skin. Several burns the size of quarters appeared beneath the dirt. The boy must have touched the bus's muffler on the long ride into town. Many of them died on the trip, so this was a lucky one.

Tears filled Willard's eyes as he cleaned between the boy's toes. How different the standards were in Kenya. He had come to another world, but love worked here the same as it did at home. Was not his mission called Agape Outreach? He had to believe that much.

SIX

Betsy awakened early on Monday morning, with the stillness of the spring night heavy on the old house. Beyond the dark blue drapes, faint streaks of light painted the sky. Dawn must be an hour or so away. She felt something wasn't right in the house, but what was new about that feeling? Most things about Amish life were troublesome to her. Betsy sighed and sat up in bed. For once she was right and wouldn't have to wait for some future event to prove her point. Josiah had left early last evening after bringing Mary home from the hymn singing. She hadn't attended, mostly because she had stayed out late on Saturday night and needed to catch up on her sleep. That had become her pattern of late. Mary moved toward her anticipated wedding date, while Betsy drifted ever closer to jumping the fence. She'd have to wait for her twenty-first birthday to make the final choice. So dictated Amish tradition, and she would give *Mamm* and *Daett* that much respect. Her leaving would bring enough sorrow to their hearts without an open display of rebellion.

Betsy threw off the quilt and dressed. She wondered why Josiah had left early last night. She had meant to stay awake and talk when her sister came upstairs, but sleep had overtaken Betsy. That meant Mary had either lingered downstairs or crept up the steps so no one would hear her. Josiah was nothing but trouble, but Betsy no longer expressed her feelings about him to her family. They didn't want her opinion because what did she know? That was their attitude. She planned to join the *Englisha*, and that took care of her sound judgment.

But Josiah was unreliable. She had been certain of that since laying eyes on him for the first time. In the meantime, Mary had been taken with his piercing blue eyes and his down-home charm. That he had fit Mary's timetable for acquiring a home and a family was a little too pat for comfort. Mary, on the other hand, could see only roses with no thorns. She had waxed eloquent these past years, scribbling her poetry on the back of Josiah's letters, yet she had never shown her expressions of love to Josiah. How had he not discovered Mary's talent? Was he not interested, or was he too taken with himself? The latter, if Betsy had to guess. But no one was asking her.

She tiptoed across the hallway and listened by Mary's bedroom door. All was silent. Had she been wrong about last night? Maybe Josiah had to leave early for his return to Lancaster…but no. That made no sense. He usually stayed until after midnight while the two lovebirds made wedding plans. The man could sleep on the bus ride back to Lancaster the next morning. Josiah would only leave early if trouble were in the air.

Betsy pushed open the bedroom door. She should check on her sister. There was a spring bug making its round in the community, so Mary could be burning up with a fever. Maybe that explained Josiah's early departure. Betsy paused in the doorway to peer at the bed. Mary was definitely under the quilt, but her breathing didn't sound heavy. Betsy had turned to leave when Mary spoke. "Do you want something?"

"Are you okay?" Betsy chirped. "I thought Josiah left early last night."

There was silence from the bed.

"You're not sick with the flu, are you?"

"I'm okay. I'll be down in a moment."

Mary sounded normal, though her voice was a little weak. Betsy pushed the question. "Why did Josiah leave early?"

"He had to get back to Lancaster." This time there was a catch in Mary's voice.

Betsy approached the bed and sat on the edge. "What happened?"

A sob burst out from deep inside her sister. "Josiah says he's not coming back. He broke off the engagement."

"What!" Betsy exclaimed. "The charlatan!"

"He's Josiah," Mary wailed. "Don't run him down."

"So what is this about him not coming back? You have your wedding planned."

"I know!" Mary gasped. "Maybe he just wants a break from our relationship. I can't imagine what else. He just...he doesn't...he left, Betsy, and he didn't say much other than that it's over." Mary buried her face in the quilt. "I tried not to cry all night. There must be some explanation I'm missing."

Betsy took a deep breath. "Don't you think *Mamm* should hear this? There are wedding plans that must be called off."

"That's not until the first Thursday in November. There's still..." Mary's voice dropped to a whimper. "That's a long time yet, and I'm sure we can straighten things out. Other couples go through things like this. We can grow and learn."

"You should still tell *Mamm*," Betsy insisted. "Just in case."

Mary gathered herself together and wiped her eyes. "I'll be down in a moment to help with breakfast, but don't tell *Mamm* anything. I'll wait a few days to see if a letter arrives from Josiah."

Betsy knew a letter wouldn't arrive, but now was not the moment to make the point. She retreated and closed the bedroom door. She ran her hand along the handrail for the descent down the steps. A soft glow of light appeared under the stairwell door before she arrived. She opened and stepped into the living room to follow the light into the kitchen.

Mamm looked up with a smile. "You're up early. *Daett's* the only one out in the barn."

"I've caught up on my sleep, I guess." Betsy tried to appear disinterested. Mary should break the news in her own way.

Mamm's smile faded. "Perhaps it's time we have another talk about your future, Betsy. With it being early, and Mary still sleeping, this might be a *goot* chance."

"There is nothing to say, *Mamm*." Betsy hung her head. This conversation would have been awkward no matter what, but with the news about Josiah's breaking off the wedding...

Mamm peered at her. "Did something out of the ordinary happen this weekend, Betsy?"

"No. I did my usual thing with Enos."

"Rachel and Annie are both praying for you." *Mamm* sighed. "Rachel told me so at the services yesterday. I guess everyone has noticed your absence at the hymn singings, and with Josiah back to visit again, and Mary's wedding coming up..." Her voice trailed off.

Betsy looked away. Thankfully, she heard Mary's step on the stairs. This conversation was almost over.

"We are all praying for you," *Mamm* squeezed in before Mary appeared.

Somehow Mary had rid herself of her tearstains and had pasted a bright smile on her face. How long would she be able to continue the charade? But then, what did Betsy know? Maybe Mary could patch up this rough spot with Josiah.

Mamm was all smiles too. "*Goot* to see you this morning, Mary. Did Josiah have any news from Lancaster last night?"

"I...we..." Mary searched for words. "Josiah left early, but everything's fine in Lancaster. They are ready for spring planting next week. He probably won't be back again until sometime in the summer."

Betsy busied herself with heating the pan for the eggs. Should she say something? Mary was in denial, and that was not *goot*.

Mamm also busied herself at the stove. "I hope Josiah didn't catch the flu bug while he was here."

"I don't think so." Mary attempted a laugh. "Josiah wouldn't catch the flu."

Betsy stifled her incredulity. There were no limits to Mary's faith in Josiah Beiler.

"Are you coming down with it? You can have a few extra hours of sleep this morning if you need them." *Mamm*'s face was filled with concern.

"I'm fine." Mary brushed past Betsy to retrieve the bacon from the refrigerator. "At least I will be soon," she muttered under her breath.

Mamm turned toward Mary. "What is wrong?"

Mary didn't answer as she rattled the bacon pan on the counter.

Mamm shrugged and continued with her work, but she appeared troubled. Why was Mary avoiding the problem?

Heavy footsteps came down the stairs, and Gerald went past the living room door. He hollered over his shoulder, "Take your time with breakfast! There's three of you and only two of us."

"I'm going to help with the chores this morning," Betsy said, leaving before either Mary or *Mamm* could protest.

She caught up with Gerald halfway across the yard.

He didn't pause in his rapid stride toward the barn. "What made you decide to help?"

"I had to get out of the house. Josiah left early last night."

He gave her a glance in the dim morning light but didn't respond.

Betsy hurried on. "There's trouble in paradise, and Mary's head is in the sand."

"So?" Gerald declared. "Lovers' quarrel, I suppose. They do happen."

Betsy sighed. "I know that nobody values my opinion, so I'll keep it to myself."

Gerald laughed. "You know there's trouble out there too." He waved his hand toward the foothills of the Adirondacks, which revealed the dawning sun.

"Of course I know that," Betsy retorted. "Things just aren't as bad as Amish life."

"Is there any kind of Amish man who would interest you?" Gerald asked in a teasing voice.

"He doesn't exist," Betsy snapped. "Or if he does, he wouldn't want me."

"You have such high standards that no one can qualify. Is that the problem?"

"Don't lecture me, Gerald. I'm not being prideful. I know what I want."

"So tell me." He paused at the barn door.

"Right here?"

"*Yah*, I can't wait for such interesting news."

"Okay." Betsy lifted her chin. "He'd have to know things you don't learn on an Amish farm. Interesting things, such as a basic knowledge of the universe." Betsy pointed up and outward. "And he'd know how to dance without stepping on toes. That would help. And if he must be a farmer, he should know how to clean up. Is there an Amish man like that?"

"You're insulting me. Maybe I don't want to hear what you have to say."

"Sorry," Betsy said. "You and *Daett* are not what I mean—"

"See?" Gerald declared as he opened the barn door. "There *are* men who fit your criteria. You just need to stop thinking so negatively. You're scaring them off."

Betsy followed her brother into the barn and muttered, "They should also be like Ronald Troyer."

Gerald seemed not to hear, but his words had stung her. Maybe she didn't have things figured out. Or maybe she had given up too easily. Maybe Ronald would return to the community and look her up.

Betsy thought about her sister. Mary was steadfast when the road became rough. Josiah was not worthy of Mary's love, and last night proved Betsy's point—but Mary was undeterred in her loyalty and affection.

Meanwhile, Betsy let a childhood injury determine the path of her life. Was she too stubborn to see the error of her ways? For once an arrow from her family had found its mark. Who would have thought that Gerald would be the one to string the bow?

"Are you helping or daydreaming?" Gerald hollered.

Daett stuck his head out from behind a cow. "Just be glad the girl came out to help."

"Thank you." Betsy sent her gratitude his way before grabbing a three-legged stool and a pail. She chose the cow beside *Daett*'s and sat down to draw milk from the udder.

Betsy's head spun. Giving in and accepting the life *Mamm* and *Daett* had planned for her would be the easy way out. She wouldn't have to venture forth on her own and learn a new way of life unfamiliar to her. *Rumspringa* wasn't a true example of the *Englisha* life. Concerts and dances with *Englisha* men weren't the same as marriage to an *Englisha* man—if she could even catch the attention of one. They would undoubtedly have expectations she might not be able to satisfy.

Betsy filled the pail with long streams of white milk. The foam rose in the bucket and rolled over the side by the time she finished.

When Betsy went to empty the milk into the strainer, *Daett* gave her another smile. "You need to come out more often to help. An extra hand makes things go so much faster."

"I'll try," Betsy responded.

Mary used to help with the morning chores before taking a job at the co-op, but no one had asked Betsy to take up the slack the men must have felt in the barn. Had *Mamm* and *Daett* been afraid she would rebel if they made her take on a greater share of the burden of an Amish farm? If they had, she could only blame herself. She had never been secretive about her disdain for Amish things.

Betsy pressed back tears. This morning had not turned out as she had expected. Maybe she was too focused on finding things wrong with an Amish life. If Mary succeeded in patching up her difference with Josiah, Betsy needed to seriously reconsider her own plans.

She sat down beside the next cow in line. Amish life might be drudgery, but that didn't mean she should take things easily in the house while *Daett* and Gerald overworked themselves in the barn.

SEVEN

Mary slipped out of her bedroom with a kerosene lamp firmly clasped in her hand. Dawn was still an hour away, and the chill of the November night had crept into the house. *Daett* would be up soon to stir the banked furnace in the basement and to call Gerald for the morning chores. She should be asleep, but she wasn't.

Half the night, she had tossed and turned until her old Texas Star quilt was a tangled mess. She had pressed her face into her pillow to stifle the sobs she couldn't silence. The pillow was dry now, and another day was about to begin. She would soon be over the last months of grief, she hoped. Someday she would look back and count the lessons learned as worth the cost. Hearts had been broken before hers.

A cry escaped her as she stubbed her toe on the banister post. The lamp tilted in her hand, and she righted herself. That was all she needed—a spill down the stairs, with an awful crash of glass at the bottom and flames bursting upward.

"She tried to burn the house down on the day she'd planned to wed Josiah Beiler." That's what the community would say.

"Couldn't get over her grief," another would add.

"She's not the first girl to walk this road," someone would reply.

She should be able to bear Josiah's rejection with grace and fortitude, she told herself. Perhaps she should even wish him and his new bride a blessing on their wedding day...a wedding day she once thought would be her own.

Mary took a careful step. Her foot didn't hurt, but her heart throbbed. Susie Wengerd! Mary had never met the girl, but Susie must be beautiful. Josiah would wed her today instead. At twelve o'clock, Susie would stand by Josiah's side and say the sacred wedding vows Mary had planned to speak. Josiah's face would glow with happiness, and his silly grin would appear as the two took their seats afterward.

"My *frau*," Josiah would whisper to Susie on the walk out of the house toward the barn, where the reception in Lancaster would be held.

She knew the tone Josiah would use—the way he would linger on that last word. Josiah had once held Mary close and told her, "Soon you will be my *frau*." Sweet words came easy to him. Had he lied to her? He had seemed so sincere. How could she have been so wrong in her judgment?

Mary reached for the doorknob at the bottom of the stairwell, and tears filled her eyes as she stepped out into the living room. The kitchen around the corner should be bustling this morning with activity, as aunts and friends gathered to cook the huge noon meal to serve later in *Daett's* barn. Instead, Susie Wengerd's kitchen in Lancaster would be filled this morning with kerosene lamps that threw their flickering light across the old wood cookstove.

Mary sat down at the kitchen table to bury her face in her arms. How she had loved Josiah and dreamed of the home they would build together. If things had gone as planned, she would have been Mary Beiler tonight. How often she had tried on the name, saying it aloud in her bedroom upstairs after Josiah left on a Sunday evening. She had been ready to settle down as a stable church member and take her place alongside the other married women of the community. They would have lived on the small farm Josiah had purchased in Lancaster. But now that future was gone, lost in the pain and sorrow of rejection. Susie would say the vows with Josiah today, and Mary would still be a Yoder when nightfall arrived.

She lifted her head to stare at the darkened kitchen window. At least her tears had stopped before the break of dawn, so that was a *goot* sign. One had to get over things, even those that tore the heart up by the roots and trampled upon one's self-esteem. What was wrong with her? What had caused Josiah to abandon their wedding plans? He had not explained himself that evening beyond a mumbled, "It's best we go separate ways, Mary."

"But I love you. We love each other," she had gasped.

"*Yah*," he had agreed, his eyes fixed on the hardwood floor. "But it would be for the best if we seek the will of the Lord for another path through life."

Then he had left, his borrowed buggy pulling out of the driveway, and she had stood beside the living room window with tears streaming down her face. The next day he made his way back to Lancaster from Little Falls, where he always caught the Greyhound bus. Maybe that had been the problem—their long-distance relationship. Maybe if she had lived in Lancaster, Josiah's affections would not have strayed. She would have been on hand to woo him back when Susie made her moves.

Mary clenched and unclenched her fists. She couldn't hate. Susie was a sister in the Lord and a solid member of the community in Lancaster. Josiah would not have settled for any other kind of girl. If Susie had captured Josiah's love, Susie had been within her right. That was the purpose of courtship, to choose the right partner for one's journey through life. Mary groaned. These philosophical thoughts did nothing to make her feel better. She had failed. She had lost the man she loved and trusted. She had been jilted, as the *Englisha* would say, six months from the altar.

Another man would come along, but not one like Josiah. There couldn't be one. She would have to settle for second best and know the truth in her heart. Her dream of home and family would never burn quite as brightly. Along with his love, that was what Josiah had taken away.

Would the memory of their sweet times together fade with the passing years? She felt them this morning as if they had happened yesterday. Memories sat undimmed in her heart even when she knew that Susie had taken her place.

Would Josiah live to regret his decision? Even if he did, there was no going back after the wedding vows were said. What once could have been could never be. Mary stood, went to the stairwell, and tiptoed upward. If she couldn't say the wedding vows with Josiah today, she would say something else. She had written the truth last night about the mistake Josiah would make today. He might never face his regret, but she had suffered enough to know that she was right. The day would come when Josiah would regret walking away from their love.

Mary entered her bedroom and glanced at the rumpled quilt. She had to put her life back in order, but last night she had mourned and wept. She set the lamp on the dresser top and found the page buried in the dresser drawer.

In a whisper she read,

> *Are you still there, as you once were?*
> *I wonder if it's true.*
> *How could you be, I ask myself.*
> *This shadow gone, this dream awakened from.*
>
> *Never real, you said, and yet we were.*
> *So near, I reached, I touched.*
> *You could have held me, claimed my heart.*
> *I offered openhanded all.*
>
> *But blind you were, and thought you saw.*
> *The future clear, what lay ahead.*

That was the dream, while I was real.
But now you hold what was not there.

Would you still be what you once were?
If we would meet, as we are now?
I ask because I wish I knew,
And yet I wonder if I do.

Would years gone by come pouring back?
Would they be strong and telling still?
Is that the fear which holds us far?
That we would break what we now are?

Must we this haunting in each other see?
This phantom of the best that's past?
Must we forever wrong now be?
This dread that ever lasts.

No breath has pain to bring us life.
No solace for this deep regret.
No agony so clear within our grasp.
As was the hour, we might have been.

Mary folded the page and closed the drawer. Obviously, Josiah felt none of this, or he wouldn't be marrying Susie today. She was the one who needed to awaken from her dream.

Mary gasped when *Daett*'s booming voice filled the hallway outside her room. "Time to get up, Gerald."

He was not calling for her and her sister. He knew she already roamed the house. *Mamm* and *Daett* had probably knelt by their bedsides while she was in the kitchen and said a prayer for her. They might not feel the depth of her pain, but they knew she suffered.

A bedroom door slammed across the hallway, and she heard heavy footsteps going down the stairs. Lighter ones followed and paused by Mary's bedroom door. The knob turned, and Betsy's face appeared. "Are you okay?"

"*Yah*, I guess." Mary tried to smile.

Betsy took in the rumpled bed, and the concern on her face increased. She stepped inside to slip her arm around Mary. "What can I do to help?"

"Nothing," Mary muttered. Tears threatened again.

Betsy caught sight of the closed dresser drawer. A piece of clothing was hanging over the edge. "Have you been writing something about this day?"

Mary looked the other way and didn't answer.

"I should read it."

"Why? To see if I'm crazy?" Mary asked with a stifled choke.

"I know you aren't," Betsy said, obviously wanting to comfort her sister. "But you should share it with someone. Being alone is the least helpful thing at the moment."

"I suppose so," Mary allowed. She brought out the paper and handed it to her sister.

Betsy read in silence. "That is dark, Mary."

"*Yah*, I loved him."

"I don't know what more to say, but come." Betsy tugged on Mary's arm. "The sun will be up soon."

"That's exactly what I don't want to see," Mary retorted. "There should be clouds and thunder all day."

Betsy clucked her tongue. "I'm sorry, and I know that you loved him—"

"I know," Mary agreed. "I'll get control of myself soon."

"I think you're doing very well, considering..."

"Thanks." Mary gave her a quick hug. "You are such a dear."

Betsy made a face. "I wish I could do more."

"You could say all the things that everyone else wants to say—that I'll find someone someday to fill a place in my hurting heart, that he'll be much better than Josiah..."

"That wouldn't be kind. And you are my sister, Mary. You know how I feel about Amish men."

"*Yah*, I do." Mary gave Betsy another hug. "But at least you are sweet and cheerful this morning."

Betsy's face darkened. "Don't get me started. I'll never get over what Josiah did to you."

"Please," Mary begged. "You were beginning to change. Don't go back on your faith because of me."

Betsy scowled. "Faith really worked for you, didn't it? But see, I shouldn't be saying anything this morning."

Mary drew in a long breath. "You don't really think—not really, Betsy—that a better life is out there than one in the community?"

"You know I do, but don't blame yourself. Now come. *Mamm* will be up soon if we don't appear. We don't want her reading that poem."

"Is it that bad?" Mary asked on the way to the door.

"*Yah*, it's that bad," Betsy said over her shoulder, "but I won't say more."

Mamm met them with a concerned look when they stepped out of the stairwell.

"She's okay," Betsy chirped. "Just mourning a bit."

Mamm didn't appear convinced. "I heard you get up earlier, Mary. *Daett* wanted to pray, so we did, but I know more should be done to help you through this day."

Mary tried to smile. "There's not much that can be done, *Mamm*. Josiah will say the vows with Susie today at noon, and that's that."

Mamm and Betsy exchanged glances.

"You should bless Susie on her wedding day," *Mamm* suggested. "Forgiveness is an important part of healing the heart."

"I know, but I can't." Mary looked away. Tears didn't come, but her pain burned like fire inside.

"The Lord will heal you, Mary," *Mamm* encouraged, "but there are things we can do to help. You must face things for what they are. Come." *Mamm* took Mary's arm and led the way to the front window. "This is Josiah and Susie's wedding day. Let's wish them well."

"You shouldn't, *Mamm*," Betsy protested.

"I know what I'm doing," *Mamm* insisted.

Mary lifted her head to gaze at the first streaks of dawn that rose over the Adirondack foothills. This should have been her wedding day. Today was the day when her dream of a home and a man who would love her would have been a reality. Yet the dream was gone, and the sun dared to rise upon a cloudless sky.

"I wish Josiah and Susie a blessing on their wedding day," *Mamm* said from beside her. "Thank You, Lord."

Sobs came from deep inside of Mary, as Betsy and *Mamm* held her tight and the sun crept higher on the horizon.

EIGHT

Mary wiped the last breakfast dish dry and glanced at the kitchen clock. The time was ten minutes till eight. She should have been on her way to open the doors of the Plain Food Co-op by seven thirty, but everything moved slower this morning. The elderly Amish owners would understand her running late today.

"You should go," Betsy said from the kitchen doorway. "I told you I would clean up."

Mary set her lips. "It doesn't matter if I'm late."

The truth was, nothing seemed to matter at the moment. She was empty of feelings after *Mamm* and Betsy had comforted her by the living room window this morning. She had faced reality, and the day should continue on its normal route—which included washing the breakfast dishes.

She felt Betsy's touch on her elbow. "Shall I walk you down to the store?"

Mary forced a laugh. "I'm not a *boppli.*"

"Sometimes we feel like one, and I should walk with you." Betsy spoke in a tone that wouldn't tolerate further protest.

Mary hung up the towel and followed her sister into the living room.

"I'm going with Mary down to the food co-op!" Betsy hollered toward the sewing room, where *Mamm's* foot-pedaled machine whirled.

"Thank you, Betsy. That's a *goot* idea," said *Mamm.*

"See?" Betsy jutted her chin. "I can do some things right. I'm doing you *goot* already."

Mary didn't argue but followed her sister outside. Betsy was concerned for her sister's welfare, and Mary did appreciate the effort.

At the bottom of the porch steps, Mary paused. "We should hitch Danny Boy to the buggy and drive down so you don't have to walk back."

"Now who's the *boppli?*" Betsy retorted. "You walk back and forth each day. What's the difference?"

Mary gave in, and they began the walk down Highway 163. Below them lay the town of Fort Plain, which wound along the river and made a sharp descent from the high ground where the community was built.

"I should have moved to Lancaster a long time ago," Mary muttered.

Usually the old town tucked into the Adirondack foothills cheered her, but the sight had the opposite affect this morning.

"It wouldn't have helped," Betsy told her. "I know this hurts to hear, but there is nothing you could have done to keep him."

"I wish I was so sure," Mary replied. "I'll always wonder what could have been."

"Forget that poem," Betsy advised. "It's not healthy to look backward."

"I know. At least I think so."

They walked together, and then Betsy took the lead. She paused for a moment and said, "You should go out with me this weekend."

"To your *rumspringa* gathering?" Mary gasped. "That's going exactly the wrong way."

"I'm just trying to help," Betsy protested. "I thought you could use a distraction, and no one needs to know."

"Don't be delusional. The community will know."

"I know." Betsy faked a smile.

"You're not jumping the fence soon, are you?"

"Not until I'm twenty-one."

"I'm so sorry this has discouraged you further, Betsy. I am partly to blame."

"Stop it, Mary. Don't take responsibility for everything. You have a right to mourn for the way Josiah used you."

Mary reached for her sister's arm. "That's what worries me."

"Don't you have doubts about your dream now that Josiah has done what he did?" Betsy's glance was sharp.

"I...I guess not. I was in love with him and the plans for our home." Tears stung. "But I don't want to jump the fence. Trouble shouldn't make us change our way of life. And I know I should have left you a better example. Instead, my life has melted down, which may be pushing you toward leaving our community."

"I considered that option long before Josiah jilted you," Betsy assured her.

Mary tried to slow her breathing. "I'll say it again. You know how hurt *Mamm* and *Daett* would be if you didn't come back from *rumspringa*."

"I know, but at the same time, think of a home out there." Betsy cast her arm outward to include the whole town and the mountains beyond them.

"The only home for our people is in the community."

Betsy didn't respond as they made their way down the incline into town. Sorrow had overwhelmed them and left destruction in its wake. Further apologies were useless. Mary would have to heal and do better in the future.

Ahead of them, the front door of Mrs. Gabert's house swung

open, and the elderly lady hollered across the lawn. "Good morning, Mary. Who is this with you on such a fine day?"

"*Goot* morning," Mary called back. She walked closer with Betsy by her side. "This is my sister, Betsy. She was kind enough to walk with me on this morning, after..." Mary stopped. Her tears would come again if she went on.

Mrs. Gabert didn't seem to mind the omission. "Good to meet you, Betsy. Is every Amish girl fresh faced and pretty?"

Betsy appeared pleased with the compliment. "That's kind of you to say, but Mary's the looker of the family."

"Amish girls are also self-effacing and kind." Mrs. Gabert smiled cheerfully. "Your sister stops in to check on me without being asked."

"I'm not surprised," Betsy replied. "My sister is a dear."

"That she is," Mrs. Gabert agreed. "And still single. But weren't you planning a wedding, Mary? I know your people are secretive, but didn't you let something slip months ago?"

"There is no wedding," Mary told her, looking away.

Mrs. Gabert clucked her tongue. "Did something happen? I'm sorry to hear that. But someone will come along for you soon, or there is something seriously wrong with this world."

"Today was to have been Mary's wedding day," Betsy blurted out. "That's why I'm walking her down to the store. Mary should be in bed mourning, but she insists on working."

Mrs. Gabert appeared startled. "You were jilted the morning of your wedding?"

Mary swallowed, but no words would come.

Betsy leaped in to help. "Not quite. The relationship was broken off six months ago. Mary's fiancé had the indecency to use the same date to marry his new girlfriend."

"There aren't that many Thursdays in November," Mary offered, her face pale.

"There were other Thursdays in November," Betsy retorted. "That's when most weddings happen in the Amish community."

The two women shared a sympathetic glance. "This is terrible," Mrs. Gabert said. "But better to know now than later."

"I guess so," Mary allowed. "But we really should be going. I'm late already."

"Don't mourn too much," Mrs. Gabert called after them. "In the end this will be a broken road that leads you home!"

"Did you hear what she said?" Betsy said once they were out of earshot. "Take that advice to heart."

"I'll try, but it's hard."

"And see? You have people among the *Englisha* who love you."

"I know, and I'm thankful for friends. Mrs. Gabert is a dear."

Betsy cleared her throat loudly. "I meant..."

"You meant what?" Mary asked.

"You are obtuse sometimes. The point is clear to me. You should consider what I said earlier." Betsy motioned toward the town again. "There is another life out there—a *goot* one. This friend of yours, Mrs. Gabert, proves that."

"And you think I should hide my dark poem," Mary muttered.

"Jumping the fence is not a crazy idea," Betsy protested. "Young people from the community have done so before."

Mary didn't answer as they continued the walk through town. She didn't want to argue with Betsy, and the effort was useless. Being a *goot* example was the best option to help Betsy—but Mary had obviously failed her.

When they approached the building from the street, they saw a buggy sitting beside the small co-op store. The beardless face of Stephen Overholt peered out at them. "*Goot* morning. The Lord's blessing to you, to each of you girls," he said in greeting.

Mary forced a smile. "*Goot* morning, Stephen. I'm sorry I'm late. Betsy was kind enough to walk down with me."

Stephen eyed Betsy suspiciously. "Why is Betsy with you this morning? Wasn't there something she could do at the house?"

"We have our priorities straight," Betsy snapped. "Mary's hurting this morning, and I wanted to walk with her."

He nodded. "I'm sorry to hear that, I really am, and I'm sorry for my words. Mary hurting is not a *goot* thing. I suppose the hurt is coming from the wedding that was supposed to take place today. But I heard that Josiah will wed his new girlfriend instead."

"How did you know about the wedding?" Betsy retorted. "That was none of your business."

Stephen ignored the barb. "I have relatives back in Lancaster—that would be cousins and such like—and they know Josiah. It's not as though everything, the going on of these two, was such a great secret. I wanted to have a few words, if Mary wouldn't object, in private, and minister to Mary in her loss."

Betsy was incredulous. "You would comfort Mary? I know what you are up to, Stephen, and why you are here. You are thinking it is now the Lord's will that *you* take the place of the shifty Josiah Beiler. Hopefully Mary has learned her lesson and will send you home at once."

Stephen winced. "My apologies for my forwardness, but I will say, with great boldness in my heart, that Josiah made a big mistake with your sister. He certainly did not, and I am sure of this, discern correctly the will of the Lord."

Betsy opened her mouth to answer, but Mary silenced her with a quick touch on her arm. "What can we do for you this morning, Stephen?"

He regarded Mary for a moment before handing her a list. "That's what I need, all of it, for my monthly trip into town. I came right after the chores, since I wanted to be on time. But I do understand, I really do, why you are late. My heart goes out to you, like I said. I am sorry that Josiah used you the way he did. Josiah, and I'm certain of this, made a grave mistake." Stephen offered her a tentative smile.

Mary nodded and unlocked the door of the co-op, with the paper clutched in her free hand.

"That is a horrible man," Betsy whispered once they were inside. "I had forgotten how horrible. Thank the Lord I came down this morning with you."

"He's perfectly harmless."

"He's an Amish man who has never married," Betsy said, as if that encapsulated the evils of the world.

"Like an old maid who has never married? Don't be too hard on him."

"That's different," Betsy huffed. "And you'll never be one anyway. How does he know about your wedding day?"

"He explained himself," Mary answered. She began to check off the list as she piled bags of food on the counter.

"I mean, but why?" Betsy insisted. She followed Mary along the aisles to help. "That's what I'm saying. Why the interest? Why's he keeping track and showing up this morning? Does he always come in on this day of the month?"

"I wouldn't know. I don't pay attention," Mary muttered, concentrating as she weighed out pecans.

"Why does the man want those?" Betsy asked with great suspicion.

"Maybe he's an excellent cook," Mary deadpanned.

They both fell silent when the front door opened and Stephen entered. Betsy scurried off in the opposite direction, while Mary carried the last of the items up to the counter. She gave Stephen her best smile. "There we are. I think I got everything right."

"I'm sure you did, I really am," he told her. "I'm sorry. I shouldn't have been so harsh about my words with your sister. I am glad that Betsy came, like family should, with you this morning of your sorrow."

"Betsy's a *goot* sister and a kind one," Mary told him. "And your apology is accepted."

"Thank you." He bobbed his head. "I'm sorry, from the bottom of my heart, for your suffering. Josiah didn't know, and I'm certain of this, what he was doing when he broke off your relationship. The man, he shouldn't have. Josiah is not, he isn't, Mary, a very wise man. I hope you know that."

"It's okay." Mary smiled again. "I'm cried out, and life goes on."

"You are brave, you are, and a strong woman," he said. He wrote out a check for the amount she showed him. "You are here this morning. Somehow in my heart I knew, which is why I set out so early in my buggy, that you would be. Not every woman, even in this community, would have held up so well."

"I did love him." Mary bowed her head. "Quite a lot, but the Lord had other things in mind."

"*Yah*, I can see, with my own eyes, what a sweet spirit you have," Stephen agreed. He handed her the check. "Josiah has made, I say this again, a great mistake. He did not know the will of the Lord."

"Thank you for your sympathy, Stephen."

Betsy appeared from around the corner of the food stands. "You have a *goot* day now, Stephen, and don't fall off the barn roof. It can be a little slippery up there."

He gathered up his bags and hurried out without a response.

"What was that about?" Mary chided her sister.

Betsy glared after him. "The man was courting you. As plain as day."

"I think you're imaging things," Mary protested.

Betsy continued to glare at the closed co-op door. Clearly, she was not convinced.

NINE

After the breakfast dishes were washed on Sunday morning, Mary slipped into her bedroom and changed into her light blue dress. The color pushed the limits of the *Ordnung*, but she had made the purchase in Little Falls a few weeks after Josiah had asked if she would be his *frau*. During that time, her spirits had flown up into the clouds on wings of happiness.

She should burn the dress in the kitchen stove, but that would be a wrong turn in her walk away from the pain Josiah had left in her heart. This morning he would drive Susie to the church service as his new *frau*, with her seated happily on the buggy seat beside him. That place had once belonged to Mary, but she must forget. The bitterest thoughts must be rejected and replaced with acceptance and resignation. That was the Lord's way. Her wedding dress must also come down from its lofty and high perch in her heart. What better way to demote the dress than to wear it to a common church service the Sunday after her planned wedding?

The bedroom door cracked open, and Betsy's face appeared. "How are you doing?" She took in her sister's choice of dress. "Wasn't that..."

"*Yah*," Mary whispered. "But I must."

Betsy stepped inside to give Mary a long hug. "You are so brave. You deserve a man who will love you like the jewel you are."

"Don't say that," Mary protested. "I've been rejected."

"Josiah Beiler isn't the end of the whole world," Betsy reminded her.

"He was of mine."

Betsy tsk-tsked her. "That's because you love with all of your heart."

"Stop it. I'll ruin this dress with a bucket of tears."

"For what it's worth, I think you're doing the right thing," Betsy told her. "A wedding dress made to wear with Josiah Beiler should not be respected. I'll go change myself. Gerald will have the buggy ready before long, and he'll be waiting impatiently as usual."

Betsy closed the bedroom door behind her, and the sound of her footsteps faded down the hall. Mary placed the last pin in the dress and adjusted her *kapp*. Then she opened the dresser drawer to pull out her tablet. *Yah*, Gerald was in a hurry, but there were still a few moments to read the words she had written last night. Writing seemed to ease the pain and bring her a measure of peace.

To moving on...

> *She gathered all her courage bright,*
> *And shed her tears through every night.*
> *But now the time had come to carry on,*
> *To bear the load and find her song.*
>
> *Each day she tells her heart to beat,*
> *That love that's lost is not the end.*
> *That with the morn the sun will rise,*
> *And shed its light for weary eyes.*
>
> *Give me, Lord, the help I need,*
> *Give me grace...and hurry, please.*

I ask with boldness, this I know,
But all this pain is hurting so.

They were bold words, and that's where she had stopped writing last night before climbing under the quilt to find blessedness in sleep. She didn't expect another man to replace Josiah, yet surely the Lord could bring healing to the deep cut across her heart. That much she could ask, and *yah*, she did wish the Lord would hurry.

Mary studied the words for a moment before placing the paper in the dresser drawer. No one would see the words, as they shouldn't. The community had moved on, and her grieving must follow.

Mary stepped into the hallway and paused for a moment to listen. Betsy's bedroom door was closed, but the sound of dresser drawers opening and closing in rapid succession reached into the hall. Perhaps Betsy couldn't decide which Sunday dress to wear this morning. A smile crept across Mary's face. Betsy was a dear sister who cared with her whole heart. Maybe someday she would get over her dream of leaving the Amish life and accept the attentions of a proper young man from the community.

Mary breathed a quick prayer heavenward before she continued down the stairs. "Don't let bitterness take root in Betsy's heart because of my own failings, Lord."

Mamm greeted her in the kitchen with a bright smile. "Ready to go? Gerald just left for the barn."

"I figured he had," Mary replied. "Betsy is hurrying to get ready."

Mamm glanced at Mary's dress. "Do you think that's wise? On your first Sunday? Maybe..."

"I'm trying to move on, *Mamm*. Don't discourage me. No one will know what this dress meant to me."

Mamm didn't back down. "But the message it sends. Your wedding dress, Mary! People will make assumptions and think you are disrespectful and flippant. You should at least look as though you cared."

Mary pressed back tears. "In that case, I should wear black."

Mamm's smile was thin. "That would be morbid. Go up and change into your dark blue dress."

"But Gerald..." Mary protested.

"Your brother can handle a lesson in patience. I'll take care of him."

Mary hesitated, but she found herself on the stairs moments later.

"What's wrong?" Betsy asked at the landing.

"I'm changing into something more appropriate."

"You decided this?"

"*Mamm* does have a point," Mary told her. "Let's not make a fuss."

Betsy huffed but said nothing more as Mary entered her bedroom. She caught a glimpse through the bedroom window of Gerald as he came out of the barn door with his hand on Danny Boy's bridle. She tried to hurry, but the pins only went in and out so quickly. Betsy ran past the window, and after an animated conversation with Gerald, waving her arms about, she hopped up on the buggy seat to wait.

Mary finished, took the stairs down two at a time, and burst out of the stairwell.

"That's much better," *Mamm* proclaimed. "And the Lord will give you comfort and courage today." *Mamm* planted a little kiss on Mary's cheek. "We love you, dear, and Betsy has explained the delay to Gerald."

Mary nodded and hurried out the front door.

Gerald eyed her as she approached. "All that over the color of a dress? Women!" he exclaimed.

Mary smiled warmly at her brother. "You'll be falling in love with a girl soon enough, and she'll have you wrapped around her little finger. The biggest ones fall the hardest."

Betsy's burst of laughter pealed from the buggy. "That's telling him."

Gerald grunted his disgust, and Mary climbed up onto the

buggy seat. Gerald threw her the lines and hopped in himself. He took the reins from Mary, and they trotted out of the driveway.

"Where's church today?" Betsy asked.

"Bishop Miller's place," Mary told her.

Gerald gave Betsy a sideways look. "If you didn't cavort around with those *Englisha* friends of yours all weekend, you'd remember such things."

"You're on your own *rumspringa*," Betsy snapped. "Don't be telling me how to conduct mine."

Gerald snorted. "You're overdoing things. That's all I'm saying. We are supposed to sample the world's things, not live among them."

Betsy pressed her lips together and fell silent.

Mary came to Betsy's defense. "She's a *goot* sister. We all have different paths to walk."

"Thank you," Betsy muttered. "At least someone has some understanding on the matter."

"That's because Mary has a tender heart. Reality must be faced, Betsy. You are way over the line with how you're conducting your *rumspringa*. The boys are talking. If you don't come back soon, your chance of getting a husband in the community will become quite slim."

"I will always have plenty of chances with farmers who have straw stuck in their hair," Betsy shot back.

"Today, but maybe not tomorrow," Gerald intoned. "Girls get old and—*poof!*—their chance is gone. You'd better listen."

Betsy pursed her lips and fell silent.

"Betsy will find her own way back soon enough," Mary said as they turned into the bishop's driveway.

Gerald didn't appear convinced, but Mary couldn't blame him. Doubt played in her own heart, and she had been wrong about Josiah.

"Whoa there," Gerald called out to Danny Boy. He pulled to a stop at the end of the walk, and with a firm grip on the horse's reins, he turned the wheel wide for them.

Mary climbed down the buggy step and said, "Thank you, Gerald."

He nodded and smiled. Betsy marched up the walk without a word.

"You should at least be civil to him," Mary whispered once she caught up with her sister.

"He deserves what he gets," Betsy muttered.

"He was only speaking the truth," Mary whispered back.

Betsy pasted on a smile as they approached two women who waited outside the mudroom door. "*Goot* morning, Miriam and Rachel. How's the baby?" Betsy cooed. She pulled back the blanket in Miriam's arm to take a peek at the bundle. "He's so sweet, I must say."

Miriam beamed. "*Yah*, and taking right after his *daett*. Benjamin Junior will be a stout young man, I'm thinking."

Mary joined in the admiration of the little one. This was Miriam's fourth child. Not that long ago Mary herself had dreamed of home and *kinner*—Josiah's *kinner*. Now he and Susie...

Mary halted her thoughts. She had to stop mourning. What was done was done, and Josiah no longer belonged to her.

Betsy held out her arms and took little Benjamin while Miriam adjusted her shawl. Then Mary followed Rachel into the kitchen.

"How are you doing this morning?" Rachel turned to ask.

Mary tried to sound cheerful. "Okay!"

Rachel was clearly not convinced. "You hide your sorrow well, but I said a prayer for you on Thursday. The Lord will be filling your heart again soon. He's a *goot* God, you know."

"*Yah*, He is," Mary agreed.

Rachel smiled her encouragement as the handshaking began around the circle of women, and Mary ended up near the living room doorway. The line of men led by Bishop Miller would soon be passing by, but there was no other place for Mary to stand. She waited while several other women came past to greet her, and she smiled and shook their hands. Betsy had divested herself of baby Benjamin and slipped in to stand beside her, thankfully blocking the view into the open living room door.

"Don't give Stephen the slightest bit of attention today," Betsy whispered in Mary's ear. "He'll be continuing his courtship efforts."

"Hush," Mary warned as the front door opened and Bishop Miller entered.

Betsy gave him a cheerful smile. The bishop nodded in greeting and took off his hat, continuing on as the other men followed behind him. Mary hid behind Betsy as they filed through to take their seats on the benches.

Mary assumed Stephen Overholt was in the line somewhere, and though she didn't want to acknowledge it, she knew Betsy was right. Stephen intended to court her, and she would have to face his advances soon enough.

"Remember what I said," Betsy whispered as Bishop Miller's *frau*, Annie, led the women to their seats.

Mary settled herself on the unmarried women's bench and kept her head down. The singing began, and she followed the words on the page of the songbook. By the time Minister Peachey stood for the first sermon, Mary's neck was stiff. She had a reason to look up now, even if Stephen was in her line of sight. One did not stare at the floor during a sermon.

Minister Peachey stood beside the kitchen doorway, pacing back and forth as he spoke. Stephen sat toward the back of the room with his attention fixed on the preaching, and Mary's gaze lingered on him for a moment. She shouldn't be afraid of the man. Stephen was a confirmed bachelor of many years. Such a state was whispered about, and a man's reputation suffered from it. But Stephen was decent enough from what she knew of him. He did speak a lot about the Lord's will when it came to love, and he was stuck in his ways, which was how men became when they lived alone. What did she really know about him? Not much. His grocery lists each month were long and varied. Maybe the crusty exterior the man carried about him covered a heart of gold.

Mary forced herself to focus on Minister Peachey. "We are all the Lord's children and are called to a life of holiness," Minister Peachey was saying, warming to his subject. "Through the ups and downs of life, through sun and shade, through the *goot* times and the tough times, the call of the Lord remains the same. Walk with Him in purity and righteousness."

What blessed words those were, and here she was, staring at a man the Sunday after her planned wedding. Betsy was partly to blame for making insinuations about Stephen, but Mary's pride may also have been touched. She wondered if Stephen wished to pick up what Josiah had tossed aside. Maybe she was wrong. Maybe Stephen's remarks at the co-op were nothing more than brotherly concern for a jilted woman who had her heart broken. That Stephen would notice her pain was to his credit, not a mark against his character.

Mary shifted on the bench to find a more comfortable spot. Minister Peachey's message on holiness was for her, and she needed to listen. Her heart must remain open to what the Lord had planned for her life. Obviously, she had been quite wrong once, so that showed how untrustworthy her choices could be. Never had she dreamed that Josiah didn't love her, considering the devotion she had felt for him in her own heart. She should be thankful that Stephen spoke with her on Thursday. Maybe she should pray that the Lord would lead her to a man who could love her instead of stir emotions in her heart that left her shattered. Maybe that was the first lesson she should learn today.

"Submit yourself to the will of the Lord," Minister Peachey thundered, his arms waving about. "Deny yourself and follow the Lord. Always! Pray and follow!"

Mary swallowed twice and caught a glimpse of Stephen in her side vision. The man smiled and nodded in apparent full agreement with Minister Peachey. She must have judged him too harshly, which was to her shame. She had prepared herself to rebuff his attentions today. Instead, Stephen was the one who was enraptured in Minister Peachey's sermon while her mind wandered.

Mary clasped her hands and listened until Minister Peachey finished and took his seat on the minister's bench. Stephen hadn't looked her way the whole time.

TEN

Early the following week, Mary descended the hill into Fort Plain on foot. The sun had risen an hour ago, and she had left the Yoders' home immediately after the breakfast dishes had been washed. Her heart still ached, but there were things for which she could give thanks. The sermon Minister Peachey had given on Sunday was full of instruction and guidance. Whatever Stephen's intentions had been, the man had not approached her again.

Even Betsy had admitted as much on the ride home on Sunday afternoon. "I know that Stephen didn't even look at you today, but I still think the man's up to something. Why else would he have shown up at the co-op on your planned wedding day to extend his sympathies? Uninterested men don't keep that close track of a girl."

Which could be true, but the Lord would grant grace for the road ahead—even if that road led to the attentions of a man like Stephen Overholt.

Mary took a deep breath of the brisk morning air. The Lord was bringing healing. She had to believe that. She could think about Josiah this morning and not feel a stab of pain in her chest. That was an improvement. Perhaps more grace would be given as the day continued.

Mary increased her pace. Ahead of her Mrs. Gabert's house

appeared in the early morning mist rising from the river. She should stop in and check on her. The elderly lady hadn't been out on her porch when Mary went past yesterday. What if some accident had occurred while she was occupied with her own troubles?

Mary turned up Mrs. Gabert's sidewalk and knocked on the door. She heard footsteps inside, but they sounded heavier than Mrs. Gabert's lighter ones. Mary stepped back and waited. The door swung open, and a tall, handsome young man stood in front of her.

He smiled. "Good morning. You knocked?"

"Oh, *yah*...I mean, yes..." Mary stammered. How foolish she must appear. An Amish girl knocking on a stranger's door—only, she wasn't a stranger to Mrs. Gabert.

"Can I do anything for you?" he asked.

"I...we...I..." Mary gave up. Let him think her an idiot. If she turned and bolted down the street, the picture would be complete.

"Who is it?" Mrs. Gabert called from inside the house.

The handsome *Englisha* man raised his eyebrows. Clearly, he was asking for her name.

"I'm..." Mary tried, but nothing worked at the moment. The man had turned her into a trembling mess.

"You are?" He obviously thought she didn't understand ordinary human communication.

"I'm Mary," she finally managed.

"Mary. Of course." He called louder over his shoulder, "Mary's here, Grandma."

"Mary," Mrs. Gabert cooed.

There was a rustling of feet and a flurry of motion.

"She knows you," he said with a grin.

Mary tried to calm herself. "Of course she does. I come here often to check on her."

"I see," he said. "That's kind of you."

"Mary!" Mrs. Gabert exclaimed, pushing him aside. "Why have you kept Mary waiting on the front porch, Willard?"

"I thought she might be an assassin," he deadpanned.

"Willard!" Mrs. Gabert scolded. "What an awful thing to say. This is Mary, the marvelous Amish girl who checks on me from time to time. And Mary, this is Willard, my grandson. He's here for a few months on furlough from his mission in Kenya."

"Hi, Mary," he said with a twinkle in his eye.

Mrs. Gabert patted her grandson on the arm. "Don't mind him. He's such a dear, and so precious to me. He's been overseas for more than a year, and I haven't seen much of him." She smiled up at him. "But I have him for a while until he has to go back. You can't imagine a more loving and doting grandson."

"I should be going, then," Mary said. "I wanted to see if you needed anything, but I see you are in *goot* hands."

"She is," Willard agreed.

"Is that all you have to say, Willard? Invite Mary in. She surely has time for a cup of tea."

"Certainly!" Willard held the door wide open. "Sorry about my manners."

"It's...I..."

Mrs. Gabert had no such inhibitions. "Come, Mary. Willard has nothing going this morning, and a little civilized company would be just the ticket. The man has a difficult time in Kenya. It would be great for Willard to see the gentle side of life while he is here."

"I don't know about that. I'm just me," Mary hastened to say. "I really should go, or I will be late."

"Nonsense!" Mrs. Gabert declared. "The kettle is on, and I know you love my tea."

"*Yah*, I do, but—"

"No protesting, Mary. Willard can drive you down to the co-op in my car, and then you won't have lost any time." Mrs. Gabert turned toward her grandson. "Won't you, Willard?"

"I'm yours to command," he said. Mirth danced in his eyes.

Mary forced herself to breathe. What could she say? Spending time with Mrs. Gabert was one thing, but drinking tea with a hand-some and charming *Englisha* man in the house was another. Her *rumspringa* was past. But in a few months this grandson would leave for Kenya again, and that would be that. She would make a point not to stop in until Willard was gone.

"Are you coming?" he asked. Mrs. Gabert had already hurried off, as if there was no question on the matter.

Mary followed him and seated herself at the kitchen table. This would be over in a moment—except for the ride with Willard down to the co-op. Well, she would have to turn it down. She had to. If someone saw her driving to work with a handsome young *Englisha* man, that would demand explaining.

Mrs. Gabert smiled and poured the tea. She waved her hand at Willard. "He doesn't drink tea, but sit down, Willard. I want to tell you about Mary."

"Please," Mary begged. "I'm sure Willard has more important things to occupy his mind."

"Now you have me curious." He grinned and pulled out a chair. "It's not like I'm scurrying about putting out fires in this sleepy town."

"This is a nice town to live in, sleepy or not," Mrs. Gabert scolded. "You grew up here, and you turned out okay. I know the place isn't populated with thieves and cutthroats like you're used to in Kenya. Mary loves the town. Don't you, dear?"

"*Yah*, I do."

Willard grinned. "So do I, Grandma. You know that, and Kenya's a nice place too. It's filled with palm trees and kindhearted people—"

"Tell Mary what happened down the street last month," Mrs. Gabert interrupted.

Willard sobered. "I thought you were going to tell me about Mary."

"That's coming."

"I have to leave soon," Mary got in edgewise, but the muffled protest was lost on both of them. She gulped down her tea while Willard gathered his thoughts.

"The tale is a sad one," he began, "even for a sad neighborhood. It's why we're there, trying to help people who have lived in darkness for many generations. We live in a well-guarded part of town, but the risks to mission workers still exist. Four men posing as policemen entered the area and forced an entrance into a home. When they couldn't find much of value, they tried to produce more by threatening the man and his wife. When this didn't work, they shot the man in front of his wife. By that time someone had heard the ruckus and called the police. Before they arrived, one of the thieves managed to escape by hopping over the back fence. The other three were apprehended, and with the man's body as evidence, they were beaten and executed on the spot. A passerby saw the other thief jumping over a fence, and because anyone vaulting a perimeter in Kenya is considered a suspect, the man was arrested by the citizens and handed over to the police. By the time all was said and done, four dead thieves were added to the body count."

"That is awful!" Mary exclaimed. "And you live next door."

"Nearby," he corrected. "We pray, and we trust in the Lord."

"But you minister in this city?" She had not intended to become drawn into the conversation.

"I do, along with others on the team, as the Lord gives us courage and grace," Willard demurred. "But not all of life in Kenya is like that. Usually that kind of thing is not happening."

"You are still a brave man," Mrs. Gabert said. Then she gave Mary a worried glance. "Are you okay? Maybe I shouldn't have asked Willard to tell you that story."

"I'm okay. I'm sure Willard is doing a *goot* work. I guess we live sheltered lives in the community." She stood. "But I really must go."

Willard jumped up. "Where are your keys, Grandma?"

"I...I can..." The objection died on Mary's lips. What was the use? They wouldn't listen to her anyway.

Mrs. Gabert produced the keys with a jingle, and Willard led Mary outside.

"You have a great day now," Mrs. Gabert called after her. "Don't forget to stop in on your way home."

"Thank you for the tea, and have a *goot* day," Mary hollered over her shoulder.

Willard opened the car door for her, and she hesitated. "I don't bite," he said, "even if I work in Kenya."

That was not the problem, but how could she explain this to him? Silence was better and easier. Willard would expect strangeness from an Amish woman anyway.

Mary climbed inside, and Willard walked around the car and settled onto the car seat. He turned the key and gave her a kind smile. "Where are we going?"

"That way." She pointed toward downtown and gave him basic directions.

"I know the place," he said as he pulled out of the driveway. "So tell me about yourself. I've dominated the discussion so far."

She kept her eyes on the road. "I'm Amish, and I work at the Plain Food Co-op."

"Interesting life. Like Grandma said, I grew up around here, but I never paid the Amish that much attention. I think I'd like to know more about your people. There is little drama, I suppose, and obviously no incidents like the story I just told you."

"That's true," Mary agreed, "but there is still..."

"Drama?" He grinned.

"*Yah!*"

His eyes twinkled. "Can you enlighten me? Amish life with drama?"

Mary's cheeks flamed.

"I'm sorry if I'm intruding," he said. "I don't understand your customs, so accept my apologies if I have been too bold."

Mary shook her head. "I guess you might as well know. Your

grandmother does, so...well, last Thursday was a little dramatic for me. That was the day my ex-boyfriend and I had planned to wed, but he had the indecency to marry his new girlfriend on the same date—some six months after he broke up with me."

"Ah, that is awful." His brow creased with concern. "Had you dated long?"

"Long enough to give him my heart." Mary looked away. Tears threatened again. Why was she telling him this?

"How are you doing?"

Mary tried to smile. "I'm here."

"And in decent spirits," he added. "Do you have some coping mechanism unavailable to people outside the community?"

Mary managed to laugh. "I'm afraid we hurt like everyone else, but the Lord is helping me."

"As He helps all who cry out to Him." He nodded soberly. "So where are you going from here?"

"I...what do you mean?"

"Coping," he said with a smile. "Continuing to heal."

"Ah. Well, I don't know."

"Could I make a suggestion?" He tilted his head apologetically. "Sometimes getting away helps. Travel, that type of thing. I could use an extra hand in Kenya. There are other people who work at the mission, and I have a woman named Tambala who serves as my cook and nurse. Her husband, Ashon, does handyman work. We could find something for you to do."

"I couldn't do that!" she gasped.

"You might be surprised! Sometimes we have more in us than we think. You might even enjoy a short excursion into a foreign culture. Kenya is much safer than the mishap next door makes it sound."

"I can't...I mean, my people..." Mary knew she couldn't explain this in a way that would make sense.

"Surely the Amish believe in mission work," he said as he parked near the front door of the co-op.

Mary clutched the door handle. "We support missions, and what you're doing in Kenya sounds like a *goot* work, but going there myself...I...we...our place is in the community, and I am single. But thanks for the offer."

"You are welcome. And I understand. I wasn't trying to push an agenda. I speak from experience, I guess. I know how to overcome disappointments in life because I've had them myself."

"We all do." Mary smiled politely and opened the car door. "Thanks for the ride."

"Are you stopping by this evening?" he called after her.

"Your grandmother seems to be in good hands for the time you are here," she hollered back.

"Come over anyway," he insisted. "I can tell she enjoys your company. I wouldn't want to deprive her of that during my visit."

Mary hesitated. "I'll think about it."

There was no decent way to say no.

"Take care, and thanks for stopping by. It's not every morning that I open the front door to such a pleasant surprise."

Mary hurried away. Willard would have to think her ill mannered. What was wrong with her? Being impressed with a handsome *Englisha* man and his passion for mission work was not a crime! This was her wounded heart talking. She opened the co-op door, determined to never think of Willard Gabert again.

ELEVEN

A few minutes later, Willard Gabert parked his grandmother's car in front of her garage and stepped out, jingling the keys in his hand.

"Well!" he exclaimed to no one in particular. Willard gave the keys another shake. "Interesting girl, though!"

He jerked his head up when his grandmother called from the front porch. "Talking to yourself isn't going to help."

He grinned sheepishly.

Mrs. Gabert's smile filled her whole face. "You were impressed, weren't you? I knew you would be. That young woman is exactly what you need, Willard."

Willard forced a laugh. "I'm not going to discuss this, and Mary comes from—"

"The second time is never the same," Mrs. Gabert interrupted. "She was impressed with you too. I could tell."

Willard chuckled. "I love you, Grandma, but Mary is Amish. Doesn't that mean anything to you?"

"Prayer overcomes any obstacle, Willard. Don't make a terrible mistake. The chance of your lifetime could be at your fingertips."

"So I'm supposed to exploit the poor girl's heartache?"

His grandmother's face brightened. "Mary told you about her

ex-boyfriend's marriage? That's bonding, Willard. Open your eyes! You are interested in her."

"Well..." Willard allowed. "Mary Yoder seems like a decent woman. She has a depth and mystery to her. She's mature and coping well with her heartache. Most girls would be a mess after being treated like that."

"Your judgment is sound, at least." Mrs. Gabert gave him a direct look. "Now, how about your courage?"

"Grandmother! That's the wrong approach. Mary deserves my respect, not my intrusion into her world."

"So you were tempted, Willard?"

He sputtered his denial.

"Mary could love you and fill that empty hole in your heart."

His face hardened. "That's what is wrong about this, Grandma. Nothing good comes out of rebounds. That's the state we're both in, and I doubt if either of us can afford another disaster."

"The road home is not always straight, Willard. Don't you tell your suffering people in Kenya that all the time?"

"That's different!"

She tilted her head to one side.

"This is about love!" he exclaimed. "And what about Mary's community? I'm not joining, and I doubt she'd consider leaving."

"With the Lord all things are possible."

"I'm *not* becoming Amish."

"I didn't say you would, but Mary would leave for a handsome fellow like you."

Willard laughed. "Your subterfuge is charming."

She moved back toward the front door. "At my age there is not a lot of time. But come inside. I'm getting chilled talking on the front porch."

He followed her and seated himself at the kitchen table. "I know I don't normally drink tea, but can I have a cup? I need nourishment."

His grandmother contemplated him for a moment. "I know

I'm right, Willard. At my age, I know." She poured him a cup and handed it to him.

He took a sip and then glanced up at her. "I don't want to argue with you, Grandma. I just can't pursue another girl, especially someone like Mary. It would not be fair to her or to me."

"Then you know it's possible?"

"What is possible?"

"Let's not go in circles!"

He thought for a second. "How can love happen again? After what Mary and I both have been through?"

She comforted him with a hand on his shoulder. "I know. Your heart needs healing. That's why you're here for these months. It's been two years since Carlene left you, and your wound is still festering. You think you're here to raise money for your mission, but this is the Lord's doing."

"It's a coincidence," he retorted. "Ean and Daisy arrived a month early to man the station, and I needed a break."

"Take a good look at the situation. This has the Lord's fingerprints on it. You should make contact with the girl, Willard. Mary can love you."

He took a long sip of tea. "So let's say you are right. Where do I begin? The Amish community is like a medieval castle with moats and no bridges. She walked away from me this morning just like that." He snapped his fingers.

Mrs. Gabert patted his shoulder again. "The Lord's already at work, Willard. I know He is. You just let Him minister His grace for a while and allow healing to begin."

"I have no idea how even if I wanted to."

"You want to, which is what matters," she assured him. "Now get busy with your church schedule and speeches, and I will pray."

He took a deep breath. "Don't you think this is reading a lot into the situation? I'm just a guy running a little mission in Kenya, and Mary is a simple Amish girl with a broken heart."

"I'm not even going to respond to that," she told him. She moved the teakettle back to the stove. "You already know the answer. It's time you believed again. In the meantime, I have wood that needs splitting in the backyard. That will keep you busy while the Lord talks to your heart."

Willard left the teacup on the table to step outside. As he opened the door, he thought about his grandmother's stinging words. He did need healing—but approaching a brown-eyed Amish girl about a relationship? Mary would reject him and that would be that...but what if she didn't? Maybe that possibility troubled him the most.

Willard found the ax in the small woodshed behind the house. He grabbed a log from the woodpile and propped it up to whack it down with his ax. When the blade stuck, he wiggled the ax loose to try again. This time the log split, and he repeated the maneuver until six small slivers remained of the round log. He straightened his shoulders. He was no stranger to hard labor, but he should have begun this project with more care. A pulled shoulder socket would benefit no one. Such haste was another indication of his injured heart.

For more than a year he had immersed himself in his work and kept up his relationship with the Lord. His heart should have been healed by now, but his grandmother was right. Tonight he was scheduled to speak at her small church in Fort Plain, but the injury remained.

Willard propped up another piece of log and brought down the ax. This time the split was clean on the first try. He thought about how Carlene had been the perfect fit for him—a preacher's beautiful daughter. He had charmed her, or so she had claimed. That he had a calling to Kenya had seemed to impress her further. He had believed their love was growing, but maybe her doubts had always been there. Seemingly out of nowhere, she had sent him a text as a way of goodbye:

I'm sorry to break this to you in this way, Willard, but perhaps
it's for the best. I'm seeing someone else. Don't worry. You
don't know him. Don't blame yourself. We weren't meant
to be. The best to you, and I hope you have many blessed
years doing what the Lord has called you to do.

And just like that, Carlene was gone. Willard had already scheduled a speaking engagement the next month in her father's church,
and he had manned up and kept the date. He knew he would have
to face her—somehow, even with the pain that blossomed in his
heart. He had cared for her more deeply than even he had realized.
Carlene skipped the meeting, and he had stumbled through the performance. She had been wiser than he had been.

Carlene's father had patted him on the back afterward. "The
Lord will be with you. These things happen, son. Don't lose heart."

But he had. He hadn't dated these past two years. There had
been opportunities—small signs of interest that seemed to indicate
an open door—but Willard had held back. Maybe he should have
asked a local Kenyan girl to be his wife. The thought had occurred
to him a few times.

Willard whacked at another piece of log in front of him. His
heart wasn't in marrying in Kenya, either, even though there were
a number of unmarried women in Tambala's church where he
attended services. Any of them would have accepted an American
man without a second thought. They would love him in their own
way, but his heart wouldn't be settled.

But an Amish girl? That was worse! A thousand times worse!
Foolish on top of everything—and wrong! Willard's ax flew as he
warmed to the task in front of him. Every reason why he should
reject his grandmother's matchmaking efforts brought a fresh spurt
of energy.

After a while, his grandmother appeared in front of him wrapped
in her long winter coat. "Arguing with yourself?"

Willard paused. "Something like that."

"I have a suggestion."

"No thank you, Grandma."

"Mary has a sister," she continued, undeterred. "Her name is Betsy. She would be on our side. I can drive up to the Yoders' home with the car and pick her up on some pretense. I know the family well enough. Betsy could come down for an hour or so, and we could talk."

"I'm not doing things like that," he muttered. He set up another log and brought the ax down with a loud crack.

"I'm just trying to help, Willard. You can't let this opportunity slip away."

"I know how you feel, Grandma." Willard gave her a thin smile. "But I'm sure Mary has dreams of love and family within the community. I would be quite the bubble buster, don't you think?"

"And you had your dreams for your life with Carlene. What would have been more natural than a preacher's daughter in the mission field? But the Lord had other plans. Don't say no, Willard."

He propped up the next log. "You make it sound as if the door is already open. Mary is from a medieval community of people. She wouldn't want me."

"You are only delaying. Can I reach out to Betsy?"

He didn't answer as he split another piece of wood.

"If you don't like my suggestion, then what is yours?" She pulled her coat tighter around her shoulders.

He noticed her shivering and escorted her back to the house. "Okay, I'll go down to the co-op and talk with Mary myself. Where are the keys?"

"On the kitchen wall where you left them." Her smile glowed. "I knew you'd do the right thing."

"What am I supposed to say to her?"

She patted him on the arm. "You're on your own with that, but the Lord will go with you."

"This is way too dramatic," he muttered. "There must be an easier path."

"I can drive you to the co-op."

He silenced her with an upraised hand. "I'm going."

He grabbed the keys and hurried out of house. At the car door he paused to brush wood chips off his jeans. Maybe he would appear more like an Amish man if he left the fresh shavings on his pants. Willard snorted at the thought and climbed into the car. Moments later he arrived in front of the small co-op.

No buggies sat in the parking lot, but there were a few cars. What did he expect? A private audience with Mary? This was more than awkward. His first date with Carlene had been the epitome of smoothness. He had walked straight up to her, smiled, and whispered, "Any chance I could take you out somewhere tonight?"

Destiny had been on their side. They had fit each other like a hand and a glove. Whereas this was... Willard grunted and climbed out of the car, and then walked the short distance to the front door. When he entered, a small bell on a chain chimed above him. Mary looked up from behind the counter, and her mouth fell open.

"Sorry," he said, stepping closer. "I didn't mean to startle you."

"Why did you come back?"

"I need bulk food products," he teased. "Lots of them."

Her lips moved, but no words came out.

He glanced around. The other customers appeared occupied at the moment, so he leaned forward. "I will be speaking about Kenya tonight at the Grandview Baptist, my grandmother's church in town. Would you and your sister like to come and listen?"

"You know Betsy?"

"Grandma does. I didn't think you would want to come alone. I can pick you up at your house if you wish."

Alarm filled her face. "Oh, you shouldn't."

"But you would come? I'm not a great speaker, but Kenya is an interesting subject. How about it?"

She looked as if she wanted to say something, but her lips moved soundlessly.

"I would love to have you come." He gave her his best smile. "Think about it."

"I...I can't promise."

"But you will think about it?"

Her face blazed.

"Please do," he whispered. "I would love to see you there, but don't run out without speaking with me. Okay?"

She stared at him in silence.

"It's at seven thirty," he added. "I won't speak that long."

He left the store and didn't look back. There! He had done what could be done. Mary wouldn't show up, and this would end where it had begun. In other words, nowhere.

But what if she does show? he wondered. His heart quickened as he walked back to the car.

TWELVE

Betsy slammed the washing machine shut with a clatter, but the sound was muffled by the loud roar of the motor in the enclosed basement. A flexible steel pipe ran from the muffler, across the wet concrete floor, and out through a small window situated high on the wall. The faint smell of exhaust fumes still hung in the air, and Betsy fanned her face with a wet washrag. Not that this did much *goot*, but the effort seemed to help a bit. Someday she would have a nice washer to work with that ran quietly and didn't threaten to suffocate everyone in the vicinity. Such *Englisha* machines could run in an upstairs utility room. *What a life that would be,* she dreamed to herself. *No more basement washing.*

"Betsy!" *Mamm* called from the top of the stairs. "Are you about done?"

"*Yah,*" Betsy responded. "I'm going out now and have one more load afterward."

She could imagine her *mamm* sighing, but the sound would've been swallowed up in the racket. Betsy could sigh too, but what was the use? Her life continued to waste away as she washed clothing in an old machine and then carried every stitch outside to hang on a wire clothesline. Her success with men, Amish or *Englisha*, had amounted to zero.

"What am I doing wrong?" Betsy muttered as she stepped out of the basement. "Why can't I find a decent *Englisha* man who is interested in me?"

Betsy glanced up at the heavens, but no answer came from that direction. Clouds had been gathering all morning, which foretold a chilly afternoon. There could even be a late afternoon snow this time of year. The weather changed easily in the shadow of the Adirondacks. If she had completed the wash before dawn, the clothes would be dry by now. But she had helped with the men's chores in the barn, and then she had worked on a new dress on the sewing machine—a bright green one with frills attached. She hadn't wanted *Mamm* to see the fancy dress, so Betsy had wasted time stuffing the material under a pile of clothing every time *Mamm* walked past the sewing machine.

Betsy was not a *goot* Amish woman, so why did everyone try to make her one? Mary was another matter. Mary was the perfect Amish woman on the outside, but her heart wasn't Amish. Betsy had always known this, but who listened to her? Everyone wondered why Josiah had dumped Mary for Susie, but it was no mystery to Betsy. Josiah was unreliable, but he had understood Mary. However, true to his character, he hadn't been man enough to admit the truth. Josiah would have been the laughingstock of the community, so a simple breakup was the easier answer. Now he was out of the picture, and Mary must be helped. They should jump the fence together.

Betsy sighed and hoisted the basket of wet clothes into her arms. Jumping the fence with Mary was not going to happen. She wrestled open the rickety basement door with one hand and went through with her back pressed against the frame. A blast of wind greeted her, and she bent her face sideways. She set the basket down at the clothesline and glanced toward the horizon. There was no sign of snow clouds, just the wind that had picked up after breakfast. With a clenched jaw, she pinned the clothes on the line and scurried back inside the basement door with the basket in one hand.

"Betsy!" *Mamm* called from the top of the stairs.

"*Yah*, coming." Betsy made her way up the stairs and forced a smile.

"Help me here in the kitchen," *Mamm* said. "You have a few moments to spare."

Betsy bit back a retort.

"And your new dress can wait until the wash is done," *Mamm* continued. "If we run late, supper must be started. That comes first."

"You're right." Quarreling with *Mamm* wouldn't help, and Betsy needed to reform her ways. "Sorry about the late start with the wash."

"The men appreciate your help in the barn, so don't blame yourself." *Mamm* hesitated. "I know about the frills on your dress. I wish you wouldn't fuss with them, but I also had a *rumspringa* once. Regardless, I'll keep saying it until you hear me. Everyone has problems, but there is nothing out there for us or for you."

So *Mamm* knew about the fancy dress? Did she know Betsy was changing dresses at the Fort Plain gas station, and then removing her *kapp* once she was away from the community's eyes? Betsy had pushed things lately, ever since Josiah had proven her opinion of him correct. Didn't she deserve some credit for judging him rightly?

Then again, why press a sore point? Betsy carried a handful of dishes over to the sink. "What did you do on your *rumspringa* in Lancaster, *Mamm*?"

Mamm shrugged. "Just the usual, I suppose."

Betsy took a deep breath. Surely this was a wild guess. "Were there any *Englisha* boyfriends?"

Alarm filled *Mamm*'s face. "Is that what is going on with you, Betsy? Are you seeing an *Englisha* man?"

Betsy laughed bitterly. "I wish, but I'm not."

Mamm stared at her, obviously unconvinced.

"I'm not," Betsy insisted. "We gather at the gas station in Fort Plain. I ride with Enos, and we travel with the other Amish young folks who are there. Occasionally, *Englisha* people are involved, but not in that way for me."

"I wish you wouldn't go out anymore," *Mamm* said. "It's time you ended this and settled down. You are setting a bad example for Gerald."

Betsy set her jaw and didn't answer.

Mamm paused before speaking again. "You're not thinking about jumping the fence anytime soon, are you?"

"*Mamm*, please," Betsy begged. "I don't want to talk about this."

"Look at the example Mary is setting in her sorrow," *Mamm* chided.

"And look how much *goot* that's doing me."

Desperation filled *Mamm*'s face. "So you *are* thinking about jumping the fence."

Mary should be, Betsy almost said. Instead, she grabbed another handful of dishes as *Mamm* lowered herself onto a kitchen chair. The pending waywardness of her youngest daughter had overcome *Mamm*'s nerves. Household work could wait.

Mamm clasped her hands on the tabletop. "Listen to me, Betsy. I was once young. I understand your temptations. I really do."

Betsy nodded and continued to work. Agreement was the best choice at the moment.

"I..." *Mamm* paused. "This is difficult to say, but I dated an *Englisha* man in my *rumspringa*."

Betsy dropped a dish on the counter with a clatter. The plate tilted on the edge, and she lunged to stop its fall before it shattered on the floor.

"I know that's difficult to believe," *Mamm* continued. "I was foolish and thought my heart could be trusted, but I was very wrong. Thankfully, your *daett* got my attention in time, and he persuaded me to return before I did something I would have regretted for the rest of my life. I would have made a terrible mistake if Kenneth hadn't loved me. 'We are not made for that life, Mandy,' he told me. I'm so grateful I listened to him. I soon loved your *daett* as he loved me. I'm ashamed of my past, and I'll always be."

Betsy clutched the dish in both hands.

"Don't be too shocked. Take courage in what I told you, because you can also change. In so many ways you remind me of myself, Betsy. I was dashing and reckless and lived for the moment. That wild heart of yours can be changed, just as mine was."

Betsy caught her breath. "You really dated an *Englisha* man? Did you love him?"

Mamm glanced down at the tabletop. "I had feelings for the man, but that is not a memory I cherish. True love is doing what is best for one's soul, regardless of one's feelings. Kenneth showed me that so plainly."

"Then you didn't love *Daett* when you married him? Is that what you're saying?"

"I am not saying that!" *Mamm* said sharply. "I truly loved your *daett*."

"But you didn't love *Daett* the way you loved the *Englisha* man?"

Mamm shook her head. "Don't misunderstand me, Betsy. I am trying to warn you. I told your *daett* I might need to tell you this story soon, and he agreed that I should. We have nothing hidden from each other. That is the way of love, Betsy." Deep concern drew creases across *Mamm*'s brow.

"The washer!" Betsy exclaimed. She made a dash for the basement door.

Mamm rose to her feet, but she didn't follow Betsy downstairs. Betsy still couldn't believe that *Mamm* dated an *Englisha* man and likely fell in love with him. *There is hope for me yet,* she told herself as she bounded down the steps.

Mamm was right. Betsy did take risks. Not that she was in love with an *Englisha* man. At this point she loved only the *Englisha* lifestyle.

Of course, she could always wind up like *Mamm*. An Amish man could show up someday to take her heart in his hands. Maybe Ronald Troyer, who had never shown his face in the community again... No, that was foolishness. Ronald was a notion more impossible than finding an *Englisha* man to love her.

Betsy lifted the lid and plunged her hands into the soapy water. She gave the switch on the wringer a thump, and the pins began to roll. Each piece of clothing was pressed flat, and the water flowed back into the tub. With the basket full, Betsy made her way outside again to pin the wet clothes to the line. She checked the first batch, but everything was still damp. If the sun didn't break through the clouds soon, she would have to set up lines in the basement and fire up the furnace. That would push the day of washing into the evening hours.

Betsy hurried back inside, where she left the basket on the basement floor. She drained the water out of the tub and shut down the roar of the motor. Then she pushed the washer back to its place along the basement wall and made her way up the stairs. She looked around, but *Mamm* was not in sight, and the counter was still stacked with dirty dishes. She busied herself, finishing quickly. Now that *Mamm* knew about the frills, she could work faster on the dress. Back in the sewing room there was still no sign of her *mamm*. Had she gone to weep in her room or pray for her youngest daughter?

Betsy pressed her lips together and sat down at the sewing machine. The white lace around the dress collar was forbidden by the *Ordnung*, but this dress would not be worn at the Sunday services. Betsy lifted it for a better look. She would appear dashing, as *Mamm* doubtless had in her youth. She was her *mamm*'s daughter.

But falling in love? Betsy had yet to cross that bridge. She couldn't imagine herself in love. Mary had been there, starry-eyed over Josiah's attentions and planning her future home. Betsy wanted a man to care about, but there wasn't one yet. In the meantime, she would occupy herself with thought of an easier life—plus adventure, travels to distant lands, and fancy dresses that weren't hand-sewn.

Betsy sighed and dropped the dress onto the sewing machine, where she worked the foot pedals furiously. She had a long way to go before she could experience most *Englisha* things. She didn't have a job that paid a wage. *Mamm* had seen to that. A paying job for her wild daughter would only push her in the wrong direction. That was *Mamm*'s way of looking at things.

Betsy stopped her sewing when she heard someone coming up the driveway from Duesler Road. Was Mary home? She wasn't due back until five or so, but the clock said the time was only a little after three. Betsy leaped up to make a dash for the front door. As soon as she stepped outside, she spotted her sister. "Is something wrong?"

Mary wouldn't look at her as she pushed past. "I came home early. There weren't many customers with the storm moving in."

Betsy glanced toward the Adirondacks. She now saw that snow clouds were forming.

"You must need help with setting things up in the basement," Mary continued.

Betsy caught up with her sister. "That is why you came home?"

Tears glistened in Mary's eyes. "No, but how do I explain, Betsy?" Mary turned to clutch her sister's arm.

Betsy didn't hide her alarm. "Something *is* wrong!"

"*Yah*, very wrong," Mary agreed. "I may as well be honest."

"What happened?" Betsy held the door wide. "Come in," she said, as if that would help with the tragedy her sister had obviously experienced. Mary never came home early.

"Mrs. Gabert, the older lady you met the other day when you walked me down to the co-op—"

"Has something happened to her?" Betsy guessed. "Did she pass away?"

Mary shook her head.

"What then?"

"I stopped by this morning..." Mary's words petered out, and she gazed toward the Adirondack foothills.

Betsy closed the front door and waited.

"Her grandson was there, and...I can't say it, Betsy. I simply can't."

"What is wrong?" *Mamm* interrupted from the bedroom door.

"I came home early because of the storm," Mary said with a weak smile. "I see that Betsy can use some help with the wash, so I'm glad I did."

"That is thoughtful of you," *Mamm* allowed as Mary hurried past them and whisked up the stairwell.

"She's home early," *Mamm* said in Betsy's direction.

"I know," Betsy said. "I'm going to the basement to set the wash lines."

Mamm didn't object, and Betsy scurried out of sight. Something was terribly out of order. *Mamm* had everything wrong. Betsy was not the daughter who had fallen in love with an *Englisha* man.

THIRTEEN

Mary paced the floor of her bedroom with the door tightly shut. She had to calm down and regain her *goot* sense. The thoughts that raced through her head amounted to foolishness. Mrs. Gabert's grandson was handsome, kind, and considerate, and from all appearances, he had a heart of gold. Who else would do mission work in Kenya? That took a sacrificial heart to say the least, but Willard seemed more than sacrificial. A light had come on in his eyes when he asked her to attend the meeting. His gaze had gone beyond her, as if he saw a distant vision that beckoned him. She knew little about Kenya, but the needs of that country must be great.

Mary paced back to the window and paused to peer past the dark blue drapes. Was her pain misleading her? That would make sense. After Josiah's betrayal, maybe she had become confused and mistook Willard's intentions. It was possible he meant nothing untoward by his invitation. Deep waves of warmth rushed up her neck and face. She rubbed her cheeks with both hands. Under normal circumstances, she would not have entertained suspicions. She was an Amish girl, and he was an *Englisha* missionary to Kenya. They lived in different worlds. Why had she become so flustered?

"Josiah Beiler!" she muttered, giving herself a fierce look in the mirror. "I'll get over you yet."

Surely she did not have feelings for a handsome *Englisha* man. Josiah had kindled emotions in her heart, but the coals would not glow again until the Lord opened the door for a proper Amish man who could be her husband. Her hopes were in the Lord's hands, and He would not lead her astray. Mary caught her breath. What a relief. Here she had thought...oh, what foolishness! Mary rubbed her face again, and the pink flush in the mirror seemed to fade slightly.

The first matter of damage control was Betsy. What a scene Mary had created at the front door before her *goot* sense returned. Betsy would think Mary was falling for the man—which was exactly the kind of conclusion Betsy would draw quite willingly.

Mary took one last glance at the mirror before she exited the bedroom and took the stairs down. *Mamm* glanced up when Mary entered the kitchen. "I'm glad you came home early. Betsy is quite behind with her work. She has been distracted all day. Thinking, I'm afraid..." *Mamm* left the familiar fear unspoken, her brow furrowed in concern.

"We'll pray for her," Mary responded. She hurried toward the basement door.

"Are you okay, Mary?" *Mamm* called after her.

"I'll be fine." Mary turned around and forced a smile. Now was the moment to clarify there was nothing to this nonsense with Willard. "Mrs. Gabert invited Betsy and me to attend her church this evening."

"Oh!" *Mamm* looked even more worried than before.

"Her grandson, Willard, is giving a missionary talk about Kenya." The man's name almost stuck in Mary's throat.

Mamm didn't seem to notice. "Are you thinking this would be a distraction from your troubles? Or perhaps would it show Betsy we aren't as backward as she thinks?"

"I guess," Mary allowed. "But I do admit that I found the subject of ministering to people in Kenya intriguing."

Mamm's smile returned. "You would with your kind heart, Mary.

That convinces me. Why don't you go with Betsy? This can only do you *goot*. What time is the service tonight?"

"Seven thirty," she said, opening the basement door.

Mary paused for a moment to catch her breath before taking the first step down. *Mamm* had allowed a visit to Mrs. Gabert's church tonight!

Betsy met her at the bottom of the stairs. "I heard what you told *Mamm*. Why don't you admit the truth?"

Mary clutched the handrail. "You've got it wrong."

Betsy gave her a glare. "How do you know what I'm thinking?"

The answer was obvious. "Because of how flustered I was when I came home. But it's not what you think. Josiah's hurt is still deep in my heart, and it colors my thoughts."

"You like the man!" Betsy declared. "But I won't spill your secret. I'll go along tonight and pretend that it's perfectly normal for two Amish girls to attend a Baptist church talk on Kenyan missions."

"Our people do things like this. You know that, Betsy."

"Not when they are in love with an *Englisha* man!" Betsy shot back. "But don't get me wrong. I completely approve. This will be an interesting journey, to say the least. You're a church member, Mary, and they could slap that horrible excommunication on you."

Mary grabbed an empty hamper. "You and your imagination. You let it run wild about Stephen Overholt, but he hasn't glanced at me since he spoke to me at the co-op."

"I know I'm right," Betsy muttered. She picked up her basket to follow Mary out the basement door.

Outside, Mary took a deep breath. "Let me assure you, Betsy, that my *goot* sense has returned. I paced awhile in my bedroom and thought about things."

Betsy shrugged. "I think I'm right about Stephen *and* about Mrs. Gabert's grandson."

"Betsy," Mary chided. "We are not going there."

Betsy set down the basket and hugged herself with both hands.

"I can't believe this. My sister is in love with a handsome *Englisha* man. He is handsome, isn't he?"

Mary ignored Betsy to fill her hamper with clothing. "These should dry quickly enough inside if we built a fire."

"You're changing the subject."

"If you speak even a word of this to *Mamm*, neither of us will go anywhere tonight," Mary warned.

"So it is true." Betsy grinned wickedly. "I am enjoying this immensely. My dark days have only been the moment before dawn. Jumping the fence will be so much easier for me if my sister is already there."

"Hush, Betsy. There will be no jumping the fence. Think about the opportunity we are being offered tonight. A glimpse into another world, a world of hurting people. Who would have thought that the Lord would send such a reminder of His work right when I needed it the most? Maybe we can help in Kenya. I'm sure suggestions will be made tonight."

"You're already in love with the man. Admit the truth."

"I don't think so," Mary said with a smile. "Tonight I'm going to accept what the Lord has sent our way. You should do the same. Just look at what we can support even though we are Amish."

Betsy didn't reply. Together they hoisted their heavy baskets of wet clothing, and the storm door in the basement slammed behind them. Betsy had a faint smile on her face as they clipped the pieces of moist clothing to the wires strung from the ceiling. After her basket was empty, Betsy went back outside to refill it while Mary piled extra wood into the furnace. When the flames crept higher, she partially closed the damper to the upstairs ducts, and the dry heat began to seep into the room.

Betsy came back inside with her basket piled high. "I'm looking forward to this evening," she teased with a bright smile.

"So am I," Mary responded.

Back outside at the clothesline, Mary filled her basket with damp pants. The wind drove the cold all the way up her arms, but it didn't bother her. The thought of faraway Kenya gripped her. How sheltered everyone was who lived in the community, while poverty and trouble stalked distant lands. She wondered, *What would it be like to visit Kenya?* Exciting and rewarding perhaps, with plenty of opportunities to touch people's lives.

The trip wasn't possible for an Amish girl. A visit to Mrs. Gabert's church pushed the limits of the *Ordnung*, so Mary would be happy with the gift she had been given. The Lord must be using this moment to show her things she hadn't seen before. Her dream of home and family hadn't been wrong, but neither was helping people to live with their own hopes for the future.

Mary lifted the basket and passed Betsy near the basement door. Thirty minutes later, they pinned the last pieces to the clotheslines in the basement. Mary joined *Mamm* in the kitchen, while Betsy headed toward the sewing room.

"She's working on a dress," *Mamm* explained. "I'm not going to complain even though she's adding extra frills."

"We'll keep praying," Mary assured her. "The Lord will be with us. Look at me. I can't believe the opportunity I have tonight to hear about mission work in Kenya."

"You can use the distraction," *Mamm* agreed. "And mission work is always a *goot* thing."

"Maybe we can help in some way," Mary said as she poured hot water out of the potato pot. "Wouldn't that be a great blessing?"

"I'm glad to see you happy, but don't forget about finding a husband." *Mamm* looked at her pointedly.

Mary laughed. "I haven't forgotten."

Mamm lifted the lid from the green beans to taste one. "Hmm... perfect." She turned back to Mary. "I trust your *goot* sense. I wasn't accusing you."

"I know you weren't."

They worked in silence, their movements honed from hours

spent in each other's presence. This was the heritage Mary wanted to pass on to her own daughter. The great needs in Kenya were doubtless the result of broken families, of children who never had the opportunity to see their parents, let alone work side by side with them.

"We have a rich heritage, don't we?" Mary said.

Mamm appeared startled. "Where did that come from?"

"I was just thinking about Kenya, and how you and I have worked together in the kitchen for my entire growing-up years. Young people in Kenya probably never experienced what I have."

Mamm nodded. "You should say as much to your sister."

"Maybe I will after the talk tonight."

"Anything would help," *Mamm* agreed. She transferred the peeled potatoes to a bowl. "But I'll feel better when both of you are safely married."

Mary laughed again. "I said I haven't forgotten, but some man has to be interested first."

"Don't let bitterness take root," *Mamm* warned. "The way Josiah used you isn't the way another Amish man will act."

"I will comfort myself with that thought," Mary replied. She finished the last potato and gathered up the scattered pieces of skin.

"You can call the men for supper," *Mamm* told her. "Tell Betsy to check on the wash in the basement. The girl should think of that on her own, but somewhere I have failed in my training of her."

"You haven't failed anyone," Mary assured her.

"I've just spent all day with your sister—who wants to jump the fence—and you're going out to an *Englisha* church tonight to find healing." *Mamm* sighed. "I do blame myself at times. I can't help it. I should have warned you about Josiah before your heart was taken with him."

"*Mamm!*" Mary scolded. "That was not your fault. How could you have known what he'd do?"

"I guess I couldn't," *Mamm* admitted. "He seemed like a nice man."

"There! See?" Mary comforted *Mamm* with a hug. "Someone will be along soon to sweep me off my feet."

A trace of a smile played on *Mamm*'s face. She waved her hand toward the door. "Go call the men, Mary. I'll check on the wash. Your sister needs to finish her sewing, now that I think about it."

Mary slipped out of the mudroom door to stand under the twinkling of the early evening stars. The Lord would be with them. He had promised.

"Supper!" she called toward the barn. "Supper is ready!"

FOURTEEN

After *Daett* had offered the prayer of thanks at the table, Mary stood and gathered up a handful of the dishes.

"Go get Danny Boy ready for the girls," *Mamm* told Gerald. "They are going out tonight. I don't want them walking alone after dark."

Gerald grunted. "So why are they traipsing around the country this evening?"

"We can hitch our own horse to the buggy," Betsy spoke up. "We don't need the help of an Amish man."

Gerald ignored the insult. "Tell me where you're going. It's a Wednesday evening, and there's no regular youth gathering."

"The girls are going to hear a talk on Kenya at Mrs. Gabert's church," *Mamm* told him. "Would you like to go along?"

Mary opened her mouth at once. "It would be great if you came, Gerald. Your horizons would be expanded."

"I don't think so," he muttered. He stood up and walked toward the door.

Daett cleared his throat at the head of the table. "So what did I just hear? Where are my girls going tonight?"

Mary began to answer, but *Mamm* spoke up. "Mrs. Gabert

invited them down for a talk by her grandson on Kenya missions. I thought this would be a suitable distraction for Mary, and it will let Betsy see the world from a different perspective."

"I guess that's a *goot* idea," *Daett* allowed, but he appeared skeptical. "Maybe you should go along, Mandy."

"My girls are old enough to travel downtown on their own," *Mamm* told him.

Daett sobered. "I would hope so. When are you ending your *rumspringa*, Betsy?"

"This has nothing to do with my *rumspringa*," Betsy objected. "I'm going with Mary."

"Are you thinking about the spring baptismal class?" *Daett* continued, undeterred. "Most of the girls your age have joined already."

Betsy pressed her lips together and didn't answer.

"This is not the time for this, Kenneth," *Mamm* chided. "I think it's okay if the girls go. Maybe Betsy will get a better picture of how differently people live out there, even in church."

"That is true." *Daett* gave in and left the kitchen.

Mary ran hot water into the sink, and Betsy brought over the last of the supper dishes. Maybe Mary should have told *Mamm* the whole story of the afternoon, including her feelings of doubt. But how embarrassing would that have been?

Mamm spoke at her elbow as if she had read Mary's thoughts. "*Daett* understands. I hope you have a *goot* time. Go change, both of you. I'll do the dishes. Gerald will have Danny Boy out in a minute."

Mary glanced at the clock. She did need a moment alone to collect her thoughts. Betsy had already run out of the kitchen and up the stairs, so Mary followed. The time to speak of this afternoon's failings had passed.

Betsy's bedroom across the hall was silent when Mary arrived at the top of the stairs. She entered her room and changed into a Sunday dress. Betsy still wasn't out in the hall when Mary came out of her bedroom. With a soft knock on Betsy's door, Mary called. "Can I come in?"

"Of course."

Betsy stood in front of the mirror with her *kapp* in one hand and her pins in the other. "I'm not wearing my *kapp* in a Baptist church," she whispered. "But I will put it on to leave the house."

"Please don't make this difficult for me," Mary begged. "We are together tonight. We're sisters, and I don't want to sneak around."

"I guess you're right. But I don't wear my *kapp* on my *rumspringa*. Surely you know that."

"I do, but this is different."

Betsy put the pins in place. "Not really, but I want you to have a *goot* evening, and hopefully a fruitful one. Wouldn't it be *wunderbah* if..." Betsy's face glowed.

Mary sighed. "I'm so thankful you don't talk like this in front of *Mamm*."

"That's because I want this to work."

"We've been over this point," Mary said. "I did fail this afternoon, and I should have told *Mamm*, but I'm okay now. Staying away from Willard would only prove that my wild thoughts were true ones."

"You think too much," Betsy muttered. She followed Mary down the stairs.

"Goodbye, girls," *Mamm* called from the kitchen. "Have a *goot* evening."

"Thanks," Mary hollered as they put on their shawls by the warm floor register. "We'll be back in time to help with the wash in the basement."

"Don't hurry," *Mamm* told them.

"Baptist services aren't too long," Betsy added.

"How do you know?" Mary asked her sister on the way out the door.

"I just know such things," Betsy said self-assuredly. "When one is serious about jumping the fence, all sorts of information comes into focus."

"This is going to help you stay Amish," Mary told Betsy as they approached the buggy. Gerald waited next to Danny Boy with his hand on the bridle.

"What really brought this on?" he quizzed them. "Isn't this sort of sudden?"

"Mary's..." Betsy began, but then she seemed to change her mind. "We're going to join the Baptist church tonight," she chirped instead.

Gerald snorted and threw them the reins. "Remember the Baptists dunk people all the way under the water when they baptize," he teased. He stepped aside to wave goodbye.

Danny Boy threw his head in the air with Betsy at the reins and trotted briskly out of the lane. Fifteen minutes later, they had maneuvered the sharp decline into town and were parked in front of the Baptist church.

"We easily could have walked," Mary commented as she climbed out and tied Danny Boy to a light pole.

"We shouldn't be walking alone after dark," Betsy replied, for once agreeing with *Mamm*.

Mary remained silent as she led the way inside. Several vehicles were parked around the building. The headlights of others had turned into the parking lot by the time Mary and Betsy reached the front doors.

Mrs. Gabert was in the foyer, obviously waiting for them. "Oh, this is such a treat," she gushed, giving both girls tight hugs. "I knew you would come. The Lord is doing such a great work through Willard's life in Kenya. You have to hear the complete story, both of you. Welcome, welcome! Willard is in a prayer meeting with the pastor in his study, but they'll be out soon."

Betsy's face was aglow as Mrs. Gabert led them down a carpeted aisle to padded pews. These seats were nothing like the backless church benches they normally sat on for Amish services.

"Isn't this something?" Betsy leaned over to whisper. "And a prayer meeting in the pastor's study. That's a little like what the Amish ministers do."

"Hush!" Mary warned as Mrs. Gabert settled in the pew beside them. She smiled approvingly at both girls.

True to Mrs. Gabert's word, Willard appeared moments later in step with a young man who was obviously the pastor. Mary had expected someone older, but what did she know about Baptist preachers? Amish ministers came in all shapes and sizes, to say nothing of age.

Willard's gaze swept the gathered group and stopped at their pew. Mary looked away. Willard appeared pleased at the sight of them, but why shouldn't he? He had invited Betsy and her. Weren't people happy when their invitations were accepted?

A piano began to play, and the smile on Betsy's face grew. Maybe this wasn't a *goot* idea after all. Mary may have played right into Betsy's desire to jump the fence. She pushed the thought away and joined in the words of the familiar hymn. Betsy must be persuaded to stay in the community, but how? Mary didn't know. She just trusted that the Lord would help them. The community offered too much for Betsy to leave her heritage for one so different from their own.

The hymn concluded, and the pastor read a short Scripture. "Thank you for coming out tonight," he said. After speaking for a few minutes, he concluded his brief remarks. "Now for the special event of the evening. We have one of our very own with us, missionary Willard Gabert. He is a man we can be proud of for his courage and compassionate heart as he works in Nairobi, Kenya, among the disadvantaged young boys of that city. Willard is back in the States for a short furlough, and he will fill us in on the progress of Agape Outreach."

The pastor smiled and motioned for Willard to join him behind the pulpit. As the pastor placed his hand on Willard's shoulder and led another short prayer, Betsy's smile nearly split her face. This was certainly different from an Amish church service. Mary was here to learn, not to criticize, but she would be able to enjoy the service more if Betsy wouldn't act so impressed.

Mary forced herself to focus on Willard as he began to speak. "Good evening, family, friends, and visitors. I want to welcome you here tonight, and I hope the Lord will give me the right words to convey His heart for the hurting and lost children of Kenya."

The man was handsome. Mary had to admit that, but there were many handsome men in the world. Willard's physical appearance had nothing to do with her. She was here to learn about his work in Kenya. She held her breath when Willard looked right at their pew.

"But before I say more, I want to welcome two Amish women who are here this evening. Both of them are dear friends of my grandmother." Willard smiled sweetly at Mrs. Gabert. "I don't know either of them that well, but Grandma speaks of them as if they are angels." There were ripples of laughter throughout the church house. "Please join me in welcoming Mary and Betsy Yoder."

After a short round of applause from the audience, Mary guessed her face must be the color of sun-ripened tomatoes. Betsy, on the other hand, appeared pleased enough to burst.

Thankfully, Willard soon turned on a projector to display a map on the church wall. In the semidarkness, Mary could breathe again.

"This is Kenya, the gateway to Africa for many Christian organizations." Willard turned and smiled at the congregation. "If you ever visit us, be sure and hang on tightly to your purses and bags. In Kenya, the opinion of the general population is that if you own two items of any object, you have too many and should share with someone else." Chuckles rippled through the congregation again. Willard grinned. "Kenya is Christian in name, but in reality vestiges of pagan customs exist, resulting in a mishmash of strange beliefs. But we will not go into that tonight. Suffice it to say that even though everyone is willing to lift your extras, they do have fierce objections to thievery. Once a thief is caught, he is often publicly executed by vigilantes. The favored method is to stack a ring of tires around the suspect, douse the ring with gasoline, and light the person on fire."

A gasp of horror went through the sanctuary, and Mary clutched the pew in front of her until her fingers hurt. The image of charred bodies sent a shudder through her. Nothing in the community had prepared her for such a vicious existence. She glanced at Betsy, who was similarly transfixed, her gaze glued to Willard's face.

"This leads directly to the mission work I do," Willard continued. "Sadly, children—mostly young boys—are either tasked by their parents or are driven to thievery by their extreme poverty, and they are often caught because of their inexperience. If a child is released or manages to escape the clutches of the vigilantes, there is no choice for him but to flee the village where he lives. Many of them do so by riding on the chassis of the buses, which connect the countryside with the large towns.

"Stories are told of boys who ride the buses into Nairobi for up to sixteen hours. Some of them don't survive the journey, and those who do end up on the streets with nowhere to call home. The police are under great pressure to keep the city presentable, so they've been known to abuse street children. After taking the children out of town, where they administer severe beatings, they tell the children to return to where they came from. With the threat of death waiting at home, the children are unlikely to choose that option. Such journeys are impossible for them."

The silence in the church was complete. Mary slid forward on her seat, and Betsy glanced at her and mouthed the words, "That is awful."

Mary nodded and turned her attention back to Willard.

"Our mission is to make contact with these lost children," Willard went on. "Many of them, by the time we find them, are addicted to sniffing glue. That is why we call them 'glue boys.' They breathe the fumes and quickly reach a numbed state in which even hunger doesn't bother them. Addiction occurs, of course, but thankfully it can be broken with greater ease than other addictions. A week of withdrawal sometimes is enough. The worst outcome is permanent brain damage, and after that has occurred, almost nothing can be done.

"Our method of contact with these boys is to develop friendships with them, because the police brutality has created an atmosphere of severe distrust. They must come to our mission willingly and stay on the same basis. Some do. Others leave after a short stay. Some leave and come back again. We offer education and opportunities for them to return to their communities, where they are often welcomed after being educated by a relief agency. If all else fails, we help them establish themselves in Nairobi. At least, that's our goal. The mission was founded some twenty years ago, and I have been the director for the past two years."

Mary settled back into her seat as Willard concluded his remarks. As the offering plate was passed, Willard stayed on the platform for a question and answer session. Her mind raced. This was a world she knew nothing about. A world of sorrow and pain far removed from the influence of the community. She desperately wanted to help. She had taken her own hopes for granted. These boys never had a chance.

The image of tires and burning flames danced in front of Mary's eyes. She dug in her satchel and found a twenty-dollar bill to drop in the offering plate. She might never go to sleep tonight.

"We should go," Betsy whispered in her ear a few minutes later. "The service is over."

Half of the congregation had begun to leave the building, while the others thronged forward to shake Willard's hand and pepper him with more questions.

Willard had told Mary to wait so they could speak, but at the moment she would be unable to say anything. Mary nodded to Betsy, and they slipped out of the church house to untie Danny Boy from the streetlight pole. Only the clip-clop of his hooves filled the silence as they trotted up the street and headed out of town.

FIFTEEN

Mary set the last dish on the breakfast table the following morning. Faint noises came from the mudroom, where *Daett* and Gerald washed up after the morning chores. She had slept restlessly all night thinking about Kenya and the glue boys. The awful image of emaciated limbs and gaunt eyes haunted her memory, along with Willard's concerned face as he told the stories.

Daett greeted her with a smile. "*Goot* morning. How did the talk go at the Baptist church last night?"

"Sit yourself at the table first, Kenneth," *Mamm* ordered. "Mary's getting ready to tell us the details. I've only heard snippets myself."

Daett's chair squeaked as he sat down.

Gerald made a face. "How much money did you leave in the offering plate?"

"Gerald!" Betsy chided. "I gave nothing, but I think Mary did."

"See?" Gerald gloated. "That's what Baptist churches do. They are only after your money."

Betsy glared at him, but Mary silenced her sister with a motion of her hand. "I did give a little, which seemed like nothing after hearing Willard talk about the great needs in Nairobi. I am thankful we were invited to attend. Never have I heard the needs in another country described in such stark terms. Here we have *wunderbah*

119

food this morning, but over in Kenya, some boys live off glue bottles and have no home but the streets."

Gerald huffed and changed the subject. "The food is getting cold. Seat yourself, Mary, so we can eat."

A retort died on her lips. She must be understanding of others who hadn't heard what Betsy and she did.

"Let us pray," *Daett* said as Mary settled in her seat. They all bowed their heads.

"Our Father, who art in heaven," *Daett* began, "we give You thanks for the abundance of food You have laid out in front of us this morning, and we remember those in other countries who are not so blessed."

Mary lifted her head at the "amen."

"So." *Daett* waited while Gerald served himself a generous helping of eggs and bacon. "What was this all about last night?"

"We should be very thankful for our sheltered life," Betsy muttered with a glare toward Gerald.

Mamm's eyes lit up. "So you did learn important things?"

"I learned about Nairobi, Kenya," Betsy retorted.

Mary hushed her sister with a shake of her head. "What Betsy means is that Willard heads a mission for street children in Kenya. Both of us were very moved, and I would like to help in whatever way I can. The twenty dollars I placed in the offering plate doesn't seem like near enough."

Gerald grunted with his mouth full. "There is always money involved."

Daett smiled as he filled his own plate. "I think you'll find that most of life needs money to function, Gerald. That is no sin."

"Especially for mission work," Betsy got in edgewise.

Gerald gave his sister a glare but otherwise remained silent.

Mamm smiled toward Mary. "We are glad to see you taking such an interest in something, Mary. Not that you weren't doing well, but you did have me worried there a bit."

"She mopes too much," Gerald agreed, before taking a huge mouthful again.

"Mary does not!" Betsy retorted. "She has been doing very well."

Gerald ignored the barb and grinned. "I heard that Stephen Overholt is ready to ask Mary home from the hymn singing. He's been talking up a storm about his plans and how he knows the will of the Lord. That would be a better distraction than Baptist meetings and Kenyan glue children."

Horror filled Betsy's face. "How can you say that, Gerald? The man is...he's..." Words for once failed Betsy.

"Am I the only one who sees any danger in this?" Gerald waved his spoon about. "Baptist meetings? Who is this Willard anyway?"

"Mrs. Gabert's grandson," Betsy shot back, as if that answered everything.

"He's an *Englisha* man, and Mary's grieving. Is he handsome?"

"How can you be so horrid?" Betsy spat. "If Mary falls for the man, I would support her totally."

Daett spoke up. "I think Mary has her heart in the right place. I'm with *Mamm* in thinking that Mary's interest in Kenyan children is *goot*. How we can help, I am not sure. Maybe we can pray." *Daett* sent a smile in Mary's direction before he turned to Betsy. "But you should not encourage anyone to leave the community, and that goes for yourself."

Betsy bowed her head and remained silent.

"I think Mary should accept Stephen's offer," Gerald continued. "At least she would be married to an Amish man."

"You...Gerald, how could you?" Betsy sputtered. "The man gives me the creeps."

"Stephen is a stable member of the community," *Daett* said. "Be careful about your personal feelings, Betsy. No one is asking you to consider the man as *your* husband."

"And neither should anyone ask Mary to consider him."

"That's up to Mary, I think," *Daett* said.

"See, you *are* considering him!" Betsy wailed. "I can't stand this."
She turned to Mary. "Please tell me you won't entertain even the
slightest, littlest, tiniest thought of allowing Stephen to bring you
home from the hymn singing. I would have to leave the house for
the evening."

Mary waited a moment before she answered. "Why are we talking about Stephen? I hoped to stay on the subject of Willard's talk
last night."

"Because the thought of you courting in Stephen's buggy sends
shivers up and down my spine," Betsy said. "After Josiah! Mary,
think! You deserve better than that."

"Betsy?" *Daett* chided. "Mary has to make her own choice."

Betsy threw her hands in the air. "Mary needs someone handsome, kind, and caring, with a heart like Willard Gabert's."

"See? I told you. There is danger in the air," Gerald said.

"Gerald, please." *Mamm* frowned at her son. "The idea of Mary
falling for an *Englisha* man is impossible. You should be ashamed
of yourself."

"Maybe," Gerald said, huffing. "I'm sorry, Mary. I didn't mean
to slight your character. I was caught up with the thought, I guess."

"Maybe other girls would cause questions, but not Mary," *Mamm*
said. "Now can we please move on to another subject?"

"We have confidence in you, Mary," *Daett* encouraged her. "And
we support any help you want to give this Kenyan venture. I don't
know how you can help, but you have our blessing."

"Thank you, *Daett*." Mary kept her head down. Her face must be
blazing red after Betsy and Gerald's insinuations. Was there doubt
in her own heart about Willard? Could she fall for an *Englisha* man?
The thought was completely absurd. She was an Amish woman who
would marry an Amish man, and that was that.

"We wish you the best." *Mamm* patted Mary on the shoulder.
"Now, if we're finished chatting, can we pray again and get on with
the day?"

Daett nodded, and they all bowed their heads in the closing prayer of thanks. Gerald bolted out the mudroom door a second after the "amen," and *Daett* followed at a slower pace. "Have a *goot* day, everyone," he called over his shoulder.

Mary busied herself with clearing the table. After *Mamm* left the kitchen, Betsy worked quietly by her sister's side. "I'm sorry I lost my temper," she finally ventured. "Gerald just gets to me."

Mary forced a smile. Her siblings should not be blamed for their concerns. She would have to walk carefully, even with the confidence *Mamm* and *Daett* had expressed in her. "It's okay, Betsy. Do you have any ideas about how we could help in Kenya?"

Betsy shrugged, her hands full of dirty dishes. "I was moved last night by Willard's words, but I don't know what could be done from here. I mean, you're Amish." Betsy made a face.

"Why is that a problem?" Mary protested. "An Amish woman should be able to help somehow."

"Your savings are pretty small." Betsy grimaced again. "That's the only idea that comes to me."

Silence fell between them as they worked in the kitchen. Once the dishes were finished, Mary left to peek into the sewing room. "I'm leaving, *Mamm*. You have a *goot* day."

"The Lord be with you," *Mamm* told her with a smile. "If you figure out how we can help the mission in Kenya, let us know."

"I will."

She grabbed her coat and shawl to step outside. The wind blowing in from the Adirondack foothills was brisk. She would have to start using the buggy to get to work soon, but she needed the bracing cold on her face this morning.

Now that she was alone, her siblings' insinuations about Willard brought flashes of heat into her face. Maybe she should abandon all interest in the Kenyan glue boys—but wouldn't that confirm Gerald's accusation? She wasn't one to back down from where her heart led, and a sudden change in interest could not be easily explained to her family.

As Mary headed down the hill, the wind whipped dead leaves

around the ditches. The chill crept through the thick shawl she wore
and chafed her face. Maybe walking instead of driving the buggy
hadn't been a wise idea. Gerald would have hitched up Danny Boy
if she had asked. Mary increased her pace at the bottom of the hill.
Mrs. Gabert's home was ahead on the right. She could stop to catch
her breath on the front porch, but that might mean meeting Willard again. What if he made assumptions from her actions the way
Gerald and Betsy had?

Mary looked sideways as she passed Mrs. Gabert's driveway. The
front porch was empty, but she wasn't taking any chances. She could
stop in tonight on the way home for a chat with the elderly lady.

At the corner of the next side street, a car pulled up beside her
and rolled down its window.

"Willard!" Mary gasped.

"What is wrong with you? Europe's warm this winter, but this is
cold. Get in."

I will not! Mary wanted to protest. Instead she gave in, and the
warmth of the car enveloped her.

"Do all Amish women walk in freezing weather?"

"Just me," she chirped, but he didn't laugh.

"You shouldn't," he chided. "Do you not have a buggy available
this morning?"

"Of course I do. My brother would have hitched it up for me, but
I didn't know it was this bad."

"A storm is approaching. The weather report was all over Grandma's TV." He paused. "But you don't have a TV."

Mary managed to laugh. "That is true."

"Don't the Amish have built-in weather forecasters?" he quipped.

His chuckle was cheerful, and Mary joined in.

"So what do you have on tap for the day? Am I driving you to
work?" he asked as he turned right on Reid Street.

"Yes, thank you. Just another day at the bulk food store, serving customers." She gathered her courage. "My sister and I were very impressed with your talk last night."

"I thought from the way you bolted that I must have offended you."

"Oh, no. Of course not. We had to…I don't know. It was late, and we were at a strange place, and—"

"I understand." He smiled warmly. "I was very pleased that you came, and I was honored. It's not every day that I have two beautiful Amish women in my audience."

Mary gave him a teasing glare. "You have quite a flowery tongue!"

"That's what it takes, I guess." He grinned broadly.

"Do you have someone waiting for you back in Kenya or in some other town?"

His grin faded. "I guess you have a right to ask that since you told me about your woes. No girlfriend. Just Kenya."

"I'm sorry. I can't imagine why not."

His grin returned. "Now look who has the flowery tongue."

Mary settled back in her seat and ignored the comment. What was wrong with her? She pasted the best smile she could on her thawing face. "Is there any way Betsy and I can help with your project? I know we are just two Amish women, and we can't do much. I write poems and letters, but that probably wouldn't mean much to starving glue boys."

She noticed interest written on his face. "You write poetry?"

"Forget I said that," Mary hastened to say. "Words seem empty in the face of the stories you told us last night. But back to the point. Amish women can sew, quilt, and make things. Would that help?"

"I had never thought of that angle." He smiled. "Let me think on that a bit, but I'm not finished with the poetry. Could I see what you write sometime?"

Mary blushed. "You would read my poems?"

"Of course. I'm sure they would be interesting."

Mary tried to breathe as they pulled up in front of the co-op. "I know nothing about poetry."

The words she had written on the back of Josiah's letters raced through her mind. *My dearest, my dearest, Josiah, my dear.* Willard would think her insane for such nonsense.

"Perhaps I should be the judge of that," he said. "But here we are."

"Thanks so much for the ride." Mary reached for the door handle. "You didn't have to."

"I can pick you up this evening too."

"No. I mean, I can't...you can't..." She sputtered her objections.

He raised his hand. "No protest, please. And if you want to pay me, you can recite one of your poems."

Mary bolted from the car and raced for the front door of the co-op store without a backward glance.

SIXTEEN

Mary pushed open the back door of the co-op and peeked out. The late afternoon sun was hidden behind a thick blanket of clouds, the view of the Adirondack foothills blocked by townhouses. She didn't need to see them to know that Willard had been correct. A winter storm was brewing. A few flakes of snow already twirled about, but at least the wind would be at her back for the walk home. If she left now, she could avoid Willard and his offered ride. She already felt rude for dashing into the store this morning without a goodbye, but she hoped Willard would understand or chalk up her behavior to Amish traditions or strangeness. Hadn't Betsy and she left the church meeting early last night?

Mary caught her breath as a fresh blast of wind hit her face. Then she closed the door and steadied herself on the doorjamb. *Willard wants to see my poems.* No man, not even *Daett*, had ever asked to read them. Josiah had known that she wrote poems, but his interest had never gone beyond a shallow "that's neat" comment. She had never dared to show him anything she had written. Now Willard had asked to see one, even though she didn't know him well at all. And he was an *Englisha* man! Her heart pounded. She should set out for home this very moment and never see Willard again.

Mary took several deep breaths. She was a sensible woman. Of course the thought of a man reading her poems unnerved her. That was what this was. If she let him read one, the flush of emotion would pass. An educated *Englisha* man could give her pointers on how poems should be written. That was the right way to look at this. Willard must find her a curiosity, but she could use the interest to her benefit. This went both ways.

Willard was not interested in her romantically. Hadn't her experience with Josiah made things clear? Men found her intriguing until a pretty face came along. Then—*whoosh!*—they were gone faster than the cars rushing past on Interstate 90.

The front door of the store opened and closed with a bang. Mary collected herself and brushed off her apron, pasting on a smile and forcing her feet forward. Customers were more important than daydreams. Mary's smile faded when she saw Stephen's face around the corner.

He cleared his throat. "I guess you're open. I mean, the door was unlocked."

"Of course we are. What can I get for you?" She held out her hand for his list.

"Ah..." He cleared his throat. "I...I mean, I came in...the storm is picking up."

"You're offering to drive me home?"

Stephen looked at her strangely. "I hadn't thought of that. I guess, I mean, it is snowing. Do you need a ride home?"

"Oh, no. I can walk." Mary clasped and unclasped her hands. "Can I have your list now?"

"There is..." Stephen struggled toward the right words. "This is, if I can say it right, not my usual visit, Mary. I was just here not that long ago. Do you remember? You should. It was the day—and I am sorry to remind you—of your planned wedding." He peered at her.

"Of course, Stephen. I am so sorry. I should not have forgotten that you recently came in." Mary steadied herself on the edge of a shelf. This day was very strange.

"There is nothing, not really, to apologize for." Stephen nodded, the problem apparently solved to his satisfaction. "I want to, if I may, ask something of you, Mary. If you would let me, if you would think about it, perhaps, if you would consider, after much prayer and thought, of course, and after consulting with your *mamm* and *daett*..." He stroked his beardless chin. "I have not done this in a long time, and never with such a lovely woman as yourself. My courage, what there is of it, fails me. You are a very godly woman indeed. I am humbled, as I should be, in your presence. But I feel as if I have seen, as best I can, the Lord's will in this matter."

"What do you want, Stephen?"

"It is not about what I want, Mary." He paused. "It is what the Lord wants, and His face is often hidden in the clouds, as the preachers say, and His ways are beyond the understanding of lowly and corrupt creatures such as myself."

"I suppose so," Mary allowed.

"Do you know, and understand, and see the full depths of the will of the Lord?" He studied her for a moment.

"Ah, I don't know. Probably not! I once thought I was marrying Josiah Beiler."

"That's...see there, that's exactly right. I say, with my spirit bowed low, that we are on the same page." He nodded again. "That is why I have dared to gather my courage, Mary, and even suppose that a woman such as yourself would consider a man like me, and see the Lord's will. Would you, even for a moment, since you can see that I have not the charms about me that your Josiah possessed—"

"Josiah is now married to the former Susie Wengerd!" Mary interrupted.

He stared at her. "Your heart is bitter about this matter?"

"It is. I hope you are not too astonished that I slip and fall in my weakness. I am praying the Lord will help me fully heal."

He collected himself. "We are all, every one of us, from the smallest to the greatest, bitter with life at times. Only the grace of the Lord, His strong and mighty hand, carries us along, and seeing His will."

"I have forgiven Josiah. I really have," Mary assured him.

"I would not—in my own great weakness and failure—argue with you," he allowed. "Which brings me back to my point—one I must get to before some else comes inside. I would have asked you, if I had dared, properly after the Sunday night hymn singing, but I am not a young man anymore."

Mary tried avoiding the subject. "You would come to the hymn singings again?"

"I could bring myself, for your sake, to go again," he managed. "Let me say, though—right up front like I did the other day—that Josiah Beiler is not a wise man. I will say no more on the subject. The Lord's will is clear to me. Would you maybe allow me to drive you home some Sunday evening? Not this Sunday evening, of course, but sometime in the future, after you have thought on the matter, and prayed—"

"I don't know." Mary hesitated. "I really don't. This is not in my plans at all."

He studied her again, and Mary hurried on. "But I guess I know what you are going to say. Josiah Beiler was in my plans, and look how that turned out. Maybe I should submit to the Lord's will, if this is the Lord's will."

"You say it, and how well you do say it!" He nodded for emphasis. "You see my thinking as plain as day."

"I don't know, Stephen," Mary repeated. "This is—"

"The Lord's will," he said. "I have seen this plainly, as if the sun came up in the morning while I was looking at the sky."

His choice of words was always odd. The man needed help, but Mary couldn't say that. Maybe she should help him, though. That was the least she could offer, since there wasn't anything better going on in her life at the moment when it came to Amish men.

"I don't love you, Stephen," she began. "I doubt if I ever will, not in the way you mean—but if you want, we can talk about this... some Sunday evening. I would be willing."

Astonishment filled his face. "You don't need a moment to pray about this?"

Mary's smile was thin. "Perhaps this is the Lord's doing, as you say. His grace on both of us? I can help you, and you can give me something to do."

"You are sure, you really are, about this?"

"I am not sure about anything, Stephen, and I don't think you fully understand me, but I will let you drive me home on Sunday evening, and we can talk. Is that *goot* enough?"

"Thank you. I do not understand, as you say, but I do at times see the Lord's ways when He is working. This is one of those times, I am sure, Mary. As the wise Solomon said, who can know the ways of a man with a maid, like a serpent on a rock—"

"I know the verse," Mary interrupted.

He seemed not to hear. "The words, those great and mighty words, touched my soul deeply when I read them the other day. I watched a serpent, a great long one, climb a rock once, and I understood a little of the wonder of it, and the Lord's work—but not much. I am not Josiah Beiler, Mary."

"Maybe that is something for which I can give thanks."

He appeared puzzled. "You have a fast tongue, not unlike your sister. But I do not criticize. I wouldn't dare. Who could complain when the Lord is in the matter? I really can't. Not me. I am a man of slow words. But thank you. You are a woman who sees the Lord's ways." A tear tricked down his cheek, and he glanced heavenward. "May the will of the Lord, His great and mighty will, be done."

Stephen retreated, and she followed him to open the door. He stepped out into the falling snow without a backward glance. Mary leaned against the door frame and trembled. Had she just agreed to a date with Stephen Overholt? Betsy would be furious.

Mary didn't love the man. She had made that clear, but Stephen had not understood. What boldness had possessed her to think she could help him? Maybe this was the Lord's way to open a door into a different kind of love—one without pounding hearts and swooning—but she doubted that.

Could she fall in love with Stephen? Betsy would say her sister was running away from Willard Gabert, but Mary was not going there. She was interested in Willard's mission in Kenya, but he was still an *Englisha* man, and she was still an Amish woman. Both of them were fully dedicated to their own causes. Willard's handsome face drifted into her mind. Mary found a piece of paper and began to write furiously.

> *He faces out into the storm with fearless eye.*
> *He touches hurting hearts with tender hand.*
> *Brave he is, and bold of soul,*
> *This man who stands and snatches from the street,*
>
> *The bruised and broken, tossed aside,*
> *The rough, the weary, lost from heaven's light.*
> *He casts on earth the shine of stars,*
> *The breath of heaven from the skies.*
>
> *He is a man so loved by God.*
> *So near, so close, so precious in His sight.*
> *Like a ship that makes her way toward land.*
> *Like an eagle searching in the sky.*
>
> *His face is set against the wind.*
> *But he will triumph. He will win.*
> *He is a man, clothed in might.*
> *A man in love with right.*

Mary stared at the paper and almost crumpled it. What foolishness. What dumb words. Willard, with his *Englisha* education, would think her mad, but he had asked to see her poems. So why not share them? Maybe if some man like Willard laughed at her poems, she would want to stop writing them.

Mary paced the empty store and began to wrap things up for the night. The clock still read fifteen minutes till closing time, but she was ready to leave. She could start out, and Willard would cross her path on the way down from his grandmother's place—if he came. Maybe the man had already forgotten about her. He must have a thousand better things to do besides driving an Amish woman around.

Mary stuck the piece of paper in her pocket and hurried out the door. She was turning the lock when Willard drove into the parking lot.

"Leaving early?" he teased from the rolled down car window.

"It's storming," she retorted.

He hopped out to open the car door. "I warned you."

"I can walk home."

"Or I can drive you." His grin filled his face.

Mary sighed. She climbed in, and he raced around to the other side. He settled on the seat and glanced at her. "I didn't want to miss any poems."

"You must be very bored sitting around your grandmother's house."

His smile grew. "Actually, I have another talk tonight in Little Falls that needed preparation, and there were emails to answer from Kenya."

"Trouble while you've been gone?" Concern flickered on her face.

"Just the usual, but nothing that Ean and Daisy can't handle. They're very capable people."

"Your staff?"

"They are filling in for me," he said. "And they might stay awhile after I return if everything works out."

"I see," she said. She *didn't* see, but this was none of her business. "I still would like to help with Kenya somehow. Have you thought of anything I could do?"

His eyes twinkled. "I did run the idea past Ean and Daisy. We can't really hand out gifts to the boys on the streets because they might trade them for glue, but we could use items at our mission center. Blankets and quilts maybe?" He wrinkled his face. "Amish quilts are expensive, though, and these are street boys. We certainly can't afford them on our budget, and they would seem a little overdone for the place they would be going. Even simple, plain blankets would be luxuries to these boys."

"They deserve the best!" Mary declared. "I'll see what I can do. Can we make contact through your grandmother once I have some items?"

"Or me if I'm still around."

"Okay then." She didn't look at him as they navigated the streets out of town.

"Back to your poems," he said. "I don't want to wait in suspense until tomorrow."

Who said anything about seeing you again tomorrow? she almost said. Mary bowed her head. "I don't know. I have never shown one of my poems to a man."

He raised his eyebrows. "Not even the mystery man who married your friend?"

Her silence was answer enough.

He winced. "I'm sorry, but I'm also honored."

"Susie wasn't my best friend," she muttered, but it didn't matter from the look on his face.

"I really do want to hear one of your poems."

"Okay." She gave in with a pounding heart. She could barely breathe. She took the poem from her pocket, and the words swum in front of her eyes. She began to read, "He faces out into the storm with fearless eye..."

She glanced at him when she finished. Willard was staring through the windshield at the road. "Was it that horrible?" she whispered.

He turned his head. "You wrote that today?"

Mary looked away. "*Yah*. Why?"

"Thank you," he said. "That was nice of you."

Mary wasn't sure what else to say.

He tried to smile. "I appreciate the words more than you could know. Life is kind of rough there." He reached over to touch her hand. "Thank you, Mary. That was the kindest thing a woman ever said about me."

Silence filled the car as they drove out of town.

"That was also nice poetry," he said. "Well put together and with the proper feeling. Thanks for reading the piece to me. I am humbled to be the first man upon whose ears your sweet words have fallen."

"Don't tease me, Willard," she managed. "I didn't mean the poem the way it clearly sounded. I'm so sorry…"

"Don't be," he said. "Can I have it?" He held out his hand for the piece of paper.

What could she do? His blue eyes pierced hers, and their fingers brushed. A jolt went all the way through her.

She gave him directions to her house. As soon as he had brought the car to a stop, she opened the door and bolted up the driveway. She didn't look back on the race up to her front door.

"What is wrong?" Betsy asked in the entryway.

"Nothing! Willard brought me home," Mary said, continuing her mad dash up the stairs.

SEVENTEEN

Willard sat at the breakfast table and scrolled through the news headlines on his smartphone. An earthquake in Chile and warfare in the Middle East dominated the list.

His grandmother set a plate of eggs in front of him. "Any news from Kenya? Or are other things on your mind this morning?"

"Ean and Daisy are handling things fine." Willard managed a smile. "I should be back before long. But you never know when trouble will rear its ugly head."

Mrs. Gabert seated herself beside him. "Can you ask the blessing?"

Willard bowed his head without answering and led out, "Dear God in heaven, thank You for this food, and for my grandmother, and for the morning You have given us…"

"Amen," Mrs. Gabert echoed when he finished. "You forgot one thing, though. Mary Yoder."

"I'm supposed to give thanks for her?"

Mrs. Gabert chuckled. "Sounds like I was right. You two are in love."

The sight of Mary bolting up the driveway toward the house last evening replayed in his head. He had her poem in his pocket, the paper already wrinkled from the many times he had read her words. His protest died on his lips.

"See, Willard? You should accept the ways of the Lord."

"The Lord?" The words exploded out of his mouth. "You want me to fall in love with a girl who will only reject me...who is impossible to reach...who belongs to another world...who..." Willard's hand flailed through the air in hopeless circles.

"A true sign of the Lord's doing," Mrs. Gabert concluded with a pleased smile. "Great things must come out of great faith."

"Faith! Love! Me! Her!" Willard sputtered. "What you are saying is impossible, Grandma. I should catch the next plane back to Kenya and leave this foolishness behind. I will soon have the funds I need. Beyond that—"

"You like the girl." Mrs. Gabert handed him a plate of toast. "Am I not right?"

"As in..."

"Don't overthink things, Willard," she chided.

"I'm not going to stop thinking," he retorted. "I did that once, and look what happened."

"The Lord gives when the Lord takes," she reminded him. "And in double portions, usually. Nothing is impossible for Him. Remember that."

Willard grunted and didn't respond for a moment.

"You should invite Mary and Betsy to your talk tonight in Palatine Bridge. Pick them up and take them out to eat afterward. That would be a step in the right direction."

Willard groaned. "You never stop, do you?"

"Not when I'm right," she said with a twinkle in her eye. "Tell me about your time together so far. You went down to the store last night to drive her home."

Willard looked away.

"Come on," Mrs. Gabert prodded. "I'm right, am I not? You find her interesting."

"She read me one of her poems." He hesitated before handing her the paper. "Did you know that Mary was a poet?"

Mrs. Gabert read silently. "I didn't, but I'm not surprised. The

Amish are talented, even in the arts. Is this poem about you? Sounds like it."

Willard studied his plate. "I don't think Mary knew or thought about... Or maybe she understands the impossibility of a relationship between us. The best thing would be to end this once and for all by leaving."

His grandmother was undeterred. "I think you're wrong."

"A man in love with right..." Willard quoted from memory, the words seared into his mind.

"Mary read this poem to you?"

"Well, I asked her to. Not knowing what it was, of course."

"You two are getting along great without my help."

"Don't let your imagination run away, Grandma."

Her smile appeared. "Let me get this straight. We have an Amish girl reading an intimate poem to a man she hardly knows. I don't think I need much imagination for this love story. The truth is plain enough to see."

"You really think I should take this risk? To say nothing of Mary... if she even would?"

"Is having your heart broken again your concern, Willard? You know that any love will break your heart eventually."

"I'm sorry." Willard reached across the table to touch his grandmother's hand. "You miss him, don't you?"

She wiped away a tear. "Your grandfather was a handsome fellow, Willard. You remind me of Benny in many ways. We were married for almost fifty years. I thought we would make the magic number, but we fell a few months short. Wonderful years, though. You should take the chance while you have it. There is only one Mary in the world. Perhaps you didn't come on furlough for the reason you thought you did."

"Your faith is great, Grandma, but..."

She patted him on the arm. "Follow your heart, Willard, and don't think too much."

"About the pain? Or about the devastation this would cause Mary? You know how the Amish are."

"Don't waste time wondering what could be or could've been. I'm not going to force you. This is your choice, but I'll keep praying for you. I'm just an old woman speaking out of her memories and wishing Benny were here."

"I know you loved my grandfather."

"I did love him, and your parents and you. I'm sure our love was only a shadow of the love the Lord has for His people. We can't see that too well except when His love is reflected in the faces of those our hearts are made one with."

"Maybe you should give the talk tonight." Willard chuckled. "The offering plate would be filled to the brim, and I could go back to Kenya next week."

Mrs. Gabert wiped away another tear. "You'll do great, dear. And you'll make the right choice with Mary. I'll keep my mouth shut from now on."

Willard gave her a skeptical look.

"Okay. I won't, but I'll try," she said.

Willard smiled. "I know you will, Grandma. I was teasing. And thanks for breakfast."

Mrs. Gabert's face lit up. "Are you going down to see her now? She walked past here an hour ago."

Willard laughed and retreated to the guest bedroom without an answer, but he sobered at the sound of a horse's hooves beating on the street pavement outside. He pushed aside the drapes to follow the slow movement of a buggy. A bearded man with a black hat sitting low on his brow drove the horse. The man studied the front porch as he passed, as if he thought danger lurked inside.

The buggy turned at the street corner, but the sound of hoofbeats lingered in the air. The Amish were not psychic, so the man couldn't know about Willard's conversation at the breakfast table with his grandmother, but the sight of the buggy reminded him of the impossibility of his situation. Mary was devoted to her faith and her community—a community they did not share.

"Don't overthink," his grandmother had said.

But how could he refrain from thinking? Every nerve in his body shouted for thinking— reasonable, logical, sensible thinking. He liked Mary Yoder. Who wouldn't? They both knew recent heartbreak, but broken hearts were known for their poor choices. Neither of them could trust their heart, let alone each other. They were headed for ruin or worse if he pursued her. Even if Mary agreed to attend the meeting tonight, choosing to love a non-Amish man would mean walking away from everything she had ever known.

Willard paced the floor. He more than liked Mary. The woman fascinated him. The depth of her soul was visible in her brown eyes. Their clearness masked no evil. She was a woman who had not walked the dark paths of the world, a world he knew well from his work in Kenya. Granted, life in the States was sheltered, but Mary's life went beyond that. She had a purity of heart that he had not encountered before. Carlene had come from a Christian home and had been a woman of virtue, but she had rejected him once his calling to Kenya had become a reality. Carlene had found him lacking, and the experience had been painful for him. The hurt would be worse if he were foolish enough to approach Mary again.

Willard glanced out the window at the empty street. The sound of the buggy had long faded from the air. He should be wise and give up any thought of Mary Yoder. She would be a pleasant memory, her words a balm to his soul, and that would be enough. He would find some other woman to marry someday, one from his world.

But could he walk away from the challenge without even trying? Grandma knew him well and had known the point to stress. What if? What could be if their love were allowed to flourish and grow?

A smile filled Willard's face. The task would be difficult— perhaps impossible. But he would try. He couldn't do anything else and live with himself. In the end, the matter was in the Lord's hands. What a miracle if a woman like Mary would love him, would come to walk by his side in Kenya. Her compassion would go into action on behalf of Nairobi's street children. Her words of faith would speak to their injured hearts.

Willard stopped himself. He was overthinking and daydreaming at the same time.

When he exited the bedroom, his grandmother looked up from her chair in the living room with a smile on her face.

"Don't say I told you so," he said.

"I never would, Willard," she replied, with a twinkle in her eyes. "But I hope she says yes."

Willard grabbed the car keys from the kitchen wall and went out the front door. In the driveway he paused, his gaze turning in the direction the buggy had gone. Why not walk this morning? The weather was better, and Mary often went past on foot. He was used to moving about on his own steam in Kenya. Maybe he was half-Amish himself?

Willard set out down the street at a brisk walk. He navigated the crossings without mishap and arrived breathless in front of the food co-op. Two buggies were parked nearby, one of them doubtless the stern-faced Amish man who had driven past grandmother's house earlier. There was no way he was going inside at the moment. With a determined stride, Willard headed up the street. He needed the exercise, and he deserved this rebuke. This is what came from acting without thinking.

A small sign pointed to the Fort Plain cemetery. That was a logical place to while away an hour or so. He hadn't been back since his grandfather's funeral. With quick steps Willard arrived at the large, double entrance pillars with complementary smaller ones on each side. Tall trees and the well-maintained grounds beckoned, and Willard found the correct path on the other side of the mausoleum. He slowed to approach the graves and knelt in the grass before the first headstone. A faded bouquet of roses lay nearby. His grand-mother had been up here not too long ago.

Benny H. Gabert, he read silently. *Beloved father and husband. May you rest in peace from your labors.*

Willard stood and moved toward other stones, getting down on his knees again. To him they were names without faces—Howard and Pricilla, his father and mother. He loved them, he knew he did, and he had loved them before they were taken—for reasons a young heart could not understand. Many memories of them had disap-peared, but love had filled his life. Grandma and Grandpa Gabert had seen to that, until one more face had vanished. Willard had loved, but not as much as Grandma had loved these people.

Death was a foe, but love and hope were still alive in Grandma's heart. And Grandpa Benny and Mom and Dad were together in glory somewhere, waiting for their loved ones to join them.

In the meantime, in the here and now, impossibilities boggled the mind. Life must have been simpler in Grandma's day. Willard stood. Times changed, but he couldn't help that. The will of the Lord was the will of the Lord, and one could not choose. One only accepted.

He retraced his steps down the hill to find the parking lot at the co-op empty. The Lord's guiding hand had provided Willard an opening, Grandma would claim. He would leave such lofty thoughts to those more mature in the faith.

Mary glanced up when he stepped inside. At least she didn't appear displeased. "*Goot* morning, Willard," she greeted him. "Can I help you?"

He hesitated. Should he make a purchase to make his visit seem more causal? Her smile began to disappear.

"I...I thought perhaps you would be open to another invitation."

"*Yah?*" She waited with no rebuke on her face.

"Would you consider coming to another talk I'm giving tonight?

You and Betsy? I could pick you up and take you home afterward. I'll even throw in supper." He attempted a smile.

"The talk is about Kenya?" Her gaze was intense.

"Of course. I don't know about much else."

Mary nodded. "Pick us up, then. Betsy would enjoy the evening out, and I'd be glad to learn more about Kenya."

"I'll see you at six thirty," he said before retreating out the door.

EIGHTEEN

That evening Betsy set the supper dishes on the table while Mary fiddled with the lid on the soup kettle. Mary had been much too quiet since she came home from the co-op. Betsy glanced toward her sister and took a guess. "Did Willard visit today, by any chance?"

Mary's face colored. "Yes, but it's not what you think. He invited us to attend another meeting on Kenya, and I accepted."

"You did?" Betsy didn't hide her delight. "At what time?"

"Willard is picking us up at six thirty, and he's taking us out to eat afterward."

"Mary!" Betsy shrieked. She glanced wildly at the clock on the kitchen wall. "Why didn't you tell me? It's five thirty, and supper is almost ready."

Before Mary could respond, *Mamm*'s face appeared in the kitchen doorway. "Did I hear something?"

Mary busied herself again with the soup kettle, and Betsy's thoughts spun. Mary was in love with Willard, but Betsy's exuberance was not going to further the result she wanted.

"What's going on?" *Mamm* glanced between the two of them.

Betsy took several deep breaths and planted a serious look on her face. "Willard invited us to attend another meeting on Kenya, and he's taking us out to eat afterward. I think we should accept."

"You and Mary?" *Mamm*'s gaze flickered back and forth again. "When is this meeting?"

"Tonight." Betsy grimaced in apology. "Mary just told me, and I really want to go. This kind of education on the suffering people of the world doesn't come every day."

Mamm regarded her skeptically. "What about your regular *rumspringa* outing tonight? You never skip that."

Betsy grasped for straws. "Maybe I'm improving?"

"You're not falling in love with this Willard fellow, are you?"

"Of course not!" Betsy pasted on a bright smile. How could *Mamm* be so blind?

"I guess you can go," *Mamm* allowed. "An interest in Kenya is better than the things you normally do on a Friday night."

Mamm disappeared, and Betsy hugged herself. Where had her inspiration come from while under such stress?

"Thank you," Mary whispered. "I didn't know how to approach the subject."

"I'm happy it worked out. Now let's get supper ready for the rest of the family." After a quick look toward the empty kitchen doorway, Betsy did a little dance on the vinyl floor. "Oh, Mary! We're going out to eat with Willard Gabert tonight."

"It's a meeting about Kenya," Mary muttered.

"You are so *wunderbah*." Betsy gave Mary a big hug. "I am so excited for you."

"I am learning a lot about Kenya," Mary retorted. "Maybe Stephen will be interested in what we learn. At least I'll have a ready topic of conversation on Sunday evening."

Betsy stared. "You...you didn't!"

"*Yah*, I accepted a date with him," Mary deadpanned. "I haven't even told *Mamm*."

"Stephen Overholt!" Betsy muffled her shriek with her apron. "What is *wrong* with you, Mary? I told you. I warned you!"

"Don't scold me." Mary shook her finger at her sister. "This is for the best, and I'll have something to occupy me. Stephen can use my help."

Betsy calmed herself. If Mary wanted to burn her hand twice in a row, there was no use trying to talk her out of it.

"It's strange how the Lord works," Mary mused. "I get to learn about a subject that deeply grips my heart, while at the same time I can help a man improve his life. How mysterious are His ways."

You have lost your mind, Betsy almost said, but she stifled her words. Mary's dreamworld was worse than she had imagined.

Mary dipped out the soup into a smaller bowl. "Maybe we should eat with the family before we leave."

"We are doing nothing of the sort," Betsy shot back. "Willard is taking us out for supper."

Mary made a face. "But we shouldn't eat too much. It might not be *goot* manners."

"You won't be eating much, believe me. Not in the shape your nerves are in."

"I'm perfectly fine." Mary drew herself taller. "I know I shouldn't have accepted Willard's invitation, but I couldn't resist."

"You did the right thing," Betsy encouraged her. "Now, call out to the barn that supper is ready."

Mary nodded and went to the mudroom door, where she hollered out, "Supper!" at the top of her voice.

There was no answer from the barn, but there never was. The men's ears were attuned to the news, and they never missed the call.

Mamm had come in to finish setting the table when Mary came back from the mudroom.

"We're going up to our bedrooms to change before supper," Betsy told her. "Willard's coming at six thirty."

Mamm appeared ready to say something, but she must have changed her mind. Betsy gave Mary a sly glance, and Mary followed her upstairs. "Let *Mamm* break the news to *Daett*," Betsy told her.

Mary nodded and appeared grateful. "You are much better at this than I am."

Because I have more experience, Betsy almost said. But why rock the boat? Was Mary ignorant of what they were doing? Apparently. Mary entered her room at the top of the stairs without looking back, and Betsy continued down the hallway to her bedroom. She changed into a Sunday dress and found Mary waiting for her when she stepped outside. Mary was similarly attired in her best Sunday outfit.

"Ready?" Betsy asked with a smile.

"We have to look our best for the important event," Mary said, as if her dress needed a defense.

Betsy took her sister's arm. "You should enjoy your time with Willard tonight. Don't forget that."

"Betsy," Mary chided. "He's an *Englisha* man. We can only be so friendly."

"Just relax and talk to him," Betsy told her. "Now come."

Mary looked at her strangely as they went down the stairs, but Betsy ignored her. Mary could pretend, but Betsy was the one with her feet rooted in reality. How strange to think that what she had dreamed of was happening to her sister, who didn't want the love of such a *wunderbah* man like Willard. But the world was a crazy place. She already knew that.

Daett looked up when they walked into the kitchen. "So what is this I hear?"

"Going out to another talk about Kenya," Betsy chirped.

"In your Sunday dresses?" He eyed them from top to bottom.

"Women," Gerald muttered from his place at the table. "They have their priorities mixed up."

Betsy nearly jumped when Mary snapped, "That is so wrong of you to say!" Her sister was not known for her outbursts.

Gerald appeared similarly stunned. "What's wrong with Mary?"

"Children," *Daett* chided. "Getting dressed for an *Englisha* church service shows proper respect."

Gerald sniffed. "Do you girls have your money ready? I told you how these things go."

"There's Willard now," Betsy sang out. Thankfully, the man had shown up at the right moment.

"Have a *goot* evening." *Mamm* bid them goodbye with a wave.

They left the house through the mudroom door and headed down the walk toward Willard's car. "I hope you know what a big favor I'm doing you," Betsy said out of the side of her mouth.

"Thanks," Mary whispered back. "I wouldn't get to hear more about Kenya without your help."

Mary missed the point, but Betsy wouldn't press it. Willard waited beside his car with a big smile on his face.

"What an honor," he said. "How many men from my world get to escort two lovely Amish women to his talk on Kenya?"

Mary had red streaks up and down her neck, which Willard appeared to graciously ignore.

"The honor is ours," Betsy told him. "We are being escorted by the most handsome of hosts."

"You flatter me." Willard grinned. He held the back door open. "But thanks, Betsy."

Obviously she was supposed to climb in. Mary began to move, but Betsy stopped her with a touch on the arm. Much as she would have loved to sit with Willard, that was Mary's place as the woman in love with him—a fact that would remain unmentioned at the moment.

"You should sit in front," Betsy told Mary, in case she didn't get the hint.

Mary's blush grew deeper. She had been in Willard's car before, but maybe having her sister along made things worse. Perhaps it rubbed salt into the wound in Mary's heart.

"So where are we going tonight?" Betsy asked from the backseat as Willard and Mary fastened their seat belts. Mary still hadn't said a word.

Willard backed the car out of the Yoders' driveway. "I'm speaking at the Valley Alliance Church. It's located closer to Fort Plain than Palatine Bridge, but Palatine Bridge is the address. Nice church." His smile grew. "I am so pleased you girls could come tonight."

Mary appeared ready to say something, but she was in no condition to utter a word.

Betsy rushed to speak. "Mary is so into Kenya that she has interested me. Isn't that something? Maybe we can go to more of your talks. How often will you be speaking?"

"Just while I'm over here on furlough, which isn't much longer. The fund-raising is coming along great. Thankfully, there are many churches interested in the work. American Christians have kind hearts and giving wallets."

"When are you going back?" Mary's voice squeaked.

"I don't know yet," Willard responded. "Depends. But in the meantime, where do you girls want to eat after the talk?"

"You really don't have to take us anywhere," Mary spoke up. "Hearing about Kenya is the important part."

Willard nodded, apparently uncertain how to continue.

Betsy spoke up. "Don't listen to her. We haven't had supper."

"Well, that decides it." Willard seemed to relax. "I thought maybe you had changed your minds, which I could understand. You have such wholesome Amish food, and I am...well, not a total stranger, I guess."

"Mary can't wait to visit a fancy restaurant," Betsy said, making Mary gasp.

Willard glanced between them. "You are teasing, I assume."

"A little." Betsy laughed. "But I know that Mary hasn't been out to eat in ages, *goot* Amish food notwithstanding. Can you take us to Delmonico's Italian Steakhouse, near Utica?"

Another gasp came from Mary. "Betsy! That's not polite."

Willard's grin grew. "I would be honored, Betsy. And I asked because I wanted to know what you like. I take it from your reaction that you know this place, Mary?"

"Faintly," Mary managed. "It sounds expensive."

"You are both worth expensive," he said.

Mary was blushing again as they turned into the church's parking lot. True to Willard's word, the building was only a few miles south of Fort Plain.

"Shouldn't we be investing money in the Kenyan glue boys instead of fancy restaurants?" Mary protested.

"Well..." Willard paused. "I guess you do have a point, but—"

"I would feel so much more comfortable someplace that's not expensive," Mary continued. "I appreciate your wanting to spend money on us, but—"

"This evening is important to me," Willard insisted.

"It's just us." Mary glanced toward Betsy. "We aren't extravagant."

"I think—" Betsy began, but Willard stopped her with a shake of his head.

"We'll eat where Mary will be comfortable, even if I believe the money would be well spent on both of you."

"Thank you," Mary whispered.

How could Betsy get a moment alone with Willard? She needed to speak to him. Obviously, no girl had ever turned down his offer to eat at a fancy restaurant. Mary meant no offense, but Betsy couldn't explain fully in her sister's presence. The poor man appeared totally confused.

"Can you wait a minute in the car?" she asked Mary. "I want to speak with Willard alone."

Mary hesitated but nodded. Betsy stepped out of the car, and Willard followed. She turned to face him once they were far enough away that Mary couldn't hear. "I hope you're not offended, Willard. Mary—"

He held up his hand. "Not in the least, Betsy. Just surprised and impressed. Mary is obviously a woman of deep faith and conviction."

"And she's in love with you." Betsy rushed the words out. "That's what I want to say."

"In love with me?" Now Willard was turning red. "Are you sure?"

"*Yah*, certain, and I think you like her, which is *goot*. I'm on your side, but I have to tell you something so you don't get discouraged. Mary is bound to mention someone this evening, which could throw you off."

Willard waited as Betsy caught her breath. "Mary has just accepted a date from an old bachelor in the community, someone she doesn't even like."

Willard tilted his head. "I thought you said—"

"I know. Mary accepted the date under the pretense of helping the man, who does need help. Mary is kind like that, but I believe the real reason is that she's trying to mask her feelings for you."

"That sounds complicated. Are you sure about this?"

"Certain as the day is long!" Betsy declared. "But we must go and get her. She'll become curious soon."

He glanced back at the car. "What am I supposed to do with this information?"

"Court her, and don't give up."

"You think that would work?"

"I want Mary to have a decent husband. That's what you would be, and she cares about your work. After what she's been through, she deserves a chance at love again. Not with someone like that old bachelor Stephen Overholt, whom she's not going to marry anyway."

Willard studied her. "And what about the community's reaction? Could Mary deal with that and still keep her faith and dedication?"

"Win her heart, and she'll be yours," Betsy retorted. "That's all I know."

NINETEEN

Thirty minutes later, Mary shifted in her seat as Willard strode toward the speaker's podium. This church service was similar to the other one they had attended. She had never dreamed the day would come when she would attend *Englisha* church services, but this was during the week and for a *goot* cause. She was here to learn more about Kenya.

Mary focused on Willard's face as he shook hands with the pastor and was introduced to the congregation. Betsy gave her a pinch on the arm and a sly smile, but Mary ignored her. Of course her sister would think Willard a worthy love pursuit. Willard was handsome, for certain. Betsy had spent a long time talking with Willard earlier, apparently over Mary's refusal to eat at a fancy restaurant. Maybe she should have indulged Willard's and Betsy's wishes. She still could, but the decision felt wrong. How could she enjoy a fancy meal when she knew that Willard was spending money that could be invested in better ways?

"Good evening, everybody," Willard said from the podium. "I'm glad to see all of you out tonight. I'm Mrs. Gabert's grandson, and I'm staying at her house in Fort Plain while on furlough. I'm also the director of a mission called Agape Outreach, stationed in Nairobi, the largest city in Kenya. But first, on less serious matters, I have brought two Amish friends with me tonight, Mary and Betsy Yoder. Please help them feel welcome."

Willard paused and grinned as several of the congregation turned to nod their heads and whisper, "Good evening, and welcome."

"Smile," Betsy spoke in Mary's ear. "And wave."

Heat flushed up Mary's neck. She had been blushing all evening, but this attention was embarrassing. She managed the smile, but she could not bring herself to copy her sister's cheerful wave to the whole congregation. Betsy was acting more like an *Englisha* woman than an Amish one, but Betsy was still on her *rumspringa*.

"Isn't he just the charmer?" Betsy whispered in her direction.

Mary didn't respond. One didn't whisper in church, and if Willard was a charmer, that was exactly what she didn't need. Josiah had exhibited all sorts of charm, but he had never shown any interest in Kenyan glue boys or in much of anything other than himself. She could see that plainly now after the man had jilted her. No, Betsy was wrong. Willard had a sense of humor, but he was no charmer. Willard had character.

He gathered the congregation's attention to himself again. "Let me get right into the stories about the work I do. I can think of nothing that better captures the burden of our mission than what happened the evening I showed Ean and Daisy Messer around town. This couple is taking care of the mission while I am gone. After driving the streets all day, we stopped to eat supper at a nice restaurant in Nairobi. The place caters to tourists and Americans, of course. The food is excellent. As we ate, Ean, Daisy, and I were catching up on news from home and their long-term plans for Kenyan missions. We exited the restaurant afterward to see one of the glue boys seated across the street from the restaurant. The boy was on the sidewalk, clutching a glue bottle in his hands. His vacant stare was fixed on the restaurant door, watching the rich, happy, well-dressed people coming and going. The three of us stopped in our tracks.

"'That's what we're talking about,' Ean said. 'Right before our eyes.'

"I agreed. There the boy was, watching the real world go by, with longing on his face but with hope stripped away, knowing that he was not part of the life that bubbled in front of him. His world was the haze of glue-induced phantoms, a world where hunger is dulled and pain is vanquished by delusion. The boys' brains become impaired by the fumes of glue. The damage is irreversible, which is why early intervention is so crucial. Detox for these young boys is not nearly as difficult as it is for heroin addicts or other drug users, which is why we keep open doors at the mission. The boys can leave or stay. Some leave, but some return once they have a taste of home, family, trust, good food, and the comfort of loving human beings."

Willard paused, and Mary glanced at Betsy. "I have to go to Kenya and visit," she mouthed.

Betsy nodded as Willard went on. "The mission offers other opportunities for the children. In one case, a small child became separated from his parents while they visited Nairobi. One of the older street children brought the boy to us, and we began an intense search for his parents by placing ads on the radio. The task was almost impossible, as we knew, unless we could pinpoint where the child was from. Kenya has two official languages, English and Swahili. Beyond that, sixty-eight languages are spoken in the villages and hamlets scattered across the countryside. The child spoke a few words, and with the help of local people, we were eventually able to narrow our search to an area north of Nairobi. By the grace of the Lord, we found the parents and facilitated a joyous reunion. Everyone expressed many thanks to the mission, as you can imagine."

Willard kept speaking, but Mary's thoughts were still on the image of the boy seated on the sidewalk outside the restaurant in Nairobi. She had lost so much when her dream of a home with Josiah ended, but hope had not died. She still had a chance at love once the Lord opened the door. There would be dinner around the supper table, Scriptures read in the living room, and affection for everyone. There were people in the world who did not have such hope. Tears trickled down Mary's cheeks as Willard concluded his remarks and the offering plate was passed. She dug in her satchel and handed over forty dollars, the last of her paycheck from the co-op.

As she placed her gift in the plate, she knew money could not buy hope for the boy seated on the sidewalk. He was past the point of help. Even love would not reach him—not with a brain destroyed by dreadful glue fumes. Could God work miracles? Wouldn't Jesus, who knew how to heal leprosy and drive out demons, know how to fix a body destroyed and broken?

There must be something else she could do. But what? Quilts and blankets were a start, but how empty the gesture seemed in the face of such need. The service ended, and smiling people shook Betsy's and Mary's hands and thanked them for coming. Mary tried to smile, but her face felt as if it were frozen.

Willard's worried face appeared above hers. "Are you okay?"

"Your story moved me deeply," Mary managed. "That boy sitting on the sidewalk outside the restaurant..."

"Now you see why I am in Kenya," he said, sober faced. "I appreciate it that you understand."

"I don't think I understand it fully, nor can I do anything," Mary protested. "I've lived an awfully sheltered life."

"I know the feeling," he said, "but to echo C.S. Lewis, the works of the devil will not be allowed to rob heaven of her joy."

"That's deep," she said with a brief glance at him. Betsy for once walked silently behind them.

"It's an answer that satisfies me," he said. "And believe me, one struggles when working in such horrible conditions. How is it right to laugh, or even live, in the midst of such suffering? Yet to surrender joy, peace, and hope in our own lives is to surrender what does not belong to the enemy."

"You thought this up by yourself?" Mary asked in a hushed tone.

Willard chuckled. "The mission field drives one to his knees—and to read the authors who have walked in difficult places. Others have pointed the way."

"I am still impressed," Betsy said as Willard opened the car doors for them and they climbed inside.

Willard seated himself and fastened his seat belt before he asked, "So where shall it be, Ms. Yoder? The choice is up to you."

Obviously, the question was directed toward Mary. She blinked. She had forgotten about the promised dinner date.

"Or do you want me to take you home?" Willard asked. "Either way is fine. Grandma has some snacks in the cupboard, I'm sure. I won't starve."

Mary grasped for that straw. "Could we stop at her place? That would be perfect, and if she doesn't have enough food for us, we'll walk home."

"That's an excellent idea," Willard agreed. "Don't you think so, Betsy?"

There was a mumble from the backseat, which Willard ignored. He started the car and pulled out of the church parking lot. They drove in silence toward town. Mary waited for another protest from Betsy, but the words didn't come until Willard parked the car in Mrs. Gabert's driveway.

"Do you think this is wise?" Betsy ventured. "I'm sure the poor woman will be shocked out of her wits."

"Then we'll say hi and bye," Mary declared, climbing out of the car. "There will be leftovers from supper in the fridge at home."

Betsy grumbled but followed her. Willard led the way up the sidewalk and into the house without knocking. "Grandma," he called out. "I've brought visitors."

Mrs. Gabert appeared from the direction of the living room. Her startled look quickly changed to a smile. "Mary and Betsy! Willard said he was picking you up for the talk and dinner tonight, but it's a little early. Did my grandson rush you through the meal?"

"We decided to come here," Willard told her. "I spoke from my heart about Kenya, and home seemed like a better place than a restaurant to gather our thoughts."

"You are so welcome," Mrs. Gabert declared. "Both of you. There's bologna and ham in the fridge, and we have chips and orange juice. If you'll give me just a minute, I'll make sandwiches."

Mary took charge. "We can do that. Why don't you sit at the table with us, and we can talk?"

Betsy joined in, and moments later the sandwiches, drinks, and chips were spread out.

Willard bowed his head and prayed, "Dear Father in heaven, thank You for the food set before us and for Mary and Betsy. They are dear people who share Your passion for lost and hurting people. Bless them as they return to their community. I thank You for the brief moment I have shared their lives. May You give them great grace and answer their prayers, which I know they will cry out from their hearts for the great needs in Kenya. Thank You, and amen."

"Amen," Betsy echoed, but Mary kept her head bowed for a moment longer. Tears had formed in her eyes at Willard's tender words. The man's compassion moved her deeply.

"So what did you share about tonight?" Mrs. Gabert asked.

"It's a story you have heard before," Willard replied. "About the boy seated outside the restaurant."

Mrs. Gabert nodded. "I remember. I'm not surprised you told that story. The Lord has blessed these weeks abundantly and has taught us much about your work. Watching Mary and Betsy open their hearts to the needs in Kenya has challenged me and warmed my heart. Mary might even write some inspired poetry on the boy sitting outside the restaurant."

Mary felt their eyes on her, and she hurried to speak. "I don't think poetry and dreams seem appropriate in the face of such tragedy."

"Ah, but they are," Mrs. Gabert said. "They sustain the soul and are of greater benefit than we can imagine. We must not languish in sorrow ourselves because of the evil in this world."

"That's what Willard said!" Betsy added.

Mrs. Gabert chuckled. "I'm glad to see he has learned his lessons well."

They laughed together.

"See?" Willard said. "I told you I didn't come up with those ideas by myself."

Mrs. Gabert beamed at her grandson, and Mary, too, snuck a glance at his face. Willard was a handsome, noble, and deeply dedicated believer. But he was also an *Englisha* man and out of her reach. She drew a quick breath and bit down on her sandwich.

Thankfully, Betsy chattered away. "You should have heard him embarrass both of us in front of everyone, Mrs. Gabert. He's done that twice now, introducing us as his special guests to the church congregation."

Willard's grin grew wicked. "It's true!"

"But we're Amish," Betsy protested. "Even I, who don't plan to stay in the community, still dislike having attention drawn to myself."

Willard didn't back down an inch. "You like my charming ways. Admit it. You looked perfectly happy waving to the crowd."

Betsy joined in the laughter. "I guess I did. So tell me, why aren't you married?"

Mary wanted to hide under the table.

Willard's face fell. "Do we have to go there? I don't want to spoil a wonderful evening."

"Sorry," Betsy said. "It just seemed the logical question."

"He had his heart broken like Mary's," Mrs. Gabert offered.

Betsy's glance went first to the one and then the other. "So you two *do* have a lot in common."

"Betsy, please!" Mary exclaimed, forcing herself to stand. "We have to be going. Thanks so much for the sandwiches, Mrs. Gabert, and for the evening, Willard. I learned so much, and the community women will be working on those blankets soon."

"But you just arrived," Mrs. Gabert said.

Willard was on his feet, but Mary rushed past him and out the front door.

Betsy was panting by the time she caught up to her sister on the steep incline out of town. "What is wrong with you, Mary? That was so rude."

"So was your remark right in front of everyone."

"I didn't say anything rude, Mary."

"Yes, you did."

"What did I say?"

Mary said nothing until they reached the top of the hill. Above them, the starry spread of the heavens opened up.

"It's not true," Mary whispered toward the skies. "I'm not in love with an *Englisha* man."

Only the stars answered her, twinkling brightly, far above the evil and wickedness of mankind. Willard had been right. Life did go on, full of the Lord's love and grace.

"I can't be!" Mary said loudly this time.

She marched resolutely onward. Betsy remained silent until they reached the Yoders' driveway, where the light spilled out of the living room window across the lawn.

"You could find your home with Willard," Betsy told her.

"Don't even say such things," Mary retorted. Then she dashed for the house.

TWENTY

The parting hymn on Sunday evening at Bishop Miller's home concluded with haunting notes of sadness and joy: "Blessed be the tie that binds our hearts in kindred love."

Cousin Esther, who was seated beside Mary on the front bench, opened her mouth—ready to ask questions.

Mary smiled politely and muttered, "I have to go."

She did have to go because Stephen had just disappeared out the bishop's front door. He had appeared totally out of place throughout the evening, seated on the second bench with much younger men. Stephen rarely came out on Sunday evenings anymore, and everyone had given him strange looks or sly smiles. That he had a date was the obvious conclusion, and Mary was the girl they landed on as the logical choice. She didn't want to answer questions about her decision to accept Stephen's offer. She did care about the man—just not in the way everyone assumed.

Mary slipped into the mudroom ahead of the other dating girls to grab her shawl and beat them out the door. Stephen's buggy was parked on the far side of the barn, and he had his horse in the shafts when Mary arrived.

"*Goot* evening," she greeted him out of the darkness.

He jumped and muttered, "*Goot* evening. *Yah, goot* evening."

Mary fastened the tugs on her side and pulled herself up onto the buggy seat. Stephen fumbled with the lines for a moment before he threw them inside and climbed up himself. Mary instinctively grabbed for the reins. She remembered that Josiah's horse would dash out of the driveway the moment someone didn't hang on tight.

Stephen settled on the seat and stared at the reins for a few seconds before he took them from her hands.

"Giddyap!" he hollered to his horse. The beast lumbered out of the driveway, and Mary pulled her head back as they passed the steady girls who were helping their boyfriends hitch up. Most of them were craning their necks to see if their conclusion had been correct.

"I'm not...I really am not used to this," Stephen stated. "Sorry if...I mean, I'm nervous, I guess. But this is, I'm sure, the Lord's will."

"It's okay," she comforted him. "They'll get used to it."

Stephen's face lifted considerably, but he said nothing. Had she just agreed to further dates with him? That conclusion seemed apparent enough to Stephen. Well, she did plan to, if needed. But first she had this date in front of her.

Stephen glanced at her from his side of the buggy. "I'm, I mean, how do I say this? I'm still surprised you are doing this—letting me take you home so we can talk. For my part, I want to say, before we get started with anything else, since it's a heaviness on my mind, that I can never fill Josiah Beiler's shoes, though the Lord knows I will try. I'll try harder than I've ever tried before in my life."

"Don't do that, Stephen. You are yourself, and you can be no one else."

He appeared skeptical.

"Everyone is the happiest when they are true to themselves," she told him.

He grunted, apparently unconvinced. The horse clomped down Tanners Road to the stop sign and shook his head when Stephen pulled the reins right. "Sorry. I mean, the horse wants to go...well, I guess you know my house is the other way."

"I know."

"You do?" His skepticism rose higher.

"I know where you live, Stephen. West on Clinton Road, the farthest place out."

"You do know, I see you do, where I live. But how is this, I mean, I never have the church services there, or any youth activities."

"You are part of the community, Stephen. I know where you live, and so does everyone else."

"I see," he said, moving about on his seat.

But he didn't see. She was sure about that.

Stephen navigated the turn at Freybush with only a quick check for headlights toward the west. His horse swished its tail as objection to the easterly direction of travel.

Mary broke the silence. "How late will you stay tonight?"

Stephen managed a laugh. "I'm an old man, you know, real old. But I suppose, now that I think about it, perhaps I could, if I really tried hard, stay up until midnight. At least, I think the rest of the dating couples do that."

When Mary didn't respond, he peered at her in the darkness.

"How late did Josiah stay?"

Mary kept her eyes on the road ahead, where the dark shadows danced with Stephen's feeble buggy lights. Josiah had stayed until well after two o'clock some Monday mornings as they laughed and told each other stories on the living room couch. Those times were gone, and Stephen didn't need to know the details.

Stephen tried again. "I'm sorry if I'm not—you know—like Josiah, but this is, I am certain, the Lord's will."

"It's okay," Mary said.

He didn't respond as they approached the Yoders' driveway. Stephen turned in and brought his horse to a lumbering stop by the barn door. Mary hopped down to wait while Stephen tied his horse.

He approached her cautiously. "What, I mean, where...how is this done? Seeing you into the house?"

Mary studied his face. "Have you never dated before?"

He dropped his head. "I once did, a long time ago, but not properly. Since then, many times, the Lord knows I have prayed. I have asked many girls, often in my younger years, but not so much anymore, when hope has failed me. The will of the Lord has grown dimmer. Only you, Mary, of all people, rejected though you were. Forgive me, but I took this as a sign, a bright sign, of the Lord's will for me."

"Come." She took his hand. "This is how it's done. You walk the woman into the house, and you sit on the couch while she gets something to eat. Then you talk."

He followed her. "Are you making fun of me, or laughing, Mary? At least, as I think the others are doing?"

Mary's eyes met his. "I'm not, Stephen. Dating a girl is not that difficult. Who have you been asking?"

He pressed his lips together. "I would rather not say, if you don't mind."

"The wrong ones, apparently," Mary muttered quietly. "I tried to be honest with you, Stephen, about why I'm letting you bring me home."

Confusion settled on his face. "Are you saying, Mary, now that we are here, that you want me to leave again? If you don't mind, may I at least sit beside you on the couch? Please, Mary? There is a reason, which I cannot say, but if you would…"

"What reason are you referring to, Stephen?"

Stephen stared at her. "I would not speak of such things that the Lord has willed. But this I know for sure. Being with you is the Lord's will."

"Come." Mary led him forward again. "We need to talk."

He didn't protest and was seated on the couch when Gerald drove in with Betsy.

"Wait here," Mary told him. She went into the kitchen and picked up a plate of brownies when Betsy burst in through the mudroom door.

"Is he in the living room?" Betsy whispered. "That awful man?"

"Go." Mary shooed her sister out. "Mind your own business tonight."

Betsy raised her voice higher. "You have lost your mind. You run away from a handsome man like Willard and take up with a crazy fleabag like that."

"I will take the broom to you if you don't go," Mary warned.

Betsy snorted and dashed through the living room without a word to Stephen, even when he wished her a *goot* evening.

Gerald had a big grin on his face when he appeared. He filled his hands with brownies, and because there were plenty, Mary didn't object.

With his mouth full, he went into the living room and mumbled, "*Goot* evening to you," in response to Stephen's greeting.

Mary waited until Gerald had climbed the stairs before she entered with a plate of brownies in one hand and a glass of milk in the other.

Stephen appeared pained.

"Well, that's my family," she told him. Apologies were not expected, so she offered none.

"If it's okay to have at least one brownie, I'll leave after that," he said.

"Stephen, you can have as many as you'd like." She set the plate and the glass of milk in front of him. "We need to talk," she said again.

His hand trembled as he took the brownie and tasted a bite.

Mary waited until he had taken a swallow of milk before she continued. "I'm going to try again, very slowly, to explain myself, Stephen. First of all, I can never be your girlfriend or love you in that way. Let's not argue about why. That's not the point, and let's not talk about the Lord's will. You are wrong on that point, but I want to help you find a woman who can be your *frau*. Widows in the community would welcome your invitation to date them and eventually marry. At least I think so, and if we can make some progress in the right direction, that would help. That's where I come in. Do you understand?"

"You are...I mean, I don't, maybe I never will understand what you mean." He stared again, a brownie halfway to his mouth.

"I will never fall in love with you, Stephen. Not enough to marry you. Spending time with me is wasting your time unless I can help you."

His puzzled look only grew. "Mary, this is the Lord's will. Why else would I be sitting on your couch and eating brownies? Mary, please do not say that...Not in a thousand years would you be wasting my time."

She let out a long breath. "Well, that is a different perspective, but that's not going to happen, Stephen. Not what you are hoping."

"You are, how do I ask this, not really truly in love with me?"

Mary nodded. "That's exactly what I'm saying."

"Then who, if I may ask, is this man—the one you are in love with?"

Mary sighed. "I'm not in love with anyone. I'm trying to help you. Can we stay focused on that point? And afterward we might talk about Kenyan missions, a *wunderbah* subject I have been learning about. Would you like that?"

He took a bite from the brownie. "I know nothing about this Kenya, wherever that is, perhaps on the other side of the world. Is it an island in the ocean? And what does it matter, Mary? I just want to be here tonight, if you don't object, with you. This is the Lord's will."

"We are getting nowhere, Stephen. Why can't you understand?"

"I do understand your words, you say them plainly enough, but where do they go? That I do not understand. Not if this is the Lord's will."

"I am not dating you, Stephen, not in the usual way. I want to help, but do not hope that I will consent to marry you. Can you understand that?"

He stared at a brownie for a moment before he nodded.

"So you *do* understand?" Skepticism was on her face now.

He shrugged. "Maybe? You want to help me, improve me, change me, tell me what the Lord's will is? And then someday I might have a *frau*?"

"But not me," Mary added.

"Not you," he agreed.

"Then we have accomplished something tonight." Mary reached for a brownie.

Beside her on the couch Stephen gulped down another one with a look of bliss on his face. She hoped they were on the same page now...but then again, maybe they weren't.

TWENTY-ONE

Mary briskly walked north on Highway 163 instead of her usual southerly direction toward Fort Plain. A chill crept into her shawl from the wind coming off the Adirondacks. She paused to take a deep breath of the early morning air. Betsy had agreed to take her place at the food co-op on the day before Thanksgiving so she could attend the sewing circle. Today the women from the community would express their gratitude to the Lord by making blankets for the glue boys in Kenya. How blessed she was, and how happy. What an honor the Lord had granted her, that she could send aid to a country she knew little about but where the need was so great.

Mamm had continued her helpfulness and spoken with the deacon's *frau*, Rachel, and the bishop's *frau*, Annie. The two women had consulted their husbands, and the project now had the community's stamp of approval. This weekend Stephen would bring Mary home again after the singing, and they would tackle his need of a *frau*. Her plate was full, to say the least. She had so many things she wanted to tell Stephen. She hoped their time together would be as fruitful as this day would be.

Mary set her face toward the north. She would not think about Josiah this morning or about Willard's handsome face. Love was not for her at the moment. She had found work to do until the Lord opened a door she could walk through that led to home and family sometime in the future. In the meantime, a thankful heart was in order even in the midst of her great lack. Did not the Scriptures say that it was more blessed to give than to receive?

The rattle of buggy wheels filled the stillness of the morning air behind her. Mary stepped to the side of the road and waved as the women drove past. She was early, but not early enough, apparently. As the person who had instigated this plan, she should have arrived first. But she wasn't late yet. Mary followed the buggies in their turn onto Nestle Road and up to Deacon Stoltzfus's driveway moments later. The two buggies were already unhitched, the horses already in the barn. Deacon Stoltzfus appeared in the door, his bearded face red and cheerful.

"*Goot* morning, Mary," he greeted her. "Where's your horse?"

"I walked up."

"*Goot, goot.* Well, I was glad to hear of your idea, and so was Rachel. You are an example for the whole community to follow—how Plain people can reach out and help faraway places like Kenya."

Mary blushed under the deacon's praise and bowed her head. "I guess the Lord is comforting my heart in my trouble."

The deacon's eyes twinkled again. "Stephen Overholt must be quite happy with the turn of events. I'm thinking he can see the Lord's hand in your sorrow."

"I guess so," Mary allowed, though she really should set the record straight. Hiding had its limits. "Not everything is quite what it seems," she began. "See, I...well, I accepted Stephen's offer of a date in order to help him. I've been honest with the man from the start and explained things to him."

"Oh." Deacon Stoltzfus's red-bearded face creased in puzzlement. "But Stephen has been saying around the community that he's taking you home again this Sunday evening. Surely you are not playing with his heart? I would not have thought such a thing of you. And I say that out of great respect."

"I...oh...this is going to sound awful, I'm afraid, but I offered to help Stephen change some things about himself. I wanted to help him find a *frau* who truly suits him. The man...he doesn't know how to go about such things," Mary finished with a groan. "I hope you don't think I'm doing something wrong?"

The deacon peered at her. "And Stephen understands this?"

Mary nodded.

A grin slowly grew on the deacon's face. "You are not wasting your time, Mary. But what else would we expect from you, even in your sorrow? Making blankets for needy Kenyan children. Helping one of our bachelors find a *frau*. I commend you, Mary. I hope this works for Stephen. The Lord knows he needs help."

"Then you don't disapprove?"

The deacon chuckled. "I give you my blessing, Mary. And I'm sure Bishop Miller will feel the same way."

Mary took a deep breath. "I really should be going into the house. This was my idea."

"You have a *goot* day, then. And the Lord be with you in your worthy projects. Someday a man will come along to fit your dreams, Mary."

A blush crept up Mary's neck, and she turned to dash up the sidewalk. She wasn't totally worthy of the deacon's praise.

Willard hadn't yet invited her to another *Englisha* church meeting, which was for the best. She wouldn't have accepted, and Willard doubtless knew this. That danger was surely past.

Ahead of her Rachel opened the front door of the house with a bright smile. "*Goot* morning, Mary. I see Mose has been telling you of his approval."

"*Yah*," Mary responded. "I appreciate this so much."

"We are the ones who appreciate your efforts." Rachel held the door open wide.

Mary entered and exchanged *goot* mornings with the two women who had arrived earlier. They were busy with quilting frames, setting them up in the living room. Mary joined in as more buggies arrived, and Rachel stayed at the front door to greet the women. *Mamm* came in by the time all the frames were set up and the quilting had begun.

"Did Betsy leave for the co-op on time?" Mary whispered to *Mamm*.

Mamm nodded. "She drove down with Danny Boy. She'll be okay for the day."

"I know," Mary agreed. She busied herself with the first small quilt, a plain dark blue with white cross-stitches. Some Kenyan boy would find great comfort with this blanket. These gifts could be sent straight to Kenya, so Willard wouldn't need to visit the co-op again. Any coordination could be done with Mrs. Gabert.

"So what gave you this idea?" Rachel pulled out a chair and seated herself beside Mary.

"Mrs. Gabert, an *Englisha* woman that I know, introduced us to her grandson's mission project," Mary began. "Betsy and I ended up going to two of his talks on Kenya. The stories he told gripped our hearts, and I asked what I could do that might help. So here we are." Mary ended with a little laugh. "I knew the blanket project was too large for me to handle by myself."

Rachel smiled. "You know we are here to help one another, and what better way than this? We should have a dozen or so blankets finished by this evening. Do you think this is something we can do again in the future?"

Mary made a face. "Maybe we should only try this once and see where it goes. I'll talk with Mrs. Gabert about how the shipping should be handled, and we'll see what kind of feedback comes from Kenya. Willard, Mrs. Gabert's grandson, said that fancy things aren't needed. They are looking for things more geared to comfort, so this should fit well, but there might still be other things that could be adjusted."

"Is this Willard a married man?" Rachel asked.

"I don't think so. Well, I guess I do know. He's not, but he's an *Englisha* man. They do things differently."

"You're dating Stephen," Rachel said. "We just heard the news. That's *wunderbah*."

"I'm trying to *help* Stephen. That's why I'm spending time with him." Mary caught her breath. "I just explained it to Mose."

"Oh." Rachel didn't appear surprised. "I wondered why you'd accepted a date with him. I know your heart is broken, but you also have a level head about you."

"You don't think Stephen is a suitable husband?"

"Not for you, Mary. You know that."

"I do," Mary admitted. Flames of red were creeping up her neck. "Maybe I took too much on myself by trying to help him. I'm not trying to be prideful."

"And you told Mose this?"

"*Yah!*"

"What did he say?"

Mary hung onto the edge of the quilt frame. "He gave me his blessing."

A smile crept across Rachel's face. "I am not surprised, Mary. Everyone can see your serving heart, but do be careful. You know Stephen will fall in love with you. What are you going to do then?"

"He won't," Mary insisted.

"You don't know men very well, do you?"

Mary winced. "I suppose I don't. Why else would Josiah…"

Rachel patted Mary on the arm. "Just don't play this out too long, okay? A few dates with Stephen can set him on the right path, but be careful, Mary. The heart has a mind of its own."

"Thank you for your understanding," Mary whispered. "I can see my faults plainer with each passing day."

"We all have weak moments," Rachel said. "Admitting our faults is half the victory, and you have been honest, so the Lord will help you. In the meantime, much *goot* is coming out of your troubles. Isn't our Lord mysterious in how He works?"

Tears stung in Mary's eyes as she nodded.

"I do want to express my regret for the way Josiah used you," Rachel continued. "Such things shouldn't happen among the people of the community, but we are failing human beings. I suppose the blessing is that he figured out where his affections lay before he said the wedding vows. You wouldn't want to live with a man who wished he had made another choice, would you? That's a hard question to face, but the truth heals."

"*Yah*, I know." Mary focused on her needle. She couldn't wipe away her tears even if the quilt swum in front of her eyes.

"Both Mose and I will be praying that the Lord opens the door for love again in your life." Rachel spoke above the murmur of the women's conversation. "We are not meant to live alone or walk the road of life by ourselves. A woman with your compassionate heart has a man and a home waiting for her somewhere. The Lord will open up the door in His own time."

"Thank you," Mary told her. "That is so kind of you to say, even with my bold ways."

Rachel smiled sweetly. "You are a jewel, Mary. We are making quilts today for Kenyan children on the basis of your own reputation. That's quite a testimony, and one for which you can give thanks to the Lord."

"I'm far from perfect," Mary objected.

Rachel didn't reply as Annie, the bishop's *frau*, leaned over their shoulders to ask, "What are you two chattering about this morning?"

"Just comforting Mary in her troubles with Josiah," Rachel told her, "and talking about her future."

"That man...that..." Annie sputtered. "He sure passed up a *goot frau*. That's all I can say."

"There you go!" Rachel smiled kindly. "I'm sure someone will be along to snatch up Mary in no time."

"What about Stephen?" Annie appeared puzzled.

"She's trying to help him," Rachel whispered under her hand.

Annie laughed. "Only Mary would do that. Just look at her. Few women in the community could have gotten a project like this together for Kenyan aid. I do wish I had a single son still available!"

"See there?" Rachel patted Mary on the arm again. "Let the Lord comfort your heart."

"I agree," Annie seconded. "In the meantime, can you spare a moment, Rachel? Susie Byler has a question about potty-training her youngest son. I thought you would be the perfect woman to give advice."

"I can try." Rachel stood. "But where's Susie's *mamm*?"

Annie made a face. "Sounds like they need a second opinion because the first one isn't working."

"Not that again," Rachel muttered. She walked off in the direction of the kitchen.

"You take care now," Annie told Mary. She left in the opposite direction.

Mary let out a long breath as she stuck the needle in and pulled the thread through the thick cloth.

TWENTY-TWO

Mary exited the mudroom door of Deacon Stoltzfus's home on Sunday evening and searched the darkness outside. She hadn't paid attention to where Stephen had parked his buggy when he drove in for the hymn singing hours earlier. The man had seemed happier and more relaxed all evening, perched on the second single men's bench while the sacred hymns had been sung. She wasn't filled with anticipation at the thought of her evening ahead. That was an emotion Josiah had always provoked, but neither did she feel dread. Stephen was a pleasant enough person underneath his strangeness.

Stephen's broad hat appeared in the barn door. His hand was on his horse's bridle, and he headed toward the far end of the buggy line. Mary stepped off the porch and wrapped her shawl tightly around her shoulders before dashing across the frozen lawn. Winter was only weeks away from the feel of things, when the snowstorms could sweep down from the Adirondacks with a furor.

"*Goot* evening," Mary greeted Stephen at the buggy.

He jumped, and the tug slipped out of his gloved hand.

Mary ignored the mishap to offer, "Shall I help on the other side?"

"If you wish, or want to, Mary. But in this cold, with the wind picking up, if you think it best, you can climb in the buggy and wait. I'm used to hitching the horse, as you can see, by myself." He gave a nervous laugh.

"Did you enjoy the hymn singing?" Mary walked over to the other side and slid on the tug, followed by the snap of the harness.

His gaze followed her, but he seemed lost in his own thoughts. "Oh," he finally said. "I'm not used to, as you can imagine, getting out on Sunday evenings—that is, for the hymn singing. But *yah*, the hymns are always a blessing to sing, as are all the Lord's ways, and His will."

Mary climbed into the buggy, and Stephen tossed her the reins before he pulled himself up the step.

Stephen took the lines and called out, "Giddyap!" His horse walked forward, plodding slowly out of the driveway. Stephen settled himself before he glanced toward Mary. "So how is your project—that one with the, you know, the *Englisha* man? Is it coming along?"

"Okay, I guess. The women's sewing circle was this week, and we completed more than a dozen blankets. I took the finished products down to Mrs. Gabert's."

"Will there be more? I mean, of these blankets in the future, with this...what was his name?"

"Willard." Mary shifted on her seat.

Willard hadn't been at Mrs. Gabert's home when she stopped by. But he was still in the country, down south in Virginia doing talks in churches. Mrs. Gabert had told her with a warm smile that Willard would make the arrangements to ship the blankets to Kenya.

Stephen was mid-sentence when Mary tuned back in. "...almost, at least it could be, if you hear the name only, an Amish man."

Mary chuckled. "Willard isn't an Amish man, believe me. Not even close, but that's beside the point. How was your week?"

"The same, much of the same. I cooked, I cleaned the house

where I could. I only get the spiderwebs when, it's embarrassing to say this, but when they get bad, which is really bad from, shall we say, through a woman's eyes."

"That's why you need a wife," Mary replied.

She tried to keep the laughter out of her voice. The image of Stephen swatting at the house ceiling with a broom after spiderwebs was hilarious.

"This is true. Like you said earlier, I need much help, which perhaps only the Lord can give. But you were gracious enough to offer, and why should I think that the Lord's hand should not be behind a *wunderbah* woman like you, if I can say that?"

Mary laughed this time. "You can say what you want, I guess, but Josiah thought otherwise, so we need to take that into account."

"Josiah was not—and everyone would surely agree with this, at least in this community—a very wise man." He shook the reins a few times for emphasis. "Josiah could not see the Lord's will."

"Well, we had best not speak of him." Mary stared off into the chilly darkness. "Have you seen a widow yet who might make a decent *frau* for you? That's what we need to speak about."

Stephen grunted. "The Lord has not shown His light on the way, at least that I can see. There is only, if I look around, everywhere I go, darkness spread upon my path."

Mary took a long breath. "Maybe that's where we should begin, Stephen. The Lord set marriage in order, but it's not a supernatural endeavor. There doesn't need to be lights from heaven shining down. You may not even have great feelings involved. Sometimes it's just practical. You work on what fits and on what is right for you. Can you think about that?"

He turned into the Yoders' driveway and parked by the barn before he answered. "That's a hard, really difficult thing to think about, Mary, let alone to think that I might...I don't know how to say it. I just always, in my mind at least, thought that the Lord, being wise and holy and all-knowing, would be glad to show me what His will must be. That is why, forgive for me bringing this up again, but when I heard, all those months ago, that Josiah had left you, I saw, in my faint understanding at least, a light cast on my path. Mary Yoder must be the woman the Lord has chosen for me."

"Stephen, please," Mary begged. Rachel's warning buzzed in her ears. *Stephen will fall in love with you.* "We've been over this before. Remember?"

"I know." He sighed and climbed down from the buggy to tie up his horse.

She followed and waited by the hitching post until he finished. They walked up toward the house in silence. Thankfully, Betsy and Gerald had left the hymn singing earlier, so she wouldn't have to deal with their snide remarks or rude behavior. But maybe Betsy was right this time. Was Mary was in over her head?

She forced a smile and held open the front door for Stephen. He entered and seated himself on the couch while she slipped into the kitchen for chocolate chip cookies and glasses of milk. He was grim faced when she returned, but his expression softened at the offered goodies.

He took a bite of a cookie and took a sip of milk before speaking. "Do you think I could change my thoughts, my understanding of the Lord's ways? That is, if you are, at least you think you are, right in what you are saying?"

"I spoke with both Deacon Stoltzfus and Rachel at the sewing circle this week." Mary grasped at straws. "I told them about what you and I hoped to accomplish. Mose and Rachel were both supportive. I don't know everything, Stephen, or even that much, but I think I am right on this. If Amish people are anything, they are practical, and your spiritual thinking is clouding your judgment."

"So, if I can say it right, why aren't you and I practical? This could be, as the Lord has shown me, a real date. In the months ahead at least, we could be speaking and planning for our future together, Mary."

Mary groaned. "There must be feelings, Stephen, and seeing eye to eye, and such things. We don't fit each other. For example, someday I would like to visit Kenya and see for myself how the work among the glue boys is going. Would you be interested in such a thing?"

Stephen eyed another cookie. "What do you mean by, how did you say it, *interested*? What does that, would you say, mean in my ways or terms of understanding?"

"Don't complicate it, Stephen," Mary scolded. "Would you travel to Kenya with me and visit the glue boys? If we were married, of course."

He grunted. "I guess that would be, at least for some people, an interesting trip."

"But would you go?" she insisted.

"I suppose, if you want to know for certain, I would not."

"Then see? That's my point. You need a *frau* who thinks like you do and fits your life."

"And you fit this *Englisha* man's life?"

"That's not what I mean, Stephen. Please don't even say that."

He shrugged. "I don't understand. Not well, at least. I am a simple man who thinks about his farm, house, and *kinner*, of course, though I am getting old in that way."

"You could marry a widow who already has children," Mary suggested. "If she fits your life and the two of you fall in love."

He appeared pensive. "What is this 'falling in love' you keep speaking of? How does one fall, or is it, *feel* in love?"

Mary smiled. "Either way works, I think. Falling in love or feeling in love—it happens."

"But we were, earlier at least, or that long ago, speaking of being practical, and yet..."

"I'm so sorry. This is confusing," Mary admitted. "Maybe I did bite off more than I can chew."

"Oh, no, not in the least. I mean, not for a moment, don't think that. This is very helpful, just being with you, Mary. Hearing you speak is very helpful and useful to me, if I may tell the truth."

"I don't think we're getting anywhere, Stephen. I'm sorry."

His face fell.

Mary calmed herself. "Okay, let's try something else. Most women like it when a man speaks directly when he has something to say. Can you practice that?"

"Like..." He shifted on the couch, the last cookie in his hand. "I don't know, not really, what you mean."

"Just say what you have to say, Stephen. Forcefully! Without going around in circles."

Mary closed her eyes for a moment. Visions of Josiah's handsome faced danced in front of her. The man was brief and even sharp at times, always sure of himself. Her heart pounded at the memory of him seated beside her on this couch those long months ago. But what an awful thought to have about another woman's husband.

Mary brought herself back and opened her eyes. Stephen stared at her, his cookie gone from his hand. She had apparently spaced out in front of him.

"Did I say something?" Her head spun.

"You were thinking about someone?"

"I'm sorry about that. I was in a dreamworld, but...What you just said was very good."

He appeared puzzled.

"That last sentence. That was simplicity itself. You said, 'You were thinking about someone?'"

"I don't know what you mean, not quite, about the question. Is that what I said?"

Mary sighed and hurried on. "Let's talk about Lavina. She is a widow with three children. Let's use her as a concrete example because I think she would fit you perfectly. On some Saturday night, you could drive into her lane, tie up, and knock on her front door. What would you say when Lavina answers?"

He appeared lost in thought.

"Try something."

"*Goot* evening, Lavina," he began. "I've come, at least it seems I have, after seeking the Lord's will—"

She stopped him. "No. Just say something simple. Once."

"*Goot* evening, Lavina," he tried again. "Have you got a minute?"

"That's perfect!" Mary clapped her hands. "So Lavina smiles and holds open the door. You step inside, say *goot* evening to any of her children who are standing nearby, and ask..." Mary rolled her hand.

"Could I, perhaps sometime—"

"No." Mary took a deep breath. "Just one straightforward sentence. Why have you come?"

"Could we speak in private, Lavina?"

Mary smiled. "That's *goot*. So she sends the children away, and you sit on the couch..." Another hand roll.

"Could I take you home from the hymn singing sometime?"

"Okay, progress." Mary hugged herself. "But not quite. You're both older, and I would suggest you simply plan to have your dates on a Saturday night. On Sunday evening, Lavina would have to find a babysitter, and that would complicate things. Think simple, direct, and practical."

"I would like to, if it's okay with you, sometime, get better acquainted with you." He smiled to the imaginary Lavina. "Perhaps I could visit on a Saturday night, if you don't mind."

"That was pretty *goot*, even with the extras," Mary mused. "So maybe this doesn't matter. Just ask the woman what you just did, and she will agree readily. I can promise you that."

"You think so?" He grinned from ear to ear.

"I'm certain," Mary assured him. "Now how difficult was that?"

His face clouded. "But what about, if I dare bring up the point, the Lord's leading? I haven't prayed or spent time on my knees, not even for an hour about Lavina being my *frau*."

Mary held on to the couch with both hands. "You really must

be practical, Stephen. Lavina would make a great *frau* for you. She would love you, and you would fall in love with her ways. Would you think about it?"

"I suppose so. And now I will be practical and leave. Is it okay with you, if we, maybe in two weeks or so, do this again?"

"How about three weeks?" she said as he stood.

He nodded and slipped out into the night. Mary didn't move until the sound of his horse's hooves clomped out of the driveway.

TWENTY-THREE

Willard crept into the kitchen in the early morning hours to find his grandmother seated at the table with a hot cup of tea steaming in her hands.

"Good morning, Willard." She greeted him with a smile. "Give me a minute, and I'll fry eggs and bacon for you."

He made a face. "I was hoping I wouldn't disturb you. Cold cereal is fine."

She stood and walked toward the refrigerator. "I need something to do, and you're not disturbing me. Remember that!"

"Okay." He gave in and settled into a chair. "I guess a warm breakfast would be delicious. Did you hear me come in last night?"

"Not enough to disturb me. How were the meetings?"

"No complaints. There's lots of interest over the Christmas season, and the funds are coming in. I should be ready to fly back to Kenya on schedule after the first of the year."

She lowered her eyebrows at him. "You know you are far from ready to go back. There's the matter of that sweet Amish girl. Have you made contact with her lately?"

"Grandma, you know that's not going to work. Carlene rejected me, and we were on the same page."

She took a carton of eggs out of the refrigerator. "You have enough faith to run a mission in Kenya. You can trust the Lord for the money you need to do that, but you cannot trust Him with your heart? Let me show you what that girl has already done."

"You were going to fry eggs for me."

"That's not funny, Willard. Come!"

He followed her to the back bedroom, where two stacks of blankets were piled on the bed.

"Look at these, Willard." She unfolded one and ran her hand over the stitches. "Exactly what I assume you ordered. Nothing fancy, yet each thread done with precision and care. Even love, I would say— deep love and devotion. You need to pursue this girl, Willard. The Lord is in this."

He winced. "Not to be disrespectful, Grandma, but mentioning the Lord's will at this point is manipulation."

"Perhaps that is pushing things. But you can't go back to Kenya until this door has closed firmly. Right now it's wide open."

A wry look crossed his face. "I'd say it's more like a closed door that you are trying to *push* open."

She ran her fingers over the small blanket again. "I am not giving up on this, Willard. I'll go cook your breakfast, and then I want to hear your plan. Just look at these and tell me you are not moved deeply."

"By a blanket?"

"You are not that blind," she chided gently. "Just hurt. But this woman will bring healing. She will be an honor to you."

"Grandma, breakfast." He tapped her on the arm. "Eggs and bacon."

"I was just waxing eloquent."

He joined in her laugher. "I always thought you a practical person."

"I am practical," she huffed. "Pursuing Mary Yoder is the height of practicality."

"Eggs and bacon," he said, and they laughed again.

Willard followed her to the kitchen and stood by the stove, heating the pan for the eggs while she brought out the bacon and turned on another burner.

"Just think," she said with a twinkle in her eye. "You could wake every morning to an Amish breakfast on the table. What greater blessing could a man want?"

He grinned. "Now that is practical."

"Am I being persuasive?"

"Not really, but tell me what I could do. How does a man pursue an Amish girl?"

"You do want to." She glared at him before she plopped the bacon pan on the stove. "Let's keep that point straight. Your faith is weak. That's the problem."

"More like my experience with women," he retorted. "The worst thing one can do is love them."

"Do you think the Lord's love for us brought Him only joy? There is pain, Willard. I won't deny that, but this girl will not let you down. I know her too well. Plus, she is Amish."

"That is the problem, Grandma."

"That is both the problem and the solution."

"There you go," he muttered, cracking eggs into the pan.

"So you agree on that point?" She glanced at him.

"An Amish woman as my wife?" He laughed. "I'm not agreeing to anything."

She sighed and fussed with the bacon in its pan.

"Her sister gave me the inside scoop."

"Oh?" Interest flickered on her face.

"Kind of. If you can believe her."

Silence filled the kitchen. Then, "Willard, don't leave me on pins and needles."

He grimaced. "Betsy told me that Mary shares my feelings. That I shouldn't take no for an answer. Something like that."

"And you still doubt?"

"More like hurt, Grandma. It's not going to work. Why put us both through this?"

"You'll never know if you don't try. Do you want to live with that?"

"There you go again." He turned over the eggs. "The pain of rejection or the pain of *what if.* Not much of a choice, I would say."

She huffed in exasperation. "I've said what I have to say, Willard."

"Okay, I'll speak with Mary this morning at the co-op. If nothing else, I'll do it to please you."

"That's better." She smiled.

He lifted the eggs out of the pan one by one. "Should I take roses? There's a flower shop in Little Falls, isn't there?"

"You shouldn't take flowers, Willard. She's still Amish."

"Doesn't that prove my point? We're worlds apart. Now I'm ready to give up before I've even begun."

"Just talk to her. Something will come to you. The Lord will guide."

Silence fell again as they carried the food to the table and bowed their heads in a short prayer of thanks. They ate, each lost in thought.

Willard cleared his throat. "I walked up to the gravesites the other day, before I invited Mary to the meeting in Palatine Bridge."

"You grandfather and father were great men." Grandma's smile was soft. "You will be the loving kind of husband they were, Willard. You take after them."

He didn't respond, and she didn't seem to expect him to. They finished eating, and then Willard gave her a quick, "I'll see you later," before going out the door.

Willard knew his grandmother would pray for him. She was investing a lot in this match for some reason. Perhaps out of her compassionate heart for him, or more likely because of Mary. If Grandma thought highly enough of a woman to put in this kind of effort, he had better listen.

He walked past the car and down the street. The air had warmed with the early morning sun, and his coat was enough to cut the chill. Mary must have walked down this morning to her job at the co-op. He hadn't heard the clip-clop of a horse's hooves on the pavement going past the house, but he might have tuned out the sound. The blasting horns and racket of Nairobi's city life immunized one to unusual noises.

He had to get back to his scheduled duties at the mission. Work was its own salve for the soul. Life was lonely, even when he was surrounded by an abundance of people and activity. His heart still ached, and he couldn't deny it. Willard hastened his steps. Grandma's faith stirred him. He had once held that faith in his heart, only to have the rug jerked out from under him. Carlene changed her mind and rejected him for someone better, more suited to her, more established in the professional world.

The missions had cost him love, yet he wasn't bitter. He walked alone, and he'd intended to continue that walk to the best of his abilities—and now this. He had to admit that Mary was interested in Kenya. That was plain to see. Was she interested enough to leave her faith, her community, her family, and her buggy? He sighed. Mary was a woman of deep faith. That much he knew.

He steeled himself before crossing the street to approach the co-op. The parking lot was filled with several automobiles. He could walk on up to the graveyard and come back later. On the other hand, buggies might have arrived by that time. Better that his own people overhear a whispered conversation with Mary than bearded Amish men.

Willard slipped inside and closed the door behind him. The fresh smell of packaged bulk foods greeted him, along with the sight of neatly organized shelves. Mary faced the other direction, deep in conversation with one of the customers. Willard turned the corner and studied the packaged nuts in front of him. There were peanuts, salted and unsalted, cashews, both halves and wholes, and pecans of various grades. The shelf continued to his right. A gourmet chef would find what he needed here. This was a store of humble origins with plenty to offer. Not unlike the Amish themselves, or Mary. Grandma was right. A man who could win Mary's heart would have won a jewel. Deep down he knew that, even while doubt screamed in his face.

"She's Amish."

"She won't love you."

"Even if she does, Mary will reject you!"

"Wouldn't things be worse than before?"

"Probably," he muttered into the empty aisle.

He wanted to bolt out the door, but he didn't. Instead, when Mary passed by the end of the aisle, he followed her to the counter.

She finally faced him. "Willard! What are you doing here?"

He motioned behind him. "Just browsing through what you have to offer."

She obviously wasn't convinced. "You shouldn't be here. Not when..."

His gaze followed hers toward the other customers. "They don't care. And yes, I have ulterior motives."

"What if a buggy drives in?" Fear flickered on her face.

"They don't know who I am." Inspiration stirred. "Also, I can help you today. Stock the shelves."

"Willard!"

"I can." He smiled his brightest. "Just show me what needs to be done."

Mary appeared pale, but she led him to the rear of the store. "I guess I could use the help. There's the brown sugar. It can be measured into five and ten pounds bags, and..." She pointed to the large burlap sacks. "We sell the bags faster than I can keep up."

"Happy to help," he chirped. He eyed the scales hanging from the wall.

"We always add a little extra to the sugar bag. There should be no doubt, you know."

"Of course not. I'll make sure."

"And the tie strips are over there. Right near at hand." She pointed. "Make sure they are turned extra tight, so no air can get in."

"Grandma showed me the blankets this morning, Mary. Thank you. They are absolutely beautiful and exactly what I wanted."

She colored and bolted back to the counter, where a customer waited. This was a strange courtship. More like a dance without a song, but maybe he simply couldn't hear it. An Amish tune, no doubt, and he was tone-deaf to the melody. What would an Amish man do if he wished to court Mary? Willard had no idea. Perhaps work hard? That seemed the logical answer. They likely didn't say much to one another.

Willard busied himself and had a small stack of bags ready when he heard footsteps behind him. "Am I doing it right?" he asked without turning around.

Mary picked up a five-pound bag, turned it in her hands, and pulled on the tie strip. "*Yah*. It's perfect."

"Just like me," he teased.

Mary didn't laugh. "What are your motives, Willard?"

"Are you still dating that Amish man?"

Confusion filled her face. "Did Betsy tell you?"

He nodded.

"I suppose she told you other things?"

"Sorry," he said.

"You know this won't work, Willard."

"But you would want it to?"

She appeared to tear up. "Willard, I am confused. There are things in my heart that shouldn't be there, but even if they were true and right, what my heart wants is not the question. There are things more worthy of our devotion than our own desires."

"This is true." He ducked his head. "I'm sorry, Mary. I'm not try-ing to make trouble for you."

"You are *not* trouble, at least not to me. I don't want to seem standoffish, or... Please, Willard. You shouldn't be here."

"Can I help you today? What is the harm in that?"

Hesitation flickered again. "Well, I could use the help."

"There you go!"

"But—"

"Just show me what I should do, Mary." He smiled his bright-est. "I won't bite."

"You won't?" She seemed breathless.

"Shall I bag more brown sugar?" He motioned toward the bur-lap bags.

"*Yah*, more," she said. "Quite a few more, if you wish."

"I wish," he said. He busied himself with the bags.

Mary waited a few seconds before she scurried off to help another customer. Willard snuck a glance over his shoulder. Not a bearded Amish man, at least. So far, so good. But he couldn't help but wonder if it was right to tempt Mary. Was this not selfishness on his part? She was dedicated to her faith, but she obviously had feelings for him—a few, at least. Why else had she allowed him to stay for the day?

Willard paused in his work to glance down the aisle, where Mary stood with an elderly woman, helping the lady make her selections. Mary looked up and caught his gaze. A smile flickered before she looked away quickly.

Willard weighed out another ten-pound bag of brown sugar. Was not all fair in love and war? That's how the saying went, but he cared about Mary's heart and her future happiness. He should leave, and yet he didn't want to. This woman drew him in, ever closer. She kept him riveted to rusty scales and burlap bags. Carlene had been about fancy restaurants and high talk around elaborate dining room tables. Her father had been the pastor of a well-respected church. Life here was simple and humble, and the hands that offered it shook and doubted.

This was why he wanted to stay. Love that sprang from this ground would have roots deep enough to withstand any storm. The certainty gripped him. Today he would believe. Tomorrow would answer for itself.

TWENTY-FOUR

That evening Betsy slipped out of the gas station bathroom in Fort Plain. She was clad in jeans and a shirt underneath a thick coat, with her Amish dress and *kapp* tucked in a paper bag. The wind blew across the street and whipped up snowflakes that lay on the curb after a momentary squall. She had walked down the hill into town because there was no place to tie Danny Boy at the gas station.

Winter would set in for *goot* after Christmas, and *rumspringa* activities would slow, but tonight there was a gathering in Little Falls. Before long Enos Troyer would pick her up in his buggy. He would have come to the house if she had asked, but that meant arriving at the gathering with no place to change. One couldn't leave home dressed in *Englisha* clothing, not with *Mamm* and *Daett* around. Betsy shivered as she waited on the street corner. She would return inside to wait if Enos didn't show soon. The gas station attendants were accustomed to Amish young people on weekend evenings. No one complained, provided a small purchase was made once in a while.

Betsy stamped her feet and glanced up the street. Thankfully, the faint beat of a horse's hooves reached her. Enos turned the corner at the light, and the animal pranced along, its head held high. Betsy smiled. Enos had wanted an automobile for his *rumspringa* time, but he couldn't afford one. His *daett* didn't volunteer the money, of course. From what she could tell, a high-spirited horse had been a compromise of sorts.

Enos whirled up to the street corner and came to a stop. The buggy door opened to reveal a strange man seated beside him. Probably one of Enos's visiting cousins. When Betsy stepped forward, her smile froze in place. "Ronald Troyer?"

"It's me," he grinned. "I see you remember."

He appeared much too pleased with himself as Betsy stood unmoving in the wind.

"Betsy, are you coming or not?" Enos hollered. "I can't hold my horse forever."

She was supposed to climb up and sit beside Ronald Troyer after years of silence? But what choice did she have? She tried to move, but her feet wouldn't work.

Ronald leaned out of the buggy to say, "Sorry to startle you. I don't bite! I'm in the area for the Christmas holidays and decided to take a whirl with Enos tonight."

He was still handsome, just as she remembered, and her heart pounded in her chest.

"Last call!" Cousin Enos sounded irritated.

Betsy lunged forward and found herself seated between the two men, almost falling into Ronald's lap on the way up the buggy step.

"*Goot* evening. Have we met before?" Ronald joked.

She would have slapped him if she'd dared.

"Surprise!" Enos sang out as his horse dashed off down the street. "Hope you don't mind riding with an extra person, Betsy, but I couldn't leave Ronald at home."

She hung on to the dash and glanced at Ronald's handsome face. "Where have you been?"

He laughed. "Oh, here and there. What about you?"

Right here waiting for you, she wanted to say but didn't. He obviously hadn't shared her feelings on that subject. Why else had he stayed away so long?

"She *can* talk," Cousin Enos said.

Enos wasn't cruel, but surely he knew about her feelings for Ronald—didn't he? She hadn't expressed her admiration for Ronald to anyone other than Mary, mired as she was in her hopelessness.

"I'll be here for a while." Ronald leaned forward to peer at her face. "Maybe I'll see more of you?"

You would if that were up to me, she almost said.

"She's still pretty," Enos said with a grin. "And feisty."

Ronald chuckled. "She appears calm to me." He leaned forward for another look at her.

"Stop it!" Betsy snapped, and they both roared with laughter.

"We were just teasing," Enos told her. "Ronald was thrilled when I told him you would be riding along tonight."

"That's right," Ronald seconded. "I couldn't wait to meet you again."

"You could have come back sooner," Betsy said, finally finding her voice.

"That's *goot* to hear." Ronald sounded pleased again. "Exactly the kind of welcome a boy dreams of."

"You call this a welcome?" Enos asked. "She's hardly said a word."

"You two are so full of yourselves," she told them, and their laughter pealed again.

"How's Mary?" Ronald asked when he had calmed down.

"Mary is too old for you," Enos piped up. "You know she was jilted and has a broken heart. She's been dating our oldest bachelor."

"Sounds interesting," Ronald said. "But I didn't have romance in mind when I asked about her."

"Mary will *not* wed Stephen Overholt," Betsy said, jumping in the conversation. "Let's keep that straight."

"You seem awful sure of yourself when you're not the one dating him." Enos regarded her with a skeptical look. "People with broken hearts do unexpected things. That's what *Mamm* always told me."

"Must never have had one of those," Ronald quipped. "A broken heart."

"Neither of you knows what you are talking about," Betsy retorted. "The best thing would be for Mary to date that handsome *Englisha* man, Willard Gabert, who runs a mission for boys in Kenya. How would that be for adventure and excitement?"

They both stared at her.

"Betsy also has wild ideas," Enos finally said.

"And *goot* ones," Betsy insisted. "I've tried my best to encourage Mary to consider the *wunderbah* chance she has for freedom and escape from the community. Just think what the *Englisha* women have at their fingertips: washers and dryers run by electricity, electric ovens, switches that turn on lights, dishwashers...and let's not forget electric beaters. Just imagine the delicious angel food cake one could make with such implements at one's disposal."

Enos smacked his lips, and Betsy gave him a glare. "Don't laugh at me, cousin. I know that you're not taking your *rumspringa* seriously. There isn't a chance you'll jump the fence."

"I hope not," Ronald muttered.

"So you're one of those too?" Betsy directed her glare toward him. "I should have known." Obviously Ronald was here for one thing—to see his relatives over Christmas.

Ronald chuckled. "I like my *rumspringa*. Don't get me wrong—"

"But you've already decided," Betsy interrupted.

"Something like that."

"Ronald's a *goot* man," Enos said. "And I don't believe for a second that Mary would consider falling for an *Englisha* man. You don't really think she'll do that, do you, Betsy?"

She made a face as they trotted down the grade toward Little

Falls on Highway 5. "I had hoped so, but I guess not. Mary is in love with him—I don't question that—but she won't fall for him."

"I don't believe she has feelings for him," Enos told her. "Your prejudices are being cast on your sister. You should consider settling down, Betsy. I'm going to take the plunge in the spring and join the baptismal class."

"Me too," Ronald echoed. "I think it's time."

"How about it?" Enos teased, as they trotted through the edge of town.

"I still dream of meeting a handsome *Englisha* man." Betsy sighed. "No straw in his hair. How long I have waited—yet my sister is the one who gets the chance!"

"There you go. The Lord protects you," Enos chuckled. He pulled into a driveway where several other buggies were parked. "This is it, I think."

Ronald jumped down as soon as the buggy came to a stop. He turned with a smile and offered his hand to Betsy. She raised her eyebrows but took the proffered gesture.

His gloved hand gripped hers. "I have an automobile back in Lancaster," he whispered. "And I can act like an *Englisha* man."

"But you aren't one," she said. She slipped but righted herself on the snowy ground.

Ronald noticed and reached for her arm. Betsy didn't resist. His courtesies were nice, but he'd be gone the day after Christmas. He held on to her arm until they reached the front porch, apparently oblivious to her stream of negative thoughts. Enos knocked and then opened the door when no one answered. A flood of light and noise came from the depths of the house, with only dim hall lamps to guide them inside.

Enos led the way with Ronald following by Betsy's side. "What are you doing with your time while you are here?" she asked him.

"Depends. I haven't decided yet."

"Have you been back to the valley since I met you all that time ago?"

He shook his head. "No. But I hadn't forgotten you."

She looked away. This kind of man would not remember her.

"You seemed much younger back then," he said with a twinkle in his eye.

The sound of the music exploded when Enos opened the door into what appeared to be the den.

Ronald leaned close to her ear. "You want to dance?"

She wondered if he knew how, but he obviously did. She slid into his arms, and they joined the other couples on the floor. Strobe lights stabbed the darkness around them, while Enos stood off to the side with a surprised look on his face.

"You're *goot* at this," she spoke into Ronald's ear.

The smell of his cologne up close was delicious. She hadn't noticed the spicy scent on the buggy ride into town. Ronald was no ordinary Amish farm boy, but being impressed with the man was a waste of time. She should know that lesson well by now.

"You're *goot* too," he said, his grin wicked. "Where did you learn?"

"*Englisha* men." She didn't hesitate. "And what about you?"

"Not from *Englisha* girls. Naughty, naughty Betsy."

She ignored the scold. Most Amish boys were bossy, but Ronald's kind of bossiness was a pleasant boldness that defied description. Almost like courage. Betsy glanced up into his face. "I didn't know Lancaster girls could dance. Amish ones, that is."

His grin was wide. "There are a few. You've lived in the valley too long."

"Why do you think I want to leave?"

"Lancaster has everything you would want," he said. "Keeps me happy."

She didn't answer. She snuggled against his chest for the rest of the song. The ripples under his shirt were not surprising. Amish men had those from hard work in the fields. But the tenderness in his strength was the surprise. His arms handled her with a deftness that made her feel as though she were flying across the floor.

The song ended, and Betsy caught her breath on the sidelines while Ronald slipped into the crowd.

"You two seemed to hit it off," Enos commented at her elbow. "You should learn how to dance."

He made a face. "Amish boys don't normally need the skill. I think I'll be fine without the effort expended."

Betsy ignored him as Ronald returned with two glasses in his hand. "They are serving champagne for a small fee," he said. "Want one?" He held out the glass to Betsy.

"See? That's how you treat a girl." Betsy took the proffered glass with one hand and shook her finger at Enos with the other. He laughed and walked off.

Ronald watched Enos leave with a pensive look. "He's a nice solid chap, isn't he?"

"I suppose so," Betsy allowed. She took a long sip from her glass.

"Like it?" Ronald teased. His glass was already half empty.

"I thought you said you were staying Amish?"

"I am." He wrinkled his brow. "This is what *rumspringa* is about."

"But you have already decided."

Ronald nodded. "How about you?"

She ignored the question. "So you are playing the system!"

Ronald laughed. "More like getting things *out* of my system. That's another purpose of *rumspringa*. So one doesn't look back and wonder, you know, years later."

Betsy took a long drink from her glass. "I could learn to like this."

"You know that's not real, Betsy. It's fun, *yah*, but..."

"I still like it." She took the last swallow.

"I'm not getting you more," he told her, his bossiness back. "Come on. Let's dance again."

Betsy took his hand, and they twirled back out on the floor. Ronald was right. Another glass and she would have been dizzy. He leaned close to whisper, "Your cheeks are rosy."

She almost stumbled. He held her tightly, and they recovered.

"You are pretty when your temper shows. Did anyone ever tell you that?"

She made a face at him, and he laughed.

The song ended, and they stood against the wall to catch their breath. He studied her for a moment.

"There's a reason I'm rosy cheeked."

"I know," he said. "Do you have a steady boyfriend?"

"No! I don't have a boyfriend."

"No one off and on?"

"No! Why are you asking?"

"That's a shame," he said. "Would you consider?"

"Dating?"

"*Yah*! Dating me?" He shrugged. "At least until I leave after Christmas?"

Betsy's head spun. "You're making me turn bright red."

"Then it's a *yah*?"

"I didn't say so."

"But you will say so?"

"I don't want to stay Amish. We've already been over that."

"You would reject a date with me because I plan to stay Amish?"

"You are awful, you know."

He chuckled. "I like you, and I'd like to know you better. Surely we can't go that wrong. You can always change your mind. It's not as if I'm asking you to say the wedding vows next week."

"But you live in Lancaster, and I live in the valley."

"All the better." His eyes twinkled. "As they say, absence makes the heart grow fonder."

"And you're depending on that?"

"Of course. And I'm also depending on my charm."

"You are so full of yourself."

"But you'll still say *yah*?" He took her hand. "We can see each other again next weekend. If we can't find a gathering in Little Falls, I'll take you to Utica."

"That's a long way in a borrowed buggy."

He leaned closer. "I have a driver's license. I'll rent something. In fact, let's plan on that. You can handle the spin, can't you? Get some of that wildness worked out of you?"

Her eyes shone. "You would do that?"

"For you, *yah*! Any day."

"You are sweet, Ronald, in addition to being full of yourself."

"Isn't that about the same thing?"

She fixed her gaze on him. "You are full of surprises, you know?"

But then again, maybe he wasn't. He appeared way too pleased with himself at the compliment. He certainly didn't act like a normal Amish man, even one on *rumspringa*. Was it possible he had not only come back to see family, but also to see her? She suddenly realized she hadn't thought about the scars on her face one time the whole evening.

The music began again, louder than before. "Shall we step outside?" he mouthed.

She nodded and followed him toward the back door. A large deck lay in front of them, with the starry sweep of the Milky Way overhead. After the warmth of the crowded room, the chill of the wind cut through her.

Ronald took her hand and pulled her close. She laid her head on his shoulder to gaze at the stars overhead.

His fingers pointed. "There's Orion with his belt, and the seven sisters. The heavens full of the Lord's glory have always drawn me in."

Betsy nestled closer. He didn't seem to need comments from her as he pointed out further constellations of stars.

"Where did you learn all this?" she finally asked.

"Always took a fascination with the solar system in school," he said. "Another luxury of *rumspringa* has been visits to the planetarium in Lancaster."

"You can go there anytime you want. Even as an Amish man."

"Maybe," he allowed. "But *rumspringa* got me started. I watch the films they show. I keep track of when the new ones come out, and then I visit again."

"You are different. I knew you were from the first time I met you." She glanced at him.

His laugh was soft. "And so are you. That's part of why I came back, Betsy, and I haven't been disappointed."

"We should go inside," she said, her fingers tight in his. "I'm getting cold, and I don't quite believe you are real."

He smiled, but he led the way without protest.

TWENTY-FIVE

The half-moon hung low in the sky as Mary slipped out of the mudroom and hurried across the lawn. With her shawl pulled tight against the chilly wind, Mary found Stephen's buggy in line behind several other men who waited for their dates.

Mary pulled herself up into the buggy and slid the door shut behind her "*Goot* evening, Stephen," she said.

"It's *goot*, it really is, to see you," he said. He jiggled the reins.

His horse plodded around the buggies ahead of them, and they pulled out of the driveway.

"So how are you, if I may ask?" Stephen glanced toward her, his face a shadow in the dark as low clouds scurried across the moon.

"Decent enough for a chilly evening," Mary replied. She tightened her shawl again.

The truth was, the cold didn't bother her at the moment. Willard's handsome face had been in her mind's eye all through the hymn singing. Since Friday, the memory of his smile and warm charm had remained. On her knees, she had beseeched the Lord for mercy—but her prayers had done little *goot*. At this moment, she imagined Willard instead of Stephen seated beside her in the buggy.

Allowing Willard to help at the co-op had been an awful mistake.

Stephen was clearly oblivious to her dreadful thoughts. He smiled gently as faint moonbeams reached inside the buggy. "I have looked forward, all week I have, to this, you know—the few hours I'd spend, at least, with you."

"I..." she began. "It's *goot* to be here with you again, Stephen." Mary caught her breath and let the words burst out. "What kind of progress have you made with Lavina? Did you get a chance to stop by her house and speak with her?"

He grimaced. "Lavina, I mean, of course not. That's not going, if I may say so, much of anywhere, Mary. Surely a woman like yourself...you are smart, and you know that such things take time. And what if Lavina...I mean, the woman doesn't even know I'm thinking such thoughts about her, if I really am. And the Lord's will. I can't, much as I try, even with your encouragement, bring myself to take the step." Stephen glanced upward. "The Lord has not spoken to my heart. And, I mean, I am dating you. Lavina? No! One doesn't, while one is dating someone else...someone whom I care about. Please don't be offended, Mary, but I care a lot. The Lord knows how much. I think you're a *wunderbah* woman."

Mary forced the words out. "Maybe you wouldn't think so if you knew what I did this past week."

Stephen laughed. "I doubt if there's anything in the world, or even in my imagination, that you are capable of, even if you tried, doing wrong."

Mary kept silent. She wouldn't change his mind, and Stephen would soon ask what she had done if she didn't leave the subject alone. She didn't regret the time spent with Willard enough to make a full confession to anyone. That was the terrifying thing about Willard. He seemed so right, so much of what she had always wanted. But how was that possible?

Mary gathered her courage. "I know you said Lavina was not for you, but we should practice making a visit to some other widow's house. That day must come, Stephen. You shouldn't live alone when there are women in the community who would take care of you."

He stared out of the buggy as they plodded into the Yoders' driveway and up to the hitching post. He hung his head, the reins loose in his hands. "I don't know, if I am honest and truthful, about that. I don't think so, Mary."

He began to climb out, but Mary stopped him with a touch on his arm. "Let's just sit in the buggy for a while. It's chilly, but the moon is still out. We can go inside if we get too cold."

Stephen nodded and settled onto the seat again.

"Tell me about your childhood." She glanced at his face with a smile. "I don't think I've ever heard much about the Overholt family."

"There's not much, as they say, to tell. Seven boys, all big men, clumsy, most of them, but none worse than me. The others—at least I think they did—turned out okay. They are all, down to the last one, married to decent women. I was the middle child. There was no reason, at least that I can see, that we were strange, which is how, as they say, I turned out. We were happy, I think, at least it seemed so to me. I was, I don't know, lost kind of...never took to things. I kept to myself for some reason—at least, that's what I was told. I just never married. That was the Lord's will."

"But that's such a sad story," Mary wailed. "There were lots of women, I'm sure, who would have taken your offer of marriage. You have a farm that must be about paid for, and—"

"*Yah*, see, there you go, like I said. There really is no reason." Silence fell in the buggy. The setting moon hung in front of them, just above the horizon.

"That's still a sad story," she insisted.

"*Yah*, I know," he agreed. "Seems like all my life, at least, that's how it's been, sad. Seeing the Lord's hand, and then not seeing it, or being told that..." His voice trailed off.

"I'm sorry, Stephen. I guess I did the same thing."

"Don't blame yourself, really, don't. At least you have—for me, I think—done much more, so much more than any of the others have."

"How many girls have you asked on dates?"

He laughed, the sound grim. "Not too many. Maybe, shall we say…" He appeared to count for a moment. "More than a dozen, I think, but I can't remember. They are all kind of lost in my mind—that is, when I'm around you, Mary. You seem like the end of the road, like home to me. Almost like the first girl, the one who was not the Lord's will."

"What did you say?" Mary asked.

His gaze was fixed on the moon as it slipped under the horizon. "Like that," he said. "Just like that—the light of my life, my hope for the future, for our plans which she spoke of. But the Lord was not with us, and she was gone forever."

"Who was this girl?" Mary studied Stephen's face.

He seemed lost in the memory.

"Stephen!" She reached for his arm. "What happened? Tell me."

He rallied himself. "It was all very long ago, as they say. I should have forgotten, but I haven't. They said we could not be, so I have worked, and waited, and prayed, but things are what they are. There is nothing anyone can do about this, at least it seems so to me."

"Maybe you should start at the beginning," she told him, still holding his arm. "Tell me about this girl."

He turned toward her. "Could we go inside the house, where it's warmer?"

"Of course."

Stephen shivered and climbed down from the buggy, while she went out the other side. He had the buggy blanket draped over his horse by the time Mary walked up to him. He dropped his gaze and followed her up the sidewalk. Mary held the door open for him and saw the pain written heavily on Stephen's face as he passed her. She closed the door and seated herself beside him on the couch. The flames from the kerosene lamp *Mamm* had left on the woodstove flickered across the room.

"You were saying?" she prompted.

"She was a beautiful girl to me," he said. "Though she wasn't really, not to others—as I wasn't, and as I am not. We were two lost souls, but we loved from our hearts. I first saw Millie at a *rumspringa* gathering in Lancaster. You know how those are, but perhaps you don't. They are much the same as here I think, or they used to be…at least, it seems so to me from the ones they have here."

Stephen gazed at the kerosene lamp flame as it danced in the glass. "Millie was from a district in the south of Lancaster County, visiting, I think, for the weekend with her brother. I heard the Lord's voice in my heart, right from her first smile, as if the heavens had come down and visited me. Millie warmed my heart and filled me with joy. I almost hurt, if you know what I mean. I suppose, at least I think, you must have known this when Josiah first paid you attention."

Mary caught her breath. This insight she had not expected. *And Willard*, she almost said aloud.

Stephen continued. "We moved closer that evening, Millie and I, each of us drawn to the other, it seemed. I dared speak, what was in my heart. I can't remember…probably something dumb, like I always say, when things are important to say. But she smiled, and it didn't matter, because she was like me. We talked, all that evening, mostly with each other. I followed her out to her brother's buggy when the time came to leave. Around midnight, I think.

"'Do you always come to this gathering?' she asked me.

"'Usually,' I told her. 'Will you be here next week?'

"'Maybe,' she said. 'If I can persuade my brother Harold to bring me.'

"But I knew she would come, because she loved me as I loved her. She was there the next week, and the next. She let me drive her home in my buggy, while her brother frowned but said nothing. A moon was out that night, much the same as there was tonight, a sliver of a moon, hanging close to the horizon. The weather was warm, though, around the middle of summer. We drove with the buggy doors open. I did not know what lay ahead of me, did not see the storm clouds coming. I was too blind to know that the Lord's will, you understand, would stop us."

Stephen fell silent, and Mary waited until he continued. "My horse was fast in those days. Wind Jammer, he was called when I bought him at the sale barn, and the name fit. Millie leaned against my shoulder as we raced along those summer nights. 'I think I love you,' she whispered in my ear once. 'I felt you would come for a long time, and here you are.' I didn't say anything for a while. I couldn't say anything. Not after a beautiful girl, at least to me, like Millie, said something like that. I stopped the buggy in front of her barn and jumped down. Her *daett* was there, ready for me, waiting. 'This will go no further,' he told me. 'My daughter is not ready for marriage.' But he meant she was not for me—how I was, poor and from a strange family, and slow. I tried to see her again, but Millie never came back to our *rumspringa* gatherings, and neither did Harold. They would not let me speak with her when I visited the house, often though I went."

"Is she married now?" Mary asked.

Stephen shook his head, his eyes fixed on the kerosene flame. "Millie's an old maid, the last I heard. She's teaching school in her district."

"But Stephen—" Mary clutched his arm.

"Can we just, how do they say, forget this?" he interrupted. "This was not the Lord's will. So do you have anything to eat? I'm sorry to bring up my past, taking up your time, but I am hungry."

"Of course." Mary leaped to her feet and hurried into the kitchen.

She didn't know who Millie was from the southern part of Lancaster County, but Stephen's story had a ring of authenticity. Likely

Millie's *daett* thought Stephen unfit for his daughter. The couple had been denied love, and Millie had refused to settle for second best. But why? Pain stabbed at her heart. That often happened when couples were broken up. Regardless, Stephen had once known his own dreams of home and family. Both of them had been betrayed by circumstances out of their control. They had more in common than she had thought possible.

Footsteps came from the living room. Mary quickly wiped her eyes, but Stephen still noticed. "I'm sorry, I really am, to unload my story on you, when I know that your own heart must still be tender...hurting, actually, from what Josiah did to you."

"It's okay," she managed. "Why don't you sit at the table? We can eat in here."

He hesitated, but he sat when she motioned with her hand. She set out brownies and glasses of milk, and they ate by the light of the lamp, with flames flickering on the dark walls.

Mary gave Stephen a smile, and he seemed to relax. "Maybe you could visit Millie again and talk to her. Things change over the years. You are both older now, and you have your farm. Millie's *daett* might be wiser after these years have passed and watching his daughter mourn for her loss. Why didn't Millie wed again?"

He hung his head. "I don't know. She was beautiful to me."

"Then Millie must still love you. The least you can do is visit."

Stephen grew pale. "But my strength, my courage...I did not tell you everything, Mary. Out by the buggy that night, her *daett* said I was rejected of the Lord. That he would not add to Millie's sins..." Stephen's voice trailed off.

Words exploded out of her. "That is horrible, Stephen! That is *awful* to say about someone. Surely Millie's *daett* has either changed his mind or seen the error of his ways by now. Why would the man say something like that?"

Stephen ignored the question while hope lit in his eyes. "You think?"

"*Yah*! Certainly!" Mary didn't hesitate. "But even if he hasn't, you must not believe such things. The Lord's blessings are on those who believe and obey. Those are the true teachings of the community."

"No one has ever said this to me." Stephen's eyes lowered.

"Have you told anyone else your story?"

"No. Those words are too awful to utter. They are true, Mary."

"They are not! You must visit Lancaster at once and pay Millie a call. After these long years..." Tears sprung into her eyes. "Another day is too long to wait, Stephen."

He stared blankly toward the window.

She held out the plate of brownies to him. "You want another one?"

He took a brownie slowly, with hope flickering on his face. "I can go see her, Mary. If you say I can."

"You can," she told him. "And the Lord will bless you."

"So perhaps I was wrong, all these years, about the Lord's will? Because Millie's *daett* was really wrong."

Mary nodded, tears stinging her eyes.

TWENTY-SIX

The following Sunday, Mary glanced up from her place among the unmarried girls as Bishop Miller led the men into the Sunday morning services. The ministers took their place on the special bench prepared for them beside the kitchen doorway. Mary searched the line of men for Stephen's face. He would be the first of the unmarried men to appear if he was still in the community.

Mamm had confirmed Stephen's story on Monday morning. "*Yah*, there was a Millie Zook from southern Lancaster if I remember right."

"Why would she never have wed?"

Mamm shrugged. "That's hard to say. Millie had a birthmark that ran up her neck and into one whole side of her face, but why are you asking?"

"Just wondering."

"This is not because of Betsy?"

"No."

But *Mamm* had not been satisfied with her answer. "You were too young to remember Millie when we moved. You wouldn't even have met."

Mary had taken a deep breath. "Stephen dated her once, and her family cut off the relationship."

"He told you this?" *Mamm* had appeared worried. "Why are you still dating the man?"

"I'm not anymore. I think I accomplished what I wanted to."

Mamm's worried look did not fade, but the conversation ended when Betsy appeared in the kitchen doorway, waving a letter from Ronald.

"It came! Another one already!" Betsy did a jig on the kitchen floor.

Joy had filled *Mamm's* face. "And he's a *goot* Amish man, right?"

Betsy had ignored the question to dash upstairs.

Now Stephen wasn't here this morning, which must mean that he had followed Mary's advice and made a visit to Lancaster. Was healing possible for him and Millie after these long years? Was the same thing possible for Mary? If so, then with who? Certainly not with Willard Gabert, though her feelings led her toward that end.

Mary caught her breath, and the girl seated beside her glanced up in surprise. Amish girls didn't draw attention to themselves by gasping in church services, but everyone in the room had also noticed what she saw. Willard Gabert, the *Englisha* man, stood in the line of unmarried men.

"Who is he?" the girl leaned over to whisper.

Mary pressed her lips together as warmth ran up her back.

The girl's look turned to disapproval. "What is an *Englisha* man you know doing here?"

Which was precisely the question. Why had he come? He hadn't been to the co-op again, and she'd felt conflicted about wanting him to return. Willard's handsome face was a memory that haunted her. Now he was here. Did he plan to join the Amish? Mary's heart pounded in her chest. Was this how the Lord would answer the cry of her heart? Could Willard Gabert be her future husband? Mary forced herself to breathe, and the girl next to her gave her another disapproving glance.

A song number was given out, and the service began. Mary snuck a glance at Willard. He seemed perfectly relaxed, even at home on the backless bench, with an Amish man seated on either side of him. One of them shared the German songbook with Willard, but there was no way the man could read a word. Willard didn't appear bothered, though, as the German hymn was sung. The plaintive notes filled the whole house, and he smiled and nodded without moving his lips. At least he didn't pretend to know what he didn't know. The man was honest, but she already knew that.

Bishop Miller stood to lead the line of ministers upstairs for their Sunday morning meeting. Willard's gaze followed them, but he didn't appear surprised—just interested in the proceedings. She had gone to his church services. Why should she complain if he came to hers?

The answer was obvious. She had been interested in Kenya, while Willard was interested in her. This was plain enough to see. Mary kept her head down as heat crept up her neck. Those were thoughts she had tried to avoid, even during the day Willard had spent at the co-op. Instead, she had focused on her own feelings and how wrong they had been. Willard cared enough to attend an Amish church service, perhaps even considered joining the community— but what would that do for his mission in Kenya? One couldn't be Amish and run a mission overseas.

The singing continued, and Mary kept her head down until Bishop Miller led the line of ministers down from the upstairs. She dared look up once the preaching began, but kept her eyes turned carefully away from Willard's direction.

"This is the Lord's day again," Minister Peachey declared. "A day in which to give thanks and rejoice for the Lord's goodness and mercy. We are but frail creatures formed from the ground of the earth. Clay is what we are, and we should never forget that we live and breathe alone by the Lord's mercy."

Which was true. Mary shifted on the bench and caught Willard's glance. His smile was warm, and shivers ran all the way through her.

She felt fragile. If only her heart would come to its senses...but what hope was there of that? Even if Willard planned to join the community, she couldn't ask him to leave his work in Kenya. In the meantime, he was here. What would happen now? Would he speak with her today? What if she gave in to temptation? Perspiration misted on Mary's forehead, but she didn't dare wipe it away. She was strong when it came to other people's trouble, but weak when she had to find her own way. She was clearly in love with Willard, in the kind of love she used to share with Josiah. What a fool her heart was to lead her down this broken road twice. Had she learned nothing from the first experience? At least Josiah had been Amish.

Mary forced herself to focus on Minister Peachey, who was wrapping up his thoughts. He spread his hands out over the congregation. "And now may the Lord bless us all, and be with us as we face another week of temptations and trials in this weary world of sorrow. Amen."

Bishop Miller echoed the "amen."

Once Minister Peachy sat down, Deacon Stoltzfus stood and began to read from the Scriptures: "'Now it came to pass on a certain day, that he went into a ship with his disciples: and he said unto them, Let us go over unto the other side of the lake.'"

The story went on, of a great storm, and the disciples' fears until Jesus calmed the wild winds. Mary closed her eyes. She was in the middle of the storm, and the Lord was speaking. She would have to believe and trust. Nothing made sense, but waves on the waters caused those emotions. They cast confusion and doubt around them.

"Help me, dear Lord," Mary prayed. "Calm my wild winds and the horrible waves."

Peace came over her as Deacon Stoltzfus took his seat and Bishop Miller began his sermon. "The Lord be praised this morning. I can freely say that what King David wrote in the holy Scriptures, 'I have been young, and now am old; yet have I not seen the righteous forsaken, nor his seed begging bread' is true and of the Lord."

Mary didn't look in Willard's direction until the sermon concluded an hour later. When her glance did stray, Willard had his head bowed. Maybe the Lord had already heard? What would she do if Willard sent another of his sweet smiles her way? Pass out, perhaps?

The service concluded. Mary scurried into the kitchen as the murmur of conversation filled the house. The girl seated beside her stayed on the bench, sending frequent glances toward Willard. Obviously, *Englisha* man or not, he had plenty of admirers.

Mary bumped into Deacon Stoltzfus's *frau* with a gasp. "I'm so sorry, Rachel! I wasn't paying attention to where I was going."

Rachel took her by the arm and leaned close. "I was looking for you anyway." She propelled Mary into the mudroom. A few small girls struggled with their coats, and Rachel helped them. They hurried away as Mary remained frozen in place. Had Rachel noticed her reaction to Willard's presence in the service today?

"There!" Rachel declared. "Now we can talk."

Mary tried to smile. "I really should get back and help with the first table."

"There are plenty of women to help," Rachel assured her. "Now, two things. I wanted to tell you how pleased Mose is with Willard Gabert and the work you introduced from Kenya. He's also pleased about Stephen Overholt. He left for Lancaster last week, after he stopped by and told Mose what you had told him. None of us had any idea what happened those long years ago. Those were awful things to say to a young man. Mose told Stephen he had our full blessing in trying to restore his relationship with Millie Zook. Hopefully, Millie's *daett* has come to the same realization by now. Wisdom does grow with the years sometimes."

Mary's mouth worked. "I...I..."

"*Yah*, I know you do things a little differently, Mary, but I want to encourage you. Not everyone would have the strength to bless the community the way you have after what Josiah put you through. Willard came by on Saturday to thank us personally for the blankets and to see if we would consider helping in the future. He even offered to attend the service to show his *goot* intentions, and Mose accepted. Not every day does the community have an opportunity to support such a cause run by honest people. You are to thank for this, Mary. You are such a blessing." Rachel gave Mary a quick hug. "I know that you will take this praise the right way and not let it go to your head."

"I...I'll try to."

"I know." Rachel gave a little laugh. "There is pain in this life, but there is also joy. The Lord will lead the right man to you when the time comes."

Mary tried to nod, but Rachel had already grasped her arm and led the way back into the kitchen.

"Why don't you help out with the unmarried men's table, as usual?" Rachel whispered on the way. "Willard is here because of you, and you should help us make him feel welcome."

Mary's mind ran in circles, but she managed to stay on her feet when Rachel let go of her arm. Willard was here to thank the community for their support and to secure their future aid. Had she so misread the situation?

Mary picked up several bowls of peanut butter spread and headed toward the unmarried men's table set up in the basement. Several girls passed her on the way and smiled but said nothing. Apparently, Rachel's news about why Willard was here had been passed around. She would have to believe the Lord would help her through this situation even if her knees knocked together. Her heart was an untrustworthy member of her body. Once again she had been totally wrong about a man's intentions.

The long table full of unmarried men came into focus, and Mary slipped up behind the broad backs and whispered, "Excuse me," before trading the full bowls of peanut butter on the table for empty ones. She had turned to leave when she caught Willard's warm smile. Mary's heart pounded furiously as she bolted up the stairs, two steps at a time. Her heart had obviously not received the message yet about his intentions.

TWENTY-SEVEN

Several hours later Mary clutched Danny Boy's reins. The steady beat of his hooves filled the silence around her and Betsy, who was seated beside her. Betsy hadn't spoken since they left the Sunday morning church service.

"Say something," Mary finally muttered. "Anything!"

Betsy smiled from ear to ear. "I am so happy. For once I am at a loss for words."

"You couldn't have had a second letter from Ronald today since it's Sunday." Mary gave her sister a quick sideways glance.

"Silly! I don't need a fresh letter. He is in love with me, and now Willard was at the Sunday services. Just think on that possibility! Is he coming back tonight for the hymn singing?"

"I didn't ask him," Mary told her. "Rachel said Willard was over to speak with Deacon Stoltzfus about the community's future support for his Kenyan mission, and he attended the church service to show his gratitude."

Betsy continued undeterred. "Did you know Willard was coming?"

"Of course not!"

"You know you are in love with him."

"I know I am!" Mary's voice rose to a wail. "But don't say it.

Willard doesn't care about me, and what if he did? We aren't made for each other."

"You two have been in love practically from the moment you met each other," Betsy said. "Apparently, I'm the only one who can face the truth of what that means around here."

Mary bit back a denial. It would not help, and she had no plans to leave the community.

"You should give in to where the Lord is leading you, Mary. Look at me." Betsy bounced up and down on the buggy seat. "I'm planning to stay Amish. Who would have thought it?"

Mary took a deep breath. "That's where you are wrong, Betsy. The Lord was not leading you to leave the community when you thought He was. Why would the Lord now lead me to jump the fence?"

Betsy's smile didn't dim. "If you'd pay attention, you'd know. You two love each other."

"Betsy!" Mary exclaimed. "Stop saying that."

"You don't understand in the least, do you? And I don't blame you, I guess. Not that long ago I wouldn't have believed that Ronald would remember me, so why should you believe that Willard loves you?"

Mary pressed her lips together. "Even if he does, my loving an *Englisha* man is very wrong."

The smile on Betsy's face didn't dim as she pulled the letter from her dress pocket. "If you won't accept what the Lord gives, that's no reason for me to drag my feet. I've read Ronald's letter at least a dozen times already. Remember when you used to get letters from Josiah? My heart would ache."

"I know, and I'm sorry for my attitude," Mary managed. "I should be more sensitive. I am too wrapped up in my own world."

"You don't have to apologize to me." Betsy unfolded the page to read silently for a moment with a blissful look on her face. She finally looked up to say, "The joy of the morning makes up for the sorrow of the night. You should remember that about Willard, Mary. And don't turn him down if he asks you to wed him and join him in Kenya."

"I'm…" Mary searched for words as Danny Boy dashed into their driveway.

Betsy's smile faded, and she glared toward the barn. "There's Stephen's buggy. You had better make up your mind quickly and send that man packing. You don't want to marry a man you don't love, Mary, regardless of how much he proclaims his affections for you. Not when you love someone else. Get that through your head." Betsy returned the letter to her dress pocket with a flourish.

"Whoa!" Mary called out to Danny Boy as they came to a stop beside Stephen's buggy.

Stephen peered at them from his buggy seat with a big smile on his face.

Betsy spoke out of the corner of her mouth. "Remember what I was willing to give up for love. You should do the same, Mary. I know I'm right."

Mary's head spun as she climbed down. Stephen came over to help her.

"Remember!" Betsy hissed under her breath. "Dump the man!"

"You are way behind the times, Betsy," Mary whispered. She greeted Stephen with a smile.

Behind her Betsy scurried off without a backward glance.

His smile didn't fade. "*Goot* to see you, Mary, really *goot* to see you. I had to stop by and share the news with you first."

"When did you get back?" Mary asked. "And do you have *goot* news?"

He unfastened a tug before he answered. "It was a quick trip, but I wasn't sure of Millie's answer, as you can imagine, and I had to find someone who could, you know, take care of the farm while I was gone. I just came back on the Greyhound into Little Falls this morning."

"So Millie said *yah*?" Mary couldn't keep the joy out of her voice.

"She did." His face glowed. "Millie's *daett* still has objections, but the years have softened his heart, and I did, once I found the courage, tell him what you said about the farm and my life in the valley."

"Oh, Stephen!" Mary gushed. "This is *wunderbah*. I am so glad for you."

"Thank you." He ducked his head. "Can I tell you something? I want to, if you don't object, return at least a little of the blessing you have given me."

"*Yah*, okay." Mary waited with her hand on Danny Boy's bridle.

Stephen's smile was gone. "Can we sit in my buggy? I can, if you would let me, take your horse into the barn."

"What do you want to say? I am happy for you, and we aren't dating anymore."

"I know. But there is a great load on my mind, and I would, if we could, speak right now, before my heart is burdened longer with it."

Mary gave in and handed Danny Boy's reins to him. Stephen disappeared into the barn while Mary climbed into Stephen's buggy to settle on the seat.

He returned after a few minutes and joined her. He cleared his throat. "It is, it really is, or it will be okay, I think. I don't mean to sound harsh, or say things which are not true, but it's just that this *Englisha* man, this Willard—"

"Please, Stephen. Don't speak of him. I—"

Stephen held up his hand. "Let me say, if you would, what I have to say. You have done so much, so very much for me, this is the least I can do, difficult though this is to say. This Willard, whom I saw the other day at the co-op..."

Mary held her breath. Someone had seen them together. But what had she expected?

Stephen rushed on. "I came back twice. I'm sorry, but I did, and I peeked in the front door. He was there both times, and you were really talking, as though you like each other. From what I can see,

Willard has eyes in his head, and he's taken plainly enough, Mary, with the woman that you are. He sees your heart for his mission in Kenya. The man has hopes in his heart that...it's hard to say this, Mary, but why would an *Englisha* man, a handsome one to boot, not think, at least consider that you might wed him?"

"I'm trying to do what's right, Stephen," Mary managed to say. "I know I make mistakes, but I'm trying."

"This time you are not understanding what I am saying. Would you, perhaps at least consider, that the Lord is leading you this way? I do know, at least it seems, something about the Lord's leading."

Mary steadied herself on the buggy seat. "We shouldn't be talking about this. It can't be, and talking about the Lord's will does not help."

He ignored her protest. "I know what love can do for a person, Mary. I know what my love for Millie has done, which the Lord has, in His great and marvelous mercy, given me. I never thought this would... Not in all my days of waiting did I think that again I would have what was taken from me. Now, here in my heart is love again, and you, by the Lord's will, opened the door. I wish to also bless your life. You do love the man, do you not?"

Mary's lips moved, but no sound came out.

Stephen nodded. "Is that not a sign enough, if you think about it, Mary? What greater sign could there be? Can you not, at least a little, see that the Lord has already sent, by His grace, help to you before you even knew it was needed? The Lord has opened up the way. He really has, Mary. By your own words, you bear witness to this."

"Are you saying...?" But she already knew what he was saying. "You would have me accept Willard's love if he gives me that love? You are from the community, yet you are encouraging..." The words stuck in her mouth.

Stephen smiled. "Those from the community were wrong about Millie and me. The Lord's ways, all of them, even the ones that are called unusual, are shining lights upon one's path. A beacon of hope for the future. You have followed that path with me, which I can bear testimony to, right into the Lord's will. There is no reason, not even one, that your love for Willard is wrong."

"You would have me jump the fence?" Mary whispered. "Right into the evil world?"

Stephen seemed not to hear. "The Lord would bless you—I know this in my heart, Mary—with great blessings that you cannot even begin, not in your wildest imaginations, to comprehend. If you chose the path the Lord has opened before you... Look where I have been taken, after I thought the whole world had come to an end, when love was ripped from my heart by Millie's *daett*. I had so many hopes and dreams, one could say high expectations, of what life would be like with Millie. You and Willard are all, and so much more, than Millie and I ever were. If you make the right choice...the same path, at least it seems to me, would open up for you. A path full of greater blessing than you could ever, in many, many years, find here in the community with a man you do not love."

"I can't do this," Mary told him. "I appreciate your advice, Stephen, but I can't. I just can't."

He peered down at her. "You cannot follow the Lord's will, then, Mary? It's so plain to see."

"I can't wed Willard," Mary tried again.

"But you do love this *Englisha* man, Willard?"

Mary didn't answer. She hopped down from the buggy to bolt up the walk toward the front door.

Betsy opened it wide. "What happened out there? Did you agree to marry the man?"

"He's encouraging me to marry Willard!" Mary kept going and took the stairs two at a time. She threw herself on her bed and pulled the quilt tight over her *kapp*. She was running away, but from what? The will of the Lord? From Willard?

From the impossible thing her heart desired?

TWENTY-EIGHT

The snow eddied around the buggy wheels as Mary brought Danny Boy to a stop on Friday morning in front of the co-op. She hopped down and unharnessed the horse to lead him into the small shelter behind the building. Several bales of hay and a bag of oats stood against the far wall. Danny Boy bobbed his head and neighed.

"I'll get you some," Mary said. She patted Danny Boy's neck. "You'll be comfy in here, and if the storm gets too bad, we'll leave early."

Danny Boy neighed again, but his attention was clearly focused on food and not on any fear of the storm that threatened from over the Adirondacks. Mary secured him to a ring in the wall and moved a bale of hay within reach. While Danny Boy munched away, she filled a bucket with oats. He plunged his nose into it the moment she set the offering down.

Mary stroked his neck and then headed toward the store. Early morning clouds scurried across the sky as she unlocked the co-op door. She paused for a moment to follow their swift passing. They were not unlike her own troubled soul at the moment. The whole week she had sought peace after Willard's visit to the church service and Stephen's surprising words afterward, but she had found none. Thankfully, Betsy hadn't pushed her point, mostly because her profound happiness dominated her every waking moment.

Mary wondered if she could find such happiness outside the community's warm embrace. How could Stephen be right? But at least his heart was honest. She knew him well enough to know that, and it had taken great courage for Stephen to speak so boldly. Her vision of home had always been wrapped up in her feelings for Josiah or another Amish man, not Willard Gabert. She was grateful that Willard hadn't shown his face since the Sunday services. Maybe these feelings in her heart would blow away like the storm clouds that scurried across the sky. Willard was honorable and true, a man worthy of her affections, but they were from separate worlds. Willard knew this. He would not be back. She should be happy, but she wasn't. She missed him terribly. He was *Englisha*, and she knew better, but those rebukes felt hollow in her heart.

Willard touched her as Josiah had never done. He was what Josiah had never been—a man of integrity. Why must he be an *Englisha* man? An automobile pulled into the parking lot, and Mary closed the co-op door to hurry inside to dry her tears. She did little but rush around of late, running from things—from the shame of her forbidden desires, the hurt and pain they would cause, and the rebukes of her community. Yet her running seemed to accomplish little. Could she face what her heart was saying for once and listen without interruption?

Mary pasted on a smile as the door opened and two women entered. She wondered if they were out-of-towners because she had never seen them before.

"Can I help you?" Mary inquired.

They both smiled a greeting.

"We're just looking around," one of them said. "We heard about the store from a friend and decided today was the day to investigate."

"With a storm brewing over the Adirondacks?" Mary forced a laugh. "I may have to close early."

"We won't be long," the woman assured her. "But plans are plans, and you aren't far off the interstate."

"That's true," Mary agreed. She retreated to the counter.

The two picked up a shopping basket and inspected the rows of shelves with intense exclamations and whispered words. When they passed the end of the aisle, the basket was half full, so the women must have been pleased with what they saw.

Mary's thoughts drifted. She hadn't written poetry in a while. The distractions had been too severe, or perhaps she had awakened from her dreamworld. Wasn't poetry an excessive indulgence of emotions? One could build dreams that never did come true. Kenya, the land where Willard was to return to soon, was a place of heartless honesty. How did one write poetry about ruined lives and broken bodies?

Her dream of home had never included violence, yet Willard lived in a brutal place. How did one raise *kinner* in such conditions? The dangers were almost too much for adults. The community would do what they could with prayers and blankets, but Willard took the biggest risk. He walked alone. What would the woman who stood by the side of such a man have to go through? She would need courage and strength. She would need a firm faith in the Lord. Such a woman must have many virtues, which disqualified her.

Mary gave a little gasp. What thoughts to have. Of course she was not qualified. Willard needed an *Englisha frau* to stand by his side. Such a woman would know how to build a home in a strange land. Mary was a simple woman raised on a farm, one who knew how to run a cash register at the local co-op but had no experience in healing bruised lives. Willard was too *goot* for her. That was the truth!

Mary managed to focus and smile as the women came around the final aisle with their basket filled to the brim.

"What a wonderful place!" one of them gushed. "I can't believe we haven't heard of this co-op before."

"The Amish haven't been here that long," Mary demurred. "Maybe ten or fifteen years."

"You are such an industrious people!" the other exclaimed. "We are blessed to have you in our area."

"Thank you," Mary told them as she rang up their purchases.

They paid with a check and exited with one last look around. "We'll be back," they chorused together.

Mary waited a few moments before she opened the co-op door to peer outside. The storm had increased. Frequent squalls blasted across the treetops and settled fresh snow on the streets. There was little expectation of new customers stopping in today. Did she dare? She wanted to see Willard. Maybe they could straighten things out with a last goodbye before he left for Kenya—if he was still at Mrs. Gabert's place. The least she could do was hurry and seize a last chance to see him. How foolish she was acting, but if she didn't...

Mary closed the door and swept the counter area clean before she exited. Danny Boy looked up at her when she entered the barn, as if he were surprised.

"I told you we might leave early."

But what if someone found out? She told herself this was only a stop in at Mrs. Gabert's place. She should have checked on the woman earlier, but she hadn't amid the kerfuffle with her emotions.

Mary untied Danny Boy and led him outside. Minutes later, the horse was hitched to the buggy, and she guided him out to the street. Danny Boy blew his nose but trotted along eagerly. A warm barn awaited the horse, and they would be home soon. Somehow she would continue to resist Willard's charms, even if he was honorable and decent to the core—a true giant of a man with a heart that could be touched by the needs of hurting and injured people. She might admire him for the rest of her life, his memory a treasure she would never forget, but...

"No, I can't!" Mary proclaimed out loud. "I never can!"

But she still turned into Mrs. Gabert's driveway. If there had been any sign of Willard, she might have driven on, but what sign could there be? Willard wouldn't be out on the porch in this kind of weather. The man never loitered anywhere. He was too occupied with helping people in need. That such a man had even noticed her was a great honor.

Mary turned her face into the wind as she tied Danny Boy to Mrs. Gabert's lamppost beside the garage. The blaze of red up her neck and into her cheeks was from the cold, not her embarrassing thoughts. At least, Mrs. Gabert would think so.

Mary wrapped her coat tighter around herself and made a dash for the front porch. She knocked, and Mrs. Gabert opened at once. "I thought I heard someone. Come in, Mary. Welcome. It's been a while."

Mary tumbled inside with a blast of snow following. "*Goot* morning. How are you?"

"Just fine." Mrs. Gabert chuckled. "You look well yourself. Are you on the way home from the co-op?"

Mary caught her breath. "*Yah.* I decided to call it a day before things get worse."

"The TV says there will be a blizzard by the morning," Mrs. Gabert observed. "Would you care for a cup of hot tea?"

Mary hesitated.

"Come on," Mrs. Gabert told her. "You have that much time to spend with a lonely old woman."

Where's Willard? The question lingered on Mary's lips, but she bit back the words in time.

"I'll have to microwave the water," Mrs. Gabert said with an apologetic look. "No slow boiling like you're used to. I don't want to keep you long."

"I'm sure that will be fine," Mary assured her.

She didn't have enough experience to know what microwaved water tasted like. That's how much she knew about the *Englisha* world. And here she thought...

"Are you okay?" Mrs. Gabert asked.

"I'm fine," Mary chirped.

Mrs. Gabert set a cup of hot water and a box of tea bags on the table, and then she settled in her chair. She faced Mary with a soft smile. "You're not fooling me, dear. What is wrong? You're flushed. Are you sick?"

"No, just troubled. Where's Willard?" To cover her embarrassment, Mary selected a tea bag and began dunking it in the hot water.

"So that's it," Mrs. Gabert mused. "I'm not surprised, but I had almost given up."

"I didn't mean it like that."

Mrs. Gabert laid her hand on Mary's arm. "Love is nothing to be embarrassed about, dear. Willard is still here. He's speaking at a church in Utica tonight. He drove up this morning because of the storm. Now that he has spent Christmas with me and raised the funds he needs, he will be flying out tomorrow morning to Kenya."

Mary looked away. "Oh."

"It's okay," Mrs. Gabert assured her. "I understand."

Mary tried to smile and took a long sip of hot tea. "So how are you taking the cold weather?"

Mrs. Gabert made a wry face. "Like usual, with aching bones, but let's talk instead about you and Willard."

"We shouldn't!" Mary rose to her feet. "I shouldn't have stopped in...I mean, I should have checked on you, but... Oh, this has to stop! It can't be."

"Did Willard disturb you by visiting your services last Sunday?"

"No. *Yah.* I mean, I wouldn't call it disturbing. Our deacon and his *frau* were quite impressed with Willard. I thought maybe...oh, it's awful to say this, but I figured Willard was up to something, like placing pressure on me. But Rachel talked to me afterward about Willard's honorable intentions. He only wanted to thank the community for their help and to see if that could continue. He didn't show up at the co-op all week, so Rachel was right." Mary ended in a gasp. There, she had said the words, and now Mrs. Gabert knew. Relief flooded through her.

Mrs. Gabert's hand reached for hers. "I knew you two were made for each other from the start, Mary."

"No!" Mary gasped. "Willard is leaving tomorrow. That's what you said."

Mrs. Gabert's smile was soft. "I'm sure a phone call would take care of that. Willard can postpone his flight for a week or whatever time is needed until you two have had time to talk. If he knows you stopped by, he'll be here in the morning."

"No! This cannot be!"

"You do love my grandson, don't you?" Mrs. Gabert's question was gentle.

"*Yah*. No. Oh, what a mess!" Mary wailed. "I love him much more than I once loved Josiah. I know what a *wunderbah* honorable man Willard is, but he's *Englisha* like you. I can't leave the community! I can't!"

"Maybe you should take one step at a time," Mrs. Gabert suggested. "Let me call Willard, and you can come back tomorrow afternoon once the storm has let up. Or on Sunday if the roads are not too bad. Will you, Mary?"

"Oh!" Mary moaned. "How can I do something so awful as jump the fence? That's what will happen! I will be excommunicated!"

"You're here," Mrs. Gabert comforted her. "Your heart is leading you, is it not, Mary? Right through your fears? Because Willard loves you, dear, as you love him. You two could bring healing to each other, and only the Lord knows what the full reach of your lives would be in Kenya. Say yes, Mary. Say yes to happiness if nothing else."

"My happiness? That's what I'm *not* supposed to think about if it involves an *Englisha* man."

"Are you sure?" Mrs. Gabert's hand pressed on hers. "Maybe the community will be more understanding than you think."

Mary shook her head and sighed. "They will not. But you are right that I must speak with him. Do you think Willard would be willing to postpone his travel plans?"

Mrs. Gabert's smile was tender. "In a heartbeat, dear. This is more than he ever dared dream would happen."

Mary gulped down the rest of her hot tea and whispered, "Thank you. That was *goot*." Then she bolted out the front door.

TWENTY-NINE

The following morning, Willard stood next to his grandmother's living room window. He watched as the snowplow barreled down the street and out of town. A plume of soft flakes lingered along the roadside long after the machine had vanished from sight. Behind him, his grandmother's Christmas tree still twinkled in the corner.

"Do you think she will come?" Willard asked without turning around. He had followed a similar plow into Fort Plain after his talk at the church last night in Utica. The flight plan change had not been cheap, so the more support he could drum up, the better.

"I told you she would," his grandmother replied from the kitchen table, her cup of coffee between her hands. "Sit down and relax, Willard."

"Maybe I should walk up and see her."

"And undo all the excellent work you have done?"

"I wasn't trying to trick her," he protested. "I wanted to thank the Amish, and I was ready to leave Mary in peace."

"Have faith, son," Mrs. Gabert chided. "You two are meant for each other."

"That's what you keep saying." Willard turned on his heel to fill a mug with coffee. If he had not already developed deep feelings for

Mary Yoder, he would never have agreed to this plan. The whole thing still seemed impossible. An Amish woman as his girlfriend, his future...

Mrs. Gabert regarded her grandson with a smile on her face. "Mary will be a wife unlike any you could have imagined. The Lord has rewarded you for your loyal and faithful service since Carlene left you."

"Grandma, please," Willard begged. "Mary is coming down to talk with me. That's a step, but I've been to their church services. Theirs is another world, believe me."

"And that world is here," Mrs. Gabert said as a soft knock came on the front door.

Willard leaped to his feet, but Mrs. Gabert waved him back. "Let me open the door and welcome her in, and then we can chat around the table. Mary will be more comfortable that way."

Willard waited as Mary entered the house. She didn't look at him as his grandmother helped her out of her snowy winter coat. Mary undid the knot on her dark scarf and stole a glance in his direction. He waved, and her cheeks grew even rosier. He stood and took a tentative step in her direction. Mrs. Gabert scuttled toward the bedroom with her wraps.

"Hi, Mary. I am glad you came down. In fact, I'm delighted. Are you okay?"

"The walk wasn't bad," she said. "I told *Mamm* I was coming to check on your grandmother, which is partly true. But I can't stay long."

He reached for her hand. "I can't say how sorry I am for the trouble this is causing you, Mary. It was only after I came to your services that I realized how deeply this affected you."

"I know. I believe you," she whispered. "You are a man of honor and integrity."

He grinned. "Have you written another poem about me?"

She managed to smile. "No, but you deserve one. A better one than I can write."

"I don't think so. Do you want to sit at the kitchen table? We can talk there."

"Of course she does!" Mrs. Gabert exclaimed from the bedroom doorway. "And I will leave you two alone. I will find my way upstairs and entertain myself in the sewing room for a few hours."

"A few hours!" Mary gasped.

"Or however long you wish to stay," Mrs. Gabert assured her. "I fully approve of you visiting, but I know that you have to live with the consequences."

"*Yah*, I will," Mary agreed, but she still moved toward the kitchen table.

Blessings to you, his grandmother mouthed to him. He smiled his thanks and then followed Mary. His grandmother's footsteps faded on the stairs behind him.

"So..." Willard pulled out a chair and sat across from her.

"Did you want me to visit?" was her first tentative question.

"Mary, of course, with my whole heart! Why else would I have changed my flight? I have...I know I have pushed our relationship too fast and without enough thought of what the consequences would be for you, but let me simply say that I greatly long for our relationship to grow. Perhaps in the future you would become very precious and dear to my heart. You already are, but I don't want to assume too much. The cost for you will be very great. I fully understand that now."

Tears formed in her eyes. "Do you really mean that, Willard?"

"Yes, Mary, I do." He reached for her hand. "With my whole heart. This has been my grandmother's doing at the beginning, but we have long moved beyond that. That day I spent with you at the co-op—you don't know how wonderful that was, how peaceful, how much I need such days in my life. You are so much more than I can put into words."

Her fingers moved in his. "That's so *goot* to hear. I never thought I would say that, or even think it, Willard. I've been running away ever since I met you, and I don't want to run anymore, even if it hurts. I want to trust a man again, one that I care about. That was difficult and almost impossible after Josiah, but no longer. You may be *Englisha*, but you make the road easy, even pleasant to travel."

He shook his head. "Trust me. I'm not all that great. I have my own fears, plenty of them, yet they grow calm when I am with you."

She regarded him steadily for a moment. "What are your fears with me? That you would be left alone again? That I would draw back if the road became tough?"

He glanced down at the kitchen table. "Something like that."

She looked away. "I was afraid to come down today. Maybe you shouldn't trust me. You've already wasted a lot of money canceling your flight."

"I've already been repaid in full, Mary. Even if I never see your face again. Your courage moves me deeply. You are greatly loved in your community—which I cannot be a part of, so you would have to walk away into a new world. You are the one who will pay the greatest price. My fears are small change compared to what you'd have to endure."

Tears began to fall. "Josiah never said anything like that. He took my love and my kisses freely."

"Mary, you don't have to go there." His hand tightened in hers.

"I want to go there," she protested. "I want to remind myself of why I am here."

"But—"

She hurried on. "I know how that sounds, as if I'm running away from my past. I really am not. I just want to know that this time things are different. I don't trust my heart...not as I once did."

"I don't blame you, and I'm not asking you to leave the community if you don't want to."

"Can we not talk about that right now?" Mary pulled out a handkerchief to wipe her eyes.

"Would you like some coffee?" He stood. His own cup had long grown cold.

"How about hot tea?" She attempted to smile.

"I don't know how to make hot tea. Grandma takes care of that."

She laughed. "You run a mission in Kenya and don't know how to make hot tea?"

He joined in with his own chuckles. "I guess I could learn."

"How about I make some?" She stood as well. "I watched your grandmother run the microwave the other day. It can't be that difficult."

"You don't know how to use a microwave?"

Mary made a face. "I come from another world, you know."

He sobered. "What is it like growing up without modern conveniences?"

"Pleasant." She filled two teacups with water. "You don't know that you are deprived, and there is plenty of work to occupy yourself."

"Sounds okay. Maybe I should join?"

"Please don't joke about that, Willard."

"I'm sorry."

She nodded. "Of course, Betsy has another tale. Her scarf caught fire one winter morning after she dumped a dustpan of debris from the kitchen floor into the open flame of the woodstove. It created a mini explosion. Her screams brought *Mamm* running, but there was permanent scarring on her chin despite the doctor's best efforts."

"Childhood accidents," Willard muttered. "They can leave lasting marks, like losing your parents when you are young. Not quite like your sister's scars, but..."

"I'd say worse." Mary sent him a sympathetic glance before she pressed some buttons on the microwave. "That is pain of the heart. I've never heard your story beyond the bits your grandmother dropped here and there."

Willard resumed his seat at the kitchen table. "There's not much to say. I was a small child and my parents didn't come home one day. People tried to explain the accident to me, telling me my mom and dad were in heaven with Jesus, but then I saw them at the funeral home with no life in them. Children struggle with that."

The microwave dinged then. Mary retrieved the cups of hot water from the appliance and set them on the table, along with a box of tea bags she picked up from the counter. "I'm so sorry about that, Willard. You came to live with your grandparents afterward?"

He nodded. "Grandma and Grandpa took me in. They gave me their best." He forced a laugh. "If I have failings, they are my own fault." He chose a tea bag and placed it in the cup in front of him.

"Willard!" A gasp escaped Mary's lips. "You don't have any faults."

He laughed. "Says who? After all..." The words died away.

"Carlene?" she guessed. "I thought I had it rough when my *wunderbah* life shattered. You've had things much worse."

"I lived, and in the end I have no complaints," he assured her.

"That's because you are such a *goot* man. Of course you don't complain, and you lost your parents well before she broke your heart."

He didn't answer, the memories of a long-ago childhood flickering in his mind. The vision appeared distant, as if he saw another person he didn't know, the form small and broken, huddled by a gravestone, tracing names with his finger.

"Willard," Mary called softly to him. "You've had a rough road to walk. Why do you want to complicate your life with me?"

"Complicate?" Surprise filled his face. "You would simplify my life, Mary. Don't you see what you offer? Peace, security, and stability I never had. Grandma tried, but this is different."

"You can minister to hurting children in Kenya without me."

"I suppose so."

"You do so now out of a broken heart. Oh, Willard, you are such a *wunderbah* man."

Tears threatened, and Willard turned his face away. Carlene had never said such things. No woman had ever said them to him, except for his grandmother.

"You haven't touched your tea," Mary whispered.

He reached for the cup and took a sip. "I want to see you again, Mary."

"You are asking to court me? That is impossible, you know."

"And yet you are here."

Tears appeared in her eyes again. "I might be able to hide my trip down today, and a few hours with you at the co-op. But beyond that...I don't know."

"Is that what we have to do? Hide the fact that we're spending time together?"

"I'm not ready for the explosion that will follow, Willard. I've just opened my heart yesterday after running away from this. Can you give me a little time?"

"I'll go back to Kenya, and you can have all the time you want."

"That won't help." She shook her head. "How long can you stay here until you have to leave?"

He smiled and reached for her hand. "For as long as you wish."

"I'm not going to take that kind of time, Willard. Can you give me next week? We can see each other somehow. I'll think of something. We're in the middle of winter, and I can close the co-op for the first part of the week. Betsy will come down with me to visit again, and she can stay with your grandmother while we go somewhere. Can you do that?"

"I will do what works for you," Willard assured her. "With all of my very willing heart."

"You are so kind," she told him. "What if I let you down? What if my courage fails me?"

"I'll take that chance," he said. When Mary stood to leave, Willard called up the stairs to his grandmother. "Mary's leaving!"

She bustled down to retrieve Mary's coat and scarf from the bedroom. He held her hand for a moment before Mary slipped into her winter clothes and went out the door.

"How did things go?" his grandmother asked.

"We're meeting again next week," he told her. "Do you really think this is possible?"

"With all my heart, Willard." Her face glowed with happiness.

THIRTY

Betsy studied Mary for a moment, seated across from her on the couch. This was a winter day in February, and *Mamm* and *Daett* were in their bedroom for a Sunday afternoon nap. Mary had been staring out the window ever since they had arrived home from the church services.

"Were you missing Willard today?" Betsy finally asked.

Mary attempted a smile. "I'd rather not answer that."

"Did Mrs. Gabert tell you he has flown back to Kenya?"

Mary appeared startled. "Did you know Willard was going to leave?"

"No, just guessing, but now I know that you knew. Did you talk with him before he left?"

"Shh...don't even say that," Mary whispered.

"Let's go upstairs." Betsy motioned with her head. "We can talk there. Something is bothering you."

Mary hesitated. "Gerald is in his room across the hall."

A smile crept across Betsy's face. "So you have something to say that Gerald can't hear."

Mary stood but didn't answer.

Betsy followed her sister into the kitchen. "What did you do? I can't imagine you have done anything too radical."

"So you have been saying those things about Willard and me without actually thinking them through?"

"I can't believe this, Mary. What have you done?"

Mary looked away. "I saw Willard yesterday at Mrs. Gabert's. I didn't tell the whole truth of why I went down to check on her."

Betsy bounced onto a kitchen chair and stared at her sister. "But this is *wunderbah*. What a great gift, and Christmas is already long past. I can't believe you followed my advice."

"I didn't. I followed my heart," Mary mumbled. "I am seeing Willard a few times in secret next week, but I'm sure you'll cover for me. After that, I'll have to tell *Mamm* and *Daett* if by then Willard hasn't decided this is enough foolishness. You know what will happen." Mary threw her hands outward. "Explosion!"

Betsy hugged herself. "Oh Mary, you have begun the journey I always dreamed of but was never able to make. You cannot know how delighted I am! This is so, so right and perfect. Words fail me. You and Willard are made for each other."

Mary's face was pained. "Maybe I'll wake up tomorrow morning and come to my senses, but I doubt it. I seemed to have crossed a bridge that has no way back. The man is so...he's honorable and noble, and he has a heart for hurting people, and...and he loves me, Betsy. I can't believe it. I can't help it that he's *Englisha*."

"You don't have to persuade me," Betsy reminded her. "I'm on your side. But why aren't you down there with him this afternoon?"

"I'm not ready for the..." Mary's hands flew outward again.

"No one needs to know," Betsy leaned forward to whisper. "I'll cover for you. I'll think of something. If you hurry, you can be back in time for the evening chores."

"I was just there yesterday."

Betsy waved her arms about. "Just go. We'll think of something next week."

Mary took a deep breath and dashed into the mudroom for her

coat and boots. Betsy waited by the kitchen door until Mary left with a whispered "Thank you."

Betsy went back to the living room and walked over to the window. Mary was already out by the main road. She disappeared moments later down the hill toward town. Betsy fanned herself with her apron. Who would have thought this moment would arrive? Mary, the solid and obedient sister, was sneaking downtown to meet with an *Englisha* man. That would have been one thing several years ago when Mary was on her *rumspringa*, but now Mary was baptized, and that changed everything.

Mary must love Willard deeply to run this kind of risk. Nothing else would cause her mature and steady sister to run off the rails. That's how the community would interpret Mary's actions. Her budding relationship with an *Englisha* man could not be kept a secret for long.

Betsy turned to go upstairs and into her room across from Gerald's. Her brother was probably reading some forbidden novel on a Sunday afternoon, something along the lines of *Tom Sawyer* or *Huckleberry Finn*. Gerald sneaked in books under his shirt when *Mamm* wasn't looking. Everyone was sneaking around except Betsy, the girl who was expected to jump the fence. The whole community had given up on her long ago because of her constant talk and determination expressed over the years.

Betsy sighed and settled on her bed. She slipped her hand under the pillow and pulled out Ronald's letters—two of them so far. The man wrote as well as he danced, with grace and skill. There was nothing forbidden on these written pages, but she liked the thrill of pretending. Who would have thought that she was the one who would choose the Plain path. Not that she had exactly chosen. Ronald had appeared when she had given up on him. He seemed to have taken over her heart, much as Willard had taken over Mary's. How strange things were turning out.

There was still time to turn back. She wasn't married to Ronald or even promised to him. That would come soon enough, and it would lead to everything she had vowed to escape. Things such as dishes that must be washed by hand, cake mixes whisked until one's arms ached, and stoves that exploded into one's face.

Betsy flinched at the memory of the flames. The years had removed none of the pain. How was she supposed to know stoves did such things? No one had blamed her for what had happened. The scars had been there to make their case and block the path to love. She wasn't ugly, but what else had kept the *Englisha* boys from showing an interest in a relationship? She had been available to date. Her desires had not been hidden, but only an Amish man had chosen to love her.

Maybe she had never wanted to escape the community in the first place. Her heart had been ready enough to love Ronald. Hadn't she dropped hints often and in many ways? Her faith had not expected love from the kind of man she had seen in her dreams. That was why she had longed for the *Englisha* world.

Mary, on the other hand, had never wanted to leave the community. Or maybe they hadn't looked deeply enough into what she wanted out of life. Had signs been there all along?

Betsy stared at the envelopes in her hand. She was confused and happy at the same time. Maybe that was how being in love felt. The joy in her heart knew no bounds, and Ronald was an Amish man unlike any she had met before. Why complain about mysteries and lives that didn't turn out as planned?

She had been determined not to submit, not to accept blindly what she could not understand—the injustice, the smiting of the innocent, the unprovoked bruising of body and soul. She had always wondered why the flames had injured her face and not someone else's.

Betsy sat up on her bed. Ronald had somehow broken past those feelings. He hadn't answered the questions that plagued her. He had loomed above them and distracted her, but they were still there.

Mary's use of the word *explosion*, once the community learned of her love for Willard, was no exaggeration. Once more the innocent would suffer. Mary carried nothing but a heart of gold and the purest of intentions. She had planned to marry a solid Amish man, and she had given Josiah her heart, only to have him reject her in a cruel manner. What man had the indecency to marry on the exact day chosen by his former girlfriend? But Mary hadn't grown bitter. She wrote poetry and submitted herself—and look at what had happened. Willard Gabert! Who could explain that?

The situation would grow worse after Mary was excommunicated. That was bound to happen. Betsy was not yet a church member, so she would not have to give her consent to her sister being under the *bann*, but *Mamm* and *Daett* would have to agree to Bishop Miller's council. How could they cast their daughter out into the darkness for loving an *Englisha* man? Mary had always dreamed of a home in the community, but she would serve side by side with Willard in Kenya among children who were truly hurting. Was that a cause for condemnation? How was Betsy to overlook that insult? How could she live in harmony with a community who did such things? Those were flames that seared deeper than skin.

She picked up an envelope and shook out the page.

> *My dear Betsy,*
> *How sweet are my memories of you and of the time we spent together. You are light on your feet when you dance. Did you know that? That must be how you approach life—a skim across the waters, a stone that never sinks. I wish you had been with me this evening. We are just back from a party north of Paradise. They played several of the songs we heard that evening I was with you. As the music surrounded us, I could imagine you with me, in my arms, your breath light on my cheek. Everything about you is light, Betsy. You lift my spirits. I thought I could wait a few months before I made*

the trip back to the valley, but I think I'm coming sooner. I'll
think of some reason while the snow flies. There's not much
going on in Lancaster. Anything I'm doing could be made
better by being with you. Or maybe you can make the trip
down to see me? I have a cousin who could put you up, or
I'm sure you have relatives here who would be glad to see
your lovely face.

Betsy smiled and continued to read. Ronald could shine into her darkest place. The letter continued on with bits and pieces of Lancaster news. Many of the people she didn't know, but she would get to know them if she dated Ronald long enough.

"Take care, sweetheart," the letter concluded. "Don't forget about me."

Betsy folded the paper. She should write back and tell Ronald about the trouble with Mary, but things had a way of spreading once they were said. Even letters to Lancaster might spill the news back into the valley. No, Mary must be given the time she needed to either resolve this issue or light the fuse herself. Betsy would stand by Mary's side through the pain, and because Ronald was special, he would do the same. Somehow Betsy knew that. Ronald was not an ordinary Amish man. He would prove equal to the task. He already loved a woman with scars on her face.

Betsy stood to push back the drapes on the bedroom window. Low clouds rolled in from the Adirondacks, but the afternoon sun seemed ready to break through. Would their life follow that pattern? A brief storm before sunshine?

Betsy saw Mary hurrying up the driveway toward the house. What had the two said to each other—Willard, the *Englisha* man, and her sister, the jilted Amish woman? Had two broken hearts found healing, perhaps even hope for the rough waters ahead?

Betsy went to the bedroom door as she heard Mary's footsteps on the stairs. She peeked out to see Mary's flushed face in the hallway.

"How did things go?" she whispered.

"I didn't stay long," Mary replied before she bolted into her bedroom.

That didn't answer the question, but Mary didn't appear heart-broken. She must be planning to meet Willard again next week.

"What's going on?" Gerald asked from behind her.

Betsy jumped. "Just talking to Mary."

He grunted. "How about some popcorn before the chores? We haven't had any in a while."

Betsy smiled brightly. "Sure, Gerald. It's snowy outside. I'll go right down and make some."

Gerald stared strangely after her as Betsy dashed down the stairs.

THIRTY-ONE

Mary drove Danny Boy down the streets of Fort Plain at a steady trot. Betsy had offered to come along this morning and stay for the day to help at the co-op while she spent some time with Willard, but Mary had said no to that idea. That would have required explaining to *Mamm* and facing questions she didn't wish to answer. *Mamm* had to know that something was afoot, but did she suspect the truth? Mary hoped not. At least not yet.

She didn't quite believe matters herself, that she was sneaking around meeting an *Englisha* man. This activity had to end, and she only had two choices. She could tell Willard goodbye this morning, or she could tell *Mamm* she planned to leave the community. By nightfall Deacon Stoltzfus would appear for a visit, and the horrors of an excommunication would begin. The third option was no option, which was to drag out the decision. She was forced to make up her mind quickly when she needed time for reflection and prayer.

Mary groaned as she approached the co-op. Stephen's buggy was parked in plain sight with his horse tied to a light pole. She had tried not to think further about Stephen's encouragement that she jump the fence, but if the man had changed his mind, his words would cut deep on the day she didn't need to hear them. But maybe this was the Lord's way.

"Whoa there," Mary called to Danny Boy.

They bounced off the street and came to a stop near Stephen's buggy. She might as well face him head-on.

"*Goot* morning," Mary said with a smile.

"*Goot* morning." He nodded. "Can I speak to you inside?"

Stephen had tied up his horse, so he was planning on a long conversation. What if Willard arrived in the meantime with his grandmother's car? Would he know enough to drive on past if a buggy was parked in front of the co-op?

"I guess you can," Mary replied.

She climbed down from the buggy. Stephen unhitched the horse for her, but he stayed behind when Mary led Danny Boy to the shelter behind the co-op. Once inside, she stroked Danny Boy's neck and clung to his mane. Both of her hands shook, and her heartbeat raced. Mary jumped when Stephen cleared his throat by the shelter door, and she let go of Danny Boy to face him.

"Sorry, I mean, I didn't intend, to startle you," he said. "Maybe this is the place, the logical place, at least, to say what I have come to say?"

"Have you changed your mind?" she managed.

He shook his head. "I have come to speak, one more time, to tell you that I know I was right in what I said the other Sunday. I have prayed, all night sometimes, since I spoke with you, and my heart is settled, Mary. I feel very, very deeply that you must accept the love that the Lord has sent your way. I am leaving tomorrow, if the Lord wills, for a long stay in Lancaster. I cannot, really cannot, find peace to begin a serious relationship with Millie until I have said this again."

Mary stared at him. "You are sure, Stephen?"

"I know what you are thinking. I am Stephen Overholt, the slow one, the one who could not have what his heart loved. But that has changed, Mary. I owe you a great debt—one that, in all my years, I can never repay. Praying for you is the least, the very least, that I can do. And I have prayed. I have given thanks for Millie's love, and for you, for what you did, I mean." A tear trickled down Stephen's cheek. "You should accept the love of this *Englisha* man. You really should."

"I'm thinking about what to tell Willard," Mary whispered. "You are very kind. Did you come down this morning just to tell me that?"

"I did. It seemed very important, heavy on my heart, to tell and encourage you to choose the right way."

"Thank you, Stephen. I am searching. That's all I can say for now. I hope that satisfies you."

He nodded. "I'd best be going. The Lord bless you greatly."

Mary stared at the empty shelter doorway for a long time. Stephen had a tender heart, which she had known for some time. But was the man right about Willard? Twice Stephen had come to her with the same advice. He thought she should leave the community to be with Willard.

Mary took slow steps out of the shelter. Thankfully, there were no cars in the parking lot, and she would have a few seconds to collect her torn emotions. What if she did decide to follow Willard to Kenya? Several roadblocks stood in her way. For one, *Mamm* and *Daett*'s approval; second, what the community would think; and third, leaving the life she had known and loved her whole life.

Was there some way her choice could be made easier? Maybe she should take a trip over to Kenya with Willard and test the ground before making a final choice. Wouldn't that be for the best? Betsy would go along if she asked. Once Mary was on the ground in Nairobi, Willard might see that she was the wrong *frau* for him. Or she might come to her senses if this was the kind of temptation the community warned about.

Such a journey would be highly irregular for a baptized Amish girl, even if Betsy came along. Amish people stayed off of planes unless they had no other choice. Suspicions would be stirred, even though no one besides Betsy and Stephen knew of her love for Willard. If she told Willard this morning to leave and never come back, she could save her reputation, her honor, and perhaps her *goot* sense.

Mary unlocked the co-op door and lit the gas lanterns. The sun had risen hours ago, but the soft glow of warm light comforted her. She needed illumination at the moment, whatever light she could find. Her life would be forever changed if she took the opportunity Willard offered her. But perhaps she was way ahead of herself. He must be struggling with the same doubts she did about the wisdom of their relationship. He had been betrayed before by a woman he loved, and his heart must be seared in ways she couldn't imagine. That he had pursued her to this extent was a credit to the man's courage. Everything about her screamed of failure, yet Willard had been so kind yesterday afternoon, so gentle and understanding.

"I have been around your people most of my life," he'd told her. "I know the risks, but I want to know you better, Mary."

She clung to the counter for a moment. She wanted to see Willard again. He had said he would come past this morning. Mary peeked out of the co-op window at the sound of a car in the parking lot, but Mrs. Gabert and Willard were not inside. Had Willard changed his mind? He wasn't like that.

"*Goot* morning," Mary greeted the customer.

Another one came in a moment later, and the morning advanced with no sign of Willard or Mrs. Gabert. A few Amish people arrived from a district to the south of Fort Plain. They were from a different *Ordnung* and had always regarded the folks who'd moved from Lancaster with suspicion. If she caused a scandal by jumping the fence after her baptism, their fears would only worsen. This was what life in the community was like. You were connected to others, and your decisions affected them. You couldn't control that.

Mary forced herself to smile. "Can I help you?"

"*Yah*," one of the Amish women replied. She returned Mary's smile. "We heard you had pecans and walnuts on sale and might be able to get peaches in early this summer for a reasonable price."

"Ah, I think we can," Mary told her. "I've only been here for two summers, and it's a little early in the year yet to know what fruit we can get in."

"I understand," the Amish woman replied. "But you do have the pecans and walnuts in bulk?"

"*Yah*, they are over in the front aisle."

"Do you have fifty pounds of each in stock, of *goot* quality?"

Mary's head spun. "I'll have to check." She turned and paused. "You can come with me."

The Amish woman followed Mary and examined the bagged nuts. "They look *goot*," she declared. "I'll take everything you have."

"Ah, let me get a cart." As Mary hurried out of the storeroom, she almost ran over Mrs. Gabert, who waited in the aisle.

"Is this a bad time?" Mrs. Gabert asked.

Mary searched the store in either direction. "Is Willard here?" she whispered.

Mrs. Gabert lowered her voice. "He's at the cemetery. Let me help you until the store is cleared, and I can handle things after that."

"Okay," Mary agreed. She came back pushing the cart, and Mrs. Gabert followed her back to the storeroom. "This is my helper for the day," Mary informed the Amish woman.

Disapproval flickered for a moment before the woman smiled. If the woman knew Mary was about to head out for a meeting with an *Englisha* man, she would not be smiling. Mary kept her gaze on the floor as they loaded the bags of nuts in a cart, and then the Amish woman paid for them at the front counter.

"I'll help you load them," Mary offered.

She pushed the cart outside and loaded the bags into the open car trunk.

An elderly *Englisha* man sat in the driver's seat and called out of the car window, "I'd help you, but getting in and out of this vehicle takes a lot of effort."

"I'm fine. Thank you," Mary told him.

They loaded the bags, and the Amish ladies climbed in. The

elderly driver gave her a wave and a smile before he drove off. Mary pressed back the tears. She needed that touch of kindness at the moment.

Mary stared down the road until the car vanished from sight. When she returned to the co-op, Mrs. Gabert was with a customer in the bulk candy aisle, prattling away. "I don't know these Amish cooks personally, but I can assure you that anything made by the community women is worth any price you pay. In fact, these prices are quite low, if you ask me."

Mary couldn't keep back a smile. Mrs. Gabert was a born saleswoman. She made the best of any situation, and improvised if she had to. That was one reason Mary had considered a relationship with Willard—because of his grandmother. Mrs. Gabert had opened the door, but no amount of sales talk could have compelled Mary to walk through unless her heart desired what lay beyond.

Maybe the Lord had known this from the beginning. Maybe her dream would have been crushed if she had married Josiah. He'd never understood her the way Willard obviously did. What if she had been on the wrong road, and this was the only way to correct her path?

Mary kept a smile on her face as she checked out six bags of bulk candy at the counter. Mrs. Gabert kept up a steady chatter the whole time and held the door for the woman on the way out.

"How did I do?" Mrs. Gabert inquired once the store was empty.

"You are quite something."

Mrs. Gabert smiled. "Thank you, dear, but you had best go. Willard is waiting. Do you know the way?"

"I do." Mary pulled on her coat and slipped out the back door of the co-op.

THIRTY-TWO

Mary paused for a moment at the twin pillars of the Fort Plain Cemetery entrance. Where was Willard? Ahead of her, the snow was light on the ground beneath the trees, with well-shoveled paths between the drifts. Was she to search for Willard across the extended grounds? Mrs. Gabert hadn't been clear on the details of where he might be.

Mary slipped around the open gate rail and behind the concrete structure. As she walked around the trees, Willard appeared among the gravestones with his back turned, apparently lost in contemplation. She approached and called his name.

He turned and smiled. "Mary. You came."

"Of course." She stilled her breathing. "It's peaceful up here."

He nodded. "No interruptions. No buggies coming by. Can I show you something?"

She followed him across the snowy ground, and he motioned with his hand. "My grandfather, Benny. My mother, Pricilla, and my father, Howard." Willard stooped in front of his father's gravestone to trace the name with his finger.

Mary moved closer and laid her hand on Willard's shoulder. "I'm so sorry. How old were you?"

He looked up into her face. "Ten. They left me with my grand-parents that evening for a date in Utica. The state police found a dead deer a hundred feet from the place where their car went through the rail and into the river canal. The fall alone, and the water…" Willard's voice trailed off. "They didn't let me close to the scene that night, but I went on my own when I could. The rail had been fixed. The new pieces blended in with the old, and the trees were bent and struggling to grow back. Grandpa did what he could to fill dad's place, but he had already raised one family. It wasn't fair, but then life isn't fair."

Mary's fingers dug into Willard's shoulder. "Your grandmother never told me the details."

"Grandma wouldn't." His eyes were moist. "She prays and does what she can, but the big things belong to God. I've never heard her say that in so many words, but that's how she lives."

"Is this why you wanted to meet me up here?"

He nodded and stood. "We should start here, if we are to begin, Mary. I don't want to hide anything, even though it hurts. I don't want to pretend. I care a lot about things, maybe too much. It's best if you know that."

Mary looked away. She would be a blubbering mess soon. The pain on his face cut deeply into her soul. She thought Josiah had caused her a great sorrow, but compared to Willard, she had suffered little.

"What did your grandma have to say about Carlene? When you… when she…" Mary stopped. She had no right to these questions.

Willard's smile was tender. "I'm glad you asked. No secrets, right? So here goes. Grandma didn't approve of Carlene, but she told me the choice was mine. I was the one who would marry her, and that was Grandma's final say in the matter. When the relationship ended, she cried more than I did."

"Mostly tears for you, I suppose." Mary reached for his hand, and Willard didn't pull away. "She cares a lot about you."

"I know. She's the closest thing to a mother that I have."

"Were you close to your mother?"

Willard shrugged. "I don't know how to rate mother and son relationships. Dad and I were close. Mom never interfered. She was there when I needed her. Smashed finger, bruised knee, hungry stomach. I miss them both a lot."

"Did you ever bring Carlene up here?"

A smile played on his face. "Come to think of it, I never did."

Mary squeezed his hand. "Then I am honored. Thank you."

"You are?" He glanced down at her.

"*Yah*. Family is important, and community and sharing."

He winced and looked away. "I am not part of your community, and I can never be. Maybe that's why I'm really up here, to make myself face what you are losing. I don't think I should ask that of you because I can never come your way, Mary. I have said that before, but I want to make that very clear again."

"I understand."

"You do? The cost to you?"

She pressed her lips together. "You are more important than my pain. That will go away."

"I don't know if I like that, Mary."

She looked up at him. "Did Carlene promise you a lot of things?"

He didn't meet her gaze. "Yes, and I believed her."

"Is that the hardest part? Believing that I would pay so much to love you? When the cost was too much for someone else?"

"So you *do* understand."

"Maybe, Willard," she whispered. "I don't know. I'm not promising. I'm doing. I want to come on a trial trip to Kenya with you. Let me see if I fit, and if you like the fit. I'm sure Betsy would accompany me."

He didn't answer for a moment. "So that's what we are, two broken pieces that seem to fit? What if we can't see clearly enough through our tears to tell?"

"Or the pain of our hearts?" she added. "At least we are honest, Willard. You have asked the same questions I have."

He nodded. "That is true, but I have only a heart to lose—one that's already broken. Not much, I would say, compared to the life you would lose in the process. Have you thought about that?"

Tears stung. "More times than you know. Yet I am here."

"Bravery, stubbornness, determination..."

"Maybe...I like you?"

He hesitated. "You would change your life on that, Mary?"

"And you would trust me after Carlene?"

"Yours is the greatest cost."

"To marry a woman who does not love your life's work is a burden no man should be asked to bear."

"Is that what I was spared from?"

"I did not mean to offend you, Willard, but would you hold her failures against me?"

"I am not worthy of you, Mary. That's the problem."

"So let me come to Kenya with you. Let's ask our questions there. I can put things back together with the community if it doesn't work. And then you would know, wouldn't you, if marrying me will work for you and the mission?"

"And you would know too. This is not a one-way street, Mary."

"I know." She held on to his hand. "Let me love you, Willard, as I love your work, your passion, your care for others. Trust me enough to take me with you so I can see it for myself. Will you do that?"

His gaze rested on the tombstones in front of them. "This is not how our conversation should be going, Mary."

"You are wrong on that," she insisted. "Very wrong."

A hint of a smile crossed his face. "So you want to come to Kenya, to the dirt and grime of Nairobi, to see the missionary in action?"

"To see your *heart* in action, Willard," she corrected. "To see more of you that I can love."

"You will be honest about Kenya?" Doubt flickered on his face.

"And you will show me the worst?"

They laughed, the sound tinkling among the bare treetops.

"It seems we do have some trust issues," he allowed.

"You know how much I already love Kenya and your work there," she told him. "I have already taken great risks with the community. I do not speak out of thin air, Willard. It's just that..."

"It's okay. I don't doubt you, and I will believe you, even if you decide that Kenya is not right for you. But will you be able to come back and mend fences with that deacon of yours? You can blame me, I guess. Tell him I lured you into danger, tempted you into the world."

She faked a glare at him. "You pulled the wool totally over Deacon Stoltzfus's eyes with your visit to our services. You are a charmer, Willard."

His eyes twinkled. "I was being perfectly honest. I wasn't trying to entrap you in the least."

"Yes, you were." Mary lowered her eyebrows at him. "You are a very naughty boy."

"So you do care about me a little bit?" Willard teased.

"I'm not going to answer that. You already know too much."

Their laughter echoed against the foothills.

He sobered and faced her. "To win your love and affection, Mary, your devotion above all, would be a dream beyond my wildest dream, because dreams are about the imagined, and I have never imagined you. I dare not think about you too much. You are a mirage, I think, or a vision would be a better way to describe you—one that might disappear in a moment, never to return."

She bowed her head. "What am I suppose to say to that? Do you want promises? I don't have them. They failed me with Josiah. I am just here, willing to take the first step with you and leave the rest to God. Is that *goot* enough?"

"You are truly something," he said. "So beautiful and open."

"Don't try the charm on me, Willard Gabert. It won't work."

He stepped closer and regarded her with a steady gaze. "So what do you think of me?"

She didn't flinch. "You are different from Josiah. You are stronger at the core. You seem encircled with a halo of pain and sorrow, but you are tender and determined at the same time. You are a man I can love with my whole heart. Why should I walk away from that? Answer me that question."

Tears were bright in his eyes. "I will not try, Mary. You are beyond me."

She took both of his hands in hers. "Don't underestimate yourself, Willard. Look at what you already faced in Kenya. The dark night you have suffered. You have walked on when you had every reason in the world to turn back. You have loved when there was no hope. You have given when you had nothing for yourself. I see a man, a tower of strength and courage, whom I can follow and trust. I don't promise, Willard. I'm telling you what is true. With you, I feel as if I have come home and found the key to the door."

"Whew..." he said. "Isn't that a little too much?"

"You will take me to Kenya, then?" She pled with her eyes.

"Mary!" he scolded. "Don't look at me like that. Of course I will take you. I am the one who should be on my knees begging you to come."

"You should not!" She tilted her head toward him.

"Are we going to argue all day up here?"

"Only if you insist."

"Then I surrender. You are coming to Kenya with me."

She reached for him and pulled him close. His gaze lingered on her face until he lowered his head and their lips met. They clung to each other under the whisper of the wind in the trees.

"Passing grade?" She peered up at him.

"You are asking me?"

Her smile was crooked. "You have never kissed an Amish girl before."

"You hope," he said.

"Willard!" Horror filled her voice. "Stop teasing me."

"I don't deserve a woman like you, Mary." He laughed. "I already told you that."

"How will I know when it's time to go to Kenya?"

He held her at arm's length to gaze into her face. "You can stop in at Grandma's, or I can come to the co-op when it's time. Either way, we'll stay in close touch."

"*Yah*, we will," she whispered. "Oh, Willard."

"To the future, then. To Kenya and to beyond. To what lies on the horizon for us."

"*Yah*," she said. "To our love."

He took her hand, and they walked down the hill, pausing to look back at the massive entrance pillars, their gazes turning and lingering on each other.

THIRTY-THREE

Mary stood in front of the flickering light of the kerosene lamp set on top of her dresser and put the last pins into her dress. She took a deep breath when a knock sounded on the bedroom door.

"Come in."

Betsy's face appeared. "We have to talk. Gerald's not up yet."

Mary nodded. She had expected Betsy's early morning visit. There had been no opportunity to speak in private before bedtime last night.

"Tell me what happened yesterday." Betsy came closer, her voice a whisper.

Mary composed herself for a moment. Her plan to defy the community's guidance was the right choice, but she had never walked this road before.

"What, Mary?" Betsy reached out her hand. "Did you do something terrible?"

Mary shook her head. "Will you come to Kenya with me?"

"Kenya!" Betsy's hand dropped. "You want me to move to Kenya with you?"

"No, to visit," Mary corrected. "Willard has agreed that I can visit so we can be sure this is the right choice for him and for me."

Betsy sat on the bed and fanned herself, speechless for a moment.

"You will come with me, won't you?" Mary turned to face her.

"*Yah*, of course." Betsy continued to wave her hand. "I'm collecting myself, that's all. So you are doing this! Finally. I...I never quite thought the day would come. Still..."

"I know how strange this is." Mary seated herself beside her sister. "Almost like a dream, and yet it's going to happen. You were right, Betsy. Willard and I were made for each other. Our hearts have walked much of the same road through life. Well, not exactly, but we have both suffered."

Mary paused, and Betsy waited for more information. Mary took a deep breath and continued. "Willard told me the story yesterday of how he lost his parents when he was ten years old, and about being abandoned by his girlfriend, Carlene, which was even more painful than what I experienced with Josiah. Yet the man continued with his duties on the mission field. He is a strong man, Betsy, a survivor who is full of faith. I cannot walk away from him, whatever the cost. I would regret my decision the rest of my life."

"I know," Betsy agreed, "but I wouldn't try this spiel with *Mamm*. Just warning you. Better that you leave quickly and not come back."

Mary paled. "I can't do that. There must be some way to explain. A visit to Kenya makes perfect sense to me."

Betsy shook her head. "It's not going to work. I would simply disappear if I were you."

"But I have to visit there first. Willard and I agreed to that. I can't push him into a decision before the trip, and neither will I be pushed into one without being certain that I am right."

Betsy shrugged. "You know I don't object to a trip with you—anywhere, in fact. Of course I'll go."

"Thanks. That's the first step, I guess. I'll have to feel my way from there."

"I'll support you, but this will not be easy."

"If only *Mamm* and *Daett* could listen to Willard the way I have…"

Betsy grunted. "That will never happen, but you can try to tell them what Willard is like. Maybe I'm wrong that they won't listen. But if you have to explain, it's only going to get worse the longer you wait."

Mary nodded. The moment had arrived. She forced herself to stand and followed Betsy out into the hallway.

Gerald greeted them with a suspicious look from his bedroom doorway. "What have you two got up your sleeve? I heard whispering in your bedroom, Mary."

"You had best come and hear this," Betsy informed him. "Hopefully *Daett* hasn't left for the barn."

"What have you done now, Betsy?" Gerald glared at her.

"Just come," Betsy told him from halfway down the stairs.

Mary waited until Gerald had passed her. That he didn't suspect her cut deep. That was about to change, and she would never be the same.

"*Daett*!" Betsy called ahead of them. "Come into the kitchen, please."

"Why the kitchen?" *Daett* asked. "Have you already burned the toast?" His laugher rumbled as he placed his winter coat near the woodstove.

Mary couldn't hear Betsy's answer, but *Daett* was seated on a kitchen chair when she walked in. No trace of teasing was left on his face. *Daett* must have picked up the seriousness of the situation.

Gerald parked himself by the stove and rubbed his hands together. "Why do I have to listen to this female drama? Did Betsy's boyfriend already dump her? What's wrong with my sisters that they can't keep their men?"

Betsy ignored him to glance at *Mamm*, who stood near the kitchen sink. "Perhaps you should sit down."

Mamm turned pale but didn't move.

"What is this?" *Daett* demanded. "You had best speak quickly, Betsy. If you have plans to reject Ronald Troyer and jump the—"

"It's about Mary, *Daett*," Betsy interrupted.

"Mary!" *Daett* and *Mamm* exclaimed together.

Gerald appeared incredulous. "What has she done?"

"That's what we're here for," Betsy said. "If you would calm down and listen and not get too excited, we can explain this. At least we can try."

Mary tried to breathe. How could Betsy be so bold in the face of *Mamm* and *Daett*'s disapproval? Years of threatening to jump the fence must have hardened Betsy to this kind of confrontation.

The room spun as Mary forced the words out. "I need to make a trip over to Kenya with Betsy and Mrs. Gabert's grandson, Willard."

Daett appeared puzzled. "I know you have been involved with the man's charity projects, daughter, but a trip over to Kenya? Do you think that is wise? It might seem as if you are taking things too far even with your interest in missions."

"I want...I want to..." Mary ran out of breath.

Betsy jumped in. "Willard is a very nice man. He's honorable, noble, cares about suffering people, and has suffered himself. You should think about that."

Daett's puzzlement had only increased, and *Mamm* had yet to make a sound. *Mamm* knew, somehow, how serious this was.

"Willard is a *wunderbah* man," Betsy insisted. "Give Mary time, and she can tell you firsthand."

"Mary?" *Daett* turned toward her. "What is this about?"

Mary kept her gaze on the kitchen floor. "I have to make a trip to Kenya so I can be sure, so Willard can be sure, that we are doing the right thing. Because we...because I care about the man a lot. Much more than I was willing to admit for some time, and now I must face the truth. I am...we may..." Mary gave up. She couldn't say the words.

Daett leaned forward in his chair. "You are what, Mary?"

"She has *feelings* for the man!" Gerald's incredulous voice filled the gap. "Now I have heard everything. I will bury my head in the barnyard mud and wear sackcloth and ashes at the next Sunday service."

"At least Mary is not marrying him without first testing the waters," Betsy chirped.

Daett and *Mamm* stared at her in stunned silence.

Mary struggled to speak. "I know this is a shock, and I am to blame for not saying something sooner, but I wasn't certain myself. I had plenty of doubts, and I resisted the temptation for a long time before—"

"You are jumping the fence." Gerald couldn't recover. "My sister Mary. Have you thought of our family's reputation? Betsy was bad enough, but she was always this way."

Daett was on his feet. "What has gotten into you, Mary? We've lived for years with Betsy's talk on this subject, but thank the Lord that's all it was—talk. With you, we..." He shook his head.

"Are you really going to do this?" *Mamm* whimpered from the kitchen sink.

"Mary wants to visit Kenya so she can find out for sure whether this decision is right for her," Betsy offered. "Isn't that a sensible thing to do? I think it is."

"Nothing is sensible about this!" *Daett* bellowed. "How has this been going on under our noses?" *Daett* turned to face *Mamm*. "Have you known about this, Mandy?"

Tears sprang to *Mamm*'s eyes. "I have many faults, Kenneth, as you know. One of them is not noticing things. I should have, but I didn't."

Mary spoke up. "*Mamm* is not to blame. I am the only one to blame, *Daett*, and I've tried to explain my reasoning. At first I saw this as a temptation and not from the Lord, but then I came to realize—"

"This *is* a temptation!" *Daett* declared in no uncertain terms. "This has always been a temptation. You had the *goot* sense to see that at first, so what changed your mind? Did your broken heart overcome you? Or did you pity Stephen Overholt and think you had to marry him? But that makes no sense. I heard that Stephen has patched things up with Millie Zook."

"I know that," Mary said. "Stephen has nothing to do with this. He has been supportive of me and Willard, but I made up my own mind."

"Stephen told you this is of the Lord?" *Daett* half rose from his chair. "How many times has the man thought the Lord had given him a certain woman? No doubt he tried the same trick on you. Stephen thinks everything is from the Lord. Why did you believe him about Willard when you didn't understand his own desire to wed you? The man is seriously confused."

Mary kept her voice steady. "I know how this appears, but I came to my own conclusion on the matter. I believe I am called to stand beside Willard as his *frau* and to work with him in his mission. I...I love the man and everything about him."

"The woman has lost her mind!" *Daett* declared. "As the Scripture says, much sorrow has cooked her brains."

Gerald choked back a laugh. "I don't think that's in the Scriptures."

Daett glared at him. "You can laugh at a moment like this?"

"Sorry," Gerald muttered. "I was overcome, but who wouldn't be with what Mary is doing?"

Daett threw his hands in the air. "It looks to me as if some other people in the house have been overcome. This is beyond me. I have chores to do, and you women have breakfast to make. Let's get those things done, and then I'll go to pick up Mose. The deacon will know what words must be spoken in a time like this."

The mudroom door slammed as *Daett* left, with Gerald trailing close behind him.

Betsy began to follow the men. "Are you two okay without me in the kitchen? I really should help the men with the chores."

Mamm nodded, and Betsy left.

Mary forced herself to walk over to the stove.

Mamm's gaze followed her. "Now that we are alone, would you mind telling me what is going on, Mary?"

"I don't think anything I can say will help, *Mamm*."

She lit the fire in the stove, her fingers numb.

"What have I done to bring this about?" *Mamm* asked. "My prayers and focus were on Betsy and her problems. Now, when the battle seems won, you give in to temptation. If I failed you, I am sorry, Mary. I should have prayed for you more after Josiah broke off your relationship. I thought you were doing so well."

"It's not your fault," Mary whispered. "I don't think anyone is to blame. What is to be, will be. The Lord's will cannot be argued with."

"You would blame this on the Lord?" Horror filled *Mamm*'s voice.

Tears stung Mary's eyes. "No, I blame myself. Is that what you want to hear? If there is blame, there must be a mistake, but I don't think I've made one. I see clearer every passing hour—and yet of course, I could be wrong. That's why I'm going to Kenya, *Mamm*, for Willard's sake and for my own. He doesn't deserve to have his heart broken the second time. Not when he dared love again after the pain he's been through. Can't you see how clearly the light is shining on this path? I know that Willard and I do not come from the same world, but I believe we were made for each other. Willard is the man of my dreams. He fulfills them perfectly, beyond what I would have imagined possible. His heart is tender yet strong. He is brave, can stand terrible storms, and yet guide me and our *kinner*—if the Lord should give us any—with a kind and steady touch. Please try to understand."

"Your sorrows have affected you," *Mamm* whispered. "I should have known better than to allow you to write poems. I thought poetry harmless, but I was so wrong. Fantasies are dangerous things. They give us wrong ideas. The soul is puffed up with great words and floods of emotion. Maybe that's what Josiah saw in you that scared him away. I have always wondered what it was."

Mary's eyes burned from crying. "I never showed Josiah my poems, *Mamm*. How can you say that?"

"Men know," *Mamm* insisted. "Just as women know. How could you suddenly take this turn, Mary? Nothing happens suddenly. Josiah must have seen what you were capable of and was simply unable to explain himself."

"I'm not going to argue with you," Mary replied. "Maybe I have always been flawed. Maybe I never should have dreamed, but I did. Now I love a man, and I can't go back...unless I am wrong. That's what the Kenya trip will show me."

Mamm clutched the countertop to steady herself.

"I'll fix breakfast," Mary told her. "I'll work fast, and it will be ready by the time the men come in. Just sit down."

Mamm hesitated before she took a chair. She stared at Mary. "You were always such a sweet baby, the easiest one of the family to care for at night. I don't think you once had colic. I had you out of diapers right after your first birthday, more because of you than me. You came to me and made yourself understood long before you could speak a sentence. You've always been that way, Mary. What happened?"

Mary finished laying bacon strips in the pan before she answered. "I don't know, *Mamm*. I would rather not talk about this."

"You know that's not going to happen," *Mamm* told her. "Deacon Stoltzfus will want a full explanation, and the community will want to know. They deserve to be told why you are breaking your baptismal vows."

"Guilt is not going to work on me, *Mamm*. I've already been over those points." Mary turned the bacon pieces over with a fork, and the sizzle from the pan rose higher.

"I ask because I want to know," *Mamm* said. "No one is trying to make you feel guilty."

"Okay. I'll try to explain. This is how I feel. I think the Lord has opened the door for me to true love this time. To a cause and a man I can give my whole heart to without reservations. My experience with Josiah appears foolish now, as if I were imagining a world that didn't exist. If you want to know the truth, that's what Josiah must have sensed. He never showed the slightest interest in my poetry, *Mamm*. Not that I thought he should have, but looking back, I think a man should appreciate what his *frau* can do. At least he should know about what makes her who she is. I had planned to show Josiah my poems once we were married, but I think he would have broken my heart. With Willard, he knew more about me in the first few days than Josiah learned in the years we dated."

Mamm had paled. "So this was going on from the first, but I was just too blind to see? Those quilts the community made for you, Mary...You knew all that time and were deceiving everyone?"

Mary removed the bacon and then cracked the eggs into the pan. "Why do you accuse me of deceiving people, *Mamm*? That's the worst thing you could say."

"It is?" *Mamm* stared out the kitchen window. "The truth is...I don't know what to say or what I'm saying. Why am I sitting here while you make breakfast? What has happened to us, Mary?"

"I don't know." Tears trickled down her cheeks, and Mary wiped them away before flipping the eggs in the pan. Her hand slipped and punctured two of the yolks, their yellow gooeyness turning solid as they ran across the hot metal.

Now *Daett* would have a spoiled breakfast on top of the news that his stable daughter planned to jump the fence.

Mary turned away from the stove as *Mamm* came closer. They embraced, the eggs sizzling on the stove as they clung to each other and wept.

THIRTY-FOUR

Mary sat on the living room couch with *Mamm* beside her, while outside the house *Daett*'s buggy rattled into the lane. Deacon Stoltzfus would be with him. The breakfast dishes sat unwashed on the kitchen counter. They could wait, and perhaps they wouldn't be washed before the sun set. Anything seemed possible at the moment.

Thankfully, Gerald was in the barn to complete the chores, and *Mamm* had shooed Betsy upstairs. No doubt her sister would creep back down to listen in the stairwell once the discussion was underway. At least Mary wouldn't have to repeat any of the painful details to her sister. Mary kept her eyes straight ahead, with her hands clasped in her lap. If Willard saw her now, she would appear a proper Amish woman, demure and submissive, but Deacon Stoltzfus would not be fooled. On their buggy ride back to the farm, *Daett* had certainly told the deacon of her rebellion.

Mamm rose from her rocker and shuffled toward the front door. She waited with her hands on the doorknob until *Daett* and Deacon Stoltzfus were outside on the porch.

Mamm opened and stood with downcast eyes.

"Mandy!" the deacon exclaimed. "Are you okay?"

Tears streamed down *Mamm*'s face. "Oh, to see Rachel at this hour of our trouble."

Deacon Stoltzfus took off his hat and stood with a bowed head. "I would have brought Rachel along, Mandy, but someone had to look after the youngest ones."

"The Lord will grant us grace," *Mamm* said, her voice choking. "But it is *goot* of you to come on such short notice."

Deacon Stoltzfus nodded and entered the room.

Mary's fingers dug into her hands, as *Daett* comforted *Mamm* with a hand on her shoulder. "Please gather yourself together, Mandy. We don't want to keep Mose longer than necessary."

"I'll stay for the time needed," Deacon Stoltzfus assured them. "And perhaps I can bring Rachel back this evening after we've had time to find one of the nieces to babysit."

Mamm wiped her eyes. "Thank you! I'm so sorry."

"You have our full understanding," Deacon Stoltzfus assured her.

Daett cleared his throat and motioned Deacon Stoltzfus to a chair. "We really must move on with this. Mose has his own place to care for. I hope you understand that I wouldn't have bothered you if this were not such a great shock to us."

"This would be a rude awakening for anyone." Deacon Stoltzfus glanced sternly at Mary. "It appears our faithful church member has not been as faithful as we thought. Is this true, Mary? Are you planning to jump the fence and marry Willard Gabert? The man who was so recently at our church services—apparently under false pretenses? Here the community opened their heart and arms to what we thought was a worthy mission project, only to learn that Willard was luring one of our best unmarried women away with him. How long has this been going on?"

"That is not what happened," Mary protested. "I can explain, but I doubt if you will agree with me."

"Not if your conclusions lead you to leave the community," Deacon Stoltzfus told her. "For us, the Lord's will is found among our own people. We love and support one another, not out there in the world. We don't stand in judgment of Willard Gabert or his mission work, but he was not raised in the community. The Lord will deal with Willard and his beliefs. You have been taught differently, Mary. You are responsible for things that Willard is not. We know that the Lord's yoke is easy and His burden light, so why are you walking away from us? You are leaving behind many broken hearts."

Mamm sobbed beside the living room window, gazing out at the morning sun. "Listen to the deacon's wisdom, Mary," *Mamm* begged. "You still have time to correct your ways before permanent damage is done."

"And listen to your *Mamm*," Deacon Stoltzfus added. "An apology to your family would be a start. Then you should cancel this foolish trip to Kenya. What has gotten into you? You have such a *goot* reputation in the community. You are a trusted woman. That's why our women made quilts for the Kenyan glue boys. The whole community was stirred in our hearts with compassion, but this is..." Deacon Stoltzfus paused, searching for words. "You have deceived us, Mary. Deception is never of the Lord. What kind of example is this to your sister, Betsy—a young woman whose life has begun to turn around? You must have prayed a few prayers on her behalf. Is this not true, Mary?"

"I did." Mary kept her gaze on the floor. "I'm not going to argue with you, Deacon, or blame anyone for what I am doing, but I have to go to Kenya. I promised Willard, and I must know for my own sake."

"Know what, Mary?" Deacon Stoltzfus spread his hands in helpless beseeching. "What is there to know in Kenya that is not already known here? The Lord warned us not to run after false prophets who promise that grace would be bestowed somewhere in the desert, or on the mountaintop, or in Kenya. Grace is given to us right where we are. I'm sure you know this."

"I do," Mary agreed. "I don't want to quarrel with you. I want to be sure I can be the kind of woman Willard needs to stand by his side. I am deeply grateful that Willard has opened his heart and considers me worthy of being his *frau*, and this after the painful rejection he has been through. A trip to Kenya is the least I can do for him—and for myself."

"The man has been rejected by his own people?" Deacon Stoltzfus peered at her. "What does that tell you, Mary? Why are you throwing away your life? Is it because you are afraid of life in the community as a single woman?"

Mary shook her head. "I know that if the Lord wills it, a life in the community as either a married or single woman brings the happiness and contentment I desire. There are always worthy causes here, but to turn my back on the door the Lord has opened would be wrong. I cannot do that with a clear conscience. I don't ask that you understand me or believe me. I'm simply answering your questions the best I can."

Deacon Stoltzfus appeared stunned for a moment. "This doesn't answer any of my questions. You create many more with your words. This sounds like one person finding her own way in the world without the council of the community, which is heresy to our people. How can so many be wrong, and you be right? Can you answer that, Mary?"

"I suppose if the Lord has moved my heart, I should obey Him," Mary ventured. "I only want to make sure of it by taking this trip."

Deacon Stoltzfus's face fell. "You speak in a way our people do not speak, Mary. We are taught humility and brokenness. We are not to think of ourselves more highly than we ought, and we certainly are not to place our own understanding of the Lord's ways above that of the brothers and sisters we love."

"Please let me go to Kenya, Deacon," Mary begged. "If I am wrong, I will be honest and admit the error of my ways. But if I am not, I also need to know it. I don't want to live a life of regret either way."

Deacon Stoltzfus stroked his beard in mournful silence before he spoke. "We have many examples of our people who have left the community, Mary. Most of them have regrets, if they would admit them. I would say the people have already trusted you enough. They opened wide their hearts. How much sorrow do you think they will feel when they learn that you used that kindness to pursue a relationship with an *Englisha* man right under our noses? And that you told no one until you were ready to accept Willard's marriage proposal?"

"I'm sorry I was not as open as I should have been," Mary admitted. "But there was a reason. I couldn't believe what my heart was telling me, and it took a long time to accept that."

"Oh, Mary!" *Mamm* wailed. "Listen to yourself talk! This is how people become deceived. You hide things in the darkness, and of course temptation overcomes you."

Mary hung her head. "I don't defend myself. I didn't do everything right, but I need to make this trip for Willard's sake even more than my own. I am quite sure of my decision."

"Then that answers your question," Deacon Stoltzfus told her. "I don't even have to consult the other ministry before I can say for certain. We cannot give our permission for you to leave."

Mamm rushed over to Mary's side. "You know what that means. If you go, you will be in disobedience, terrible disobedience. This is the community speaking, Mary, not just *Daett* and me. They would have no choice but to..." *Mamm*'s voice ended in a whimper, and she collapsed on the couch.

Daett covered his face with his hands and groaned. "My daughter, cast out into the darkness."

Deacon Stoltzfus nodded, his face grim.

"Just think, Mary!" *Mamm* tried again. "You can't be right. Your pride has completely eaten you up."

"This has gone far enough," *Daett* said before Mary could protest. "We are thankful that Mose came over this morning and spent so much time with us. His godly wisdom is something we have to dwell on, especially Mary. I hope he has patience with us as a family while we work through this problem."

"I agree." Deacon Stoltzfus stood up from his chair. "You can have the time you need, Kenneth, but Mary must not make the trip to Kenya. On that, I think I speak for everyone."

"We will do what we can," *Daett* said. Then he ushered the deacon out the front door.

Mamm appeared to have passed out on the couch. Should Mary say something? What was there to say? She had known things would be rough, but the waves were higher than she had imagined. But she couldn't turn back now. She simply couldn't.

Mary slipped into the kitchen and began to run hot water in the sink. Soft footsteps approached from behind.

"That was awful," Betsy whispered. "I heard everything they told you."

"Don't become bitter," Mary warned. "We both knew what was going to happen."

"I didn't think it would be that bad," Betsy continued, undeterred. "I need support from someone quickly, or my courage will fail me. I will become bitter and rethink my own plans."

"Please," Mary begged.

Betsy's face brightened. "I'm going to write Ronald and tell him he has to join us on this trip to Kenya. I'm sure he'll agree. That's what I need."

Mary wrung her hands. "Do you think it's wise to drag Ronald into this? I should have been more open about the whole affair with *Mamm* and *Daett* instead of dropping a bomb on their heads. They said what needed saying. Remember, I would have said the same thing not so long ago."

"You are always too kind," Betsy grumbled. "But I am going to involve Ronald. In fact, a letter is much too slow. I'm calling the Troyers' phone shack this afternoon. I'll leave a message if I have to. Ronald is flying with us to Kenya—somehow, somewhere. Willard will make it work. I need someone by my side so you will have someone by yours during this awful time."

"You would do that for me? You really would?"

"You poor dear." Betsy gave Mary a long hug. "Remember, I will always be your sister. We will stand together, even through excommunication. I know it's coming because I know what you will find in Kenya, but you can make it, Mary. In fact, when you see that the way is clear in Kenya, you should not come back. I will tell *Mamm* and *Daett* the news."

Mary's mouth worked soundlessly for a few seconds. "I can't run away from things. Once I know for sure, I'll have to come back and face my excommunication."

Betsy hushed Mary with a shake of her head. "Times are changing. After a few years, when everyone sees that you are living a decent life with Willard and caring for troubled boys in Kenya, I will have Ronald make a personal appeal to Deacon Stoltzfus that the excommunication be lifted. Everything will be okay. But don't think about that right now. We'll cross the bridge once we get there."

Betsy's kindness overcame her. "You are dreaming," Mary sobbed. "But you would do that for me—you and Ronald? You have me weeping and wailing at the thought."

"Ronald is a very special man," Betsy assured her. "He thinks outside the box, and things are changing, I'm telling you. I even think he will come to live in the valley. I don't know for sure, but he's like that, unlike your horrible Josiah Beiler."

"Don't bring Josiah into this," Mary protested. "We must love and understand regardless of what happens."

"So says the saint!" Betsy muttered. "But not me!"

"You will love too," Mary replied through her tears. "I know you will."

THIRTY-FIVE

Willard leaned back in his seat as the Air France flight climbed through the clouds and burst into the starlit sky. Through the small window beside him, the full moon hung above the plane wing. The hurried arrangements of the last few days were behind him—the last-minute checks, the uncertainty, the wondering if the schedule he wanted could be achieved. Grandma had helped with a call to a travel agency in Utica. Ronald Troyer, Betsy's boyfriend, had met them at JFK at five with his connecting flight.

Willard took a deep breath and glanced toward Mary, who was sitting in the seat beside him. "Are you okay?"

"Maybe I shouldn't look out the window. I'm a little queasy." Mary made a face. "That's a nice moon, though."

"You've never flown before." This was more a statement than a question.

Mary's smile was wry. "I know. Are you having second thoughts about me? Already?"

Willard chuckled. "Not a chance. And you?"

"No second thoughts," she said, gazing up at him.

He reached for her hand, and Mary leaned over to rest her head against his shoulder.

"Do you want to talk, now that we have some time?" he asked her. "The flight won't land until the morning, Paris time."

"We have to get some sleep. Or are you a night owl?"

He grinned. "Would that make a difference?"

"Looks like I'm learning a lot about you."

"I'm not a night owl," he said. "Are you?"

"Amish night owls?" Mary laughed. "Hard work will take that characteristic out of you quickly."

"I suppose so," he allowed with a look over his shoulder. "Those two seem to hit it off well."

Mary followed his gaze to where Betsy and Ronald were seated a few rows back on the other side of the plane. Betsy noticed and waved, her face aglow with happiness.

Mary's eyes filled with tears. "Betsy's such a dear. I don't know how I would have made it through the last few days without her support."

Willard squeezed her hand. "Catch me up on the news. I've been around the Amish community my entire life, but I can't imagine what you have been through since I saw you up at the cemetery."

"Nothing really," Mary said, in a tone that belied her words. "Two visits from Deacon Stoltzfus. His *frau*, Rachel, came along the second time. I'm glad we're flying on a Saturday evening. I don't think I could have handled the church service tomorrow."

Willard reached his arm around Mary's shoulder to pull her close. "I'm so sorry. You don't have to do this."

"I want to," she said, smiling through her tears.

Willard looked away. Her devotion and the love in her eyes were more than he could handle. He didn't deserve a woman of Mary's character.

"Open your heart, Willard," Grandma had told him before he left to pick up Mary and Betsy. *"Do not be afraid to love again."*

Willard swallowed. They were both teary-eyed, and the trip had only begun.

"Thank you for the work you put into planning this trip," Mary whispered into his ear. "And the cost. I can only imagine."

"I don't want to hear a word about that," he warned. "Ronald is paying for his ticket and Betsy's, and the cost you pay in heartache makes any money I spend pale in comparison."

"You are worth it." She smiled up at him again. "I hope I pass every test you put me through with flying colors."

"There will be no test, Mary," he chided. "I already know my answer. I told you that."

"That's what you said, so we are just making sure."

"Allowed," he agreed.

"Then we are in unity," she said, her gaze fixed on the bright globe of the moon still visible over the plane's wing. "There are few things as valued in the community as unity."

"Do you want to tell me about the talk with the deacon?"

"You wouldn't understand." Her tears sprang up again.

"I can try."

"Why can't we just leave that part of my life alone?"

"Burying pain isn't wise." He held her hand in both of his.

She struggled to speak. "Okay, I'll try. There is a part of me that knows this is right...you and I, what we are doing. On the other hand, the community speaks to another part of me. It's the one I've lived with most of my life. I grew up with them and believed as they do that the world out there is not for us, that we have the best already, that we can't improve on community life or our devotion to one another. The Amish believe that the Lord blesses us when we submit to the council of others who watch for our souls. By going with you, I am going against my past, Willard. Maybe it would be easier if I had bitterness in my heart to drive me, like Betsy used to, but I don't."

"I wouldn't want bitterness," he told her. "This is the best way, though perhaps more painful. Are you going to make it?"

"I think so." A smile finally came. "I have something to help me along."

"That would be?" He tilted his head toward her.

A blush rose into her face. "I'm not saying it."

"You don't have to. I already know," he whispered.

"You do?"

"Yes, and I feel the same. I love you, Mary Yoder, more each moment that I am around you."

Her blush deepened, and she lowered her eyes, burying her face in his shoulder.

"You are a sweet girl."

A soft sob escaped her, but Willard held her close.

"Betsy and Ronald will see us," she finally whispered.

He looked over his shoulder. "They are quite involved in themselves at the moment, and we are not doing anything wrong."

"I know." She sat up to reach for a handkerchief in her dress pocket.

He waited as she wiped her eyes. "Don't the Amish believe in excommunication?" he asked. "Has the deacon spoken to you about that?"

Mary covered her face.

"I'm sorry," he muttered. "I shouldn't have brought that subject up at the moment." He held her again until her sobs ceased.

She sat up straight and composed herself. "You're right, Willard. We shouldn't bury my pain, so let me explain how the community thinks. Their belief goes back many years to a time when heretics and false prophets were drowned, strangled, or burned at the stake by the church. Many of our people suffered that fate, all while they rejected violence as a method of resolving church disputes. Instead, they believed that casting the person out of the community was the extent to which the church was allowed to go in its defense of heartfelt beliefs. So that's what they do. They cut you off."

Willard waited a moment. "What does that mean for you practically?"

"I...we..." Mary sniffed. "First the deacon talked to me, warning me that I am doing what the community does not approve of. There is a further consultation, which has already happened. After that comes the informing of the church. In the meantime, I imagine that Deacon Stoltzfus has spoken with Bishop Miller and the others on the ministry team. If I had listened and called off the trip, I suppose the matter would have been dropped. Anyone from the membership may speak with me at the service, to add any further warnings—but because I am not there, everything will be on hold until I return. After that, if I persist in my supposed rebellion, a set time will be determined, perhaps four weeks or so. By then, if I have not repented and am willing to make a confession of my sins in a church service, a vote is taken. That vote will pass because no one will want to support my actions, and I will be cast out."

Mary paused, and Willard cleared his throat. "I am so sorry, Mary. I really am. So what happens with your family?"

"I can go back to the valley, but contact with me, other than brief conversations, is forbidden. I can't help around the house or live at home, or do any of the other things I'm used to."

"This is so wrong, Mary. I have no right to ask you to go through this."

"You are not asking. I want to. You are not to blame, Willard. Perhaps the community isn't to blame either. They have to uphold what they believe is right, and I have to..." Mary's voice died out.

"You have to what?" he prompted.

Her gaze found his. "You already know. I have to be true to my heart."

"I love you, Mary, so very much," he whispered.

She avoided his eyes. "Enough about me! Tell me where we are going. You said we would stay an extra day in Paris."

Willard took a deep breath. "We will come back to this, Mary. There is more to be said." When she didn't answer, he continued. "I planned a two-day stay in Paris, if you count tomorrow and we can stay awake. They've had a mild winter on the mainland this year, so there shouldn't be too much snow."

"Won't that cost a lot of money?"

He squeezed her hand. "You are worth any money I spend on you, Mary, so stop saying that."

"I am not," she protested.

He continued with a smile. "I want you to see Paris, not just Nairobi. Either one would be half the story, but together you will have a better, more complete picture of what lies out there, as your people would say."

"Out there," she muttered. "I never planned to go out there."

"You never dreamed of moonlit walks by the Eiffel Tower with me by your side?" he teased.

"I barely know what the Eiffel Tower is, Willard," she scolded. "I read of the place in school, and of other things in Paris, but I never thought I would see them."

"Really? What else did you read about in Paris?"

A smile formed on Mary's face. "There is the Louvre Museum and the Mona Lisa."

"You know of her?"

"*Yah*. Why? Is that wrong?"

"Mary, stop the guilt." He touched her hand. "What did you think of the Mona Lisa? That's what I want to know."

She sighed. "I thought her beauty of the sad sort, or rather a prettiness that comes out of enduring the troubles of life."

He chuckled. "Are you always this deep?"

Mary grimaced. "No, I'm just common Mary Yoder, an Amish woman."

He gave her a skeptical look. "Did you write poetry about the Mona Lisa?"

Color crept up Mary's neck as she stared at him. "How did you know?"

"I didn't."

"But you asked!"

"You write poetry, and you were obviously moved. It was a guess!"

Mary took a deep breath. "There is one, I will admit. I haven't read it since..." Mary rushed on. "Anyway, I went into my cedar chest upstairs when Betsy told me we were staying in Paris. I didn't expect you to ask, though. It's..."

"Let me see." Willard held out his hand.

Mary's face flamed, but she bent forward to find her satchel under the seat, and soon she handed him the piece of paper. Willard read silently.

> *The world is drawn to your face,*
> *To your quiet beauty and your grace.*
> *They hang your portrait in their lofty halls,*
> *They captured you upon their walls.*
>
> *Some man conceived with paint and brush*
> *To touch your heart and show the hush.*
> *Which sorrow wrote upon your life,*
> *The peace that came amidst the strife.*
>
> *For beauty does not rise in mortal eyes,*
> *Unless the lines are written from the skies.*
> *With pain you showed us heaven's touch,*
> *And so your smile is loved so much.*

"You wrote this?" Willard held out the paper.

"*Yah!*" Her fingers brushed his as she took the paper back. "Are the words terrible?"

He blinked back the sting of tears. "No. You moved me deeply."

"Is that okay?" Mary leaned forward to replace the poem in her satchel.

"Of course," he said. "You seem to know a lot about suffering."

"Not really, unless you count what Josiah put me through. I should have known better than to open my heart so wide to him."

He shook his head. "Don't blame yourself. I don't have a better record."

She settled back in her seat. "Shouldn't we get some sleep if we plan to tour Paris in the morning?"

He grinned. "You expect me to sleep after reading your poem?"

She made a face at him. "I'm going to doze off and forget I showed the poem to you."

He laughed and glanced over his shoulder. "Looks like those two are in la-la land."

"See?" Mary chided. "We should follow their example."

"I agree," he said, as Mary leaned back on the headrest. "We are in unity."

Mary seemed not to hear. The faint smile on her face didn't fade as her breathing deepened. Mary had fallen asleep in the blink of an eye. She was either exhausted, totally at peace, or both. A lifetime of honesty and openness before the Lord and others had shaped her spirit and written grace in every line.

Willard looked away. That such a woman would love him took his breath. The beauty of her face would fade as the years passed, but the glory of her heart would grow brighter with each new day. He should never ask Mary to walk with him through life as his wife. She was much too good for him.

Willard studied the bright twinkle of the stars outside the window. Showing Paris to Mary was the least he could do for her.

THIRTY–SIX

Betsy hung on to Ronald's arm in the brisk early morning air. She should be exhausted after the seven-hour flight across the Atlantic and scant hours of sleep on the plane, but energy ran through every muscle. This was Paris, the city of love, and she was here, a scarred Amish girl who had planned to jump the fence. No fence jumping would have accomplished this. Not with the happiness that filled her heart to overflowing.

"We're in Paris!" Betsy squealed. She let go of Ronald's arm to dance a jig in the street.

Ronald grinned. "I would say I was sleeping, but I know I'm wide awake. This is nice, even in the wintertime."

Betsy pinched him and he hollered.

"That's to convince you that you really are awake." Betsy giggled.

He chuckled and moved away a few steps for a better view of the gaunt, four-legged tower. "Sure is ugly, this Eiffel Tower thing," he muttered.

"Ronald!" Betsy scolded. "How dare you? I thought you were educated."

He made a face at her. "I'm an Amish farm boy far from home."

Betsy linked arms with him again. "You're not going to convince me of that. I know you too well. You are my hero, my lucky star, my dream come true, my love."

"Oh, my. Such sweet praises." Ronald's smile split his face. "My hat won't fit once we're back home."

"You should have brought your hat. No *goot* Amish man leaves the house without his hat."

"Who says I'm an Amish man?"

"I do." Betsy puckered her lip. "You're not changing your mind because of Mary, are you? Not after you didn't think I had a case to stand on."

Ronald glanced toward the other side of the tower, where Mary and Willard stood holding hands. "Your sister has a rough road to walk, but that doesn't change my plans. Further, let me assure you that you did have a complaint about your scars. But you are beautiful, Betsy, just the kind of girl I like. Fit for Paris." He leaned toward Betsy to give her a quick peck on the cheek.

She hugged him and didn't let go for a long time.

"Pretty soon I'll be kissing you on the mouth in public," he warned.

Betsy giggled again. "This is the city of love."

"I know," he said. His gaze drifted back to Mary and Willard. "How do you think they are really doing?"

"Mary's happy," Betsy replied. "Which is a miracle after what she's been through. Deacon Stoltzfus came over twice, and Mary just sat there and didn't say much. I know, because I heard both conversations from the stairwell."

"You should act your age," Ronald scolded.

Betsy pinched him again.

He regarded her soberly this time. "How are you going to take this, Betsy? Seeing your sister suffering up close? People you both love will injure her, and it will be hard to take—worse than a fire and scars on your face. I'm sorry to tell you that."

Betsy considered his words. "I was angry, but Mary, the saint, counseled love and forgiveness. Maybe my first bout with bitterness was a warning not to indulge myself."

Ronald appeared quite pleased. "That's *goot*. There will always be things in life to cause us injury. Injustice is baked into a pie. Wasn't our Lord crucified for His efforts to reach this world with love and *goot* deeds?"

"*Yah*!" Betsy agreed.

Ronald's spiritual observations still caught her by surprise. Everything about the man caught her by surprise. That was what she loved about him.

"You want to go up there?" Ronald motioned toward the line at the lift, which Mary and Willard had joined.

"I don't know." Betsy hesitated. "It's nice enough down here. What will we see, more of the city?"

"I thought you would jump around on one foot the entire day in Paris," Ronald teased.

"I am excited! But...well, it is Paris, I guess."

He winked at her. "I knew you were a down-to-earth girl at heart from the moment I laid eyes on you. You are just like me. You enjoy the world, but you'll settle for home."

"You know way too much about me. I tell you what. I'll climb the tower to the second floor with you, but no lift."

Ronald grunted. "I wasn't expecting that."

"You stay here," she teased. She made a dash for the much shorter line at the base of the exterior steps.

He followed moments later. "I didn't come to Paris to work."

"You are grumbling," Betsy gloated.

"I am. And I like it for some reason. Seems I like everything about you, even the bad parts."

"Ronald!" Betsy warned. "I can get the next plane ticket home, and you can stay in Paris by yourself."

"You can't because you have no money," he retorted. "But I will be nice and behave myself."

"That's impossible."

"You say such kind, tenderhearted things."

She paused on the first step to reach back and ruffle his hair. "I like you very much, Ronald. Did I ever tell you that?"

"No!"

"Liar." She slapped his head.

He laughed, and Betsy joined in as they raced up the steel steps. They fell silent as they climbed higher. "It is nicer up here than I expected, and not too cold," Betsy observed.

"Changing your mind about Paris?"

"You know I'm not. Like you said, we do enjoy the world."

"Do you think we'll come back here after we're old and settled down?" he mused, his gaze fixed on the meandering river far below them.

"I'm not thinking that far ahead. Look what has already happened. Who would have thought?"

"But at your sister's expense," he observed wryly.

"No, from supporting Mary," Betsy corrected. "That's why we're here now, and we are going to help her in the future."

He paused to survey the city below them. "You know we're only getting away with this because we're still on *rumspringa*."

"Agreed," she said. "But let's talk about something else. We are in Paris."

He laughed. "The view gets better the higher we climb."

"That's because we're working for it instead of riding up to the deck on man-made contraptions."

Ronald grinned from ear to ear. "Only an Amish girl would think in those terms."

"Well, I am Amish," Betsy grumbled. "But I'll probably never be a *goot* one."

"*Goot* enough for me." He tugged on her hand and winked.

"Stop teasing me, Ronald," she warned. "I'll tumble over the railing."

"I'll catch you, or fly after you like Superman."

"Who is that?" Betsy turned a puzzled face toward him.

Ronald grunted. "You are an Amish girl."

"And you are my Superman. I do know that."

His eyes grew big. "She sings my praises even in her great wrath."

"Isn't that the kind of girl you want?"

"You know too much about me," he grumbled this time.

She didn't really. Each moment simply tumbled into the next, devoid of much knowledge on her part. But hadn't life been that way for her? The stove, the flames, the scars, the bitterness—and here she was with a man who tugged on every heartstring.

"I do like you," Betsy whispered.

Ronald was not supposed to hear, but from his smug look he clearly had. She made a face at him, and his smugness increased. Nothing she did seemed to faze him.

The second floor drew nearer, and the line ahead became thinner. People had been dropping out behind them, but she had hardly noticed. In a dash, Betsy scaled the last steps with Ronald right behind her. She glanced around for any sight of Mary and Willard, but they must have been here and gone again. Mary and Willard would wait for them on the ground below. They had the day and tomorrow yet to explore the city.

"Whee!" Ronald exclaimed from beside her. "What a climb."

Betsy drew a long breath. That she wasn't huffing and puffing was a matter of pride, and Ronald was impressed. She could tell by the glance of admiration he had given her. She wanted to stay up here forever with him, and yet he was right. This only made home, in spite of its troubles, seem dearer.

"Shall we see the other side?" Ronald suggested. He led the way around.

The viewing deck was just as crowded on that side, and the view much the same. Once seen, Paris was Paris, apparently.

Ronald pointed. "There is the Arc de Triomphe. See that spot where all the streets run together? The structure was inspired by the Arch of Titus in Rome many years ago. I read that it's the fifth most popular tourist site in Paris."

"Will we see it up close?"

"There may not be time."

"We should see everything," Betsy muttered.

Ronald chuckled. "Be practical, my dear. Practical."

Chills ran up and down Betsy's back at Ronald words, enhanced by the high altitude and the empty space beneath her. Maybe the effects of the city of love came simply from a combination of elevation and sleep deprivation. Betsy giggled.

"Is something wrong with you?" Ronald asked.

"I was born with something wrong with me," Betsy retorted. "Just thinking, that's all."

"Care to share with me?"

"No."

"Ah, please, Betsy," Ronald begged. "No words are so sweet as those that drip from your lips."

Betsy dissolved into laughter. "Even you have outdone yourself."

He joined in her laughter. "It's Paris, I suppose."

"So you didn't mean them?"

He came closer. "I meant every word. Now tell me what you were thinking."

Tingles chased each other up and down her spine. "Okay, my prince. I was wondering if I'm only sleepy and dizzy from being up here, or if I do really love you as much as I think I do."

"Now that's an important question," he said, with a twinkle in his eye. "Have you found the answer?"

"I think it's you," she said, "although I am dizzy and sleep deprived."

Ronald gazed into her eyes for a long time before he leaned over the rail to watch the sightseers moving far below them. Betsy joined him and waited. She could exercise patience the whole day for what was to come next. The moment had arrived.

He finally turned his face toward her. "I want to stay Amish, Betsy, but it's right that I should ask you here, on the top of the Eiffel Tower...Will you be my *frau*? My beloved one, for the rest of our lives, until we grow old and sit on the front porch swing together? Will you?"

"Ronald!" She tried to breathe. "You know I will."

He came closer. "I love you, Betsy, so much. We were made for each other, by the Lord's own hand."

"Ronald!" His name came loudly this time. Several tourists turned to stare, but grins grew quickly on their faces.

"Betsy," he said, reaching for her.

She opened her arms with a heart that pounded in her chest. His face was a blur and heat burned up her neck as he kissed her. Betsy's ears rang, but the sound was the clapping of the tourists around them. They must make a strange sight in their Amish clothing, which Ronald had insisted they wear. Lovers were undoubtedly a familiar sight on the Eiffel Tower, but not Amish lovers.

Betsy buried her face in Ronald's chest. His arms were still wrapped around her, their strength a comfort and a deep joy. There was no reason she should be embarrassed because of their love, even in this public place. Amish customs gave way for this day when Ronald had chosen the Eiffel Tower to ask her if she would marry him.

Betsy peeked out of Ronald's arms and forced a smile. "Thank you, everybody. That was nice."

"Congratulations," several people called back.

A jolly-looking fellow in bib overalls asked, "Can the wife and I come to the wedding? I've never been to an Amish one."

"We'll have to plan the date," Ronald told him. "We're just in love at this point."

"The best to both of you!" someone else called.

People smiled even as they moved away.

"We are strange. Do you know that?" Betsy whispered into Ronald's chest.

He pulled her closer. "You are perfect. That's my only concern."

"Ronald!" Betsy gasped. "You have to stop saying these *wunderbah* things."

He grinned and let her go. "Should we find Mary and Willard? They are probably wondering what became of us."

She nodded and clung to his hand for the long journey down the stairs. This day was meant to be, this climb up and down the Eiffel Tower. She would look back and become more certain as time continued. Mary would leave the community and marry Willard. They had known this before the trip, and the certainty only increased. Betsy would be Amish and speak for Mary, and Ronald would do the same. Perhaps that was the purpose of their lives. Was not service the highest calling? Deacon Stoltzfus would not understand that reasoning, but they didn't have to persuade him. They only needed to climb the stairs of life the Lord had laid before them.

Ronald took the last step with a great leap and turned to give her a warm smile. "You are so beautiful, Betsy, my sweetheart."

She giggled and leaped into his arms.

THIRTY-SEVEN

Mary awoke in the early morning light to throw off the bed quilt and sit bolt upright in the bed. Where was she? Betsy was asleep in the bed beside her, and this was obviously a hotel room. Paris! The memories rushed back. The night spent flying across the Atlantic with Willard seated next to her. The sleep-deprived day in which they had toured the legendary Eiffel Tower, the Grand Palais, and the Petit Palais next door. She could no longer think straight by the time the day ended.

Mary lay back in bed and pulled her covers up under her chin. She was in Paris, the city of lights. A soft smile crept over her face. Willard could not have been more charming yesterday. He was not trying to impress her. He was always a kind and gentle man.

Then she blinked, and her smile faded. The sorrow from home had also followed her. The peace and quiet of the community lay in sharp contrast to the bustle and roar of the Paris streets. Quiet came to the soul in the museums with their beautiful art pieces, but this was a different peace from that of the farm. Willard wanted her to see his world, here in Paris and in Kenya. And Willard was right. He would never live in Paris, but there was more to his life than the mission. Willard had been wise to bring her here. She must be certain of what lay ahead. Surprises and regrets were not in Willard's plans. He was an honest man, with a true heart.

Tears crept into Mary's eyes and trickled sideways down her face.

"Crying in Paris!" Betsy exclaimed from the bed across from Mary. "What is wrong with you?"

Mary attempted a smile. "I know. I shouldn't be crying."

"Are you having doubts?" Betsy sat up straight.

"No, just memories of home."

Betsy sighed. "I suppose you're allowed to feel that way. I'm going back there, but you..."

"I don't think I should go back," Mary ventured. "I think you were right that day in front of the kitchen sink. It's not that I'm afraid anyone will change my mind, but the pain doesn't seem worth it. I can't change things anyway. The die is cast, unless I repent, which..."

"You shouldn't go back," Betsy agreed. "But how will you live over here, all by yourself?"

Mary shrugged. "There's the mission in Kenya, and there is another couple staying there, so it's not as though I would be alone with Willard."

"I agree, but I'm not thinking about details right now!" Betsy threw off her bedcovers. "We are in Paris, and what a day lies ahead of us. A gorgeous day like the one we had yesterday." Betsy walked over to the window drapes and pushed them back to blow a kiss through the glass. "Paris! I do love you."

Mary smiled in spite of herself. "I guess I ought to enjoy the day since I'm here."

"That's the spirit," Betsy said. "Up and at it. Willard told us last night they have breakfast across the street, or have you forgotten? You looked dead on your feet by the time we arrived at the hotel."

"I was," Mary agreed. "But I haven't forgotten."

"Paris," Betsy whispered at the window again. "How beautiful thou art."

Mary laughed this time. "What were you and Ronald doing so long up on the Eiffel Tower yesterday?"

Betsy colored quickly. "Just..." Betsy turned as the glow spread into her face. "Ronald ask me to wed him, Mary."

"And you're the one who's staying Amish!"

"I know." Betsy danced in front of the window. "Nothing makes sense, but I'm so happy."

"And I'm glad for you," Mary told her. "Congratulations."

Betsy beamed with happiness. "I just love the man. Don't you think Ronald is the most charming, the most handsome, the most lovable man who ever walked the face of this earth?"

"Ronald is the Lord's answer for you," Mary agreed.

How many prayers had Mary prayed along with *Mamm* and *Daett* for this moment to arrive? Now she was on the other side of the fence when the answer came. That, no one had expected.

She blinked back the sudden tears and climbed out of bed. They dressed quickly and knocked on the men's room across the hall.

"Coming," Willard answered. He opened a moment later and ushered them in. "Ronald just has to put his shoes on, and then we'll be ready to go for breakfast."

"I am ready," Ronald protested, one sock still in his hand.

Betsy rushed over and gave him a long hug.

Ronald grinned. "Now that's exactly what I needed. *Goot* morning, Betsy."

"And a *goot* morning to you!" Betsy squealed.

"I think something happened between those two yesterday on top of the Eiffel Tower," Willard commented with a wry smile.

"It did," Mary informed him. "So are you ready? Those two can find their own way."

Willard chuckled. "We'll be at the diner down the street. You saw it last night when we came in, Ronald."

There was no response from Betsy and Ronald, who were engaged in a whispered conversation.

Willard took Mary's hand once they were outside the room. He smiled down at her. "How are you doing?"

"I'm hungry, and I didn't even work yesterday."

Willard's smile grew. "I think traveling works up more of an appetite than working." A look of concern crept over Willard's face. "Everything is so new for you."

"I'm fine," she assured him. "And I'm happy to be here, and happy that you are showing me Paris. That was wise of you."

"I am a wise man," he teased, sobering quickly. "Life won't be easy for us either way, not after we've been together in Paris and Kenya. Even if you go back to your life in the community, I'll never forget you Mary, or the moments of joy I have shared in your presence."

"Willard," Mary scolded. "You don't have to say those things."

"I want to." He let go of her hand to open the door into the street. "But I don't want to embarrass you...I just want to make sure you know how full my heart is. I thought I would burst a few times yesterday, being with you. Don't let that change your decision about us. Once this trip is over, you can always go back to the community. I'm just saying how I feel."

Mary took his hand as they walked down the street, and she leaned her head against his shoulder. The words she wanted to say didn't seem right. Willard obviously thought she was still in a state of indecision. She was not an *Englisha* girl who could make her own marriage proposal.

"I love you, Mary," he whispered.

"I will always be an Amish girl at heart," she warned him. "I hope you know that."

"I wouldn't want it any other way," he assured her. "Shall we?" As they arrived at the restaurant door, he motioned her inside.

Mary nodded and they entered. French voices murmured around them, and the food appeared strange for a breakfast menu.

Willard chuckled, obviously reading her thoughts. "There won't be anything you would commonly find in America. Probably more like cheeses and bread rolls with coffee."

"Sounds nourishing," Mary chirped as they seated themselves. Betsy and Ronald appeared a moment later, hand in hand, still chattering away.

"Over here!" Willard waved to get their attention. "You two would walk into a wall if someone didn't guide you."

Everyone laughed, and a waiter appeared.

"I'm sorry, but we don't speak French," Willard informed him.

This provoked a frown and further words still in French. The man slapped down the menus and left abruptly.

Willard raised his eyebrows. "At least we are allowed to order, it seems. French charm on full display this morning."

"I've heard they are that way," Ronald muttered. "Even in the city of love."

Betsy pinched his arm. "Don't mix the city of love with bad rumors."

Ronald grinned. "Whatever you wish, dear."

"Are you practicing for married life?" Willard teased.

Ronald laughed wholeheartedly. "Betsy will turn into a proper submissive woman once we get back to the community."

Betsy joined in the teasing. "He can sound tough on the outside, but he doesn't fool me. Ronald's a jewel."

"Sounds like you've made your case well," Willard observed.

Their laughter rippled until the stern-faced waiter reappeared. Willard pointed to several plates of food on the menu. "Whatever you bring, we eat, but try to keep it to morning food."

The waiter's head bobbed, and he grabbed the menus and disappeared into the kitchen.

"I hope you know what you are doing," Ronald said.

"I don't." Willard grinned. "But he'll bring something decent. French pride will demand that, at least."

Mary clung to Willard's arm while they waited, and Ronald and Betsy chattered away.

"The Grand Palais was awesome yesterday!" Betsy exclaimed. "If only we'd had time to tour the inside to see that glass ceiling. But at least we got to eat dinner in the structure." Betsy caught her breath. "Just think! I have eaten dinner in Paris at the Grand Palais, and with you." She wrapped her arm around his.

He smiled. "Maybe we should come back to Paris every year, sweetheart."

"I would love that. But you know that's not possible. We'll just have to keep our memories and think on them as we grow old together."

Mary sent a smile toward Willard as they listened. Betsy's chattering soothed her soul. The Lord's hand was plain to see. She would never have imagined that Betsy and Ronald would meet each other, let alone that they would travel together to Paris and Kenya.

"Here's the food," Willard whispered in her ear as the waiter reappeared from the kitchen.

He set plates on the table, cups of coffee, and vanished again with only a grunt in their direction.

"Croissants and éclairs," Willard muttered. "At least they thought to bring the poor starving Americans slices of cheese."

Ronald stared at the offerings in horror. "You call that breakfast?"

"I'm afraid that's all we'll get, my friend." Willard thumped the table. "Let's pray so we can fall to it."

"I think one trip to Paris is enough in my lifetime." Ronald stared at the plates, while Betsy held his hand and shook her head in sympathy.

"Let's pray," Willard repeated and bowed his head. "Our gracious Father in heaven, thank You for this food, and for this day, and the days which You will grant us after this one. Bless what we are to eat, and bless the hours we will spend in Paris. I thank You for Ronald and Betsy, who have so graciously agreed to come with us, and especially for Mary. You are a great God, and thank You. Amen."

"Amen," Ronald echoed. He grabbed a croissant and a slice of cheese. "Might as well do as the Romans do while in Rome."

"Or the French while in France," Willard added.

Betsy's and Ronald's faces turned red.

"What? What did I just say?" Willard asked.

"They were doing what the French do on to Eiffel Tower yesterday," Mary told him with a smirk.

Betsy's face turned pink. "Hush! Don't say that in public!"

"I didn't," Mary protested. "But you were!"

"I think we had best eat." Ronald chewed his food, staring straight ahead.

"We did nothing wrong!" Betsy declared. "We would have done the same thing at home on the living room couch during a proper Amish date."

"That's right." Ronald grunted and took another bite.

Willard said nothing, but his shoulders shook with laughter.

"You should try a kiss yourself on the Eiffel Tower," Ronald said. "Downright exhilarating."

"Ronald!" Betsy exclaimed. "You make it sound so..."

"Romantic?" Willard teased. "Who says we didn't? Both of you were climbing up the hard way."

Betsy's eyes grew large. "Did you? Are you hiding something from me, Mary?"

Now her face was glowing. She was not going to speak about kissing Willard in public or in private.

"Are you two engaged?"

Willard shook his head. "I love your sister deeply and have told her so, but we are still finding our way. I want Mary to feel totally free to follow her heart without any pressure from me."

"That is *goot*," Betsy declared. "But I think I already know the answer to Mary's question."

"Leave them alone and eat your food," Ronald ordered.

Betsy huffed for a moment, but soon complied. Mary realized that her fiery sister had found her match. Willard winked at her, and she leaned against him for a moment. They finished their food and waited while Willard paid. No one left a tip, which must be the custom. That had not been the strangest thing about their breakfast this morning. The food had fit that bill.

Willard consulted his tour guide outside the restaurant, and they walked down to the bus stop for the short ride to the Louvre Museum. When the correct bus arrived, they all climbed aboard and paid their fares.

"First stop," Willard declared. "Perhaps our only one, depending on how much time we spend here."

Mary and Betsy said nothing as they stepped off the bus, clearly enraptured with the view in front of them—the glass pyramid in the center of the ancient courtyard, ringed by the three-sided rectangle of castle-like buildings. Mary took Willard's hand, and they followed Betsy and Ronald inside. After buying their tickets, they moved slowly past the old paintings and sculptures, past the unfamiliar names. Mary waited for one thing: the face she had seen many years ago in a little one-room Amish schoolhouse.

"She's smaller than you might have thought," Willard whispered in her ear once they arrived.

Mary studied the frame—the stout woman, the open fields behind her with jagged mountain peaks and water. Her hair was long and black, falling straight down over the shoulders the way an Amish woman would wear it without her *kapp*. Mary would look like that if she married Willard. Customs from childhood would have to fall by the wayside.

"Your poem fit perfectly," Willard said from beside her. "You are a Mona Lisa."

"Please," Mary begged. "Not out loud."

"I will say what I want to say," he replied.

Mary held him close as the crowd bustled around them. Betsy noticed, giggled, and punched Ronald, but Mary didn't care. Willard loved her. He loved everything about her, and that was enough for now.

THIRTY-EIGHT

The pickup truck wheezed down a crowded Nairobi street. Mary sat in front between Willard and Ashon, the mission's handyman, who had picked them up at the airport. Ronald and Betsy were in the open back, simultaneously hanging on to each other and their luggage.

"You watch these close, now. Many thieves in Kenya," Ashon had said with a toothless smile. "They come right on the truck and snatch from before your eyes."

Mary could almost believe the words. As he weaved in and out of the tangled lanes of traffic, she flinched at a horn blast from an approaching automobile. All drivers used the horn at the slightest provocation, or apparently to vent their grievances at the world.

"Terrible drivers in the city," Ashon muttered, his elbow jabbing the center of the steering wheel. The hood of the vehicle seemed to vibrate from the sound. Did these people enhance the volume of their car horns? Mary could not remember such a racket from driving in *Englisha* vehicles in big cities at home.

"Are you okay?" Willard asked.

"It's certainly not Paris," she told him.

The concern written on his face only grew.

She tried to laugh. "I'm teasing."

The sound was more cackle than mirth. She needed a drink of water. Plus, the sleep deprivation she'd felt in Paris seemed unnoticeable compared to the exhaustion she felt at the moment.

"The mission is coming up soon." Willard took her hand in his. "You'll have food, water, and rest there."

She smiled up at him. "That sounds *goot*."

The German word slipped out, a reminder of home in this strange land. What would *Mamm* think if she could see her daughter, dust strewn, *kapp* askew, stuck between two men on the front seat of a pickup truck? Betsy sat in the back in no better condition. At least she was enjoying each moment, pointing at the passing sights, and jabbering to Ronald while they hung on to the suitcases. Betsy was carefree and happy, while Mary was here to make a life-altering decision—or rather to confirm one. In reality, the choice had been made before she boarded the plane in upstate New York for the short connecting flight into New York City.

"You been here before?" Ashon beamed above her.

"No. It's my first time," Mary told him.

"You like Nairobi, the big city?" he continued.

"It's okay." She gave Willard a sideways look. "I like him."

Ashon's smile nearly split his face. "He a good man, yes. A very good man."

"Have you known him long?"

"Ah, I know him well, Mr. Willard!" Ashon's face glowed. "He the Lord's hand in this city."

"Don't listen to him," Willard protested. "The mission helped Ashon's son pay some hospital bills. He's prejudiced."

"Willard, he pray, and my son get well!" Ashon proclaimed. "And get medicine."

"Willard is a wonderful man," Mary agreed.

"You his loved one?" Ashon continued. "I no hear that Mr. Willard get married."

"We're not married," Mary said with another glance at Willard. "But I think he likes me."

Ashon guffawed and laid on the horn at the same time. "Then that is cause for much celebration. Willard a lonely man. He need wife. Are you coming to live in the city?" He gestured at the passing streets. "After the wedding?"

"That's the plan," Mary chirped.

Ashon laid on the horn a few more times. "You will make a great woman for Willard," he proclaimed.

"Ignore him," Willard said out of the side of his mouth.

"Is that your marketplace?" Mary asked, changing the subject.

Wooden shanties lined the street below the larger buildings, and garbage was strewn everywhere amidst merchandise for sale, boards of trinkets, and sodden garden produce.

"Something like that." Ashon grimaced. "I no buy there. Not anymore. There is a better place closer to the mission. And Mr. Willard taught us how to grow garden. Much better. Good to eat with no rot." Ashon gestured at his stomach.

Mary wrinkled her face. "I can believe that. So Willard raises a garden and taught you?"

"In his classes, yes." Ashon shrugged. "Same thing."

"It is the same thing," Mary agreed. "He is a wonderful man."

"Stop talking that way!" Willard ordered, and they laughed together above the sounds of blasting horns.

"You have these marketplaces at home where you come from?" Ashon asked. As they drove, the streets began to widen.

"Not really," Mary told him. "Maybe in the big cities, but I don't go there. We live in the country."

"You like this city better, yes, once you see the mission. You not go home straight thing in the morning?"

Mary shook her head. "I haven't seen anything to scare me away."

"You brave woman." Ashon gave her a bright smile. "I like you."

"You'll like her more the longer she is here," Willard told him.

"Stop talking about me," Mary ordered this time, and they laughed again.

They were tired, thirsty, sleepy, and hungry, but there was no panic. She could make this place home, even in the middle of a big city. The streets and houses had continued to improve the last few blocks, with tree-filled yards and clearly defined boundaries.

"Here we are!" Ashon announced, turning the pickup into a paved driveway. A long row of well-kept buildings were set a distance from the street, with trees and landscaping arranged randomly in the yard. Peace and quiet settled in as they moved away from the racket behind them.

"Do you like the place?" Willard asked nervously.

"*Yah*, I do." Mary surveyed the scene around her. "I don't know what I was expecting, but this is very nice."

Willard smiled with relief. "It's better quarters than we can afford, but there's not much in-between, and this is where I landed. The Lord provides, I suppose." He opened the creaking pickup door and offered his hand. "But we pinch pennies with our vehicles."

She lowered herself to the ground with her hand tight in his. "Thank you."

They stood for a moment in silence. Agape Outreach was written in large letters under a dark green tin roof. As she took in the grounds, the garbage-strewn street from the other side of town felt like a distant memory.

A large local woman appeared in the front doors to wave at them with both hands. She hollered, "Welcome back, Mr. Willard! You have a good trip coming home?"

The smile broadened on Mary's face. That familiar word—*home*—had been applied to this strange place. She saw a light in Willard's eyes as he approached the woman and gave her a hug. This was Willard's home in the same deep way she felt about her community.

"My wife, Tambala, she keep the mission running tip-top!"

Ashon proclaimed with pride. "We live here a long time before Mr. Willard come, but he the best of them all."

"I'm sure he is," Mary agreed.

Betsy and Ronald had climbed out of the pickup and set out on their own tour of the grounds.

"Lots better than the dumps we saw driving in," Betsy called over her shoulder.

"This is the most beautiful side of town," Ashon agreed, with obvious great pride. "This is where the work of the Lord is done by Mr. Willard."

Ronald came back with his hand in Betsy's. "I could almost make myself at home here," he declared. "Shall we take the suitcases inside? We kept them from being spirited away."

"That good." Ashon clapped him on the back. "Now I know you no thief."

Confusion played on Ronald's face for a moment. "Oh, you are teasing?" He joined in Ashon's laugher.

Behind them the doors opened again, and a white couple appeared. Willard hurried forward to shake their hands. Then he brought them back to the small group gathered around the pickup.

"Meet Ean and Daisy Messer, my dedicated coworkers. These are my friends Ronald, Betsy, and Mary."

Willard slipped his hand around Mary's shoulder and pulled her close. The message was clear. She belonged here when it came to matters of the heart.

"How was your journey?" Daisy inquired. "I heard you planned to lay over in Paris on the way here."

"Oh, we did!" Betsy gushed. "What a *wunderbah* time we had. Ronald and I are so happy that we had the chance to travel with Mary and Willard."

"I'm glad to hear that." Daisy's smile grew.

"So this is where Willard spends his time ministering?" Betsy continued.

"It is." Daisy motioned around with her hand. "We've tried to hold down the fort while Willard was gone, but it's not the same without him."

"I'm sure you did very well," Mary assured her. "This looks like a place I can call home. Maybe you could show us around."

"Certainly! Follow me." Daisy lowered her voice. "Looks like the men are taking the outside tour, so let me ask. Are you and Willard serious?"

"We are," Mary said. "I know I've already made up my mind, but Willard wants me to see everything first before he agrees—which is reasonable, I suppose."

"Willard is a wise man." Daisy held open the front door for them. "If I am any fair judge, he cares a lot for you. I could tell from the way he looked at you when we were introduced, and he has told us so much in his emails."

"I am happy to hear that you agree with me!" Betsy said. "I have never seen anyone better matched than those two."

"From what I understand, you come from a different culture?" Daisy's glance took in Mary's Amish dress.

Mary colored. "I guess I should begin the change. But I want Willard's concerns satisfied first. Otherwise he might feel pressured."

Daisy appeared pleased. "I see you share Willard's wisdom."

"They are perfect together," Betsy pressed.

Daisy showed them the kitchen, where Tambala waved and called out, "Here are bottles of water. When will you be needing food?"

Mary took a long drink before she answered. "I am starved, so whenever you have the meal ready, we can eat. But please don't bother yourself too much for us."

"Nothing is big bother for you," Tambala assured them. "But I will get you something right now. Mr. Willard has brought great blessing to our lives, and we can never fully repay him."

"I agree. Willard is a wonderful man," Mary told her.

Tambala beamed at them as she brought over a platter with strips of meat on it. "Here is something until I can make a proper meal for starving people."

Mary took a piece and chewed slowly, and Betsy did the same.

"Delicious!" Betsy declared. "I didn't know how hungry I was."

"Another piece or two," Tambala ordered. "Then you must wait, but soon the meal is ready."

Daisy led them down the hall as they finished their snack. "That's your first taste of Tambala. She is our combination cook, nurse, and housemother for the boys we have in our care," Daisy told them. "I try to help where I can, but they bond better with someone from their own culture."

"I can see that," Mary agreed. "But I'm sure you do more than you know. I'll look forward to the wisdom you have to impart. Just tell us where we need to help, and your word is our command."

Daisy laughed. "I think today should be a day of rest from your travels, but let me quickly show you the housing and schoolrooms on the back side." She walked them past a long line of bedrooms to their right. "You and Betsy will have a room nearest to the kitchen, Mary, with Ronald next door. Ean and my room is next, and the boys' bedrooms start after that. Willard is at the end. His and hers bathrooms are across the hall. Most of our housing is humble compared to stateside standards, but this complex is a luxury to the boys. That's part of the lure we use to keep them here. No one is kept against their will, and the door to the street is always unlocked. They can go when they wish, and some do. A few come back, but not everyone." Daisy's face saddened and then she said softly, "We do what we can, but the glue and the gangs are a deadly game on the streets. Some of the boys have the fever in their blood, and nothing seems to break the disease."

"You do such worthwhile work here," Mary said as they headed deeper into the house.

A courtyard opened in front of them, where a dozen boys sat on chairs in front of a crude lectern. They held open notebooks in their laps and twiddled pencils between their fingers. A few looked up and smiled at the approaching group. Others showed little interest, and a few expressed outright hostility.

"Boys, we have visitors from the United States," Daisy announced. She lowered her voice to say to Mary and Betsy, "Ean was in the middle of teaching the English and writing class when you came. They have nothing else to do, so they are waiting until he comes back."

"Why don't I help?" Mary suggested.

Daisy raised her eyebrows. "You don't have to."

"Can I try?"

"Certainly, if you wish. The class is not organized in any particular fashion." Daisy handed her a textbook. "This is what Ean's been using for English 101."

Mary took her place at the lectern. Her heart beat wildly, but this was what she wanted to do.

"Greetings from the States," Mary began. "What are your names?"

A few raised their hands, and Mary moved closer to them as they spoke. The ones who wouldn't speak, she laid her hand on their shoulders until they looked up into her face.

"I'm Mary," she told them, her face bearing her brightest smile. Everyone gave their names except a skinny boy with glazed eyes and a distorted frame.

"I can see why Willard loves her," Mary heard Daisy whisper to Betsy.

Tears threatened to flow as she took her place at the lectern again. "Let's speak English, boys, and see how many words you know. Then we will write them on my piece of paper, which I will hold up for you. Okay?" Mary caught her breath. "Let's begin with, 'The Lord God is good.'"

THIRTY-NINE

The long dining room table was filled with boys on one side and the Americans on the other. Porridge bowls and cups for tea were set at regular intervals along the full length. Mary stood beside Betsy and waited for the men.

"*Goot* morning," she called to Willard when he walked in with Ronald.

"And a good morning to you. Up bright and early, I see."

"I had to help Tambala in the kitchen," Mary chirped. "This place invigorates me."

He laughed. "I'm sure the food is extra special this morning if you had a hand in it."

She made a face at him. "I was raised on a farm, so yes, I can cook. But I don't know anything about thin porridge, chai tea, flatbread, and yams. I only helped, and from the samples I tasted, everything turned out delicious. You have a devoted staff, Willard, which doesn't surprise me. You are a kind man." Mary gave him a sweet smile. "You are doing an awesome job running this mission."

"You've only been here one day." He took his seat and motioned for her to sit. "That's too early for you to know for sure."

Mary settled in beside him. She had made up her mind before

the plane landed, and everything she had seen so far only confirmed that decision.

"Do you think the time we have planned is long enough? I mean..." Willard fumbled for words. "We took that extra day in Paris, and I'm glad we did, but I can change the plane tickets if you need more time here in Nairobi to decide."

"I'm okay, Willard," she assured him. "No need to spend money on plane ticket changes."

"Money is no concern when it comes to you."

"I'm okay," she repeated. "If I had any doubts, I would tell you. A community of people is waiting back home to take me in with open arms. I promise you I will not condemn myself to a life I don't want."

He appeared satisfied and turned his attention to the breakfast table. Then he called to Tambala in the kitchen. "Are we ready?"

She bustled out with her apron flapping. "Yes, Willard. Ready when you are. I didn't want to interrupt your conversation with the excellent woman who helped me in the kitchen this morning."

Willard grinned. "I think Mary and I can eat and talk at the same time."

"Then we should start. The boys are hungry."

Willard stood, and everyone bowed their heads while Willard led a prayer. "Dear Father in heaven, gracious and merciful Lord. We give You thanks this morning..."

"Amen," Mary echoed when Willard finished. The cheerful clinking of bowls began around the table as the boys dished out the porridge. Ean and Daisy had everything running in an orderly fashion. Even the quiet boy from yesterday behaved himself and waited for his turn at the porridge bowl.

"So you like the strange food you helped make this morning?" Willard asked.

"Yes, I do. Kenyan food is not difficult to enjoy." Mary motioned toward Betsy and Ronald. "Listen to them talking. They like it too!"

His grin was broad. "Both you and Betsy have settled in well, and in a day's time. I'm impressed."

"It's easy with you around," Mary whispered under her breath.

Willard had to have heard. His hint of a smile betrayed him.

"I regret I didn't hear the English lecture yesterday," he said. "Daisy said you were a natural. You didn't tell me you had a degree from the Amish Barn Institute."

Mary laughed. "I guess the simple life lends itself to teaching. There's the farm, the chores, and the need to explain things to younger siblings. None of our parochial schoolteachers had degrees, just on-the-job training."

Willard grunted his agreement. "That may be the best kind of education. With the schooling American children receive, I'm not sure students learn that much."

"You turned out okay." Mary patted his arm.

He smiled down at her. "Thanks. I appreciate your trying to acclimate. More than I can say. You touch my heart deeply."

"I am glad I can help out." Mary straightened in her chair and then looked away.

She was not used to Willard's praise. Thankfully, Betsy and Ronald were deep in their own conversation and had not noticed.

Willard filled his bowl of porridge again and glanced at Mary. "I'd like to show you around the city today. Would you like that? See more of what I do here?"

"Certainly! That would be great. I'm sure I'll be impressed."

"You do much more than I deserve or ever imagined that you would," he told her.

"Please, stop saying these things," Mary begged. "I'm still Amish at heart, and we don't sing praises this early in the morning."

Willard laughed. "Or perhaps ever."

"Oh, sometimes," Mary objected. "Everyone needs a little encouragement, but within limits."

"You'll just have to get used to it."

"Maybe I won't," she warned.

The warmth in his eyes flowed all the way through her. His were the most *wunderbah* words she had ever heard. But was that not how love felt? She was very much in love. Josiah Beiler had never been anything like this.

Willard reached over to hold her hand before he stood and announced, "Don't stop eating, but it's time for our Scripture reading."

Tambala must have anticipated Willard's move because she was ready to hand the book across the table.

"Thank you, Tambala."

He opened the Bible and turned a few pages before he began to read. "'The Lord is my shepherd; I shall not want. He maketh me to lie down in green pastures: he leadeth me beside the still waters…'"

Mary listened to the familiar words. She had heard them so often in the community, where the open fields of the farm lay outside the living room window, and the clip-clop of horses' hooves passed on the road outside. Here she heard the distant roar of automobiles on the streets beyond the landscaped front yard, and the crush of a populace squeezed into small places. Yet the words of the psalm were the same, and so was the peace that came over her heart.

Willard finished and closed the book. "These words of the Lord are fresh and new this morning. They speak to my heart. I have been gone from the mission awhile, but I am back and have brought a lovely lady, Mary Yoder, with me for a short visit." Willard's voice caught as chuckles rose from the Americans at the table. Most of the boys stared with uncomprehending looks.

Mary clasped her hands under the table as Willard collected himself and continued. "I cannot begin to explain what Mary means to me, or the wonder I feel that she has come, along with Betsy and Ronald, to Kenya. Truly the Lord has been my Shepherd, and He has led me to green pastures."

Laughter rippled at the table this time, and Mary lowered her head to hide the heat that colored her face. A few of the boys across from her smiled once comprehension had begun to dawn. Love was a universal language that could be understood by even the most street-hardened children.

"Let us pray and give thanks for the great things the Lord has done, and for the good food we have eaten," Willard concluded. Everyone bowed their heads.

Mary waited for the "amen" to open her eyes. Willard's warm smile was the first thing she saw above her. He was so handsome, standing there with his hands by his sides, and the words of his prayer still on his lips.

"Come." Willard reached for her hand. "We should be on our way."

"Where are you going?" Betsy called after them as Mary followed Willard out of the dining room.

"I'm showing Mary the streets," Willard told her. "Do you want to come along?"

Betsy made a face. "I don't think so. I'll help with the dishes and work around the house."

"You're welcome to come with us," Willard assured her, but Betsy shook her head and returned to her conversation with Ronald.

Willard and Mary walked out the front doors hand in hand. She let go when he opened the passenger's side of the pickup.

"I'm driving," Willard said with a big grin. "Mind that?"

"Of course not! I trust you."

He hopped in and turned the key.

"Where are we going?" she inquired.

He drove down the landscaped driveway and into the street before he answered. "The slums."

"Did we go past them yesterday?"

"No." He gripped the steering wheel as they lurched into the traffic. "Ashon brought us past the market, but the slums are much worse. The mission is based in the better part of town. The boys come here in the daytime, but few can stay the night in the streets. The police are too vigilant, and getting caught isn't a pleasant experience." Willard frowned. "We don't offer a place to stay at the mission unless the boy is willing to enter the programs we have in place. We want them to get off the glue, stop stealing in the streets, and take any education course we are offering at the time."

"Doesn't sound like much of a sacrifice," Mary mused.

"You wouldn't think so." His face was pensive. "But things can get turned around easily. God has made us social creatures, and we are adaptive to our environments. We feel at home with what we are used to or have grown up with. We Americans can forget that when we deal with cultures unfamiliar to us. Even the slums can become home for many. Thieving becomes their way of life. The streets tug at the hearts of these boys, and glue sniffing is like the familiar embrace of a father. Strange how that works, but it does. I have seen boys leave the mission and return to the dirt, the grime, the filth, and the suffering of the street because they were homesick." Willard shrugged. "That's the only way I can explain it."

"Do you think I will become homesick for the community?"

"I know you will." He gave her a quick glance. "That's not a guess."

"Is that the real reason I'm here?"

He took a moment to answer. "Partly. You have more reason to return than these boys do."

"How am I going to persuade you, Willard?"

"It's not a matter of persuading me. It's simply walking through the valley that lies ahead of you and seeing things as they are. I want you to have a choice in that valley before you commit. The worst thing for me would be to see tears of loneliness well up in your eyes and know there was no way back."

"I love you, Willard. You know that."

"I know, Mary." He forced a smile. "I feel the same, which makes things worse, I think." A horn blasted beside them, and Willard swerved away from the offended vehicle. "Looks like I had better pay attention to my driving."

Mary moved closer to him and reached for his hand. "I will be honest with you. I know there will be pain if I join you in Kenya, but there will also be joy in a life spent ministering with you."

"You are a saint," Willard said. His attention focused as they weaved in and out of the traffic.

"You are a better driver than Ashon," she finally told him.

He chuckled. "That wouldn't be difficult to beat."

Mary stared as they reached the edge of town. The changes had begun a few streets back, but that didn't diminish the stark devastation in front of them.

"Welcome to the slums," Willard told her, as if words were needed.

A railroad track cut through the shacks, which were constructed with boards set on end and bound together by the flimsiest of means. The roofs were rusted metal, and in some cases strips of metal laid horizontally on top of each other. Laundry hung on wires that were strung from one side of a structure to the other. The pieces of clothing were brightly colored but threadbare. People walked slowly in the streets, the pattern haphazard and fuzzy, as if no one was certain where they were bound.

"We're stopping here." Willard brought the pickup to a rattling halt. "We can walk in a ways, but we can't leave the vehicle out of sight. There wouldn't be much left when we came back."

Willard jumped out, and Mary didn't wait for him to open her door. The ground squished under her feet, but she kept her gaze on the people around them. Most stared blankly, except for a young boy who stood alert at the street corner.

Willard waved to him, and the boy moved closer. "You want me to watch your vehicle, Mr. Willard? I will for a price."

"Thank you, Chane," Willard told him. "You keep asking, but you know I can't. We'll stay in sight as always. Anything going on that I need to know about?"

The young lad spat on the ground. "The police raided here yesterday. What they looking for, you know? They found nothing of that sort, but two of my boys were taken. I send someone to look this morning, but I know what I will find—if I find them." Chane spat again. "Bloody and beaten, that I find. Can I bring them to you?"

Willard nodded. "You know you can. In fact, we will wait and take them back with us."

"They come soon," Chane assured Willard. "You can take them."

The lad resumed his post at the street corner. Several young boys appeared from a side street, engaged Chane in a short conversation, and left again.

"The gangs," Willard confirmed. "They are experts at stealing. Somehow they manage to keep things hidden from the police raids. None of them would survive if caught."

"Will you ever let him guard your vehicle?" Mary asked.

Willard shrugged. "He never stops offering. Someday I'll take the chance, I guess."

"I can tell Chane already trusts you."

Willard gave Mary a smile. "That's what I want, but I never know how to read these street boys. That would be one advantage of having you with me. You read people well."

Mary looked away. She had not read Josiah well at all. Thankfully, Willard didn't notice her grimace.

His attention was focused down the street. "Here they come now."

Mary followed his gaze to where four skinny lads struggled with a blanket strung between them in a makeshift litter. Chane also noticed and ran toward the approaching party. Willard followed with Mary close behind him. Chane's face was contorted with rage when they arrived. "One is dead. The other looks like this. The soldiers, we hate them. Now you see why."

Mary peered into the blanket at the frail form crisscrossed with lashes. Blood oozed from the open wounds, with dirt crusting the edges. Mary reached for the boy's head and cradled the matted hair in her hands.

"Bring him over to the pickup truck," she ordered. "I will ride in the back with the boy on the way home."

"The hospital," Willard corrected her. "We are going there first."

FORTY

Mary awoke in the early morning hours to the blasting horns and the faint roar of street bustle outside the mission's thick walls. Big cities never slept. Surprisingly, she had adapted well in the few days they had been in Nairobi. Betsy had done well until Mary returned to the mission in the back of Willard's pickup truck holding the bandaged head of the street urchin.

Mary studied her sister, who slept in the bed across from her. Betsy had two pillows stacked on her head, as if to shut out the horror she had witnessed. For the last two nights, Betsy had moaned and cried out frequently. Thankfully, she slept soundly at the moment. Betsy would emerge for breakfast bleary-eyed and short tempered until Ronald teased her back into *goot* spirits.

Mary exited the bedroom and made her way down the hallway. Betsy belonged back in the community. Ronald managed city life a little better, but he had also begun to mope around during the day with a homesick look in his eyes. Their scheduled departure at the end of next week would not come soon enough for those two.

Mary paused to catch her breath. The truth of how she felt was clear this morning. She didn't want to go back to the community. Only pain awaited her there. Distance and time might heal the wound between her and the ones she loved, but immediacy would deepen the cut. That certainty had increased each day she had been here. This was where she belonged. Nairobi and Willard's mission work were not a dream, but her dream had led her here. Would Willard allow her to stay? Would he ask her to marry him? Was he satisfied with how she had adjusted to life in the big city? If not, she would have to walk the road back to the community, agonizing though that would be.

Mary pushed open the door into the injured lad's bedroom. The boy appeared to be resting well, so she seated herself beside his bed and took his hand. Fever had wracked the thin frame since they had brought him home from the hospital. The emergency staff had washed and sewn up the worst of the boy's cuts, but that had been the end of their care.

"Gang warfare," several of the nurses had muttered darkly. "We no want him here."

Willard hadn't objected. Apparently, protests would not be believed. That they were Americans who could pay was likely the only reason the hospital would treat the boy at all. The nurses had helped place the boy into the pickup bed with a clean blanket under him, and Mary and Willard had headed back to the mission. Tambala had resumed his treatment from there, with the help of antibiotics purchased at the corner drugstore. No prescription had been given at the hospital.

The fever had come fast, but the boy had lived. They still didn't know his name. Street Boy, Tambala had called him, until something better would develop. The name sounded familiar on Tambala's lips. She must have used the moniker before to peg the children who came through the mission doors. In a way, all the boys from the street were nameless, faceless children caught in a world without a home.

Willard supplied them a place where they could be something

beyond unwanted cogs in the city's wheels. Where would this child go when he awakened and was able to move about? Would he wish to stay, or would the strangeness of the place, removed from the dirt, filth, and violence of the street, be too much change? How strange that this mountain must be climbed, a mountain she had never seen before. Mary had imagined the boys would line up outside the mission for a chance at a fresh start, a chance to live in a real home where you were loved. Perhaps the definition of love changed on the streets. Chane, with his street corner, cared in his own way for his charges. Did that suffice or pass in this boy's heart for affection and acceptance?

From what she could see, Willard didn't offer freebies to the boys as enticements. He required a lot of those who stayed. They were cut off from the freedom of the streets, from the excitement of city life, from unexpected disruptions, and from the promise of thievery to supply needs without labor. In the slums, the deprived were surrounded by those with abundance. The temptation to take must be overwhelming, and this boy had succumbed. Would he be able to resist temptation, once wellness returned to his body?

A soft knock came on the bedroom door, which cracked open to reveal Willard. A smile crept across his face. "At your post early again. How's he doing?"

"His hands are cooler." Mary brushed the boy's forehead. "I think the fever has broken. He's sleeping soundly."

"You are quite the nurse. Tambala is impressed."

"So I passed the test?" Mary teased.

Willard chuckled. "With flying colors, but you always do."

Mary stilled a quick intake of breath. This was a conversation made in jest. She had to keep that in mind.

"Can I talk to you?" Willard motioned toward the hallway.

The boy stirred, and Mary waited until his breathing evened. Willard had left the doorway, so he must be in the kitchen where Tambala would be busy with breakfast.

A flood of light from the kitchen appeared ahead of her, where Willard leaned against the counter.

"Good morning," Tambala called to her. "How's the street boy? Willard told me you were up early to see him."

"Much better, I think, due to your excellent nursing."

Tambala shook her head knowingly. "That was you and not me. The boy can feel your love. That's what brought him through so quickly." Tambala turned toward her. "And don't you argue with me, Mary. Willard knows this is true. Don't you?"

"You know I do," Willard agreed with a broad grin. "But you also are an excellent nurse and cook, Tambala."

"See, you are the *goot* one," Mary insisted.

Willard glanced at her. "I was just ready to ask Tambala for a favor this morning. I want her to fix us a breakfast that we can take along to the park."

"The park!" Mary exclaimed. "You have a park in this city?"

The question was lost to Tambala's wagging finger. "You know I cannot do that, Mr. Willard. I make you food right now, and you can eat early, and then you go. Breakfast is not in a box you can take with you. Now you listen."

Willard chuckled. "I guess taking breakfast to a park is a little impractical, but I wanted Mary to see the sunrise with me away from the city." Willard turned his attention to her. "I discovered this place by accident one morning, driving in from a trip into the country. From the park, the city lies on the horizon, and the sun is a beautiful sight coming up over the skyscrapers. This morning the skies should be clear."

"Then let's go!"

Tambala's finger punched the air. "You eat here! I not tell you again."

Mary joined in Willard's laughter before she asked, "Will there be enough time to eat and still get there when you want to?"

"Depends how fast we eat," Willard replied.

But she could tell there would not be. "Let's take something with us and go," Mary decided.

A look of alarm filled Willard's face. He apparently was not used to defiance in the face of Tambala's orders.

Mary hurried on while Tambala stared at her. "We can take fruit, cheese, and bread. We ate like that in Paris."

Tambala finally found her voice. "You would starve Willard of his breakfast?"

"I'll pack it myself," Mary told her with a sweet smile. "You don't have to worry about a thing."

"But...but...Mr. Willard..." Tambala sputtered.

"I'll take care of him. He will live." Mary gave Tambala another smile as she began to gather up what she needed.

Tambala sent a few baleful glances her way but soon gave up. The bridge had been crossed safely. Mary could tell from the look on Willard's face that he was impressed. He followed Mary out the front door, and they climbed into the pickup. Willard gave her a wink but said nothing as they drove out of town toward the south.

"How far is the park from here?" Mary inquired when the first sign appeared for Nairobi National Park.

"A few miles. We'll be there before the sun is up. Thank you for handling Tambala so well at the mission."

"I was glad to help out."

Willard kept his focus on the road until he turned into the main gate and followed the arrows to the picnic area. He seemed to know his way around.

"You've been here a few times."

He grinned. "I've come back since my discovery, but never with a breakfast basket or a beautiful woman."

"I should hope not," Mary said in mock horror.

Their laughter filled the pickup truck. Willard parked and turned off the headlights. The first colors of dawn had begun to rise above the skyscrapers outlined on the distant horizon. Mary climbed out and carried the basket with her to the first picnic table. Animals stirred on the plain below them. Giraffes mingled their long necks with the skyscraper silhouettes, and ostriches strode about, barely recognizable in the low light.

"What do you think?" Willard asked as he slid onto the seat beside her.

"It's beautiful and peaceful." Mary caught her breath. "I can see why you come often."

Willard winced. "True. I find rest here when the going gets rough at the mission."

She leaned toward him on the park bench and wrapped her arms around him. "Thank you for sharing this with me. The place is very precious."

He gazed across the grassy plain toward the brightening horizon. "What can I say, Mary? Words fail me. I don't deserve you."

"Hush," she told him. "Let's eat."

He nodded, and they bowed their heads in a brief prayer of thanks. Mary laid out the bread, cheese, and fruit. As they ate, the sun rose higher over the distant skyscrapers. The giraffes were in motion, their tapered necks softening the steel outlines of the buildings. The ostriches fluffed their feathers and strutted, happy with the dawn of a new day. Striped zebras came into focus, and rhinoceroses raised their arched noses in the morning air.

"I want to settle our future this morning, Mary," Willard began, "in my heart and in yours."

Mary held her breath. The moment she wanted had arrived, and she had no words.

Willard continued. "I have struggled with how I dare ask so much of you, Mary. And don't protest. I know the cost you will have to pay and have paid already. Add to that my inclination not to trust a woman, which must tear at your heart. If you return to the community and I never see you again, I will let you go without grudges, and I'll be thankful for the short time I have known you. I want to be clear about that."

"I know," Mary whispered. "You have been nothing but kind to me. That's one reason among many why I love you so deeply, Willard."

"Are ready for this, then?" His gaze was on the horizon and the sunlight bursting over the skyscrapers.

"For what?" she whispered.

He took a deep breath and reached for her hand. "Will you be my wife, Mary? Live with me here in Nairobi and wherever else the Lord may lead us?"

"I will." She squeezed his hand in hers and looked into his eyes. "I've known the answer for a long time, Willard. I am greatly honored to accept with my whole heart."

"You will?"

"*Yah*, Willard. What can I say to convince you?"

He shook his head. "I don't need convincing, I guess. I just need to believe that something so wonderful could happen to me—that such a perfect gift, which can only come from heaven, would be given to me." He looked away, his eyes moist. "I'm sorry, Mary. You deserve so much better."

She wrapped her arms around him and pulled him close. "I want to marry you here, Willard. On this spot...as soon as you can fly your grandmother across the Atlantic and before Betsy and Ronald fly back to the community. That's the only request I have. I know that's a big one, but it's important to me."

He stared. "What about your family and the community?"

She blinked back the tears. "We've already spoken about that, and Betsy is right. She can break the news to my parents when she gets back. They wouldn't attend the wedding anyway, even if we were to have the ceremony at the church in Fort Plain. I'm not strong enough to face that pain right now. Maybe later when the years have passed. Forgive my weakness, but that's what I want."

He held her tight. "I would give you anything I have in the world, Mary. Grandma feels the same way. I will email her this morning and make the arrangements."

"This is my home," she whispered, and they clung to each other as the sun rose higher and flooded the prairie with glowing light.

FORTY-ONE

Willard awoke in the early morning hours to the silence of the mission house. Nairobi street life would be stirring outside the walls, engines backfiring among the ever present horn blasts. The sound would increase as the city stirred. Underneath the surface racket were the silent cries of the neglected, who populated the sidewalks and stone niches in the daytime and went wherever shelter could safely be found for the night. Lost souls lived from moment to moment with bitterness in their hearts against a world they found cruel and unforgiving. He'd come here to minister, and the Lord had sent a woman to walk by his side. Adam couldn't have been more blessed when he was presented with Eve as a helpmeet. Never had Willard understood that story better or felt greater thanksgiving rise up in his heart. The vision of Mary's beautiful face as she gazed at him that day in the park outside of Nairobi still rendered him speechless.

Willard slipped out of bed to kneel on the floor. "Dear Father," he prayed. "I am unworthy of this great gift. Mary is more than I deserve. She is leaving so much to love me and stand by my side. I can never repay her for what she is doing, and will do. How great is Your grace, and what a debtor I will always be. Mary is so like You with her giving and open heart. Thank You. A thousand times I say it, and still that will not be enough."

Willard buried his head in his hands for a moment before he stood and dressed. Outside the bedroom door a low light shone from the direction of the kitchen. He followed the beam down the hallway, to find his grandmother busy at work with Tambala by her side.

"Greetings on this morning of your wedding," Tambala sang out, her face creasing with a bright smile. "You have been blessed with a beautiful day by the Lord. The sun is rising on a cloudless sky, beautiful as your bride is beautiful."

"I have much for which I can give thanks." Willard slid onto a chair. "I know this well."

"Mary is a bride of brides!" Tambala gushed. "She will be like the queen of Nairobi today decked in flowers and a dress which is the most beautiful, the most..." Tambala nearly dropped the bowl in her hands as one hand flew upward. "The best the city can supply. That's all I can say," she finished.

"And Mary likes this dress?" Willard directed the question to his grandmother.

Mrs. Gabert's smile was gentle. "Tambala exaggerates a little in her enthusiasm. We found a very fitting dress for Mary, and Mary highly approved. We wouldn't do anything that Mary didn't like, Willard."

Willard sighed in relief. "Thanks again for coming over, Grandma. I don't know how we would have prepared for this day without you."

Mrs. Gabert shook her finger at him. "I'm still insulted that Mary was the one who insisted I come. You should have known I wouldn't miss your wedding for anything in the world."

"I know." Willard grinned. "But our wedding day coming so soon was a surprise, to say the least. I would never have dared suggest a wedding date before Mary returned to the States."

"And so it should be!" Tambala declared. "The woman runs things best in the house, and on the day of the wedding."

"And most of the time," Mrs. Gabert added with a laugh. "Just teasing, Willard. But I must remind you again that I was right from the first. Mary is the woman for you."

"As you keep saying." Willard nodded soberly. "I just came off my knees thanking the Lord for His great grace, so I agree fully. You were right."

Mrs. Gabert gave her grandson a wise look. "Faith is always the best choice, Willard, even when our heart is wounded and bleeding. I know that's difficult at times, but old age teaches the lesson well. As King David said in the Old Testament, 'I have been young, and now am old; yet have I not seen the righteous forsaken, nor his seed begging bread.' I can assent with my whole heart."

"Those are great words," Tambala agreed. "But in this city they are not listened to by many people."

"May their number increase by leaps and bounds," Willard muttered.

Mrs. Gabert beamed a smile at him. "With Mary by your side, I think your prayers have been answered, son. Here she comes." Mrs. Gabert tilted her head toward the darkened hallway.

Willard leaped to his feet. Mary came out of the shadows and held her hands out for him.

They embraced as Tambala cooed in the background. "It is so good to see such sweet love in this broken city."

Willard brushed loose strands of hair from Mary's face to whisper, "You are so beautiful, sweetheart."

"I haven't even washed the sleep from my eyes," Mary protested. "Why didn't someone awaken me? I want to help with breakfast."

"You are not helping with a thing," Mrs. Gabert retorted. "Sit down and relax this morning. The Lord knows you will have your hands full after the wedding."

"My wedding," Mary whispered. "The day of my wedding." Tears sprang to her eyes. "I couldn't have planned this better if I had a hundred years of advance warning. Your grandmother is here, Willard, and I am where I belong. I cannot thank the Lord enough for leading me to you."

They held each other for a moment. "Shall we step outside?" Willard suggested.

Mary followed him without hesitation.

"We'll be back," Willard hollered over his shoulder.

With Mary's hand in his, they went out the front door and onto the front lawn, which Ashon had manicured to perfection. Tambala had been correct. The sun was rising in a cloudless sky. The first beams rushed over the treetops and into the street beyond the mission grounds. Several young boys standing on the sidewalk turned their heads toward them.

Mary's grip tightened in Willard's hand. "We have chosen a *wunderbah* day for our wedding."

"Any day when I marry you would have been wonderful," Willard whispered back.

"I'm just glad to be with you, Willard."

"The feeling is mutual, Mary." He pulled her closer.

"Do you think any of those boys have been to the mission?" she asked.

"They know about us," Willard replied. "And they know about you."

"They do not," she objected. "How could they?"

"They do!" he insisted. "The whole city knows. They know that Mary has arrived."

Mary leaned her head against his shoulder and laughed. "You say the kindest things, and to think that you will be my husband today."

"Sure you have no regrets?"

She shook her head, her gaze on the sunlight streaming over

the housetops. "I like this place, and there will always be the park outside the city. We can go there to refresh our faith in the Lord's goodness."

"I know," he agreed. "I feel the same way."

She glanced up at him. "Thank you for sharing so much with me. Your mission, your secret hideaway in the park—the place that so ministered to you and so deeply blessed my heart the first day you took me there. We will make our first memories as husband and wife in that place."

"We will," he said. "Shall we go inside? Grandma will have breakfast ready, and your sister should be up by now."

"Just a moment," Mary told him. "Can we pray for my parents? That the Lord will comfort their hearts? *Mamm* must feel what is to happen today."

"Grandma could have told them before she flew over," he told her.

"I know you offered, Willard, but it's better if Betsy tells them when she gets back. We'll visit in a few years, and the hurt will have healed to some extent. These things take time. If I had returned before the wedding, things would have been said that could have wounded us further. *Daett* might have been forced to banish us, and then we could never have gone home."

"You think your father would have done this?"

"He might not have had a choice. This way..." Mary clung to him.

Willard held her and prayed, "Dear Father in heaven, merciful and gracious Father. Comfort the hearts of Mary's parents this morning. Allow Your grace to minister to their pain, and let healing come between us quickly. Make us not strangers from Mary's community, but give Mary a place there that she can also call home."

"Thank you." She smiled up at him, her face beautiful in the soft morning sunlight.

He wanted to kiss her, badly.

"We'll save the kiss for later," Mary whispered, as if she had read his thoughts. "Don't the *Englisha* kiss the bride after the vows?"

"They do," he said.

"I'm *Englisha* now. I can kiss my husband in front of everyone."

He chuckled. "You sound as if that might be a problem."

"Oh!" She buried her face in his chest. "You don't know how much I love you, Willard. But I'll always be Amish, I guess."

He brushed his fingers along her cheeks. "We don't have to follow our customs today. In fact, we won't. I want you to have this day exactly the way you want it."

"Then I want to kiss you."

"In public?"

She groaned.

"See?" he said. "It is decided."

"Thank you," she whispered. "So kiss me now, Willard. Please."

"You don't have to beg. I'm the one who—"

Mary silenced him, pulling his head down. He lingered long, and the wonder of her closeness filled his being.

She pulled away. "We should go inside. Breakfast is ready."

He concurred and followed her.

"There they are!" Betsy sang out. "I was beginning to think the lovebirds had eloped."

"Good morning. How are you?" Ronald added.

Mary hugged her sister while Willard took his seat at the table beside Ronald.

"Good weather outside?" Ronald inquired.

"Nice day, that's for sure. But Mary's still hurting over the break with her family. Any suggestions?"

Ronald didn't hesitate. "Mary is making the right decision with a clean break. You don't know how messy these things can become. Betsy and I will do what we can to smooth things over."

"I don't understand fully, I guess," Willard admitted.

"There's not much to understand," Ronald said. "The community has their way of life to maintain, and I like that life. No one has come up with a better way so far, so there we are. Sorry for the contradiction."

"I have no hard feelings," Willard assured him. "Mary is the one who suffers."

"She'll be okay. Mary feels sorrow when there is pain, but joy comes in the morning. Quite fitting, don't you think?"

"I hope she wasn't crying all night?" Willard glanced toward Mary and Betsy.

"She doesn't look like it." Ronald gave him a smile. "Betsy keeps me up-to-date. Mary did her crying before she left. The morning is here, my friend, and you are blessed."

"That I am," Willard agreed.

Tambala clapped her hands in front of them and declared, "Time to eat, and time for the wedding soon. We must hurry and not be late."

"Late!" Willard chuckled. "How can anyone be late in Nairobi?"

Tambala glared at him. "You get saucy now that you have a wife. I no like this."

Everyone joined in the laughter, and the food was served after a short prayer of thanks. Mary came over to sit beside Willard while they ate, but she dashed off the minute her plate was cleared.

"The wedding dress!" Tambala beamed. "Mary has gone to put on her wedding dress. Even you will like this wedding dress, Willard."

"I like the woman I'm marrying more," Willard corrected.

Tambala left with a snort, and followed the other women as they scurried after Mary.

"Quite the deal, this wedding dress," Ronald said. "Have you seen it?"

"Must be quite a marvel," Willard seconded. "And no. I haven't."

They sat in silence for a few moments, their faces turned toward the hallway.

"So what is an Amish wedding like?" Willard asked.

Ronald laughed. "Not like this one. More like a formal three-hour church service, with premarital counseling in the morning from the ministers. It includes two sermons, each an hour long, and the vows, of course. The ceremony is completed by a full meal afterward for the guests, and a young folks' supper and hymn singing in the evening."

"You will have such a wedding?"

"Plan to!" Ronald grinned from ear to ear. "Betsy accepted my proposal in Paris."

"Congratulations." Willard extended his hand. "I should have guessed."

"No offense taken."

A commotion in the hallway drew Willard's attention. Mary appeared in a long flowing white dress with an overlapping gown that hung from her shoulders. Embroidered rings of traditional Kenyan art ran the full length of the edges and followed the neckline. Mary made her way toward him with slow steps, while he stood, his mouth falling open.

"Wow!" Ronald proclaimed. "That is some dress."

Willard stepped forward to meet Mary. "Words fail me," he said, reaching for her hands.

Mary's face glowed. "That's exactly how I like it."

"This from an Amish woman."

"I'm *Englisha* now." Mary smiled.

"Come! We must go!" Tambala interrupted, shooing everyone outside.

Two new trucks waited in the street, bedecked with ribbons and streamers. Ashon was seated in the first vehicle, and the hired pastor stood in the back waving his hands about. "The Lord's blessings to the happy couple!" he hollered. "You have been given a beautiful day as a sign of the Lord's goodness."

"He would say so," Tambala grumbled. "Though it is true."

Willard helped Mary into the front seat and climbed in after her.

"Good morning. Good morning," Ashon greeted them. "This is a great day."

"Yes, it is," Mary agreed. "I am to wed Willard today."

"Ah...he is so blessed," Ashon gushed. "And you are so beautiful."

Mary turned a deep red, but she still managed to tell him, "Thank you, Ashon. You are kind to say so."

"We wait now until the food is loaded," Ashon declared. "Then we be off."

"Can't forget the food," Willard muttered.

Mary smiled sweetly at Willard. "Do I really look okay?"

"You are heaven's bride itself," he told her as he took her hand. They held each other tightly, and Ashon took off and headed out of town with the other vehicle behind them. Both of them blasted their horns until the edge of town was reached. With the gates of the park in front of them, silence settled over the party. The animals raised their heads to follow the progress of the procession. Ashon maneuvered across the grassland and pulled into the overlook with a flourish.

"There we are!" He hopped out.

Willard climbed down and reached back to help Mary. They stood together, close to where they had sat that day when he had first brought her here. The pastor was waving his arms again, escorting everyone into place. There were no seats, but the ceremony would be short. Mary had insisted.

"And now a wedding the American way," the pastor began, standing in front of Mary and Willard. "We will have a Scripture reading." He opened the Bible and read, "'Praise ye the Lord. I will praise the Lord with my whole heart, in the assembly of the upright, and in the congregation. The works of the Lord are great, sought out of all them that have pleasure therein...'"

Willard listened. Mary could not have chosen a better Scripture, as he could not have chosen a better wife if he had gone on a long arduous search. The gift of the Lord had been given with an open hand, even while he doubted.

"'The fear of the Lord is the beginning of wisdom: a good understanding have all they that do his commandments: his praise endureth for ever.'

"And now we will come to the vows," said the pastor. "Will you, Willard Gabert, take this woman, Mary Yoder, as your wife, to love, to honor, and to hold while you have life on this earth?"

"I will," Willard said.

The words seem to hang in the air, before they distilled across the open grassland in front of them.

Softly, Mary's answer joined his.

FORTY-TWO

The connecting flight from New York City to Albany circled to land and lowered its wheels with a thump. Betsy flinched, seated in the window seat beside Ronald. The sound should be familiar by now. They had logged many air hours flying to Kenya and back, but she was still an Amish girl at heart. Plane travel would be forbidden to her once she ended her *rumspringa* and settled down in the community. In the meantime, she had to face *Mamm* and *Daett*. They would be hoping and praying that Mary had seen her mistake and was ready with her church confession, but Mary wasn't on the plane. Mary was Willard Gabert's *frau*. A worse fate than a church confession awaited her sister.

In her heart *Mamm* must know that Mary would not return. *Mamm and Daett* both knew Mary well, and surely they would see reason once Betsy explained. They would agree that Mary had been wise to wed Willard quickly and avoid a protracted struggle with Deacon Stoltzfus that could only end with Mary's excommunication.

"Are we ready for home?" Ronald muttered from the seat beside her.

The plane wheels touched the ground with a lurch, and Betsy forced a smile. "I guess so."

"I'll stay a week and help you work through this," he encouraged her. "Longer if needed."

"Thank you," she whispered as the plane taxied to the gate. "But I'll be okay."

"We still have our wedding to plan," he teased.

"I know." Betsy leaned against his shoulder. "You are so sweet. I'll never forget our days in Paris. Not if I grow old enough to wither and wrinkle like a prune."

Ronald laughed. "Spare me the image, but I'm sure you will still be the most beautiful prune in the world."

"You are terrible. Hush!"

Mrs. Gabert had turned to give them a bright smile from the aisle seat across from them, but she couldn't have overheard their endearments. If she had, what did it matter?

The plane parked, and the stairs were lowered. Betsy waited until Ronald was in the aisle and had taken their carry-on bags from the overhead bin. Mrs. Gabert was already on her way, and they followed.

Silently they took the short walk down the stairs and into the terminal, with the roar of the plane's engines in their ears. Signs pointed toward the luggage carousel. Ronald took her hand, and she clung to him. The wait for their bags wasn't long, and after Ronald grabbed the suitcases, they made their way to Mrs. Gabert's car.

Little was said as they drove north, the stillness heavy in the automobile. Betsy rode in the front with Ronald in the back. Coming up Interstate 90, the outlines of the houses in Fort Plain took shape in the distance.

"You want to go straight to your parents' place?" Mrs. Gabert asked.

Betsy nodded. "I'll drive Ronald to Cousin Enos's in the buggy afterward."

"I hope he's staying with you until..." Mrs. Gabert let the sentence hang.

"*Yah*, until," Betsy replied.

She bit her lip. "Until" could be awhile. Until the first words had been spoken to *Mamm* and *Daett*. Until the wrath of the storm had passed. Until the evening, when Deacon Stoltzfus and Bishop Miller would arrive and hear the news. Until Sunday, when Mary's excommunication would be declared.

Mrs. Gabert's car slowed as they approached the familiar driveway and turned in to park beside the barn. The door flew open, and *Daett* appeared. He hesitated until *Mamm* came out of the house and hurried down the snowy walkway toward them. Ronald gave Betsy's shoulder a quick squeeze before he climbed out of the backseat.

"Can I pay you for the drive in from the airport?" Betsy offered. "And for the other things you have done?"

Mrs. Gabert patted Betsy's arm. "Just be kind to your parents and remember they are hurting. I am the one who owes your family, not the other way around."

Daett arrived at Mrs. Gabert's window. "*Goot* morning."

"Good morning, Mr. Yoder," Mrs. Gabert replied.

"Thanks for bringing our daughters back from Kenya," he told her.

Silence fell. *Daett* had to see that Mary wasn't along, but perhaps he thought Mary had stayed down at Mrs. Gabert's place with Willard. *Daett* stroked his beard, his face fallen. Was the storm to begin before Mrs. Gabert could leave?

"Just go, dear." Mrs. Gabert touched Betsy's arm.

Betsy forced her legs to move, and she exited the vehicle. She stayed frozen in place while Mrs. Gabert's car disappeared down the hill toward town.

Daett's voice was like a thunderclap. "Where is Mary?"

Mamm stood a few feet behind *Daett* with her face buried in her apron. Clearly her parents expected the worst.

Thankfully, Ronald slipped to Betsy's side and took her hand. "Maybe we can discuss this inside," he suggested.

"Discuss what?" *Daett* demanded. "Tell me where Mary is."

"Look!" Ronald held out both of his hands. "A lot of things have happened in the weeks we have been gone. Mary has made her choice, and that can't be changed—but let's not plunge into the end of the story before you have heard the beginning."

Mamm moaned. "I knew it. She married the man. Just up and married him! Tell me at least that my daughter is okay."

"She's okay, *Mamm*," Betsy managed.

"But I want to see her!" *Mamm*'s voice rose higher.

"Stop this, Mandy." *Daett* laid his hand on *Mamm*'s arm. "We'd best leave this for Deacon Stoltzfus and Bishop Miller."

"She's not coming back," Ronald added.

"She's married!" *Mamm* shrieked. "My daughter has left us." With another cry, she muffled her sobs with her apron.

Daett's face had paled. "So Mary really did marry this *Englisha* man? Your *mamm* told me she might, but I didn't want to believe it."

"*Yah*." Betsy tried to move, but her feet didn't seem to work at the moment.

"We should go inside and talk this through," Ronald said. "This is not a fitting place to break this news."

Daett appeared not to hear. "Deacon Stoltzfus must be told at once!" he declared. He turned and headed toward the barn.

Mamm let out a loud cry and ran to the house with her apron flying.

"I'm so sorry," Betsy told Ronald. "I thought I would do better with this."

"Don't blame yourself," he comforted her. "My method didn't work either. There is apparently no discussing this matter in a civilized and decent manner."

"Don't blame *Mamm*a and *Daett*," Betsy begged. "Anyone in the community would have acted this way."

Ronald agreed with a long sigh. "You are right." He moved their suitcases to the side of the lane. "What are we supposed to do now?"

As if in answer, *Daett* appeared with his hand on the bridle of their family driving horse. He hurried the animal across the barnyard toward the buggy.

Ronald stepped forward to help, but *Daett* waved him away. "I will do this myself, son." Without a sideways glance, *Daett* completed the task, hopped in the buggy, and dashed out of the lane.

"So much for that," Ronald muttered.

"I can't believe this," Betsy moaned. "Their reaction was much worse than I imagined."

Ronald placed an arm around her shoulder. "You didn't do anything wrong, dear. What was the right thing to say? We've never been through this before."

"We should go in and speak with *Mamm*," Betsy suggested.

"Speak with her?" Ronald peered down at her. "I'll get thrown out of the house. Your *daett* wouldn't even let me help him with the horse."

"He called you 'son,'" Betsy told him. "Count your blessings. *Daett* is in shock."

"I guess he did say that. Come. Let's go in."

Hand in hand, they approached the front door to hear *Mamm's* loud sobs coming from the living room. Betsy entered to find *Mamm* seated on the couch with a pillow pressed to her face.

"*Mamm*, please?" Betsy begged, slipping in to sit by her side.

"My daughter is married to an *Englisha* man," she wailed. "Thank the Lord we had the presence of mind to send Gerald away for the day. He was spared this awful moment when we learned the news."

"Mary is...she's so happy..." Betsy wanted to give up. What was the use?

"We understand what you are feeling," Ronald tried again, standing in front of the women. "If there had been another way, she would have chosen it."

Mamm moved the pillow away from her face. "She must have had this all figured out before she left. How could she not tell us?"

"That's not true," Betsy retorted.

"Then what is true?" *Mamm* sobbed. "My daughter has left the community, and I'm acting like a woman who can't control herself. We told Mary not to go over there. We tried. The community tried, and we failed."

Ronald pulled up a chair and sat in front of them. "I would like to tell you the story, Mandy. I know it's not what we are used to, but hear me out. I think I have the right, since I plan to marry your daughter."

"You are jumping the fence with Betsy?" *Mamm*'s face had lost all color. "I had my heart prepared for...but not both of you together."

"We're not leaving." Betsy pulled on *Mamm*'s arm. "Listen to what Ronald has to say."

Mamm appeared uncomprehending. "You're not leaving?"

Just tell her, Betsy mouthed toward Ronald.

He nodded. "Mary has a true heart, Mandy. She really does. I wouldn't say that just to comfort you or ourselves. I've been out there in the world, and I don't want the problems they have. That's why I've come back, and why I plan to marry Betsy. We will live in the community, perhaps even here in the valley for a few years, now that..." Ronald paused for a second. "You may not find that a comfort at the moment, but at least listen to what I have to say. I was there in Nairobi, and I saw Mary struggle through her decision. She wanted to find the Lord's will. Maybe I should judge more harshly, but I can't bring myself to do that. I saw too much, and Mary is acting out of an honest heart. She wanted to see what Willard's life was like and whether she could fit in it. And from our first day in Kenya, I could see plainly that Mary's heart grew larger and fuller as she considered working at the mission with Willard."

"Don't say these things." *Mamm* sat with her hands clasped on her lap, but at least her sobs had ceased.

Betsy nodded encouragingly to Ronald, and he went on. "Willard runs a mission for boys from the streets of Nairobi, but you already know that. We stayed there and got to see firsthand the work that he does. There are many boys who are truly being helped. Mary felt that she couldn't walk away from that ministry to them, and she loves Willard."

"She really does," Betsy seconded.

"Tell me about the wedding," *Mamm* whispered.

Betsy stared at Ronald. *Mamm* wanted to know about the wedding?

Ronald spoke softly. "She wore a simple white dress. A long, flowing traditional dress, I think, with local symbols embroidered on the edges. We had breakfast at the mission and then traveled in two trucks to a park outside of Nairobi, where Mary exchanged her vows with Willard on a little overlook. Giraffes, zebras, deer, and other creatures from the park were below us. It was lovely. It really was. I wish you could have been there."

"I wish so too," *Mamm* said, but her face hardened when *Daett*'s buggy pulled back into the driveway.

Ronald stood.

Mamm tottered to the front door. Rachel and Annie rushed in, with Deacon Stoltzfus and Bishop Miller close behind them. *Mamm* appeared ready to collapse, but Rachel steadied her and helped her back to the couch.

Bishop Miller took off his hat. "What have you two got to say for yourselves?" he demanded.

Betsy would have fallen to the living room floor if Ronald hadn't lent his steady hand.

"We are merely messengers," Ronald said simply.

The bishop nodded. "Well, then. We have a lot to discuss with Mary's parents." Bishop Miller motioned toward the front door, clearly dismissing Ronald and Betsy.

"I'm taking Ronald back to Cousin Enos's place," Betsy called over her shoulder on the way out the door.

No one seemed to hear.

Ronald helped her into *Daett's* buggy. He drove as they pulled out of the lane.

"Will you be okay?" Ronald asked.

"I'll be okay." Betsy smiled up at him. "Thanks for what you told *Mamm*."

Ronald grunted. "The bishop should be gone by the time you get back."

"I suppose so. But we have a long journey ahead of us. Do you think there will be peace between *Mamm* and *Daett* and Mary someday?"

"There has to be peace."

She leaned against him on the buggy seat, the strength of his arm against her face. He held fast to the reins as Danny Boy's hooves beat steadily on the pavement beneath them.

DISCUSSION QUESTIONS

1. What was your first impression of Josiah Beiler when Mary and Betsy met him? Would your conclusions have lined up with Betsy's or Mary's?

2. Could you identify with Mary and her dream of home and family nestled in the peaceful valley under the shadow of the Adirondacks?

3. Have you experienced a heartbreak similar to Mary's when Josiah broke off the relationship? What advice would you have given Mary?

4. Have you known a person like Mrs. Gabert, who took a grand-child into her home? How did his or her experiences compare to raising Willard?

5. Describe Willard's state of mind when he first met Mary. Do you know anyone who has walked through bitterness and found their way to healing?

6. Betsy was determined to leave the community at the first opportunity, but do you think her heart was in the effort?

7. Trace Mary's caring heart through the story, from her under-standing of Betsy to her compassion for Stephen Overholt. Were you surprised when Mary was able to help Stephen? How did Mary's character fit with Willard's needs on the mission field?

8. As Mary opened her heart to Willard, were you on Mary's side? On the community's side? Did both have reasons for how they felt?

9. What advice would you have given Mary's family when they learned of their daughter's romantic attraction to Willard Gabert?

10. How do you think this story will continue in the years ahead when Mary returns from Kenya with Willard for a family visit?

ABOUT THE AUTHOR

Jerry Eicher's Amish fiction has sold more than 800,000 copies. After a traditional Amish childhood, Jerry taught for two terms in Amish and Mennonite schools in Ohio and Illinois. Since then he's been involved in church renewal, preaching, and teaching Bible studies. Jerry lives with his wife, Tina, in Virginia.

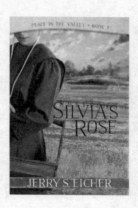

A Beautiful Rose, like True Love, Never Fades

Esther Stoltzfus considers herself to be down-to-earth, the way most Amish women do. Her marriage to her now-deceased husband was one borne out of practicality, and Esther sees no reason why God won't replace what He was taken away.

When Esther moves to a new community with her daughter, Diana, she meets the handsome minister Isaiah Mast, who has experienced his own loss and appears to be a logical fit to complete their family. But everything changes when Esther is introduced to Joseph Zook, her widowed neighbor down the road.

While tending to his treasured roses, Joseph tells stories of his passionate love for his late wife, Silvia—stories that stir a place in Esther's heart she never knew existed. What if she and Isaiah could have the kind of love Joseph and Silvia shared?

Meanwhile, Joseph gets his own second chance at love with the eccentric Arlene King, even as he knows he will never find another *frau* like his beloved Silvia.

Silvia's Rose is a beautiful story filled with redemption, romance, and risking it all for the reward of true love.

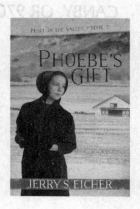

Dreams Never Die When You Believe in Them

Phoebe Lapp's grandmother was *anything* but ordinary. Before her death, the eccentric elderly woman purchased three Assateague ponies, seemingly for no reason. But after her passing, Phoebe learns of her beloved grandmother's wish to start an Amish pony farm in a lovely little valley near the Adirondack Mountains for hurting *Englisha* children. That dream now lies with Phoebe if she decides to fulfill it, but a teaching position is available as well. Which path should she choose?

Further complicating her decision, before her passing, Grandma Lapp asked a neighbor, David Fisher, to be involved in running the farm and help Phoebe. David agrees, but his sister Ruth has yet to abandon her *rumspringa*, and the only reason she hasn't left the church already is because of Grandma Lapp's kindness. Unbeknownst to Phoebe, David has secret hopes of attracting her affection, but Ruth's decision to stay or jump the fence could make things difficult for him.

Phoebe knows she has choices to make—whether or not to honor her grandmother's legacy and what to do about David's growing attentions toward her. But she's not alone. God is with her every step of the way.

To learn more about Harvest House books and
to read sample chapters, visit our website:

www.harvesthousepublishers.com

HARVEST HOUSE PUBLISHERS
EUGENE, OREGON